Praise for Nalini Singh and the Psy-Changeling Series

SLAVE TO SENSATION

'I LOVE this book! It's a must read for all of my fans.
Nalini Singh is a major new talent'

New York Times bestselling author Christine Feehan

VISIONS OF HEAT

'Breathtaking blend of passion, adventure, and the paranormal.
I wished I lived in the world Singh has created. This is a keeper!'

New York Times bestselling author Gena Showalter

CARESSED BY ICE

'Craving the passionate and electrifying world created by the
megatalented Singh? Your next fix is here! . . . One of the most
original and thrilling paranormal series on the market . . .
Mind-blowing!'

Romantic Times

MINE TO POSSESS

'Singh has done it again. *Mine to Possess* grabs you and
never lets you go. This may be the best book of an already
outstanding series'

Fresh Fiction

HOSTAGE TO PLEASURE

'Singh is on the fast track to becoming a genre giant!'

Romantic Times

Also by Nalini Singh from Gollancz:

Guild Hunter Series

Angels' Blood

Archangel's Kiss

Archangel's Consort

Psy-Changeling Series

Slave to Sensation

Visions of Heat

Caressed by Ice

Mine to Possess

Hostage to Pleasure

Branded by Fire

BLAZE OF MEMORY

A PSY-CHANGELING NOVEL

NALINI SINGH

The right of Nalini Singh to be identified as the author of this work
has been asserted by her in accordance with the
Copyright, Designs and Patents Act 1988.

First published in Great Britain in 2011 by
Gollancz
An imprint of the Orion Publishing Group
Orion House, 5 Upper St Martin's Lane, London WC2H 9EA
An Hachette UK Company

5 7 9 10 8 6 4

A CIP catalogue record for this book is available
from the British Library

ISBN 978 0 575 10007 7

Printed in Great Britain by Clays Ltd, St Ives plc

The Orion Publishing Group's policy is to use papers that are
natural, renewable and recyclable products and made from wood
grown in sustainable forests. The logging and manufacturing
processes are expected to conform to the environmental regulations
of the country of origin.

www.nalinisingh.com

www.orionbooks.co.uk

To Anu fua, for loving books . . .
and for loving my books!

DEATH

Death followed the Forgotten like a scourge. Relentless. Without pity.

They'd sought to find hope when they dropped from the PsyNet, wanting only to build a new life away from the cold choices of their brethren. But the Psy in the Net, their hearts iced over with the emotionless chill of Silence, refused to let the dissidents go in peace—for the Forgotten, with their hopes and dreams of a better life, were a roadblock to the Psy goal of absolute power.

Among their numbers the defectors counted a large contingent of telepaths and medical specialists, men and women gifted in psychometry, foresight, and so much more. These powerful individuals, these *rebels*, stood as the only real psychic threat to the increasingly omnipotent Psy Council.

So the Council cut them down.

One by one.

Family by family.

Father. Mother. Child.

Again and again and *again*.

Until the Forgotten had to run, to hide.

In time, memories were lost, truths were concealed, and the Forgotten almost ceased to exist.

But old secrets cannot be kept forever. Now, in the final months of the year 2080, the dust is rising, light is shining through, and the Forgotten stand at a crossroads. To fight is to face death once more, perhaps the total annihilation of their kind. But to run... is that not also a kind of annihilation?

CHAPTER 1

She opened her eyes and for a second, it felt as if the world shifted. Those eyes, the ones looking back at her, they were brown, but it was a brown unlike any she'd ever seen. There was gold in there. Flecks of amber. And bronze. So many colors.

"She's awake."

That voice, she remembered that voice.

"Shh. I've got you."

She swallowed, tried to find her own voice.

A raw hiss of air. Soundless. Without form.

The man with the brown eyes slipped a hand under her head and tilted it up as he put something to her lips.

Cold.

Ice.

She parted her lips, working desperately to melt the ice chips in her mouth. Her throat grew wet but it wasn't enough. She needed water. Again, she attempted to speak. She couldn't even hear herself, but he did.

"Sit up."

It was like trying to swim through the most viscous of fluids—her bones were jelly, her muscles useless.

"Hold on." He all but lifted her into a sitting position on the bed. Her heart thudded in her chest, a fluttering trapped bird.

Beat-beat.

Beat-beat.

Beat-beat.

Warm hands on her face, turning her head. His face shimmered into view, then twisted impossibly sideways.

"I don't think the drugs are fully out of her system." His voice was deep, reached deep, right into her beating, fluttering heart. "Have you got—thanks." He raised something.

A cup.

Water.

She gripped his wrist, her fingers almost sliding off the vivid masculine heat of his skin.

He continued to hold the cup out of reach. "Slow. Understood?" It was less a question than an order—in a voice that said he was used to being obeyed.

She nodded and let him bring something to her lips. A straw.

Her hand tightened on him, she was so thirsty.

"Slow," he repeated.

She sipped. Rich. Orange. Sweet. Despite the ruthless edge in her rescuer's voice, she might've disobeyed and gulped, but her mouth wasn't working right. She could barely draw up the thinnest of streams. But it was enough to soothe the raw flesh of her throat, fill the empty ache in her stomach.

She'd been hungry for so long.

A flash of something in the corner of her mind, too fast for her to grasp. And then she was staring into those strangely compelling eyes. But he wasn't just eyes. He was clean, almost harsh lines and golden brown skin. Exotic eyes. Exotic skin.

His mouth moved.

Her eyes lingered on his lips. The lower one was a little fuller than seemed right on that uncompromisingly masculine face. But not soft. Never soft. This man, he was all hardness and command.

Another touch, fingers on her cheek. She blinked, focused on his lips again. Tried to hear.

"...name?"

She pushed away the juice and swallowed, dropping her hands to the sheets. He wanted to know her name. It was a reasonable question. She wanted to know his name, too. People always exchanged names when they met. It was normal.

Her fingers clenched on the soft cotton sheets.

Beat-beat.

Beat-beat.

Beat-beat.

That fluttering bird was back, trapped in her chest. How cruel.

Not normal.

"What's your name?" His eyes were piercing in their directness, refusing to let her look away.

And she had to answer. "I don't know."

Dev looked into that cloudy hazel gaze and saw only a confused kind of fear. "Glen?"

Dr. Glen Herriford frowned from the other side of the bed. "Could be a side effect of the drugs. She was pretty doped up when she came in. Give it a few more hours."

Nodding, Dev put the juice on the table and returned his attention to the woman. Her lashes were already dropping. Not saying anything, he helped her down into a position flat on her back. She was asleep moments later.

Jerking his head to the door, he walked out with Glen following. "What did you find in her system?"

"That's the funny thing." Glen tapped the electronic chart

in his hand. "The chemicals all add up to plain old sleeping pills."

"That's not what it looks like." She was too disoriented, her pupils hugely dilated.

"Unless..." Glen raised an eyebrow.

Dev's mouth tightened. "Chance she did it to herself?"

"There's always a chance—but someone dumped her in front of your apartment."

"I went inside at ten p.m., came back out at ten fifteen." He'd left his phone in the car, had been irritated at having to stop work to return to the garage. "She was unconscious when I found her."

Glen shook his head. "No way she had the coordination to get through security then—she'd have lost her fine motor skills well beforehand."

Fighting the rush of anger provoked by the thought of how helpless she must've felt, what might've been done to her in that time, Dev glanced back into the room. The bright white overhead light glinted off her matted blonde hair, highlighting the scratches on the face, the sharp bones slicing her skin. "She looks half-starved."

Glen's usually smiling face was a grim mask. "We haven't had the opportunity to do a full checkup but there are bruises on her arms, her legs."

"You telling me she was beaten?" Raw fury pulsed through Dev's body, hot and violent.

"Tortured would be the word I'd use. There are old bruises beneath the new ones."

Dev swore under his breath. "How long before she's functional?"

"It'll probably take forty-eight hours to flush the drugs out completely. I think it was a one-time hit. If she'd been on them longer, she'd have been even more messed up."

"Keep me updated."

"Are you going to call Enforcement?"

"No." Dev had no intention of letting her out of his sight. "She was dumped in front of my door for a reason. She stays with us until we figure out what the hell is going on."

"Dev..." Glen blew out a breath. "Her reaction to the drugs says she has to be Psy."

"I know." His own psychic senses had picked up an "echo" from the woman. Muted but there. "She's not a threat at this stage. We'll reassess the situation after she's up and around."

Something beeped inside the room, making Glen glance at his chart. "It's nothing. Don't you have a meeting with Talin this morning?"

Taking the hint, Dev drove home to shower and change. It was just ticking over six thirty when he walked back into the building that housed the headquarters of the Shine Foundation. Though the top four floors were sectioned into a number of guest apartments, the middle ten were taken up with various administration offices, while the floors below the basement housed the testing and medical facilities. And today—a Psy. A woman who might turn out to be the latest move in the Council's attempts to destroy the Forgotten.

But, he reminded himself, right now she was asleep and he had work to do. "Activate. Voice code—Devraj Santos." The clear screen of his computer slid up and out of his desk, showing a number of unread messages. His secretary, Maggie, was good at weeding out the "can-waits" from the "must-responds" and all ten on-screen fell into the latter category—and today hadn't yet begun. Leaning back in his chair, he glanced at his watch.

Too early to return the calls—even in New York, most people weren't at their desks by six forty-five. Then again, most people didn't run the Shine Foundation, much less act as the head of a "family" of thousands scattered across the country, and in many cases, the world.

It was inevitable he'd think of Marty at that moment.

"This job," his predecessor had said the night Dev accepted the directorship, "will eat up your life, suck the marrow from your bones for good measure, and spit you out on the other end, a dry husk."

"You stuck to it." Marty had run Shine for over forty years.

"I was lucky," the older man had said in that blunt, no-nonsense way of his. "I was married when I took the job, and to my eternal gratitude, my wife stayed with me through all the shit. You go in alone, you'll end up staying that way."

Dev could still remember how he'd laughed. "What, you have a very low opinion of my charm?"

"Charm all you like," Marty had said with a snort, "but women have a way of wanting time. The director of the Shine Foundation doesn't have time. All he has is the weight of thousands of dreams and hopes and fears resting on his shoulders." A glance filled with shadows. "It'll change you, Dev, turn you cruel if you're not careful."

"We're a stable unit now," Dev had argued. "The past is past."

"Dear boy, the past will never be past. We're in a war, and as director, you're the general."

It had taken Dev three years into the job before he'd truly understood Marty's warning. When his ancestors had defected from the PsyNet, they'd hoped to make a life outside the cold rigidity of Silence. They'd chosen chaos over control, the dangers of emotion over the certain sanity of a life lived without hope, without love, without joy. But with those choices had come consequences.

The Psy Council had never stopped hunting the Forgotten.

To fight back, to keep his people safe, Dev had had to make some brutal choices of his own.

His fingers curled around the pen in his grip, threatening to crush it. "Enough," he muttered, glancing at his watch again. Still too early to call.

Pushing back his chair, he got up, intending to grab some coffee. Instead, he found himself taking the elevator down to the subbasement level. The corridors were quiet, but he knew the labs would already be humming with activity—the workload was simply too big to allow for much downtime.

Because while the Forgotten had once been as Psy as those who looked to the Council for leadership, time and intermarriage with the other races had changed things in their genetic structure. Strange new abilities had begun to appear...but so had strange new diseases.

But that wasn't the threat he had to assess today.

If they were right, the unknown woman in the hospital bed in front of him was linked to the PsyNet itself. That made her beyond dangerous—a Trojan horse, her mind used as a conduit through which to siphon data or implement deadly strategies.

The last spy stupid enough to try to infiltrate Shine had discovered the lethal truth far too late—that Devraj Santos had never left his military background behind. Now, as he looked down into the woman's bruised, scratched, and emaciated face, he considered whether he'd be able to snap her neck with cold-blooded precision should the time come.

He was afraid the answer might just be an icily practical yes.

Chilled, he was about to leave the room when he noticed her eyes moving rapidly beneath her lids. "Psy," he murmured, "aren't supposed to dream."

"Tell me."

She swallowed the blood on her tongue. "I've told you everything. You've taken everything."

Eyes as black as night with a bare few flecks of white stared down at her as mental fingers spread in her mind, thrusting, clawing, destroying. She swallowed a scream, bit another line in her tongue.

"Yes," her torturer said. "It does seem as if I've stripped you of all your secrets."

She didn't respond, didn't relax. He'd done this before. So many times. But the next minute, the questions would begin again. She didn't know what he wanted, didn't know what he searched for. All she knew was that she'd broken. There was nothing left in her now. She was cracked, shattered, gone.

"Now," he said, in that same, always-patient voice. "Tell me about the experiments."

She opened her mouth and repeated what she'd already confessed over and over again. "We doctored the results." He'd known that from the start; that was no betrayal. "We never gave you the actual data."

"Tell me the truth. Tell me what you found."

Those fingers gouged mercilessly at her brain, shooting red fire that threatened to obliterate her very self. She couldn't hold on, couldn't protect them, couldn't even protect herself—because through it all he sat, a large black spider within her mind, watching, learning, knowing. In the end, he took her secrets, her honor, her loyalty, and when he was done, the only thing she remembered was the rich copper scent of blood.

She came awake with a jagged scream stuck in her throat. "He knows."

Brown eyes looking down into hers again. "Who knows?"

The name formed on her tongue and then was lost in the miasma of her ravaged mind. "He knows," she repeated, desperate that someone understand what she'd done. "He *knows*." Her fingers gripped his.

"What does he know?" Electricity arced like an inferno beneath his skin.

"About the children," she whispered, as her head grew heavy again, as her eyes grew dark again. "About the boy."

Gold turned to bronze and she wanted to watch, but it was too late.

PETROKOV FAMILY ARCHIVES

Letter dated January 17, 1969

Dear Matthew,

At today's meeting of government heads, the Council proposed a radical new approach to the problems we've been facing. I knew it was coming, but still, I can't quite imagine how it will work.

The aim of this new program would be to condition all negative emotion out of the coming generation of Psy. If we could cure rage, what a boon that would be—so much of the violence could be stopped, so many lives saved. But the theorists have gone even further. They say that once we have a handle on rage, we may be able to control other damaging emotional events—things that cause the fractures that lead to mental illness.

I'm cautiously optimistic. God knows, this family has paid the price for its gifts one too many times.

With all my love,
   Mom

CHAPTER 2

He knows...About the children. About the boy.

Having forced himself to wait till nine, Dev coded in a call to Talin with impatient hands, his shoulders tight with strain. The blonde woman had fallen straight back into unconsciousness after uttering those words, but Dev hadn't needed anything more—his gut told him there could be only one answer.

"Dev?" Talin's sleep-rumpled face appeared on the transparent screen of his computer, her yawn unsurprising given it was just hitting six in her part of the country. "I thought our meeting was at ten thirty Eastern."

"Change of plans." He considered his next words with care. Talin was pragmatic, but she was also very attached to her charges. "I need to ask Jon something."

She made a face. "He's not going to change his mind about entering a Shine school. But I make sure he reads everything Glen sends him, and the Psy in the pack are helping him train his abilities."

"He's settled in DarkRiver." Dev had come to that

conclusion after a personal visit to the leopard pack's home base in San Francisco. "I think that's the best place for him."

"Then . . . ?"

"How many people knew about Jon in the Psy labs—after he was kidnapped?" The boy was—genetically speaking—over forty-five percent Psy and had been born with a unique kind of vocal ability. Jonquil Duchslaya could literally talk people into doing whatever he wanted. It was a gift many would shed blood to control.

Tiny lines fanned out from the corners of Talin's eyes as her gaze sharpened. "Ashaya, of course. She was the head scientist."

Ashaya Aleine was also now mated to a DarkRiver leopard, and would do nothing to put either Jon or other Forgotten kids in danger. "Who else?"

"No one alive." Talin's voice vibrated with the echo of purest rage. "Clay took care of Larsen, the bastard who was experimenting on the children. And you know the Council destroyed Ashaya's lab after she defected, killing all her research assistants."

Ice speared through his chest, cold, rigid, deadly. "How certain are you of that?"

"DarkRiver has contacts in the Net. So do the wolves," she added, referring to DarkRiver's closest ally, the Snow-Dancers. "There wasn't even a hint of a survivor."

But the Psy, Dev knew, were adept at keeping secrets. Especially Psy like Ming LeBon, the Councilor rumored to have been behind the destruction of the lab. "If I send you a photo, can you see if Jon recognizes the person in it from his kidnapping?"

"No." An absolute answer, her expression as fierce as that of the leopards in her pack. "He's finally starting to act like a normal kid—I don't want to remind him of what he went through in that place."

Dev had known Talin long enough to understand that she wouldn't budge. "Then I need Ashaya's number."

"She was pretty broken up about losing her people." A pause. "Just be careful with her."

Dev heard what she wasn't saying. "You afraid I'll beat the answer out of her?"

"You've changed, Dev." A quiet response. "Become harder."

It was an accusation he'd faced many times in the past few months.

You heartless bastard! You put him in the hospital! How can you live with yourself?

Shelving the knife-edged memory, he shrugged. "Part of the job." That was true as far as it went, but even if he stopped being the director of Shine tomorrow, his ability would ensure the spreading cold in his soul. Paradoxically, that very ice made him the best person to run Shine—he knew how the Psy thought.

"Here."

He noted the number Talin flashed on the screen. "Can we postpone our meeting?"

A nod. "Let me know what you find out."

Ending the call, Dev coded in Ashaya's number. It was answered on her end by a gray-eyed child with silky straight black hair. "Hello. May I help you?"

Dev hadn't thought anything could make him smile today, but he felt his lips curve at the solemn greeting. "Is your mom around?"

"Yes." The boy's eyes sparkled, suddenly more blue than gray. "She's making me cookies for kindergarten."

Dev couldn't quite reconcile the idea of Psy scientist Ashaya Aleine as a mother who made her little boy cookies at six fifteen in the morning. "Shouldn't you still be asleep?"

Before the boy could reply, a frowning female face filled

the screen. "Who are you talking—" Her gaze fell on him. "Yes?"

"My name is Devraj Santos."

Picking up her son, Ashaya hitched him over her hip. The boy immediately snuggled his head onto her shoulder, one little hand spread on the pale blue of her shirt. Intelligent eyes watched Dev with undisguised interest.

"The Shine Foundation," Ashaya said, adjusting the collar of her son's pajama top with the absent movements of a mother used to doing such things.

"Yes."

"Talin's spoken about you." She tucked back a strand of curly black hair that had escaped her braid. "What can I do for you?"

Dev's eyes flicked to her son. Taking the hint, Ashaya kissed the boy on the cheek and smiled. "Keenan, you want to cut out some cookies while I talk to Mr. Santos?"

An enthusiastic nod. Mother and child disappeared from the screen for a minute, and as he waited, Dev found himself wondering if he'd ever hold a child of his own in his arms. The likelihood was very low—even had he trusted his genetic inheritance, he'd done too much, seen too much. There was no softness left in him.

Ashaya's face returned to the screen, her eyes filled with the remnants of laughter. "We'll have to be quick—Keenan's very good, but he's still a four-year-old alone with cookie dough."

Knowing he was about to wipe that shimmering joy from her eyes, he didn't try to soften the blow, didn't try to sugar-coat the implications. "I need you to see if you can identify someone." Then he told her about the woman he'd found dumped outside his apartment door.

Ashaya's face went pale under that dusky skin. "Do you think—"

"It could be nothing," he interrupted. "But it's a possibility I have to check out."

"Of course." Her throat moved as she swallowed. "If the Council knows about the unique abilities being manifested in the children of the Forgotten, there's a chance they'll begin to try to experiment on those children once again." A pause. "I think Ming would kill them if he couldn't use them."

Dev's jaw tightened. That was exactly what worried him— the Council would never countenance the idea of another group with access to psychic powers—much less the increasingly strong ones being manifested in some of his people. "Is this line secure?"

"Yes."

He sent through a photograph. "She may not look like she used to."

Nodding, Ashaya took a deep breath and opened the attachment. He knew the instant she recognized the woman in the photo. Crushing relief, anger, and pain—it all swept over her face in a violent wave. "Dear God." Her fingers covered her mouth. "Ekaterina. It's Ekaterina."

CHAPTER 3

The Psy Council met in their usual location—a mental vault deep within the PsyNet, the psychic network that connected every Psy on the planet but for the renegades. An endless vista of black, each Psy mind represented by a single white star, the Net had a stark kind of beauty. But of course, those within the Net no longer understood beauty.

Like their Council, they understood only logic, practicality, economics.

Shut inside the solid black walls of the vault, Nikita looked to Ming. "You had something to discuss?"

"Yes." The other Councilor's mind was a blade, precise, ice-cold. "I've been able to retrieve some of the data Ashaya Aleine obfuscated before her defection."

"Excellent." Shoshanna Scott's mental voice was as coolly elegant as she was in person. That was why she was one of the two public faces of the Council. Her "husband," Henry, their relationship a front to pacify the human and changeling media, was the other half. Though, Nikita thought, the two hadn't been working as a cohesive unit these past months.

"Anything we can use?" Shoshanna again.

"Possibly." Ming paused. "I'm uploading it now."

Streams of data scrolled down the black walls, a silver waterfall comprehensible to only the most powerful Psy minds. Nikita absorbed the information, scanned through the salient points. "This concerns the Forgotten."

"It appears," Ming said, "that their most recent descendants are being born with abilities unseen in the Net."

"That's hardly surprising." Kaleb's smooth voice.

Nikita considered him the most lethal member of not only the Council, but of the Net itself. At present, he'd allied himself to her on certain issues, but she was in no doubt that he'd kill her without hesitation should it prove necessary.

"Councilor Krychek is correct," Tatiana said, speaking for the first time. "We've made a practice of eliminating mutations from the gene pool except where those mutations are essential to maintaining the functionality of the Net."

Nikita knew the dig was directed at her, a reminder of her daughter's unacceptable genetics. "The E designation isn't a mutation," she said with a calm that had been conditioned into her from the cradle. "Empaths form a critical component of the Net. Or have you forgotten your history lessons?" The last time the Council had tried to suppress the E designation—by destroying all embryos that tested positive for the ability—the PsyNet had come critically close to collapse.

"I've forgotten nothing." Tatiana's voice was utterly without inflection. "Getting back to the issue at hand—the deletion of mutations has made our core abilities stronger, purer, but with the inevitable side effect of stunting the development of new talents."

"Is that really a problem?" Anthony Kyriakus asked, matter-of-fact as always. "Surely if the Forgotten had developed any dangerous new abilities, they would have used them against us by now."

"That was my conclusion," Ming said. "However, if no one disagrees, I'd like to devote a small fraction of Council resources to monitoring the Forgotten population for evidence of more serious mutations—we need to ensure they never again become what they once were."

There were no objections.

"Nikita," Tatiana said as Ming's data disappeared from the walls, "how is the voluntary rehabilitation going in your sector?"

"The pace is steady." Allowing the populace to choose to have their conditioning checked—and, if necessary, bolstered—rather than coercing them into it, had reaped dividends beyond anything Nikita had expected. "I suggest we continue to permit people to come in voluntarily—the Net is already becoming calmer."

"Yes," Henry said. "The eruptions of violence have ceased."

Nikita hadn't been able to unmask the individual who'd orchestrated the recent surge of murderous public violence by Psy, but she knew it had most likely been someone in this room. If that individual's goal had been to drive people to cling to Silence, he or she had succeeded. But those bloody events had left a psychic echo—the Net was a closed system. Whatever went in, stayed in.

The other Councilors appeared to have forgotten that, but she hadn't. She was already building her shields, waiting for the moment when they paid the price for that violent piece of strategy.

CHAPTER 4

Six hours after their early morning call, Dev found himself leading Ashaya Aleine down to the medical floor. Her mate, Dorian, walked by her side, his mouth grim. "If Ekaterina was taken from the lab when it was destroyed, she's likely been in Council hands for over five months."

Ashaya uttered a choked-off sound of pain, making Dorian swear under his breath. Dragging his mate to his side, he nuzzled the electric curls of her hair. "Sorry, Shaya."

"No." She sucked in a breath. "You're right."

"And if that's true," Dev said, "they now know everything she did."

Ashaya nodded. "Ming LeBon would've torn her mind open. He was behind the destruction of the lab—it had to be him that took her."

The mental violation, Dev thought with a burst of cold anger, *would've been all consuming.* A psychic assault left the victim with not even the slimmest avenue of escape, no place where she could even pretend that everything was okay.

"Why leave her on your doorstep?" Ashaya said, voice shaken. "A warning?"

"A taunt, more like it." Dev had made it his business to study the enemy. "Psychological warfare."

Dorian nodded. "Could be Ming wants to spook you into doing something rash."

"All the Shine kids are safe and accounted for," Dev said, having spent the past few hours verifying that. "Unfortunately, we've still got the gray area where we've tracked them down, but they haven't yet agreed to accept our help." The last Council mole had taken advantage of that gray area, fingering children for experimentation after they came into the field offices but before they'd been brought safely under the Shine umbrella.

Every single death haunted Dev. Because Shine was about safety, about locating those Forgotten who'd been lost, cut off from the group when the Council first began hunting their ancestors. But instead of safe harbor, it was only death the children had found . . . while the old Shine board sat by, their heads in the sand.

Dev had been ready to kill them for their blindness, their refusal to see that the culling had begun again—and according to some, he'd almost succeeded. One board member had had a heart attack after Dev threw pictures of the children's broken bodies in front of him. Several others had come close to nervous breakdowns.

But no one had stopped him when he took over, when he went after the mole with single-minded focus. "This way," he said, leading them down a silent corridor.

"Tally said you shut down the recruitment process last time." Dorian looked over, his eyes a brilliant blue even more vivid against his distinctive white-blond hair. "You going to do that this time, too?"

"They need a mole to find those kids," Dev said, his tone flat. "And the mole is dead."

Ashaya blinked, glancing from him to Dorian, but didn't say a word. Her mate nodded. "Good."

Dev used his palm print to scan them in through a security door. "I can't justify shutting down the program again so soon without solid proof of trouble—we spend so much time and effort on finding descendants of the original rebels for a reason. There are kids out there going insane because they think they're human."

After a hundred years of Silence, of the Psy remaining locked within their own culture, no one bothered to test for psychic abilities. No one realized that some of those crazy kids actually *were* hearing voices in their heads. Some were latent telepaths whose gifts had broken through during puberty. Some were weak empaths, overwhelmed by the emotions of others. And some . . . some were secret treasures, gifts rising up out of a century of genetic drift.

Seeing Glen exiting a room, he waved the doctor down. The other man hurried over, dark circles under his eyes.

Dev took in his friend's wrinkled clothes, the way his ginger hair stuck up in untidy tufts. "I thought you were off shift."

Glen thrust a hand through his hair, further electrifying the strands. "I wanted to be here in case our guest woke. Caught some sleep in the break room."

Introductions took only a couple of seconds, and then they were walking into Ekaterina's room. To Dev's surprise, she was awake and sitting up, sipping something out of a small cup. He glanced at Glen.

"Just ten minutes ago," the doctor murmured.

Ekaterina looked straight at Dev, her eyes skating off Ashaya as if her former colleague didn't exist. "The cobwebs are starting to part." Her voice was husky, as if it hadn't been used for a long time . . . or as if it had been broken in the most brutal way.

Walking to her side, Dev took the cup she held out, caught

by the shadows that swirled in the green-gold depths of her eyes. "How much do you remember?"

She swallowed but didn't break eye contact. "I don't know who I am." It was a plea, though her voice didn't shake, her eyes didn't glisten. Yet Dev heard the scream—a thin, piercing cry that stabbed him right in the heart.

Part of him, a small, barely salvageable part, wanted to offer comfort, but this woman, simply by existing, was a danger to his people. She was Psy. And Psy connected to the Net could not be trusted. No matter that she acted more human than her brethren, he had to treat her as a weapon, carrying within her the seeds of Shine's destruction. And if she proved to be that, he'd have to make the most lethal of decisions... even if it killed the last bit of humanity left in him.

"Ekaterina." Ashaya's voice, gentle, coaxing.

The woman on the bed blinked, shook her head. "No."

"That's your name," Dev said, refusing to let her look away.

Those changeable hazel eyes flickered and went out, a flame dying. "Ekaterina's dead," she said with absolute calm. "Everything is dead. There's nothing lef—" Her teeth snapped together as her body convulsed with vicious strength.

"Glen!" Catching her before she twisted off the bed, Dev tried to keep her from hurting herself, her bones startlingly fragile under his hands.

"Say it."

She kept her lips closed.

"Say it."

No. No. No.

"Say it."

He didn't tire, didn't stop, didn't shove into her mind. The horror of waiting for the pain, the terror, was somehow worse than the violation itself.

"Say it."

She held on to her sanity through the first days, the first weeks.

But still he wouldn't relent.

Her tongue felt so thick, so dry. Her stomach hurt. But she held on.

"Say it."

It took three months, but she did. She said it.

"Ekaterina is dead."

"She's unconscious." Glen shined a light into Ekaterina's eyes as she lay slumped on the pillows. "Could be the residue of the drugs in her system, but I think the trigger was her name—some kind of a psychic grenade."

"More likely a combination," Ashaya said, then reeled off the chemical compounds of the sleeping pills Glen had noted on the chart. "Some of these agents cause memory loss in Psy."

The doctor's eyes brightened at having found a colleague. "Yes. There's a possibility some of the drugs were used sparingly in conjunction with other methods to psychologically break her."

Dev stared down at Ekaterina Haas's scratched and bruised face, wondering what she'd given up to come out of the torture alive... what she'd let her captors put in her. His hands fisted inside the pockets of his pants—whatever bargain she'd made, it hadn't saved her. "What you said when you first arrived," he murmured to Dorian while the doctor and Ashaya were distracted, "it can't happen."

"Shaya wants her close." Dorian folded his arms, eyes on his mate. "It devastated her when she thought Ekaterina died."

"Whatever happened to her," Dev said, unable to take his own eyes off the thin figure in the bed, "whatever was *done* to her, she's not the woman your mate knew. We're far more capable of monitoring her."

"And if she proves a threat?"

Dev met the other man's gaze. "You know the answer to that." Dorian was a DarkRiver sentinel. And the leopard pack hadn't reached its current status as one of the most dominant changeling groups in the country by being weak...or easily forgiving.

Blowing out a soft breath, Dorian returned his attention to his mate. "You make that decision, you bring me in. You let me prepare her." His voice was a harsh, low order.

Dev was more used to giving orders than taking them, but Ashaya had saved the lives of Forgotten children at risk to her own. Then she'd blown the Council's secret perversions wide open. She'd earned his respect. "Fair enough." However, as he watched Ekaterina's chest rise and fall in what seemed to him to be a dangerously shallow rhythm, he wondered once again if he'd be able to do the deed if it came down to it. Could he break that body that had already been broken so badly?

The answer came from a part of him that had been honed in blood and pain. *Yes.*

Because when you fought monsters, sometimes, you had to become a monster.

PETROKOV FAMILY ARCHIVES

Letter dated May 24, 1969

My dear Matthew,

Your father says that one day you'll laugh at these letters I write to you, to the son who is, at the moment, trying to suck both thumbs at once. "Zarina," David said this afternoon, "what kind of a mother writes political treatises to her seven-month-old son?"

Do you know what I told him?

"A mother who is certain her child will grow up to be a genius."

Oh, how you make me smile. I wonder, even as I write this, if I'll ever let you read these letters. I suppose they've become a kind of journal for me, but since I'm far too sensible to write "Dear Diary," instead I write to the man you'll one day become.

That man, I hope, will grow up in a time of far less turmoil. The psychologists' theories notwithstanding, early indications are that it'll prove almost impossible to condition rage out of our young.

But that isn't what worries me—I've heard disturbing rumors that the Council is looking more and more to Mercury, Catherine and Arif Adelaja's secretive group. If those rumors prove true, we may be in far more trouble than I believed.

It's not that I have anything against Catherine and Arif. Indeed, I once considered them friends and have only admiration for their courage in surviving the worst tragedy that can befall a parent. I don't think it's an exaggeration to say that they are two of the most extraordinary minds of our generation. And, having spent considerable time with both of them, I know one thing with categorical certainty—they want only the best for our race.

But sometimes, that depth of need—to save, to protect—can become a blinding fervor, one that destroys the very thing it thinks to safeguard.

I can only hope the Council sees that, too.

Love,

   Mom

CHAPTER 5

Two days later, the woman everyone called Ekaterina stared at the stranger in the mirror and tried to see what they saw. "It's not me."

"Still no memory?"

She swiveled to find the man who'd introduced himself as Devraj Santos standing in the bathroom doorway. Dark hair, dark eyes... and a way of moving that reminded her of some unnamed predator, sleek, watchful, dangerous beyond compare.

This predator wore a perfect, charcoal-colored suit.

Camouflage, she thought, her most basic, most animal instincts whispering that he was anything but safe. "No. That name... it's not mine." She couldn't quite explain what she wanted to say, the words locked behind a wall she couldn't break through. "Not now."

She expected him to brush off her statement, but instead he leaned one shoulder against the doorjamb, hands in the pockets of his suit pants, and said, "Do you have another preference?"

A choice?

No one had given her a choice for . . . a long time. She knew that. But when she tried to reach for details, they whispered out of her grasp, as insubstantial as the mist she'd felt on her face as a child.

She grabbed onto the fragment of memory, desperate for even a glimmer of who she'd been, who she *was*, her psychic fingers curling almost into claws as she tried to rip away the veil.

Nothing. Only blankness.

"No," she said. "Just not that name." The shadow-man had used it. His voice haunted her. Saying that name over and over and over. And when he said it, pain followed. So much pain. Until the phantom memories made her jerk awake, certain he'd found her, put her back into that hole, that *nothing* place.

"How about Trina?" Dev's voice snapped her back to the present, to the awareness that she was with a man she didn't truly know, a man who might be another shadow. "It's close enough to jog your memory."

The hairs on the back of her neck stood up. "Too close."

"Kate?"

She paused, considered it. Hesitated.

"Katya?"

Somehow she knew no one had ever before called her that. It felt new. Fresh. Alive. Ekaterina was dead. Katya lived. "Yes."

As Dev walked farther into the room, she realized for the first time how big he was. He moved with such lethal grace, it was easy to overlook the fact that he was over six feet three, with solid shoulders that held his suit jacket with effortless confidence. There was considerable muscle on that tall frame—enough to snap her in half without effort.

She should have been afraid, but Devraj Santos had a heat to him, a reality that compelled her to move closer. He was no shadow, she thought. If this man decided to kill her, he'd do so with blunt pragmatism. He wouldn't torture, wouldn't torment. So she let him get close, let him lift a hand to her hair and rub the strands between his fingertips, the scent of his aftershave soaking into her skin until the fresh bite of it was all she could smell.

Her body began to sway toward his the moment before he said, "You need to brush this out."

"I washed it." She picked up a brush, fighting the urge that threatened to destroy what little control she'd managed to cobble together. "But it's so knotted, I couldn't get it smoothed out. It might be easier to cut it."

"Give it to me." Sliding the brush out of her hand, he nudged her back toward the bed.

The slight touch jolted her, made her move unresisting. But she headed away from the bed and to the chair instead. "There's no sunshine here." *Sunshine.* The word ricocheted around her head, echoes upon echoes. *Sunshine.* A painful thudding in her heart, a sense that she'd forgotten something important. "Sunshine," she whispered again, but the echo was already fading, lost in the fog of her mind.

"It's snowing up above," Dev said. "But the sun's out— we're just too far down." He waited until she was seated before beginning to brush her hair. She didn't know what she'd expected, but the patience with which he untangled the knots wasn't it.

Some small part of her knew that he was fully capable of using those same gentle hands to end her life. And yet she continued to sit, her body vulnerable, the tender skin of her neck tingling where his fingers grazed it. *More,* she wanted to say, *please.* Instead of betraying the depth of her need, instead of begging, she gripped the sides of the chair, the metal growing warm under her palms. But no matter the touch of heat, it wasn't real, wasn't human.

"I know things," she blurted out.

He didn't pause. "What things?"

She found herself leaning back toward him, so hungry for contact that her skin felt as if it was parched, dying of thirst. "I know about the world. I know I'm Psy. I know I shouldn't be able to feel emotions." But she did. Need, fear, confusion, so many things that twisted and tore at her, demanding attention, wanting to surface.

And beneath it all was terror. Endless. Wordless. *Always*.

Dev's fingers touched her nape, vivid warmth and silent demand. "How much do you know about the world? Politics?"

"Enough. Pieces." She breathed deep, found that the scent of him, rich and dark below the crispness of the aftershave, was in her lungs. It made her heart race, her palms go damp. "When people speak, when I watch the news channel, I understand. And I know other things…I know who—what—you are. I know what Shine is. It's only me I don't know. Nothing comes."

"That's not true." Firm strokes, little tugs on her scalp. "You dream."

A pulse of dread, bile in her throat. "I don't want to."

"It's a way for your brain to process things."

Her arms hurt, and she realized she was holding herself so stiffly, her muscles were beginning to burn. Forcing herself to let go of the chair, she focused on the repetitive strokes through her hair, the feel of the bristles, the aggressive male heat of the man behind her. "I'm a threat."

"Yes."

That he hadn't lied almost made her feel better. "What will you do with me?"

"For now? Keep you close."

"Don't." It came out without thought. "There's something wrong with me." That *wrongness* was an alien silhouette in the back of her skull, a wave of whispers she couldn't quite hear.

"I know." He didn't sound too worried, but then, she thought, he was a man who'd likely never known fear. She knew it too well, until the acid of it stained her very cells. But she still had her mind, fractured though it might be.

"You want something from me." Why else would he keep her alive, keep her close?

"Do you remember the research you were doing with Ashaya?"

Pale blue-gray eyes, dark hair in wildfire curls, coffee-colored skin. *Ashaya*. "She was here?" Her skin stretched as lines formed on her brow. "She was here."

"Yes." Long, easy strokes through hair that no longer needed to be smoothed out. "She wants you to go stay with her."

Katya was shaking her head before he finished speaking. *"No."* Fear closed around her throat, brutal hands that choked her until she couldn't breathe. Pinpricks of light in front of her eyes, agony in her chest.

The tugs on her scalp ceased and a split second later, Dev was crouching in front of her, his hands over hers. "Breathe." A ruthless order, given in the voice of a man who would *not* countenance disobedience.

Staring into those not-brown eyes, she tried to find some sense of balance, of self. "Breathe," she repeated in a thin whisper that was barely sound. "Breathe." Air whistled into her lungs, heady with the exotic taste of a man who'd never see her as anything but an enemy.

At that moment, she didn't care.

All she wanted was to drown in the scent of him, until the fear inside her was nothing but a vague memory, a forgotten dream. She drew in another deep breath, luxuriating in the wild sweep of her senses, in the unforgiving male beauty of Devraj Santos. He smelled of power and an unexpected stroke of wildness, rich cinnamon and Orient winds—things she somehow knew, words her mind supplied. Almost without deciding to do it, she raised her hand to the thick silk of his hair. It was soft, softer than should've been possible on this man. "Will you promise me something?"

For the first time in years, Dev found himself facing an opponent so opaque, he couldn't get a handle on her. He'd come down here in order to make up his mind about whether or not she was nothing more than a truly clever actress. Instead, he'd found his Achilles' heel given human form—a woman who appeared utterly without barriers, without protections.

Then she'd touched him, and he hadn't pushed her away... though he was a man who'd never been easy with touch, with the casual intimacies so many took for granted. Dev preferred to keep his distance. Except her hand was still in his hair, her skin soft under his rougher grip.

Even now, he had to fight the primitive need to protect, to shelter, to save. What some called his stone-cold heart apparently had some warmth left in it. But that warmth wasn't enough to blind him to the cynical truth—she might be the best move the Psy Council had ever made, a weapon tailor-made to provoke instincts so basic, Dev had little to no control over them. "What do you want me to promise?" he asked, hardening himself against a plea for mercy.

Instead, she stroked her hand through his hair, as if fascinated by the texture, and said, "Will you kill me?"

He froze.

"If I prove too broken," she continued, "too used up to fix, will you kill me?"

There was, he thought, nothing lost about her at that instant. Her intent burned off her, a bright, decisive fire. "Katya—"

"He did something inside me," she whispered with a restrained violence that was all the more powerful for being contained. "He changed me. I don't want to live if that's who I am. His... creation."

The horror in her face, in the inescapable ugliness of what she was saying, curled around the iron shields that caged his soul, threatening to erode everything he thought he knew about himself. "If," he said, unable to look away from those eyes streaked with gold and green, "you were going to give up, you'd have done it by now."

Her hand fell from his hair, but she held his gaze, unflinching in her naked honesty. "How do you know I didn't?"

EARTHTWO COMMAND LOG:
SUNSHINE STATION

21 February 2080: The new staff rotation arrived at 0900. All personnel are in good physical and mental condition. Work will begin in one day's time, after the team members have had time to acclimate to the conditions.

Councilor Ming LeBon has requested a report on the continued viability of this site, to be delivered at the end of this rotation. According to current calculations, the site should yield valuable compounds for the foreseeable future, but all data will be confirmed prior to the completion of the report.

CHAPTER 6

An hour after Katya asked him for a promise of death, Dev pushed a plate across the break-room table. "Eat."

Not touching the food, she pinned him with eyes more gold than green at that moment, streaks of brown bursting from the pupils. "Will you keep your promise?"

He knew when he was being played. But most people wanted favors of a far less final kind. "I'll kill you if it proves necessary."

She paused, as if considering his words, then picked up the fork. "Thank you." While she ate in small, birdlike bites, he wondered what the hell he was going to do with her. Dev knew full well what he was becoming, but he wasn't—not yet—so much the monster that he'd throw her back to the wolves. But neither could he permit her to become intimate with Shine.

Katya might look fragile, might appeal to instincts born in the darkness of a childhood that had ravaged his soul, but she was Psy—and Psy cared for their physical appearance only to the extent that it got the job done. It was her mind that he had to consider—she couldn't be allowed near any computers, any sources of data, certainly none of their most vulnerable.

Pushing away the still mostly full plate, the woman at the center of his thoughts shook her head. "My stomach can't take any more."

"Another meal, in an hour."

Her expression remained unchanged, but he saw her fingertips press down hard against the edge of the tabletop. "You're used to giving orders."

"And having them obeyed." He made no effort to hide his nature, his will. It was what had gotten him this far, and it was what would protect the Forgotten from the Council's murderous attempts to stamp them out forever. "Can you handle some questions?"

"Would you stop if I couldn't?"

"No." He had to assess the level of threat—outwardly, she was as fragile as glass, but then again, most poison didn't look like much either.

In contrast to the majority of people when faced with him in this grim mood, she didn't break eye contact. "At least you're honest."

"Compared to?"

A shake of the head, one answer she wouldn't give him. "Ask your questions."

"Are you in the Net?"

She blinked. "Of course." But her tone was unsure, her forehead furrowing.

He waited as her lashes came down, as her eyes moved rapidly behind the delicate lids. An instant later, they flew up. "I'm trapped." Her fingers curled into the table, nails digging into the wood veneer. "He's buried me in my mind."

"No. If he had, you'd be dead."

The harsh words acted as a slap. Katya jerked up her head, saw the cold distance in the eyes looking into hers, and knew there'd be no gentleness from him. He was no longer the Dev who'd brushed her hair and let her touch him. This man wouldn't hesitate to fulfill her promise. But she hadn't asked this man.

Paradoxically, the ruthlessness of him made her spine straighten, a new kind of resolve rising up out of her battered soul. Where she would've softened for Dev, she didn't want to surrender and give the director of the Shine Foundation the satisfaction. "Yes," she said, forcing herself to still the panic. "The biofeedback has to be coming through." The logic of it was irrefutable—she wouldn't have lasted more than a few minutes without that feedback from the neural network that every Psy linked to instinctively at birth. "But I don't think I can enter the Net itself."

"Doesn't mean someone can't find a way inside you."

Her stomach revolted. It took everything she had to keep down what she'd eaten. "You think he already has," she whispered, looking into that pitiless face. "You think I'm nothing but a puppet."

Heading back up to his office after Katya—and yes, he found himself thinking, that name suited her far better than Ekaterina—began to slump from exhaustion, Dev considered who might know the answer to the mystery that was Katya Haas. He had a network of spies and informants that was as byzantine as the PsyNet. However, a direct channel to that net was the one thing he hadn't been able to achieve. But, he thought, DarkRiver counted more than one full-blooded Psy among its numbers—chances were very high that an open line of communication existed somewhere.

Looking down at the frenetic energy of New York, he weighed his next move. If Katya had been dumped at his home as a warning, then the powers in the PsyNet already knew she was alive and were—as she herself had said—controlling her. However, he had to consider the converse possibility—that she'd been rescued and left at his home because her rescuer knew the Forgotten would never cooperate with the Council. If so, any ripple in the pond could put her life in danger.

"Dev?"

He turned to find Maggie, in the doorway. "What is it?"

"Jack's on his way up." Her eyes were sympathetic.

Dev's gut twisted, his mind filling with images of William, Jack's son. The last time Dev had seen him, Will had still been a laughing, energetic little boy. Now... "Show him in when he arrives."

Sleet began to fleck the window as Maggie withdrew, every blow more cold and brittle than the last. Moving away from the sudden darkness, Dev returned to his desk. To his responsibilities. There was only one decision he could make when it came to seeking information about Katya—she wasn't as important as the thousands of Forgotten he'd pledged to protect. A ruthless line, but one he could not cross.

Several floors below, her eyes closed in sleep, Katya found herself back in the spider's web.

"What is your secondary purpose?"

"To gather information on the Forgotten, to discover their secrets."

"And if you fail to find any useful data in the designated time frame?"

Fear rose, but it was dull, a feeling she'd endured so long, it had become a bruise that never faded. "I must shift all my focus to the primary task."

"What is that task?"

"To kill the director of the Shine Foundation, Devraj Santos."

"How?"

"In a way that makes it clear he was assassinated. In a way that leaves no room for doubt about who did the task."

"Why?"

That threw her. "You didn't tell me why."

"Good." A single, ice-cold word. "Your job isn't to understand, simply to do. Now repeat what you are to do."

"Kill Devraj Santos."

"And then?"

"Kill myself."

A pause, a rustle of fabric as he crossed his legs, his face as expressionless as when he'd shut her in the dark again though she'd begged and pleaded on her hands and knees.

"Please," she'd said, scrabbling to hold on to his legs. "Please, don't. Please, please!"

But he'd kicked her away, locked the door. And now he sat—a god on his throne while she huddled on the floor—speaking to her in that cool voice that never changed, no matter how much she screamed.

"That task is the sole reason I'm leaving you alive."

"Why me?"

"You're already dead. Easily expendable."

"If I fail?" She was so weak, her bones seeming to melt from the inside out. How could she possibly kill any man, much less one reputed to be as lethal as the director of the Shine Foundation?

There was no immediate answer, no movement from the spider who'd become the only living being in the endless pain that was her universe. He was a true Psy. He didn't make gestures or movements without purpose. Once, she'd been like that. Before he'd torn into her mind and snapped the threads of her conditioning, wiping out all the things that had made her who she was.

Before he'd killed her.

"If you fail," he finally said, *"Devraj Santos will eliminate you from the equation. The end, for you, will be the same."*

Katya gasped awake, her clothing sticking to her skin, her head pounding. Fear and horror clawed at her chest until she kicked off the blankets, certain something was sitting on her ribs, crushing her bones.

Nothing.

Nothing but madness.

Shoving a fist into her mouth, she curled onto her side, wrestling with the jagged fragments of a dream that had drenched her body in the sick chill of fear-sweat. But no matter how hard she tried, she couldn't connect the pieces, couldn't figure out what it was the shadow-man had wanted her to do.

She just knew that when the time came...she'd do it. Because the shadow-man never left anything to chance. Most especially his weapons.

PETROKOV FAMILY ARCHIVES

Letter dated December 3, 1970

My dear Matthew,

It's as I thought—the attempt to condition rage out of our young is failing. But that isn't the most disturbing news. Today, I read a confidential report that says the Council has begun to consider the effective elimination of all our emotions.

My hand shakes as I write this. Can't they see what they're asking? What they're destroying?

Mom

CHAPTER 7

Three days later, Dev had the answer to his question.

"We've rechecked with our source," Dorian told him over the communications panel. "She's officially listed as deceased."

"Ming had to have taken her out beforehand. Unless your intel says otherwise?"

"No. With Ekaterina—"

"Katya," Dev corrected automatically.

"Right." The sentinel gave a single sharp nod. "Well, with Katya, he really cleaned up his tracks—apparently, there's not even a whisper that she survived the explosion. Ashaya's starting to think the amnesia could be the side effect of a psychic block of some sort, something that stops her from betraying herself on the Net."

"We're working on that." The Forgotten had changed over the years, but they still had telepaths in their midst, still had those who could work with minds wrapped in a mental prison. Dev knew the painful certainty of that far too well.

"You need any of us, all you have to do is say the word. Sascha, Faith, Shaya," Dorian said, naming three of the powerful Psy in his pack, "they're ready to drop everything to help Katya."

"Until we know how dangerous she is, I can't chance that," Dev answered. "Shine might be the main target, but if I know the Council, they'll use the opportunity to hurt anyone they can. DarkRiver is a real thorn in their side." All true. But there was another truth—in asking him to end her life, Katya had put that life in his hands—he'd allow no one else to interfere. "I'll let you know if we find anything more."

Dev had just hung up when Glen paged him down to the medical floor. "She's ready to be discharged," the doctor told Dev as soon as he arrived. "I've given her several bottles of supplements—combine those with a steady diet and she should bounce back fairly quickly."

Dev's shoulders tensed as he was reminded of exactly how badly she'd been treated, but he made himself focus on the issue at hand. "Any indications of her abilities?"

"According to the tests we've run, she's midlevel in terms of strength. Can't yet tell you what type of ability she has, but what I can tell you is that she doesn't appear to be accessing it at present."

That lowered the level of threat, but—"We need to keep her close until we figure out why she was sent in."

"I can't justify holding her down here." Glen's boyish face set in stubborn lines that might've surprised many. "It's a nice-enough clinic, but she needs sunlight, fresh air."

"I can't set her free, Glen, you know that." Yeah, it made him feel like a bastard, but his ability to be a bastard was why he'd been chosen as director. Metal was his gift, and perhaps his curse, but that growing layer of metallic ice meant he didn't hesitate to do what needed to be done.

The doctor pinched his nose. "The Hippocratic oath doesn't differentiate between friend and enemy."

"I know. That's why you have me." Squeezing the other man's shoulder, he turned toward Katya's room.

"Dev." Glen's expression was troubled when Dev looked back at him. "You can't keep being responsible for all the tough decisions."

"I made that choice when I took the job." Or perhaps he'd made it decades ago, the day the cops found him lying half-broken in the corner of his parents' bedroom. That was the day he'd first felt the metal, first begun to sense the cold intelligence of the machines around him.

Glen shook his head. "It doesn't have to be you. Shine has a board."

Yes, it did. And that board was now made up of men and women who wouldn't simply look the other away when reality became too harsh, too uncomfortable. But—"A good leader never asks his troops to do anything he can't." Shifting on his heel, he said, "Go home, Glen. Get some sleep."

"Not until I know what you're going to do with her."

That was when Dev realized Glen didn't trust him to not hurt the woman who, by her simple existence, her *survival*, reached parts of him he preferred to leave in darkness. It was a blow . . . and it showed just how much he'd changed from the man Glen had first called friend. "I'm not that far gone yet," he said softly.

"No . . . not yet," the doctor echoed as Dev crossed the doorway into Katya's room.

He found her sitting on the bed dressed in a new pair of blue jeans and a white T-shirt, having thrown on a heavy gray sweatshirt over the top. Her shoulder-length hair had been plaited into a tight French braid, and there were out-of-the-box-white sneakers on her feet. Her lips lifted in a tentative smile when she saw him. "Hi."

And that quickly, the metal threatened to retreat, to leave him wide open to the raging protectiveness that slammed into his skin with brutal force. "Where're your boots, your coat?" he asked, and the words were hard.

"In here." Smile fading, she patted a khaki-colored duffel

with a quietly possessive hand. "Thank you for the clothes. And the other things."

"Maggie bought them." He jerked his head toward the door as he reached for her bag. "Come on, you're leaving this place."

She tugged the bag away from him. "Where are you going to take me?" The finest thread of steel.

Not that surprised, he dropped his hand. "For now, to my place in Vermont."

"What about your work?"

He looked into that still-pale face, wondering if the question was simple curiosity or something far more sinister. However, the answer wasn't exactly a state secret. "I can handle things remotely." His team was solid, used to working with him regardless of location. "If necessary, I can commute." Shine had access to several jet-choppers, but Dev preferred to drive most of the time—the trip took less than three hours in a high-speed vehicle, and it gave him time to think free of distractions.

"Why?" Katya's eyes were crystal clear as they met his, each shard—brown, green, yellow—perfectly defined. "Why not just dump me on someone else?"

"Because I don't know how big a threat you are," he answered, and it was *a* truth. She had no need to know about the complex, unwanted emotions she aroused, the buried memories she unearthed. "You'll be staying with me until I can figure out what to do with you."

"You could let me go." Her fingers curled on top of the duffel.

"Not possible."

"So I'm a prisoner again."

The point hit hard, stabbing into the core of honor he'd somehow managed to retain. He wondered if it would still be there after this was all over. "No, you're the enemy." This time, he took the duffel without waiting for her agreement.

Katya watched the broad wall of Dev's retreating back and

forced herself to get off the bed. For the first time since she'd woken in this place, she felt not fear, not terror, not worry. Instead, something else burned in her, a hot and sharp and violent thing.

"Move it." It was a command from the doorway.

That raw new emotion flared so high, she had to fight to find her voice. "Are we going on the train?"

"No. I'll drive."

She walked to him, then with him down the corridor, aware he was keeping his stride short to accommodate hers, his big body moving with a grace that told her she'd never be able to move fast enough to escape him. Still, a pulse of excitement bubbled through her, lighting up her mind—the car, she thought, it had to do with the car. *If she had the car, she could find—*

Another black screen, her memory cutting out like a badly tuned comm panel.

Her nails dug into the soft flesh of her palms so hard she felt skin break. Relaxing her fingers with effort, she lifted her hand to look at one palm. It was hers, she knew that. Those life lines, they were hers. But there were other lines, thin white lines that crisscrossed skin unbroken except for the bloodred crescents she'd just created. How had she gotten those lines? Head beginning to pound in a dull, heavy beat, she stared, determined to divine the truth, no matter how ugly.

Warm male fingers gripped her hand. Startled, she jerked up her head—to meet Dev's scowl. "Don't force it," he ordered, squeezing her fingers. "Glen said the memories will return when it's time."

She didn't pull her hand from his, in spite of the violent chaos of her emotions. When he touched her, she felt real, a living being instead of a ghost. "I can't help it. I hate not knowing who I am."

"Hate—strong word." He led her through a pair of automatic glass doors. "Emotions come easily to you?"

"Yes." She swallowed as he paused in front of the elevator. "There's only so much the mind can take. After that, it splinters." Taking the lines of conditioning with it.

The elevator doors opened and Dev tugged her inside. She took one step across the threshold before freezing, her breath stuck in her throat, her spine so rigid she literally couldn't move.

Dev's hand flexed around hers and for an instant she was terrified he'd pull her inside. He was so much bigger, so much stronger, she'd never be able to stop him. Fear was a fist in her throat, blocking her airway.

Then he dropped her hand to wrap an arm around her waist, carrying her out and back into the corridor. "You don't have to go in there." One palm cupped the back of her head as he spoke in a voice as harsh as sandpaper. And yet his hold...

Her entire body began to shake, terror transmuting into a painful kind of relief. Not stopping to think, she buried her face in his chest, her arms locking around him. A rough word. The thud of the duffel hitting the floor. Then his own arms came around her with bruising strength. She wanted more, wanted to strip him to the skin and touch his heartbeat, convince herself that he existed, that *she* existed. Deep inside, she was so scared that this was all just another madness-induced fantasy, her mind trying to come up with something to fill the endless void.

"Shh." Spoken gently against her ear, the hot brush of his breath another tactile anchor.

Daring to move her hand, she placed her fingers against the side of his neck, feeling his pulse strong and steady against her fingertips. Real. So real. "I can't be in a box again." The last was a whisper as she caught a wisp of memory. "There was no light, no sound, no touch, no Net." How could there be so much pain in nothingness? But there was, excruciating, agonizing, relentless pain—pain that had turned her from a sentient being to something lower than an animal. "It was like I didn't exist."

Dev stood unmoving under Katya's hesitant touch. What she was describing was one of the cruelest forms of torture known to man, one that left no marks but destroyed the victim from within—sensory deprivation. Leave a thinking, living being without feedback long enough and the mind began to break, to turn inward, going so deep that many never came back out. And for a Psy to be cut off from the Net—

He blocked the wave of pity before it could rise. Because sensory deprivation wasn't only about hurting the victim until that person shattered. It could be used for a far more ominous purpose—to break down an individual and then build him or her back up again according to the torturer's requirements.

Katya might be precisely what she feared—Ming's creation.

The bruises, the scratches, the starvation, it had in all probability been nothing but the most calculated kind of window dressing, meant to make her appear weak, to arouse pity... and protectiveness.

Even understanding the bleak truth, he couldn't let her go, not when tremors still quaked through that unbearably slender frame. If he squeezed her too hard, he thought, he might break her. Psy bones were already more breakable than human, and she'd been starved on top of that—just because it was window dressing didn't mean she hadn't felt every blow, every kick, every hour of hunger.

He made a conscious effort to loosen his hold, but the instant he did, she began trembling so hard he thought she'd shatter from the inside out. Crushing her closer, he moved his hand until it lay underneath her braid, on the soft skin of her nape. That skin felt bruisingly delicate under his much rougher touch, but she calmed at the contact. So he held her that way, murmuring wordless reassurances as her fingers stroked over his pulse, as her body all but melted into his.

It took ten long minutes for her to stop shivering. The hand on his neck slid down to linger at the knot of his tie. He held his breath as her lashes lifted to reveal eyes filled not with the fear he'd expected, but with an almost impossible calm. "I survived that. I must be stronger than I think."

He knew it was a dangerous step into enemy territory, but he couldn't help the pride he felt in her—it was a swell of emotion, primitive in its ferocity. "Yes."

"Yes." Pushing off his chest, she stepped out of his arms. "Do you know—sometimes I remember being chased by a panther."

The change of topic stymied him for a second. Then he understood. "Do you want me to find out if it might have happened?" He could still feel the imprint of her body against his, a quiet brand that disturbed him on the deepest level.

"If you can. I need to know if I can trust the things in my head." She rubbed her hands down the front of her jeans. "It's such a strange thing to remember. Maybe everything I remember is a fantasy."

Dev didn't think so. He knew one changeling panther—but what the hell would Lucas Hunter, alpha of DarkRiver, be doing going after Katya in his aggressive animal form? "Do you think you can handle the stairs?"

A pause. "I believe so. There's always a way out with stairs."

That told him more about her captivity than anything else. Muscles tense with a rage that had no outlet, he bent to pick up her bag, then, in an act he'd never expected to come so easily, held out a hand. She took it at once, acting nothing like the Psy he knew her to be. The Silent race never touched, not if they could avoid it. Tactile contact was a slippery slope, they said, one that could lead to sensuality in other areas of life. But Katya openly craved contact.

There was no light, no sound, no touch, no Net.

Tightening his fingers on the already familiar warmth of hers, he held open the stairway door until she nodded that she'd be alright. And though she gripped his hand so hard he could see her every tendon, she didn't halt once on the way up—he wasn't sure she even breathed until they exited into the airy lobby.

Her gasp as she saw the soaring arches of the atrium made him appreciate the beauty of the building anew. In a clever bit of design, the square footage of the ground floor was wider than that of the solar-paneled office tower that stood atop it. The architect had used the extra real estate to bring light into the lobby—curving glass archways covered both the entrance and the large island manned by the receptionists. As part of the building's eco-rating, greenery crept over that glass, healthy and lush below a second protective layer of glass.

The end result was that on a cloudless day like today, walking through the lobby felt like crossing a sun-dappled clearing. But the architect had gone even further, using clever positioning of glass and mirrors to make optimum use of the natural light. That ingenuity not only minimized the use of artificial light during daylight hours, leaving more solar power for Shine to sell to the city grid, it bathed the entire area in a golden glow.

That glow lit Katya's face, caressing the translucent beauty of her skin as she stared, enraptured. "There's so much light"—she reached out as if to touch it—"it's so bright."

As he watched her, his gut went taut with an anger that had nothing to do with her being an enemy, and everything to do with the evil that had trapped her in the dark. No one had the right to savage another living being that way.

No one.

Yet . . . he knew that every time he "connected" with metal—and now—with machines, he took another step toward the kind of emotionless mentality that might green-light torture of the worst kind. The last time his great-grandmother Maya had seen him, she'd clasped his hands and begged, *pleaded* with him, to shield himself, to "stay human." But, just as an empath couldn't not sense emotions, Dev couldn't not feel the metal all around him. Metal *was* his shield.

And if that shield was slowly stealing his humanity... that was a price he was willing to pay to safeguard his people. His eye fell on Katya then, and something in him rebelled against what had always been an absolute acceptance. Her face was still lifted up to the light, her hands hanging loosely by her sides. Simple pleasure suffused every inch of her, until he was tempted to reach out and touch, see if he could absorb that joy into himself.

Dangerous, he thought, she was dangerous in so many ways.

CHAPTER 8

"Dev!"

Looking away from Katya's delighted face with reluctance
that sparked a blazing red warning light in his brain, he found
himself facing one of his vice-directors. "Aubry."

"Hi." Aubry smiled at Katya, his teeth flashing bright
white against skin the color of "the most luscious dark chocolate" according to Maggie. Like most of the women in Shine,
his secretary had lost her heart to the tall black man the first
time he smiled at her.

Dev waited to see Katya's reaction, aware he was pulling
metal from the building itself. She reached too deep, made
him feel too much, slipped under his defenses as if they didn't
exist.

Katya gave the slightest of nods. "Hello."

Aubry appeared a little startled at the formal greeting. But
he recovered fast, gentling his smile, tone. "You need to eat
more, darlin'." The slow music of Texas wove through every
easy syllable.

Dev was aware of Katya shifting closer to him, even as

she nodded. "Dev keeps putting food in front of me and saying *eat*."

The calm shook, threatened to break. He drew more metal, letting the chill work its way down to his very bones. But then Katya's fingers brushed his, and the metal boiled, a sudden, violent heat he'd never before experienced. He should've moved away. Instead, he allowed her to tangle her fingers with his, closing his hand firmly around hers.

Aubry chuckled. "Sounds like the boss." His eyes shifted to Dev.

Tempering the unfamiliar internal heat with more metal, Dev met the other man's gaze, knowing he couldn't give Aubry the answer he wanted—he couldn't promise to take care of the woman by his side, no matter that she aroused his most primal instincts. "Did you need me for something?"

"Yeah." Aubry frowned. "I wanted to go over some new—"

Dev cut him off before he could reveal anything sensitive in front of Katya. "Later. We'll set up a comm-conference. I'm heading out of town."

For all his lazy charm, Aubry was nothing if not intelligent. Picking up the subtext, he closed the small electronic organizer he'd flipped open. "I'll e-mail you the details—we can talk after you've had a chance to look things over. See you later, beautiful."

As Katya said, "'Bye," Dev sent a message to his car's onboard computer, telling the vehicle to meet them in front of the building.

Katya didn't speak again until they were almost to the curb. "That man—"

"Aubry," he said as the car rolled to a stop in front of him, the computronic system purring smoothly in the back of his mind.

"Aubry was very handsome." She sounded almost puzzled.

Dev used his thumbprint to unlock the car though he could

have as easily used his link with the computer. Only a very few trusted individuals knew of his gift with metal, even fewer of his developing affinity to machines. "Hop in." As she settled in beside him, he answered her earlier comment. "Women like Aubry." Age, culture, class, none of it mattered. The other man walked into a room and women smiled.

"I can see why," Katya murmured, watching him guide the car out into the traffic. After almost a minute of silence, she added, "A true Psy wouldn't have noticed his looks."

"Why not?" Dev suddenly realized he'd stopped drawing metal the instant he had Katya to himself.

"True Psy are Silent."

"Correction," he said. "Psy in the Net are Silent. Psy outside the Net are not. Both are Psy." And none of them affected him as viscerally as this woman who'd been dumped outside his home like so much garbage.

"The Forgotten," she whispered in a voice so soft he had to strain to hear her through the rush of protective anger. "I remember…the boy, he was one of yours. One of the Forgotten." Scrunching up her face, she paused for several seconds before uttering a sound of absolute and utter frustration. "I know something, but I can't reach it yet. Something about the boy."

Dev could guess exactly what she was trying to remember— Jonquil's ability to literally sweet-talk people into doing whatever he wanted would be considered the most perfect of weapons by Ming LeBon and his fellow Councilors. Psy in power killed with cold-blooded precision when necessary, but they preferred to work under the radar if at all possible—it made it far easier to disclaim all responsibility for the brutal acts they put in motion.

Glancing over, he saw Katya press her fingers to her temples, as if trying to still an ache—or force open the locked vault of her memory, no matter that it might incite even worse pain. Instinct rose, wiping out the civilized man and the cold control of metal both. "You *want* to cause an aneurysm?"

Katya felt her entire body tense at the unsheathed blade of his voice. "I just want to remember." The edgy response came from a new part of her, a part that hadn't existed before she woke in the hospital bed; a part, she thought with wonder, that was fresh, unbroken...the phoenix part.

"The memories won't make you who you were before."

"I'm not sure anything could." Her throat dried up as she glimpsed a flicker, a bare splinter of lost time. "I was so cold."

"You were Silent."

"Yes." She stared out at the traffic in the next lane, everything moving at a crisp pace that ensured there were no logjams inside the city as there had been in the late twentieth century. If a manual driver deviated too much from the optimum speed range, the car's backup system would kick in, putting it back in sync with the rest of the traffic. It was all about programming. Just like her mind. "I'm a blunt instrument."

There was no warning. One moment she was speaking, the next she felt her eyes snap shut as her spine arched in screaming pain. Then...nothing.

"Katya!" Reaching out as Katya's head fell limply to the side, Dev grabbed her wrist. Her pulse was strong, but irregular.

Where the hell was the exit? *There!* Pulling off, he managed to get into the parking lot of a huge mall situated on the very edge of the off-ramp. Undoing his safety belt and moving around the car to open Katya's door took only another few seconds.

"Come on," he said, cupping her face, "wake up."

When she didn't respond, he focused his residual telepathic ability and spoke to her, hoping the call would reach her on some level, stir her back to consciousness.

Katya.

A hiccup in her pulse.

That's it, your name is Katya. "Come back to me. You're

stronger than this." Another hiccup. "Katya." It came out as a caress, a spoken kiss.

Caught in the sticky strands of the cobweb that seemed to be growing ever stronger, Katya stilled, listened, heard a name. Hers? *Yes,* she thought, fighting the fog, fighting to wake up. It was hers. The first breath was a coughing rush, the second full of the exotic scent of a man with not-brown eyes and skin of such a beautiful shade that she wanted to taste it. "Katya," she said, her throat strangely raw. "That's me."

Dev's hands tightened on her face, his cheekbones cutting against that golden brown skin. "We need to get you back to the clinic."

"No." It came out without thought, an instinctive response. If he took her back, she'd be trapped again—and she needed to get moving, get there. *Where?* Shaking her head to clear the fog, she reached out to touch his shoulder. Muscle flexed under her palm, and her thoughts threatened to scatter.

Then she saw the determination in his eyes and knew she had to speak. "I think it was a response to a trigger of some kind. The words I said…there was something in them that my brain couldn't process, so it shut down for a few seconds to allow me to reboot."

Dev's expression changed, becoming almost ascetic in the stark purity of its focus. "It's coming back to you, isn't it?"

"Things come out of my mouth," she told him, her gaze locked to his, "and then I know them." It made sense to her, but she could see he wasn't convinced. "I'm not misleading you on purpose." It was so important that he believe her, that he know her, though he was all but a stranger.

But Devraj Santos wasn't a man who'd ever give her an easy answer.

Now, his lashes came down to hood his eyes for a second before he said, "I guess we'll find out soon enough." Getting up, he motioned her out of the car. "We might as well take a break so you can eat a bite."

She stared at the mall, at the mass of people, and felt herself shrinking back. "I'd rather stay here."

Dev's gaze rested on her for a long moment. She knew he hadn't missed her retreat when he said, "I'll bring you something." Closing her door, he walked around to the driver's side and pressed something on the dash. "Wouldn't want you taking off with my car." A piercing glance.

It was difficult to keep her face expressionless, her frustration contained. "If I wanted to, I could simply walk away."

"You're too weak to go far." A highly pragmatic answer. "And, I'm not taking that chance." The doors locked around her as he stepped back, activating the car's antitheft systems with what she guessed was some kind of a remote.

Katya waited only until his back was turned before trying to restart the car. *She had to get there, had to see, had to bear witness.*

It was a drumbeat in her head, that strange compulsion, but she didn't know where she had to go, didn't know who or what she had to find. All she knew was that if she managed to get free, she had to keep going, keep running until she ended up *there*.

But first, she had to escape.

Looking up, she saw Dev's tall form disappear into the mall—just as she located the panel that concealed the car's computronic safeguards.

PETROKOV FAMILY ARCHIVES

Letter dated February 24, 1971

My sweet Matthew,

Debate is raging across the Net. I can't set foot in the slip-stream without getting caught up in it. There's a sense of dis-belief at this proposal, this Silence the Council is calling "our best, perhaps our only, hope."

Maybe my fears were for naught. It appears that no matter the demons that savage us, in the end, we're far too human to do such irreparable harm to our young. For that mercy, I thank God with everything in me.

Love,
Mom

CHAPTER 9

Katya broke several nails but the panel wouldn't shift. It took her ten precious seconds to realize it had been locked in place by a second layer of security. Frustrated, she moved on, trying things she hadn't even known she knew until her brain put her fingers into motion.

All for naught.

The car's systems were as impregnable as a tank's. Giving up when it became obvious she was wasting her energy, she slid back into her seat and pressed two fingers to her forehead in an attempt to follow the thread of the compulsion, find out if her need to go there...go *north*—yes, north!—was nothing but another booby trap.

At first, there was only the sticky blankness of the cobweb, a prison that trapped her hands, muted her mouth. But then, she found herself standing in a quiet, hidden part of her psyche, a part protected by the phoenix's wings. That part whispered that this need, this urge, came from within herself. Yet how could she trust that it did when her mind was a cracked and fractured thing, full of holes and lies, illusions and nightmares? What if the phoenix she'd glimpsed was only a madness-induced fantasy, something she'd clung to when all else was taken from her?

A click of sound.

She snapped up her head to see the driver's-side door sliding back. Dev got in, his tall, muscular body taking up what felt like every inch of spare space. "Here."

Accepting the take-out drink container he held out, she frowned. "This is heavy for juice."

"Milk shake," he said, unscrewing the lid on a bottle of water and putting a spare bottle in the holder between them. "That's for you, too."

"Thank you." The cold of the milk shake seeped through the insulated container, a small thing, but she luxuriated in it, in the reminder that she was no longer in the dark.

"I made a call while I was in there," Dev said, surprising her. "The panther? It's a real memory."

"Oh." A slow bloom of hope unfurled. "Are you certain?"

A quick nod that sent his hair sliding across his forehead, drawing her eye. Pushing it back, he looked at the container she held. "Drink."

Aware she'd likely never tasted such a thing before, she took a cautious sip. Nothing came up. "The straw's defective."

Dev shot her a quick grin. It altered his face, turning him strikingly beautiful. But that wasn't the odd part. The odd part was that seeing him smile made *her* heart change its rhythm. She lifted her hand a fraction, compelled to trace the curve of his lips, the crease in his cheek. Would he let her, she thought, this man who moved with the liquid grace of a soldier...or a beast of prey?

"Did I say milk shake?" he said, withheld laughter in his voice. "I meant ice cream smoothie—with enough fresh fruit blended into it to turn it solid." Glancing at her when she didn't move, he raised an eyebrow.

She felt a wave of heat across her face, and the sensation was so strange, it broke through her fascination. Looking down, she took off the lid after removing the straw and stared at the swirls of pink and white that dominated the delicious-smelling concoction. Intrigued, she poked at it with the tip of her straw. "I can see pieces of strawberry, and what's that?" She looked more closely at the pink-coated black seeds. "Passion fruit?"

"Try it and see." Handing her his water bottle, he started the car and got them on their way.

"How would I know?" She put his water in the holder next to the unopened bottle. "And I need a spoon for this."

Reaching into a pocket, he pulled out a plastic-wrapped piece of cutlery. "Here."

"You did that on purpose," she accused. "Did you want to see how hard I'd try to suck the mixture up?"

Another smile, this one a bare shadow. "Would I do that?"

It startled her to realize he was teasing her. Devraj Santos, she thought, wasn't supposed to have a sense of humor. That was something she just knew. And, it was *wrong*.

That meant the shadow-man didn't know everything, that he wasn't omnipotent.

A cascade of bubbles sparkled through her veins, bright and effervescent. "I think you're capable of almost anything." Dipping in the spoon, she brought the decadent mixture to her lips.

Oh!

The crisp sting of ice, the cream rich and sweet, the fruit a tart burst of sensation. It was impossible not to take a second bite. And a third.

Though he kept his eyes on the road, Dev was acutely conscious of Katya eating up the smoothie. She was concentrating so hard on the treat she appeared to have forgotten all about him. The clawing protectiveness in him relaxed—he'd found something she'd eat. And if he had to feed her those things for the next month, she *would* put on weight.

She was of enemy blood. It would be in his best interests to keep her weak.

His hands tightened on the steering wheel. That ruthless voice was as much a part of him as the protectiveness, no getting around that—but these days, it dominated more and more. On the flip side, he thought, the Santos family tree was also lucky enough to contain an empath, a woman gifted with the ability to heal emotional wounds—maybe his great-grandmother's blood would save him from becoming a complete and utter bastard. That was what she'd predicted the last time he'd seen her.

"So much iron in your heart, boy," Maya had said. "I touch you and I taste metal."

"It's part of who I am."

"You think it makes you strong."

He hadn't argued.

"This isn't why my parents left the Net," she'd said, a scowl marring her delicate features. "They fought for our right—*your* right—to feel, to live as you wanted. Instead, you're becoming so cold you might as well be Psy."

His great-grandmother had been a child at the time of the defection, and, as with the others of her generation, it had been the defining moment of her life. What the old ones didn't understand was that the war had never ended, that iron-hard choices were all that kept the Forgotten from extinction.

And Dev wasn't yet bastard enough to shatter the heart of an empath.

Katya sighed, and that quickly, he was wrenched very much into the present. "Good?" he asked.

"I want to eat more but my stomach is protesting."

He let the ice of control go for the moment, the dark heat

of his nature filling the empty spaces within. "I'll pull up at a rest stop so you can throw away the cup."

"I don't want to throw it away." She licked the spoon with an innocent relish that hit him as anything but.

His entire body went taut, fixated on the lush softness of her mouth, the pink dart of her tongue. *Jesus, Dev,* he told himself, *this is hardly the time to be thinking of sex.*

His body had other ideas. Weak, fragile women had never attracted him. And Katya, she was all of that. But he'd glimpsed the steel frame beneath that translucent skin, those lost eyes— when this woman found herself again, she'd be a force to be reckoned with.

"I'll make you another one at home," he managed to say, his voice raw. "We'll stop at a grocer's on the way and pick up supplies." He couldn't stop looking after her. Another small weakness, another chink in his armor.

"Can I choose the fruit?"

Her excitement was both a balm to his hunger and fuel for the same. "How will you know what to choose?"

"I'll take one of each, then decide what I like." An eminently practical answer...and yet the shimmering joy in her voice was nothing practical, nothing remotely Psy.

If she was a weapon, she was a masterstroke.

A little more than two hours later, Katya walked across a wide porch and into a graceful house isolated at the end of a long drive and surrounded by what seemed to be acres of trees. A fine layer of snow had turned the area into a wonderland, but it was the house that captured her interest. "You consider this your home?"

Dev gave a short nod. "When I can get to it. Give me a second to put these groceries in the kitchen."

Deeply curious about the man behind the director, she turned slowly, taking in everything. The split-level house was wide and full of light, with furniture that was stylish yet appeared lived in. Blown-up photographs graced a few walls—she found herself moving toward one in mute fascination. It was a shell lying on the beach, its every precise angle illuminated by the lens. But there was warmth in the black-and-white shot, a sense that the photographer had been entranced by the beauty of the simple object. "Art," she whispered, hearing Dev's footsteps, "is not something the Psy appreciate."

"Perhaps that's why the Forgotten held on to it so hard." He leaned a shoulder on the wall beside the photograph, his arms loosely folded. "Almost all Forgotten children are brought up with a strong appreciation for art and music."

Katya considered whether that was a piece of knowledge that could be used to harm Dev and his people should she ever be thrown back in the hole, in the darkness, and decided not. "You prefer art."

A slight nod.

"You're very good." Psy didn't truly understand art, but there was a store of data in her head that told her she'd learned how to value it. Because, to those of her race, anything that gained in value was a sound investment, whether or not the owner actually found the piece aesthetically pleasing.

Dev's eyes gleamed when she looked to him. "How do you know they're mine?"

"They echo with you." Even as she spoke, she wasn't sure what she meant. She just knew she'd sensed his fingerprint on each and every piece. The clarity, the focus, it rang with his personality. But that warmth...something had changed. "When did you take these?"

"A few years back."

She wondered what had happened in the ensuing time. Because while he'd laughed with her, she sensed a cool kind of distance in Dev, a feeling that he held everything behind multiple shields. But then again, she was the enemy. Why should he share anything of himself with her?

Dev tapped the photograph of the shell. "Ever been to the beach?"

Sand in her shoes, in her hair, in her clothes.

"Yes." Grabbing the memory with frantic hands, she held on. "Once, when I was a child. It was...an accident. Our vehicle had a malfunction and my father had to pull to a stop near the beach."

"You grew up with your father?"

"Yes." Again, fragments of memory, sharp, almost vicious, as if they were being rammed out through the cells of her very brain. "No. Both."

"Both?"

"Yes." She shook her head, searching through the scraps for the piece that would complete the puzzle. Pain resonated down her spine, but she found that last, broken fragment. "They had a joint-parenting agreement."

"Sometimes," Dev murmured, "I think the Psy have it right with their agreements." The expression on his face was strangely remote. "Leaves no room for human error."

"There's no room for anything." Her mind continued to withhold so much, but she remembered the sense of isolation she'd always felt, even as a child. "There are no emotional bonds. My father could as easily have been a stranger—to him, I was an investment, his genetic legacy."

"Yet you feel strongly about him—you mentioned him first."

That halted her. She blinked, looked into those eyes she'd begun to see in her dreams. "Yes. I suppose...but isn't that a paradox? I didn't feel in the Net. I was Silent."

"Or maybe," he murmured, reaching out to slide a strand of her hair behind her ear, the touch inciting a shocking burst of sensation along her nerves, "you were simply silenced."

EARTHTWO COMMAND LOG:
SUNSHINE STATION

18 May 2080: The medical team is reporting a higher than average number of minor illnesses, with headaches being the main complaint. Tests to date have revealed that a small number of staff are suffering from recurring pinprick hemorrhages in the cerebral cortex.

Those affected are being regularly monitored, while a biomed team has been instructed to scan the area for any toxins that may be causing the problem.

However, no one has been disabled or seriously compromised as a result of these illnesses, and productivity remains high. There is no need for replacement personnel.

CHAPTER 10

Dev's words—the impact of his touch—circled endlessly in Katya's head as he showed her upstairs and to her bedroom. That room proved lovely and airy, the sheets on the double bed a rich cream shot with rose. "It's perfect, thank you."

"Unfortunately, they don't open." He nodded at the two wide windows on the opposite side of the room. "The wood swelled last winter, and I haven't gotten around to replacing it. But you'll get plenty of fresh air if you leave your door open during the day."

Katya looked at that handsome face and saw a merciless conqueror, a warrior king whose sense of honor would never allow her to be mistreated. And yet... "It's a very comfortable prison." A low curl of anger unfurled in her stomach.

He didn't flinch, didn't pretend surprise. "What I said about why the windows don't work? Truth. But yeah, that's why you're getting this room and not one of the others."

"What do you expect me to do?" She waved at the endless spread of green and white beyond the glass. "We're in the middle of nowhere—I doubt I could find my way out if you gave me a map and a compass."

"But the car has a nav system," he said with quiet implacability. "It also has security features that tell me when someone's tried to start it without authorization."

Ice trickled down her spine, extinguishing the anger. "I'm a captive. It's my duty to escape."

"And go where?" A harsh question from the warrior, all traces of civilization stripped away. "You were dumped on my doorstep like trash."

She was the one who flinched. "That doesn't mean I'm not wanted by someone. My father, for one."

"Never lose an investment?" The razor of his words sliced over her flesh, slitting her open.

"Yes," she whispered, wanting to believe that the cold man who'd raised her, with a woman as cold, cared whether she lived or died. "He'll help me."

"Against the Council?"

No, she thought. Her father was no rebel. He'd brought her up to be a good Council soldier. But she'd chosen her own path—and in that truth, she had found her strength. "I'll help myself."

Dev shook his head, sunlight gleaming off the black of his hair, highlighting the hidden strands of bronze. "You can't even stand for ten minutes without your legs getting shaky."

It angered her, his sheer disregard for her abilities. She was—*a blank.* No one. She was no one. But she would become someone, she vowed, looking into that arrogant face. Devraj Santos was going to eat his words.

Walking over on the legs he'd mocked, she pushed him in the chest.

He didn't shift so much as an inch, but his eyes narrowed. "What was that for?"

Her palms tingled where she'd touched him, her skin tight

with painful craving. "I want you to leave." Fighting the need for tactile contact, she folded her arms and tilted her head toward the door. "Right now."

"And if I don't?" He stepped closer, until they were toe to toe, those impossibly beautiful eyes of his staring down at her.

He was good at intimidation.

But she was through with being intimidated. "Then you'd better eat carefully," she said sweetly. "I am a scientist, after all."

"Poison?" His lips curved. "Bring it on."

"I just threatened you and you smiled. I tried to escape and you got angry?" She didn't understand him.

"The threat," he said, touching his fingers to her cheek in a slow caress, "is permissible. After all, I'm keeping you prisoner, and it's hardly as if you can overpower me. But the escape attempt? That, I won't allow—you belong to the Forgotten, and until I figure out what you're meant to do, you're staying right where I can see you."

She understood the distinction. When she dealt with Dev, the man, she might get away with a great deal. But when it came to Devraj Santos, director of the Shine Foundation, rebellion could cost her everything. The heat that had reignited within her during the argument, the sudden spurt of fire, chilled under the ice of understanding.

She didn't know what she would have said, didn't know how he would have responded, because his cell phone beeped at that moment. Except... he made no move to retrieve it from his pocket. The sustained eye contact stole her breath, threatened to pull her under. "Aren't you going to answer that?" Her voice sounded strained to her own ears.

"No."

The sheer *iron* of the answer made her heart crash against her ribs. "Has anyone ever talked you out of anything?"

"If I'm in the mood."

His answers kept confounding her. He didn't behave according to how her brain, how her knowledge of the world said he *should* behave. "What do you want?"

The phone stopped beeping.

Dev blinked, a slow, lazy thing at odds with the wild energy that she'd felt under her palms. "That's the problem, isn't it?"

PETROKOV FAMILY ARCHIVES

Letter dated November 30, 1971

Dearest Matthew,

Today you fell off a swing and bloodied your knee rather spectacularly. But you know what? You never cried. Instead, you stood there, your face all scrunched up and tears glittering in your eyes as I cleaned and bandaged the wound. It wasn't until I kissed it better that you threw your arms around me and told me it "hurt." Oh, my baby, you make my life a joy. And soon, you'll have someone else to play with—your father has charmed me into giving him another son or daughter, you a little brother or sister.

I love him, your father, exasperating man that he is at times. But I wonder at bringing a child into this world. The tide is changing, Matty. Today, Mrs. Ennis told me that maybe the Council is right, that maybe we should embrace Silence. I wanted to argue with her, but what could I say in the face of her loss? She's still grieving for her husband. As soon as Enforcement catches one serial killer, another takes his place. Mr. Ennis was simply one victim among many—and that horrifies me.

And yet, I can't accept a protocol that would steal your smiles, your tears, your very heart. You're more precious to me than all the peace in the world.

Love,
   Mom

CHAPTER 11

Changing into sweatpants and a sleeveless tee, Dev continued to ignore his cell phone in favor of a hard workout in the gym set up at the back of the house. Pounding his fists into the punching bag worked off some of his frustration, but left him with no new answers.

Katya drew him. Simple as that. And it was about time he admitted it.

She was the enemy, had even warned him that she was a grenade waiting to blow up in his face, but still, she drew him. Part of him wanted to protect her, take care of her, while the other part, the hard-nosed pragmatist, warned him that doing so would just come back to bite him on the ass.

He'd almost kissed her upstairs, his entire body humming with the raw excitement that came only from arguing with a woman who aroused a much more intimate passion. She *shouldn't* have been able to get through the metal of his shields, shouldn't have been able to affect him on such a visceral level, not without a conscious decision on his part.

And yet she had. She did. Every fucking time.

Slamming his foot into the punching bag, he spun and came down feet flat on the exercise mat.

"You're good."

He didn't turn, focusing on his next round of punches. "Been doing it since I was a teenager." Since the day he'd realized he carried within him the seeds of the very violence that had shattered his life as a child. "Good stress relief."

Katya stayed in the doorway, and he was blindingly aware of her gaze as she watched him. It took all his concentration to maintain his focus. "We'll get you into doing some easy stretches, strengthen those muscles."

"Are you sure I have any?"

It was a kick to the gut, that hint of humor. He glanced at her, pushing damp hair off his face, conscious of the fact that his tee was sticking to his body, his arms shimmering with sweat. "I'm sure there're one or two hidden away in that scrawny body of yours."

Hazel eyes darkened. "Do you always insult the women you kidnap?"

A temper. Interesting. "Depends on the woman."

"How many have you brought here?"

None. Dev didn't share his personal spaces well. "That's for me to know." Wiping off his face with a towel he'd thrown in the corner, he strode to the door. "I'll make you that smoothie after I shower."

She shifted away as he walked past. It was a very Psy thing to do. They hated any kind of physical contact. But Katya had seemed to crave it. Irritated at the change, he took the steps with angry confidence. And when the shower came on ice-cold, he left it that way.

Katya bent over, bracing her hands on her knees as all the breath simply rushed out of her. Dear God, she'd known he was in shape, but...

She swallowed, tried to relearn to breathe. She'd once seen a tiger in a wildlife reserve in India. Her job had been with a multinational lobbying for permission to mine in the region, but it was the image of the tiger that had always stuck with her. The lethal grace, the beauty of it—even her Psy mind had understood that it was something extraordinary.

Dev's muscles slick with sweat, his biceps defined as he punched the bag—he'd been as wildly beautiful as that tiger, as far from the man in the dark suit and formal shirt as she was from the Ekaterina who'd once worked for the Council. It had taken every ounce of control she had not to reach out and stroke him.

He'd probably have snapped off her hand if she'd dared.

Drawing in another shaky breath, she walked across the exercise mat to put her palm on the punching bag. It was heavy. And he'd been sending it back and forth like it weighed nothing. Her memories of the details might be scattershot, but she knew that all her life, she'd valued psychic strength over physical. But after seeing Dev move, she was revising her opinion.

The physical plane was just as powerful as the psychic.

Especially between male and female.

And for the first time, she felt very much female.

She drew in a deep breath, trying to find her balance… and catching an echo of Dev's distinctive scent instead, harsh, sensual, unforgivingly masculine.

Something low in her body tightened, a sensation for which she had no name, no comparison. It was hot and tight and… needy. And it craved Devraj Santos.

CHAPTER 12

Dressed again after the welcome chill of the shower, Dev picked up his phone to see three missed calls. One from Maggie, two from Glen. Maggie had left a message saying she'd rescheduled his meetings, but Glen had hung up both times.

Running his fingers through his damp hair in lieu of a comb, he coded through a call to the doctor as he headed downstairs. The house's security was undisturbed, which meant Katya was inside somewhere. Deciding to finish the call before he tracked her down, he walked into the kitchen and pulled out the blender.

"Dev?" Glen's voice came on the line. "Where were you?"

"Busy." He put the milk on the counter. "What is it?"

"One of the Shine Guardians picked up a kid in Des Moines. Looks like a true telepath."

Dev froze. "They sure?" True telepaths were extremely rare outside the PsyNet—after their exodus, the Forgotten had intermarried with humans and changelings, had mixed-race children. Their abilities had changed in remarkable ways, but they'd lost things, too. The first to go had been the purity of certain Psy abilities—some Psy in the Net could telepath around the world without blinking an eye. None of the Forgotten had been able to do that since the rebel generation.

"Very," Glen said. "You know the Guardian—Aryan—he has some low-level telepathy himself, and he did a phone consult with Tag and Tiara. All of them agree the kid's showing clear signs of strong telepathic abilities."

Tag and Tiara were the strongest telepaths in the ShadowNet— the neural network created by the original rebels when they dropped from the PsyNet—but even their range was limited to a distance comparable to the length and breadth of the United States. Of course, that was impressive on its own. "Is he salvageable?" Dev had to ask that question, though the weight of it was a rock on his chest. He hated losing any of his people, hated it with a vengeance that had turned him merciless.

"Kid was in a state home." Glen's voice was tight. "Parents died in a car crash, leaving him an orphan. The grandparents apparently never passed on the fact that the father was descended from the Forgotten, so the poor kid's been doped up on meds most of his life for his apparent schizophrenia."

Anger roiled in Dev's gut. That knowledge should never have been lost. All the Forgotten who'd scattered after the Council began hunting them had been told to keep precise records for the very reason that latent genes could awaken with devastating results in their children. "Mother had to be one of us, too, if the kid's a true telepath."

"Aryan tracked her records down. Her great-great-grandmother was part of the original rebel group." Glen muttered something blue under his breath. "The boy's fragile, Dev. He's going to need you—you've got a way of getting through to these kids. If I didn't know better, I'd say you had some kind of empathic ability."

Dev knew it was the opposite the children sensed in him— that he was a pit bull, one who'd let no one and nothing get to them. "I'll be there."

"What about Katya? You want one of the others to keep an eye on her?"

"No. She comes with me." It was an instinctive response, threaded with an almost brutal possessiveness. Something in him flinched at that description, at the realization that he was losing the cold faster and faster.

But Glen didn't argue. "With the meds currently in his system, the boy isn't going to be coherent for at least two days, so we don't need you until then."

Hanging up after getting a few more details, Dev set his senses to searching. This aspect of his abilities, while very minor in the scheme of things, was an interesting offshoot of telepathy. He could literally scan a discrete area, correctly identify the individuals in each room, and if he was emotionally linked to someone, accurately guess at his or her mood.

Katya was sitting in the sunroom out front.

Her mood was opaque to him, her secrets hidden.

Slamming a glass on the counter, he poured the milk into the blender and scooped in some vitamin-laced protein mix. "Katya!"

She appeared in the kitchen doorway a minute later. "Yes?"

"What fruit?"

For an instant, he thought she'd tell him she wasn't hungry, in which case, this would've gotten ugly—his need to take care of her was a fucking fist in his gut, a violent protectiveness that demanded release. But she stepped closer and picked up a mango.

He gave her a knife. "Peel and chop."

Taking a second mango, he quickly did the same. He was done before she got halfway...because she kept licking at her fingers. His entire body became one giant pulse as he watched her close her lips around a finger and stroke it through. "Katya."

She colored, misreading that single strained word. "It tastes so good."

He couldn't help it. Raising a piece of the juicy yellow flesh to her lips, he said, "Open."

Eyes locked with his, she obeyed. Her lips—soft, lush, wet—brushed his fingertips as he fed her the fruit and it was the most erotic thing he'd ever felt. "Good?" he asked, his voice husky.

A nod, blonde hair catching the light. "Where's the ice cream?" An ordinary question, but the way she was looking at him said something else altogether.

Reminding himself that, everything else aside, she'd been unconscious not that long ago, he shut the door on a desire that threatened to undermine his every vow, his every promise. "I'll get it." Adding it to the mix, he finished blending everything and poured her a glass. "You're eating a sandwich, too."

"I'm not really hungry."

"Tough."

The glass she'd picked up met the counter with a bang. "What will you do if I don't eat?"

"Tie you to a chair and wait until you decide to cooperate. Then I'd feed you every bite." Shoving bread across the counter, he began to take out the fixings. "Start making your own, or I'll do the choosing."

This time, the look she shot him was pure female fury. "Just because you're bigger doesn't mean you have to be a bully."

"Just because you're a woman doesn't mean I'm going to let you get away with bullshit."

She slapped butter on her bread, then reached not for the ham or cheese, but for the raspberry jelly. "Quiet," she said when he opened his mouth.

Raising an eyebrow, he went to the pantry and brought back a jar of crunchy peanut butter. "Goes well together."

She shot him a suspicious look but took the jar. Not saying anything, he quickly put together his own sandwich, then took it and her smoothie to the table. Katya followed him a minute later, after putting away the jam and peanut butter with slow deliberation—as if hoping he'd be gone by the time she was done.

When she did sit, she kept her eyes resolutely on her meal.

He was, he realized, being ignored. Grinning, he sprawled back in his chair, his legs encroaching on her space.

Katya had spent her life in science. She might not remember much of it, but she knew she'd been cool, calm, collected, even beneath the Silence. But today, with Dev, she'd come startlingly close to losing her temper. And right now, she wanted to kick his feet away from her chair, aware he was deliberately pushing into her personal space.

Big shoulders, long legs, muscled power, and contained arrogance. No wonder he made her mad. But— She put down her sandwich, her mouth suddenly bone-dry. "Why isn't my emotional state leaking out into the Net?" Betraying her, warning the others that she was a traitor to Silence.

"You said you were trapped." The hairs on her arms rose in response to the ice in every word. "It makes sense that the shield isn't only meant to serve as a cage. It has to hide you, too—the fewer people who know about a Trojan horse, the more damage it can do."

"Why do you sound so calm about that?" She leaned forward, searching for answers. "For all you know, my task might be to kill you." A chill snaked up her spine, and she found herself whispering, "There's a good chance it is that."

One shoulder lifted in a negligent shrug. "I'm not easy to kill."

"Don't be so overconfident. I'm a telepath, after all."

A silence.

She blinked. Shook her head. "Yes, I'm a midlevel telepath... and M-Psy. Dual abilities, with both my telepathy and my medical talent measuring at around the same level. Below 5 on the Gradient."

Dev knew the Gradient was the scale the Psy used to measure power, with 10 being the highest level. Apparently, cardinals were unmeasurable beyond that point. "Send to me."

"Dev! If they find me—"

"Council already knows we've got some remnant abilities— and I don't intend to let you go." Soft words, lethal as blades. "I've only got a touch of telepathy. I want to know if it's enough to 'hear' a Psy."

She sent the first thing that came to mind. *Don't you consider yourself Psy?*

Dev tipped his head slightly to the side, a furrow between his eyebrows. "I almost caught it. Like a too-soft murmur. What did you say?"

She repeated her question aloud.

"No." His mouth firmed. "The Psy cut off my ancestors without a thought—then they tried to annihilate them. Far as I'm concerned, that removes any family connection." He reached forward with a speed she had no hope of avoiding and gripped her chin, his hold gentle but firm. "Do you? Consider yourself Psy?"

"It's what I am." But his question raised ones in her own mind, stabbed phantom pain into her heart. "They threw me away."

Dev rubbed his thumb over her chin, a slow, intent stroke. "Or you could see it another way." Golden brown eyes watching her with the same absolute focus she'd seen in that tiger's gaze.

"What other way?" she whispered, realizing she was leaning toward him.

But she couldn't pull back, couldn't be the Psy her fractured memories told her she was. Every atom of her being was focused on the roughness of Dev's skin against hers, the angles and planes of his face in the sunlight, the shape of his mouth as he said, "That they gave you to me."

CHAPTER 13

Nikita stared out at the patch of the Net that was simply "dead." "How long has this been here?" she asked the mind at her side.

Councilor Kaleb Krychek sent her a psychic image. "Threads have been running through the Net for some time now, but nothing like this."

"What's caused it?"

Kaleb paused, as if considering how much to reveal. As a cardinal telekinetic, perhaps the most powerful Tk in the Net, he wielded considerable control over the NetMind, the neo-sentient entity that *was* the Net given form. It provided Kaleb with a conduit of data no other Councilor could match. But all he said was "You have your own suspicions."

She decided there was nothing to be lost in sharing them. "The surge of violence in the past months—the compulsion killings—they left a mark. I think this is a psychic scar."

"Possible."

"But you don't agree?"

"I think the echo of that violence will ripple through the Net for some time, but this speaks of a deeper malaise."

"You think the Net itself is...sick," she said, for lack of a better word. "If that's true, it's going to start affecting the populace." All Psy were linked to the Net on the most basic level—there would be no way to avoid the insidious effect if these "dead" areas continued to grow.

"Maybe it already has—perhaps cause and effect are now locked in a feedback loop." Kaleb touched a psychic tendril to the edges of the darkness.

Nikita kept back. "You could become infected with whatever it is that's caused this."

"No," he murmured, almost absently. "I'm shielded."

She knew it was more than that. Could it be that Kaleb had some affinity to the spreading stain? "Where else is it this bad?" This patch was small and isolated—as if the disease was hiding. Nikita would've considered the anthropomorphization absurd in any other context, but in spawning the NetMind, the Net had clearly proven it was an organism of some kind.

"This is the worst," Kaleb responded, drawing back the psychic tendril he'd used to explore the darkness. "It's as if all the dead threads have been migrating here, collecting in a pool."

"That means it's going to keep growing."

"Unless we can find a way to negate those threads of darkness."

She felt a flicker of warning. "Why are you showing this to me rather than to the Council as a whole?" They were allies of a kind, but there had been something else in that statement.

"I thought it'd be obvious," he said. "Your daughter is a cardinal E-Psy."

"I see." And she did. The last time the Net had threatened to self-destruct, it had been because the E-Psy had been systematically eliminated. But the situation was completely different now. "There are millions of E-Psy present in the Net." The Council had stopped the deletion orders on all E-designation conceptions once it became apparent that their simple presence—no matter if their empathic powers were kept ruthlessly contained—helped keep the mental fragmentation at bay. "This is something else." The problem was, she had no idea what.

CHAPTER 14

It was dark. *So dark. Darker than the night, than the midnight sun. No, that didn't make sense. There was no such thing as a midnight sun. No...Alaska had a midnight sun. But that meant there was light all day long. Here there was no daylight, no sunlight, no hope.*

She tried to curl her fingers and toes but couldn't feel them. It was as if they'd been eaten up by the darkness. It was tempting to scream, to hear sound even if she couldn't see, couldn't feel, but she held it inside, locked within the walls of her mind. The monster had taken everything else she had.

She wouldn't give him her screams.

But minutes, hours, days later, she lost the battle and her anguish poured out of her in a wave of sound.

Except...she heard only silence. The darkness absorbed even her scream.

And that was when she knew.

She truly was dead.

* * *

Heat.

Touch.

Life, electric in its fury... a kiss that demanded her participation.

Shuddering in surrender, she drowned in the scent of him. Wild and exotic. Dark and male.

A man who'd snarled at her, caged her... fed her.

"Dev." Spoken against his lips, she was so loath to break contact.

His mouth took hers again before she could say anything more, his teeth sinking into her lower lip. She jerked, dug her fingers into solid masculine shoulders. Never, she knew, had she experienced anything even remotely similar. He was so hot, she wanted to crawl into him. His skin burned her fingertips, and she wanted more, wanted to be naked, to have him crush her to the sheets, his weight a heavy, immovable blanket.

Gasping in a breath when he released her, she stared into his eyes, wondering if he could read the clawing depths of her need.

"You back?" His voice was harsh, his eyes glittering fever bright.

Her breasts brushed against his chest with every breath, the tips so tight with need, it was almost pain. "Where did I go?"

"You were screaming your lungs out." He continued to hold her in an embrace she knew she'd never be able to break. "Wouldn't wake up no matter how much I shook you."

"So you kissed me." It had been, she was forced to admit, a highly practical decision. Even a broken Psy would react to something so completely against her conditioning. "Thank you." It would've been prudent to pull back, but she'd never felt more alive, more *real*. "I think... that was my first kiss."

A low, rough word. "Hell, I'm sorry."

"Do it again."

His lashes came down. Once. Twice. She expected refusal. Instead, he tugged back her head and brushed his lips over hers, a single hot caress. When she tried to get closer, he refused to let her. "Dev."

"Don't rush." And then he touched his mouth to hers again, but this time, he lingered.

Acting on instinct, she sipped at the fullness of his lower lip, felt the rough warmth of his body tense against the palms she'd pressed flat on his chest. For a second, she was afraid he'd stop. But he deepened the kiss with slow, sweet strokes that made her fingers dig into the firm muscle under her hands as her body filled with a liquid kind of heat. Hips twisting in a hunger she barely understood, she tried to pull him closer.

"Enough." Harsh, spoken against her lips.

"A little more." Every hot breath, every stroke, every lick, it anchored her in the most sensual, most earthy of ways. "Touch me."

His fingers tightened in her hair instead, his jaw setting in a way that was already becoming familiar. "Why were you screaming?"

Somehow, the softness of the question, the strength of his hold, made it easier to return to the nightmare. "I dreamed I was in the hole, the nothing-place, again."

Something flashed across his face, something so razor sharp in its fury, it should've made her run. But all she wanted to do was strip him to the skin, feel his body hard and unashamedly male over hers. "Dev—"

"You're scared," he said, fingers on her jaw. "I'm not going to take advantage."

Her eyes dipped to the straining bulge of his arousal. "You want to."

"What we want"—a voice as unbending as stone—"isn't always good for us."

Hearing the finality in that, she swallowed the need that urged her to keep pushing. "Thank you for coming to me."

"Are you going to be alright now?"

The truth came out before she could censor herself. "No." Without the erotic shield of Dev's kiss, fear was already crawling up her legs, creeping into her lungs.

He didn't say a word, simply got up and nudged her over on the bed. She shifted with alacrity, feeling the mattress dip to his side as he lay down beside her seated form. He was, she noticed, wearing only a pair of sweatpants, his chest a lithely muscled plane sprinkled with dark hair. Fingers curling into her palms, she found her gaze dropping, following the trail that—

"Come here." He held up an arm.

Jerking up her head, she felt her cheeks burn.

"I don't bite."

She wasn't so certain. This man, he confused her. As hard as he was beautiful, and yet capable of a gentleness that left her floundering. Now, he just watched her, let her make up her own mind. There was only one choice, only one place she wanted to be.

The erotically charged taste of him still in her mouth, she scooted over and laid her head down on his arm. It curled around her shoulders, curving her into his body. And the contact—hot, real, Dev—shoved the fear aside. When he pulled a sheet over them, she didn't protest, tucking her head against his chest, her fingers curling into the crisp hairs on his chest. The last thing she was aware of was his heartbeat.

Dev brushed Katya's hair off her cheek and studied her sleeping face, his eyes lingering on the lush sweetness of her mouth. Hunger and innocence, it was one hell of a potent combination. His body surged at the memory, defying his efforts to keep it under control. Gritting his teeth, he sought out all the metal in the house.

The cool kiss of iron and steel brushed his mind, invaded his limbs. It wouldn't last long, not with Katya's slight form resting trustingly against him—but he'd use the calm while he had it, see if he could find answers to some of his questions in the ShadowNet. He'd heard stories of the PsyNet, that it was an endless field of black littered with millions of white stars, each star representing a mind, but it was a concept he had trouble understanding.

How could minds remain completely separate?

Closing his physical eyes, he opened a psychic gateway and stepped out into the organized chaos of the ShadowNet. Given their comparatively small numbers, the "skies" of this psychic network were stretched thin in comparison to the endless breadth of the PsyNet, but it was a riot of color, of connections.

From where he stood, he could see the solid threads that tied him to both sets of grandparents—his bond with his maternal grandmother was the strongest, but he was linked indelibly to all four, and the two couples were also connected to each other, though those links were much weaker. More threads linked him to uncles, aunts, cousins, friends, some thin, some strong, some on the verge of breaking.

And then, there was the strange, almost invisible dark thread that tied him to his father.

All the crisscrossing bonds made the ShadowNet a busy place to navigate. Most people tended to follow the lines of connection until they found the person they wanted—sometimes even then, the lines were so tangled that it took a few tries to locate the right thread. But the one that Dev wanted stood out like a beacon—bright silver and tough as titanium.

His maternal grandmother took no shit from anyone.

Smiling inside at the thought of the woman he'd loved since the day he'd first opened his eyes and seen her watching over him, he shot along the silver thread and "knocked" on the door to her mind. She responded a moment later. Conversation in the ShadowNet itself was difficult because of the amount of psychic "noise," so they both hooked into the emotional line that connected them, creating a direct conduit for speech— and affording unbreachable privacy.

"Devraj." His grandmother's energy was strong, beautiful, carrying within it the echoes of incense and spice, silica and molten heat. "A little late to come calling, *beta*."

Only his grandmother ever called him "beloved child" in the language of his mother. "I figured you'd be up working on your designs."

"The glass is becoming more and more stubborn with age. Today, I meant to finish a stained glass window except the red refused to cooperate. It turned orange instead."

He was used to the way she spoke of her precious glass as if it were a sentient being. "You still haven't sent me my birthday present."

"Cheeky boy." A psychic brush against his mind, an affectionate kiss on his forehead. "You'll get what's coming to you."

He laughed, and it was perhaps the only time he ever truly did that anymore—with her, the woman who'd loved him even when he'd hated himself. "Nani," he said, using the Hindi word for maternal grandmother, "I need some advice."

"You've been walking a lonely path these past few years."

"Yes." He'd never lied to his grandmother. Perhaps he'd withheld his darkest secrets, but he'd never lied.

"The metal—I know it kept you sane at a time when another child might've broken," she said, the warmth of her love a gentle wind across his senses, "but you must see what it's doing to you."

It was, Dev knew, becoming fused into his very cells.

Sometimes his mind was so cool, so flawlessly quiet that he wondered if it was blood that ran in his veins, or something far less human. "I can no more stop reaching for metal than you can stop shaping glass." Steel and iron, copper and gold, it all called to him, resonating on a psychic frequency he alone could sense. "It helps me do what I need to do."

"Understand the Psy?"

"Yes. And make decisions that need making."

A sigh. "Metal melts, too, *beta*. It is not always hard, not always cold."

"That's the problem. Something's penetrating my shields."

"Without your conscious control?"

"Yes." He told her about Katya. "I'm the director—I can't afford that kind of a chink in my shields."

"No."

"I should remove the threat."

"Kill her, you mean."

"Yes."

There was no shock from his grandmother. In her youth, she'd been one of the foot soldiers for the Forgotten. "This woman, this Katya," she now said, "she plays on your weaknesses."

Katya's screams echoed inside him, full of so much terror, he didn't know how she'd survived. "I don't think it's deliberate."

"Perhaps." A pause. "If she is a sleeper assassin, it may be that she was chosen...no, that she was *made* to disarm you. Your history isn't public knowledge, but neither is it completely hidden—you may believe you're refusing her entry, but your subconscious has clearly opened a door for her."

Something twisted inside him, shooting barbs into his heart. "If she was designed to get under my skin, they did a good job." She'd slipped inside him with such stealth, the perfect stiletto in the dark.

"Ah, Devraj, don't sound as if you've been played for a fool." A pulse of loving energy that was as familiar as the melting silica of her precious glass. "I'm happy for you."

"Why?"

"It shows you still have heart, that you didn't immediately move to strike. And I'd rather you have that than be a cold-blooded general who thinks of nothing but power."

"Her mind," he said, "do you think you might be able to unravel the programming?" His grandmother was only a midrange sender, but she was very, very good at untangling psychic knots—an odd skill that the Psy in the Net seemed to have lost. Perhaps it was no longer necessary now that they were Silent.

It was very much necessary for the Forgotten.

Nani was the one who'd untangled the ribbons of madness that had ravaged Dev's father. The ribbons always came back—faster each time—but now they knew what to watch for. The first time...Dev shook his head in violent repudiation.

For a second, his attention split between the psychic and physical aspects of his nature as Katya stirred. Putting his hand on the back of her head, he gentled her into sleep once more before returning to his grandmother.

"I'd have to see her." Her mental tone was serene, yet no less sharp for it. "But you know the problem—we're not the same as the Psy in the Net. I may not even be able to sense the bonds that lock her in, much less the deeper programming."

"I don't want you trying yet in any case." A midrange Psy telepath could do a lot of damage to one of the Forgotten who'd lowered her shields.

"You call me when you need me." Another psychic brush. "Do you want to talk to your *nana*?"

"No, let him sleep."

"You know he never sleeps while I'm awake. Stubborn man."

He sent her a good-bye kiss before dropping from the

ShadowNet. Coming back into his own mind was an easy glide, a familiar truth. He understood exactly how the woman in his arms felt at being cut off from the psychic plane. It must be akin to having a limb amputated, a claustrophobic terror.

If, of course, she was telling the truth.

This woman, this Katya, she plays on your weaknesses.

How could he not have seen it? It was as if someone had gone into his very psyche and created a woman he simply *could not* harm, no matter what he'd told himself to the contrary. Even now, with the truth of his grandmother's words ringing in his head, he couldn't repudiate Katya...couldn't send her back to the dark.

Her hand spread over his chest.

He sucked in a breath through clenched teeth. He was a healthy male in his prime—he liked women, and most of the time, women liked him back. But never had he felt so close to the edge, so close to going out of control. Too many emotions clashed inside him—including a dawning possessiveness that might yet spell his death.

"Dev." It was a complaint. "Stop broadcasting."

He froze. "Have you been listening to my thoughts?" That should've been impossible. He'd never been able to send to anyone but his mother. When she'd died, that part of him had simply gone silent.

A shake of her head, fingers rubbing at sleepy eyes. "It's a drumbeat against my skull—bam, bam, bam."

Intrigued, he ran his fingers through her hair. "How do you know it's me?"

"It feels like you." A yawn and her lashes lifted. "And you're giving me a headache."

He should've been penitent. Instead, he moved to brace himself on his arms, her body slender but intrinsically feminine beneath his. It was her eyes that did it, huge pools that asked something from him he'd never be able to give— to her, to anyone. He'd left that part of himself behind in a sun-drenched room the day he watched his father close those always careful hands around his mother's throat.

Shadows moved in the clear hazel, awareness sparking out of sleep. "Dev."

"Shh. No words." He ensured that by claiming her mouth, by stealing her breath. There was no gentleness in him this time. He crushed her to the bed, used his teeth on her neck, fisted his hand in her hair.

Just one kiss, he thought, *just one.*

Then she wrapped her arms around him. And he gave himself leave to take this much of her. Their lips came together in a darkly sensual connection, every gasp filled with the inevitable truth—this moment, this kiss, was a stolen one. All too soon, reality would claim them both. And when it did, Dev would either have to destroy her fledgling smile, savage her heart... or betray every vow he'd ever taken.

PETROKOV FAMILY ARCHIVES

Letter dated March 4, 1972

Dear Matthew,

Something extraordinary happened today. I'm still not sure I believe it. Catherine and Arif Adelaja appeared in public for the first time in a decade—with their twins, Tendaji and Naeem. The boys are teenagers, strong and quite beautiful. And they are Silent.

Arif made a speech, said that he and his wife had—wait, I have an idea. I'll paste a copy of the relevant part of his speech into this letter. When you're older, it will give you a glimpse of the strange world in which you grew up, in which your sister will be born.

> *Like many of you, Catherine and I have lost too many family members to the ravages of their gifts. Some have simply crumpled under the pressure, while others have broken in a more violent way, taking countless men, women, and children with them.*
>
> *We lost our infant daughter to a psychotic outbreak that destroyed a close family friend, turning her into a malevolent creature no one could recognize. Tilly was a sweet, gentle woman who loved children, and yet that day,*

she used her telepathy to shatter our Margaret's mind as our precious baby screamed and screamed.

In truth, we lost two people that day. Margaret to Tilly's madness, and Tilly to her own horror and guilt.

We refuse to lose any more of those we love. Which is why we've been working to condition emotion out of our sons since the moment of their birth. Perhaps some of you will call us monsters, but today, our children stand alive beside us, in full control of their gifts. We've given them life.

I understand Arif's grief—I was only twenty when he and Catherine lost Margaret, but I'll never forget his keening agony the night he found their poor, sweet baby. It ravaged him, ravaged them both. The man I saw today bears the emotional scars still. They're so deep and true that he can't see the paradox in his own words. To save those he loves, he's willing to destroy the capacity to love itself?

How is that in any way an answer?

Mom

CHAPTER 15

Katya accepted Dev's offer of a walk without hesitation the next morning. Something had shifted between them the previous night—she could feel it deep within: a subtle tug, a bond barely formed.

But that wasn't the change that distressed her.

Dev walked beside her, but gone was the man who'd kissed her with a passion that had seared her to the soul. Only the director, hard, focused, unreachable, remained. As she watched his teeth sink into the crunchy flesh of a bright red apple, she couldn't help but remember those same teeth grazing her neck, nipping at her ear. Yet it seemed impossible that this cool stranger was the darkly sensual man who'd taken her mouth until she felt branded to the very core of her being.

"Perhaps he did me a favor," she said when the silence became too crushing.

"He?"

"The shadow-man." The spiderweb in her mind pulsed, a constant reminder that she was, in the end, nothing but a puppet. Her hand clenched into a fist. "By breaking my Silence."

"There are ways to do that without destroying the individual." He threw his apple core into the undergrowth, his jacket dusted with snow that fell from an overhanging branch. "Let's go down here."

She followed him through the snow-covered firs, but her mind had turned inward. For the first time since she'd woken, she looked deep within, examining the strands of control—of compulsion—that swirled around her psyche. Each was barbed. Ripping them out would destroy parts of her, maybe cause brain damage. It would've been easy to give up—but she chose to let the brutality fan the simmering flames of her anger.

And when she saw the pathway, she didn't hesitate to take it. The vines of control ripped at her from every side, drawing blood that felt real, the acrid scent of it thick in her nostrils, but she pushed through, determined to find answers, determined to find herself.

Two steps later, terror silvered into her mind, into her very heart. "Dev." A husky plea to a man who seemed to have frozen his own heart with the dawn.

He took her hand, the heat of him soaking into her skin, through her blood, into her very cells. The terror remained, but she understood it now. It was an implanted fear, designed to stop her from reaching the end of this road. Her mind felt as if it was awash in blood by the time she completed the task, but she didn't stop.

And there it was, buried so deep that it was as much a part of her as her heartbeat—her link to the PsyNet, to the biofeedback that kept her Psy brain from dying. She looked at the solid column of light, brilliant and beautiful, and understood that it offered no means of escape. The link jacked her directly into the fabric of the Net itself, but it was no tunnel. No, this was the most solid of conduits, its only purpose to keep her alive. To get out, to actually surf the Net, she'd have to find a doorway.

She'd tried to do that once before, but then she'd been physically weak, her mind in chaos. It was possible she'd missed something. Today, she took every step with slow deliberation... and she found it. The psychic doorway was hidden behind several layers of barbed wire. Swallowing, she thrust her hands through the viciousness of the coils and cracked it open the barest millimeter.

Black.

Not the black of the Net, but the black of a shield. She knew the shield had been created by her torturer, that it linked back to him on some level. But... "It's not mind control," she said out loud. "It's not an open link. That would take too much energy." So he'd immured her in her mind, given her instructions, and set her free. "He doesn't know what I know, doesn't see what I see." The fist around her heart fell open.

"You're probably programmed to contact him if you discover something important." Dev's tone was flat as he came to a stop in a small clearing pierced by a ray of sunlight. "Could be as simple as a phone call."

Closing the psychic door, she backed down the path and returned completely to the world. It was an effort to keep her feet on the glittering white of the snow, to tell herself she wasn't truly bleeding. "I don't think I was ever meant to come out of this alive."

The tendons of Dev's jaw pulled white over bone. "What did you see?"

"The roots of *his* control, they're buried deep. I can't see a way to pull them out—even if I could figure out how—without killing myself in the process."

"He must have the psychic key to unlock it safely."

"Not like he's going to give it to me." She slid her hands into the pockets of her coat, chilled to her very soul. "So since I'm dead either way, do you know what I want to do?"

Dev simply watched her with those amazing, amber-flecked eyes.

"I want to follow the only thing I have left—my gut."

"What's it telling you to do?"

She met his gaze, hoping for understanding, for freedom. "To go north."

But it was ice that met her. Cold, blank...metallic.

Dev had every intention of continuing their conversation, but returned home to find a situation in progress. "We'll talk about this later," he told Katya.

"There's not much to talk about. Will you let me go?"

"You know the answer."

"Say it." Her body trembled, her hands fisted at her sides.

Angry at her for demanding something he could never give her, he answered with a curt "No."

Still feeling the impact of her flinch several minutes later, he switched the clear screen of his computer to comm mode, dialing through to Aubry. "Maggie says we've got an uprising in progress."

The other man nodded, face grim. "It's the young ones, twenty-year-olds who think they know everything there is to know."

"Are they with Jack?" His cousin stood on the opposite side of the fence to Dev on the most critical issue facing their people, but he'd never gone behind Dev's back before.

Aubry shook his head. "Looks like some kind of 'radical' college group. Snot-nosed punks aren't as radical as they think."

"Give me the short version."

"They think, and I quote, that 'there's no need for their families to be tied to Shine.' According to Beck, the pretty-boy academic leading the charge, we're an 'anachronism' that serves no purpose in today's society." A snort. "I think it's time we showed them the fucking reality—those tortured kids last—"

"No." Rage infused Dev's blood at the reminder of the children Shine had lost to the Council's coolly logical evil, children who'd been murdered simply for being who they were.

Aubry's scowl was pure thunder. "Why the hell not?"

"I won't use those children again." It was a line he'd drawn in the sand. He'd had to use them once, to save the ones who were still alive. It had scarred him. One more time and he'd be so far on the wrong side of the line there would be no redemption for him.

"Yeah, okay." Aubry rubbed a hand over his face, having had the nightmare branded into his memories, too. "What do we do with Beck's group, then?"

"Give them what they want. Take them off the Shine register, let them know we no longer expect them to come to our assistance if called." Those with money contributed to the coffers, but the basic requirement was for service.

"Dev." Aubry looked troubled. "They're just stupid kids—they don't know how much we do, how badly they might need us in the future. What about their own children? Some of the recessive genes can express out of nowhere."

"I know. But we can't afford to baby them." It was a ruthless decision, but he had to focus on the ones he *could* help, could save. "They're old enough—if they want out, give them out."

Aubry met his eyes. "Tough love?"

"You don't agree?"

"As a matter of fact, in this case, I do." A sharp grin. "Let's see how long they hold out without the Shine information line."

"Yeah, yeah, crow all about it." Aubry was the one who'd come up with the idea of setting up an information line manned by older members of the Forgotten, people who—between them, and with recourse to Dev and the board—could answer pretty much any question the descendants might have.

"I will, thanks." Aubry's eyes gleamed. "I did a shift on

the phones the other night and had this anonymous kid call in. He wanted to know if it was normal to be seeing everything in triplicate."

"What'd you tell him?"

"To get his eyes checked and call me back."

Dev laughed, but it was a hollow sound. Nothing could ease the vise around his heart—because no matter how hard he tried to keep Katya at a distance, the metal still melted for her, still burned for her... for the one woman he could never have. "Anything else I need to know about?"

"Jack's quiet—don't know if that'll last."

That vise twisted, powered by another layer of emotion. "I understand what drives him," Dev said, staring out at the snow-covered landscape that spread beyond the windows. "Makes it a hell of a lot tougher to play hardball."

"The fact that he's your cousin doesn't help."

"No." Dev thrust a hand through his hair. "If he's quiet, let it be for now. It's not exactly an issue we have an answer for."

"We're going to have to think of something soon. Or there's a chance the Forgotten will splinter again."

"I know." Leaning back in his chair, he caught a glint of pale gold on his desk... a strand of Katya's hair. It could've been transferred to the study on his body, but there was a chance she'd been in here. She'd have gotten nothing, but Dev was well aware she shouldn't be this free to move, to sabotage.

Looking away from the golden strand, he made himself return his attention to the matter at hand. "You okay to keep an eye on these college kids?"

"Yeah. I'll tag them in the files—if they do decide to go lone wolf, we need to be able to step in if they have children with active Psy genes."

"That's what Shine's always been about." Protecting the children. And if that meant the death of a Psy scientist... Dev's hand clenched on a paperweight hard enough to crack it.

PETROKOV FAMILY ARCHIVES

Letter dated June 7, 1972

Dearest Matthew,

I don't know quite what to write, so perhaps I should just write it as it was and let you make up your own mind. This morning, through the oddest sort of coincidence, I met Tendaji and Naeem Adelaja.

The family was scheduled to come to the government block for a meeting with the Council, and security, as you can imagine, was tight. Their older brother, Zaid, there's such pain in him, and yet such conviction, too. As soon as I looked into his eyes, I knew he'd do anything for Mercury.

But I'm getting ahead of myself. My job as aide to Councilor Moran allows me a certain security clearance, though not high enough to meet the Adelajas now that they've become so very important to our race. Today I went in early, because I had a report to complete, and as I was heading through the lobby, I saw three men enter the elevator that goes up to the secure level. I thought nothing of it until someone called out my name.

When I turned, there was Zaid, holding the elevator open. He'd remembered me from when the Adelajas lived on the same street as your father and me—back when we were first married. Well, I went to them and all three boys stepped back out into the lobby, and we were able to talk for a few minutes before their meeting.

Zaid... I always liked Zaid. He was such a solemn child—I knew in my heart that he carried the burden of terrible power. Now he reminds me of a soldier, strong, determined, proud. Beside him, his twin younger brothers were slender and so cold I could almost feel the ice on their breath. Tendaji spoke for them both—they were polite, precisely so, and their intelligence can't be doubted. And yet I kept feeling as if I was talking to two shadows—it was as if something critical was missing.

No, I'm not saying it right. Not missing, dead. Killed. As if part of them had ceased to exist. I said nothing of the sort, of course, spent most of that short time speaking with Zaid. I'd hoped he'd one day find peace. And I can't argue that today, there was a sense of purpose in him that spoke of peace.

If that's true, then perhaps this Silence has a chance? But Zaid, with his courage, his strength, and his will, isn't the future. The twins are. And they're so removed from humanity that I fear what such a course will do to the wild beauty of our race. Will the PsyNet one day turn dark, our minds cold, isolated stars?

I don't know. And it terrifies me.

With all my love,

Mom

CHAPTER 16

Katya jumped when Dev walked into the sunroom, where she was viewing archived news footage in the hope of triggering new memories. His eyes went to the trail mix in her hand.

Heat burned across her cheekbones. She'd all but thrown it back at him when he'd handed it to her after that flat-out "no" about going north. Now frustration, anger, *need*, it all tangled inside her, stealing her voice. The only thing she could do was watch the contained strength of him as he walked around to sit on the sofa beside her. "NewsNet," he said, taking the remote. "That's the Council's propaganda machine."

Her paralysis snapped in the face of his arrogance. "It is not." She tried to get the remote back, but he held it out of reach. "What're you doing?"

"Here." His body a line of heat against her side, he switched to an unfamiliar channel. "CTX is what you want to be watching—they're the ones who broke Ashaya's story, and they're currently running a series on the recent surge of public violence by Psy."

Unwilling, unable, to pull away from him in spite of her

simmering anger, she watched. "It's very energetic." No NewsNet reporter would ever gesticulate as wildly, much less use such emotive language.

"Hmm." Reaching over, Dev stole some of her trail mix, popping it into his mouth in a smooth gesture that hijacked her interest from a report on what appeared to be some kind of political turmoil in Sri Lanka.

Drawing in a deep breath, she tried to focus. But the scent of Dev—rich and wild, with an edge that tasted of steel— settled over her senses, holding her in thrall. He glanced over at that very moment and for the space of a single frozen second, everything stopped. Dev broke the electric contact by putting his arm around her.

She resisted. Because in that fleeting instant, she'd glimpsed a thousand shadows in his eyes. "What's going to happen when we get back to New York?"

"Later, Katya."

Shaking her head, she turned to push at his chest. "The pretense ended last night." With the painful honesty of that kiss.

He closed his hand over hers, holding her palm against those pectorals she ached to have the right to stroke. "A few more hours," he said, his expression stark with things unsaid. "Do you want this to end so soon?"

No, she thought, *no*. Even if their relationship was a fragile construct formed of hopes that would never survive in the harsh light of day, she wanted to cling to it with all the strength in her. Giving in, she settled herself back by his side, curling her fingers lightly into his chest, her knees scraping against his thigh as she sat with her legs bent, feet pointing away from him.

His chin brushed her hair as he said, "Watch this."

It took her emotion-torn mind several seconds to realize the import of what the reporter was saying about trouble in Sri Lanka's legislative capital. "She's talking about Psy." Her mouth fell open. "The reporter's saying Psy attacked a government building!"

Dev's free hand came to rest on her knee. "Only four people," he murmured, "but that's four more than should exist under Silence."

"That's Shoshanna Scott!" Blasted by memory, by reams of connected knowledge, she would've jerked upright had Dev not been holding her.

On-screen, the slim brunette waited until the reporters had quieted to make her statement, her pale blue eyes striking against the darkness of her hair, the creamy white of her skin. Shoshanna Scott was the Council's public face for a reason—she had an appearance of such delicate beauty that people forgot the Psy ruled with their minds, not their bodies.

"This was," she began in a clear voice, "an incident provoked by Jax."

Katya couldn't believe it—her memories, shaky as they were, told her the Council liked to consign the Psy drug problem to the darkest of corners.

"The psychological weakness," Councilor Scott continued, "inherent in those who succumb to Jax is unfortunately not a genetic abnormality we can screen against."

"Councilor!" A short man with stiff black hair stood up, his eyes that of a rottweiler. "There are rumors this incident was caused by Psy who've given in to their emotions. What's your answer to that?"

"It's a ridiculous assertion. Normal Psy do not feel."

"Clever," Dev muttered, stroking his hand down her calf in a caress that shattered her concentration. "She's sidelining those four, effectively making them non-Psy."

Another reporter stood up even as Katya realized he was tugging her feet out from under her, placing them on his lap. "Dev—"

"Shh." His eyes were on the screen, but his fingers continued to stroke lightly over her calf. "Listen."

She forced her attention back to the screen, hearing only the last part of the newest question.

"—Jax is a problem for Psy?"

"For the weak among us, yes," Shoshanna said. "Some individuals are intrinsically flawed."

The report cut off at that moment, with the anchor doing a short analysis. "She took the less damaging blow," Katya said, skin stretching tighter with Dev's every languid stroke, "acknowledging the Jax problem rather than admitting Psy are beginning to break Silence."

"Yeah, that's my take, too." His hand closed over her ankle in a grip that screamed possession. "It's not really admitting anything, is it? Everyone knows some Psy do Jax. The junkies are hard to miss." The lazy stroke of his thumb over her anklebone.

Her thighs pressed together in an instinctive response she barely understood. Dragging in a breath, she tried to find her train of thought. "But it's the deeper issue that's really interesting—the public nature of the breakdowns."

"These four aren't the first," he said, his breath mingling with hers as their faces came ever closer. "There was a rash of similar incidents not that many months back. They'll be in the CTX archives."

It should've been a startling piece of information, but— "I worked with Ashaya for years. I always knew there was something imperfect about her Silence." And if there was one, why not more?

"Stop that."

Only then did she realize she'd been petting him through the thin cotton of his T-shirt. "I—"

His hand curled into her hair, tugging back her head and cutting off her words. She found herself looking up into a face that could have as easily belonged to some dark age of war and conquest. Devraj Santos, she thought, made a good show of being civilized, but peel that away, and this was who he was at the core. Hard. Ruthless. Quite possibly without mercy.

"Such big eyes," he murmured. "Don't you know you shouldn't play with what you can't handle?"

"I figured," she said through a throat that had gone as dry as dust, "my status as a likely enemy spy would save me." Except somehow, she was draped across his lap, her heart thudding in time to his.

"No one said," he murmured in that low, compelling voice, "I couldn't have it both ways." His lips touched hers.

The intensity of it made her toes curl. "You can't." But her hand was on his neck, though how she dared touch a man this dangerous, she didn't quite know—no matter how tame he appeared, he wasn't, never would be.

"No?" Another fleeting touch, the hand that had been on her leg closing gently around her throat.

"No," she whispered. "I'm either the enemy or..."

"Or?" He sipped at her lower lip, a tiny, suckling kiss.

"Exactly." It came out ragged, her heartbeat pulsing in every inch of her skin.

He gave her another one of those maddening little kisses, making her fingers clench on his neck, her body twisting impossibly closer. Something flickered in his eyes, a glimmer of what seemed to be gold. Then his head dipped and she forgot everything but the pleasure that arced through her body.

Taking her lips in a slow, so slow kiss, he drove her mad even as he gave her just what she wanted. The heat of him was a wave against her body, making her nipples ache, the soft cotton of her bra suddenly unbearable. It would've made a "normal" Psy pull back, scramble to reinitialize the conditioning. But Katya craved the sensations, the feeling of being alive, of *existing*.

Here, with Dev, there was no room for the madness that had stalked her in that lightless, formless chamber, where the temperature never changed, and no one spoke to her for so long, she would've debased herself for a simple human kindness.

Teeth sinking very deliberately into her lower lip.

She opened her eyes to find him watching her with the

glittering gaze of a tiger who'd sighted prey. When he released her kiss-wet lip, she stayed in place, feeling his pulse against her palm, his skin hot and somehow intriguingly rougher than hers, his body so big, so strong that it blocked out the world. What would it be like if he covered her with that raw male heat, if he simply took her over?

She shivered.

Rubbing his thumb over the sensitive hollow at the base of her neck, he said, "Top or bottom?"

"What?" Had he read her mind?

"Top or bottom?" he repeated softly.

She was suddenly very certain she was in over her head. Devraj Santos wasn't the kind of man a woman "learned" on. He'd not only take, he'd demand, and if those demands weren't met...He'd be no easy lover.

As his next words proved.

"Would you like me to kiss you here"—the brush of his knuckles across her breasts—"or go lower?" A big hand closing over her thigh.

Dev knew he should stop, that she'd hate him the next day if this went any further. But he'd used up his self-control last night. No amount of metal on earth could stop him now. All he wanted was to strip her naked and taste. "I'm a selfish bastard."

Her eyes were almost pure green as she looked at him. "Not if you're the one being kissed."

He froze.

Before he could snap himself out of it, she was pushing up his T-shirt, her intent clear. He wasn't about to argue. Releasing her only for the seconds it took to rip the soft cotton over his head, he shifted their positions until she sat straddling him, her hair brilliant in the sunshine pouring in through the huge windows to his right. "I'm yours," he whispered, his voice husky with the ferocity of his hunger. "Do whatever you want, whatever you like."

She spread her fingers on his pectorals, the shock of it going straight to his cock. "I want to..." Her voice whispered away as her fingers caressed him, light, so light that his entire body arched upward, begging for more. She shuddered, leaned forward...then shook her head. "No."

It took him almost a minute to find his voice. Even then, it came out gravel rough. "Are you sure?"

"What happens when I insist on going north?" Her hand swept out, accidentally knocking the trail mix to the floor.

And he knew the time of illusions was over. "I can't let you go."

Hazel eyes locked with his, the intent in them unmistakable. "You can try to hold me. You'll fail."

"I'm not used to failure."

"Dev, I have nothing to lose." Quiet words, but her will—it was a steel blue flame. "I know I'm looking down the barrel of a gun that *will* go off in my face. So if necessary, I'll cut off my hands to get them out of cuffs, break my own ankle, do whatever it takes to escape."

The bloody images slammed into him, hard, brutal, unforgiving. He'd heard words like those before. From the men in his old army unit when they'd been boxed in, with no way out. All seven had survived—because they hadn't cared whether they lived or died. Better to go out fighting than live as a prisoner of the enemy.

Katya would do exactly as she said if he tried to hold her.

And he would do everything in his power to keep her. "You're still a threat," he said, knowing he was tearing apart the fragile new bonds between them, damaging them beyond repair. "I'll do whatever it takes to contain you."

Katya felt an unwelcome start of surprise.

Dev, she realized, had been very careful with her. She'd thought she'd known, but he hadn't truly shown her the utterly ruthless side of his nature until this moment. Though his voice was soft, everything about him said he was speaking the unvarnished truth. He'd lock her up and throw away the key if that was what it took.

And she had no way to fight him.

Angered by her own helplessness, by her foolish hope that he'd change his mind, she pushed off him. His hands tightened on her hips for the merest fraction of an instant before he let her go. Moving to a separate armchair, she folded her arms around herself. "I want to see Ashaya." It was a small rebellion, a reminder that she wasn't as alone as he might think.

He didn't put on his T-shirt, a bronzed god in sunlight. "You didn't seem keen on talking to her when she visited."

"I was ashamed." Unable to stop her eyes from drinking in the addictive beauty of him, she got up and walked to stare sightlessly through the windows. "I didn't understand why then, but now I know."

"She'll have guessed—"

"It doesn't matter!" Thrusting a hand through hair that had begun to lighten even under the winter sun, she leaned her forehead against the glass. "I need to face her, tell her what I did."

Dev's voice came from inches behind her. "You've remembered more."

"I dream." Such horrible dreams. "But last night was different—for a while it was as if I'd wiped the grime off a particular lens, making everything crystal clear."

He leaned forward, one hand palm down on either side of her head. "How much?"

She found herself desperately fighting the urge to lean back, to surrender to the illusion once again. "Pieces, but enough that I know I need to tell Ashaya, warn her."

A long silence, broken only by their breaths, the window fogging over to lock them in a still, quiet intimacy. "You could be a threat to her family, the children. You were pretty adamant yourself about not going to her when I mentioned it at the clinic."

Her stomach dropped. "Yes...yes, you're right." Legs weakening, she braced herself on the glass rather than on him, not sure she'd be able to pull back a second time. Emotion was a feedback loop without rules, without boundaries. It scared her how susceptible she was to this man who seemed almost Psy in his ability to lock away his emotions when they became inconvenient.

Forcing herself to think past her turbulent awareness of him was almost impossibly hard, but something in his words drove her forward. "Dev," she whispered, "you said children. Ashaya only has a son."

The solid warmth of Dev's body stroked over her as he spoke. "The two kids who were kept in the labs while you were there..."

"The boy and a little girl." So young, so vulnerable.

"Ashaya didn't kill them—she helped them escape."

Panic beat in her. "Wait—"

"The Council knows," Dev told her. "The kids were adopted by a DarkRiver couple and after Ashaya's defection, there was no need to hide them."

Emotion—relief, worry, joy—buffeted her on every side. "I guessed that Ashaya got them out, but I was never sure." And she hadn't asked, conscious that the fewer people who knew the truth, the better. "I suppose," she managed to say through the chaos in her body, her mind, "I'd begun to think that since I hadn't been compelled to head toward her, Shine had to be the target, but the reality is I could be programmed to hit her or the children. I'd never know until that particular component of the compulsion activated." Her hand fisted so tight, she felt her entire hand throb. "I *hate* this, not knowing what's in my own head."

"How far would you go to fix that?" Dev asked, and there was a darkness in his voice that should've scared her.

But she'd gone past that kind of fear. "As far as it takes!"

"Would you leave the PsyNet?"

That halted her. It was a question she'd never even considered. "I can't. I need the biofeedback provided by my connection to the Net." Psy who lost that feedback died within a matter of minutes. "I know—I remember—the ShadowNet can't take pure-blooded Psy anymore."

His arm muscles went rock hard. "I didn't realize Psy knew that."

"Not Psy...well, I suppose the Council does now." She wrapped her arms around herself, ashamed of how utterly she'd broken, how much she'd betrayed. "Ashaya and I, we made that assessment. It was a best-guess scenario. We had to know, you see."

"Yes." A silence. Then, a wave of heat, as if he'd shifted an inch closer. "If the ShadowNet could support full-bloods, rebels would have the perfect escape hatch."

Katya bit her lip, wanting him to close the final, minuscule gap between them and hating him at the same time for inciting such need inside her. Because, unlike Dev, she didn't know how to go cold anymore. This want, this hunger, she'd never be able to put it back in its box. But she didn't turn, didn't pound him with her fists as she wanted.

"It wasn't mercenary," she said. "There's just so much we can't do because we're trapped by our need for feedback. If we could somehow neutralize that..." More and more of her memories were starting to come back, as if her mind had picked up enough steam that it could part the curtains, even if it was only segment by slow segment.

"The thing is, Katya," Dev said, his lips grazing her ear in a hot caress that almost broke her, "the ShadowNet would probably drive most Psy to insanity. It's chaos given form."

"What about the ones who are already mad?" she asked, seeing another painful truth. "What about the ones like me?"

CHAPTER 17

Jack looked up as William walked into the garage. "Hey, kiddo. What's up?"

"I have a question." All big moss green eyes, Will hitched himself up on his usual spot on top of the closed tool chest.

"Yeah? Homework?" Setting down the old-fashioned saw he'd been using to shorten a length of timber in preparation for building a tree house, Jack headed over to hunker in front of his son, glad Will was acting more like his normal self. After the last incident... "Hit me with it."

But Will didn't respond with his usual mock punch. Instead, his lower lip trembled. "How do you know if you're bad?"

Jack touched his son's knee, fear a knot in his throat. "Did you do something, Will?" It had been two months since the dead birds on the lawn. Not one or two, dozens of them. All appearing as if they'd simply fallen from the sky.

Will had woken screaming in terror that morning, and while Melissa had cuddled his shivering form, Jack had gone out into the dark edge of dawn to prove to Will that it had only been a dream. He'd found a nightmare instead. But Jack had buried the birds before full light, and Will had never known. "Come on, son," Jack said, raising one little hand to his mouth for an affectionate kiss. "Did you break a window or something?"

Will shook his head. "No. I haven't done anything yet."

Something in those words made Jack's heart chill. "You think you're going to do something?"

"I'm bad," Will whispered. "I'm bad inside."

"No, Will, you're not." He would not allow his son, his precious child, to become a victim of his own gifts. "You're a good boy."

But tears filled Will's eyes. "Help me, Daddy."

CHAPTER 18

What about the ones who are already mad? What about the ones like me?

Katya's question haunted Dev as he finished working out that night, trying to exhaust himself in an effort to forget the delicate heat of her hands, the lush warmth of her body. But the exercise did little to assuage his frustration. He was angry at fate itself—why bring Katya into his life if he was meant only to destroy her?

"Dev."

He looked up, having sensed her arrival. "What're you doing here?" It had taken all his control to leave her that afternoon instead of pressing her to the glass and taking her in every way his body demanded...then doing it again. "Go back to bed." Because he couldn't trust himself. Not after walking away twice, and now with the night a secret blanket that hid them from the world.

"I need to ask you something." Stepping into the gym, she padded across on bare feet, until they were separated by only a single step.

His fingers curled into his palms as she looked up, eyes luminous. "I've been thinking about what happened this afternoon."

"Katya—"

"*No,* it's my turn to speak."

He gave a short nod, unable to talk past the need in his throat.

"I've decided," she said, "that I was shortsighted. I want—"

"No." Gritting his jaw, he went to walk past her.

She stopped him with a hand on his arm. "You don't know what I was going to ask."

Pushing her back against the wall, he found he'd fisted his hand in her silky soft hair. "I know what a woman's got on her mind when she looks at me that way." And his body was only too happy to reciprocate. Except he couldn't do that to her. She had no idea what she was asking for, what she was risking.

This afternoon, he'd been drunk on his hormones, but if he did this tonight, it'd be a conscious choice, one that would haunt him forever. "The answer is no. It'll continue to be no."

A blush of color across her cheekbones, so fucking innocent he called himself every name in the book for letting things get this far. But then she parted her lips and he couldn't remember what he meant to say.

"Why not?" she insisted. "There's a connection between us."

It was all he could do not to take what she was offering. His cock pounded with every beat of his heart, hard and painfully ready to take her, *mark* her. "Have you ever been with a man, Katya?"

"You know I haven't."

Yeah, he knew. Psy didn't believe in such intimate pleasures. "Then let me tell you something—we do this, it won't only be physical sensations you experience."

A steady look, but he felt the fine tremors that snaked over her body, they were pressed so close. "I'll feel more bonded to you."

"That's one way to put it." He couldn't let go, couldn't step back. "This afternoon, you learned to hate me a little."

She didn't answer.

"Tell me."

"Yes," she said, jaw setting. *"Yes."*

It felt like a fucking lance through the heart, for all that he'd known it already. "We do this, think about how badly it's going to hurt when I have to throw you into a cell."

She physically flinched. "I know things will change. I'm ready."

It would be so easy, so very easy to let her talk him into it. "Are you?" He spoke with his lips against hers. "Or are you just hoping I'll spare your life if we fuck?"

Her entire body went stiff at the deliberately crude statement. "Let me go."

He gripped her hip instead. "Hate me enough yet, or—"

"You've made your point!" She pushed at his chest with angry hands. "Now let me go!"

He heard the break in her voice, and it broke him, too. "God help me, but I can't." Crushing her to him, he held her tight.

She didn't stop fighting till he whispered, "Shh, I've got you."

A pause. "You said that to me before." Her arms slipped around him, her voice a trembling whisper. "You saved my life that night."

Unspoken were the words that it was a life he could no longer protect.

When they slid to the floor, he leaned back against the wall and held her as close as humanly possible. They sat that way for hours, until dawn streaked its way past the horizon.

CHAPTER 19

"The situation in Sri Lanka," Shoshanna said to Henry, "were you responsible?" They'd been a team for years, working to increase their combined power in the Council, but after the incident with Ashaya Aleine's prototype implants, he'd changed. She was certain he'd sustained brain damage when the implants malfunctioned, but instead of lessening him, whatever had happened had unleashed another part of his personality—one that could lead to their downfall.

"And if I was?" He sat across from her, eyes dark, without expression.

She checked her shields to ensure they were locked tight. Henry was a telepath, 9.5 on the Gradient. He could sweep through a mind with lightning speed. Satisfied she was still safe, she sat back in her own chair. "It wasn't you," she said slowly. "You're smart. You learn from your mistakes." He'd never confirmed it, but she knew he'd been behind the spate of public violence by Psy approximately two months ago, violence that had led to renewed support for Silence. "Given the way the PsyNet functions, violence will only spawn more violence. And you want Silence to hold."

"Not just hold, my dear," he said, the endearment meaningless. They'd both learned to use such little "humanisms" to make themselves more palatable to the human and changeling media.

"No?"

"No. I want it to consume the Net, until there isn't even a whisper of dissent."

Pure Silence was what Shoshanna wanted as well, but... "What about the Council?"

"Perfect Silence will eliminate the need for a Council." He met her gaze. "We'll all think with one mind."

"Impossible." For the first time, she wondered if Henry would go so far as to kill her to achieve his aims. "Without an implant that impels a merge, we're too individualistic to form a universal mind."

"One of us will be proved right, one not. Shall we wait and see?"

She gave a slow nod, moved to the true reason she'd asked to meet. "We're stronger together than we are apart."

"Yes."

"Then we remain a team?"

"No. We remain two Councilors with aligned goals."

That wasn't quite what she was used to hearing from Henry. However, it was far better than the current situation. "Agreed."

"I believe Nikita may have something of the same arrangement with Councilor Krychek."

"Nikita would strike a deal with Satan if he existed, so long as it advanced her business interests."

"And you wouldn't?"

"Of course I would." She rose from the chair. "That's how I became a Councilor."

"Have you been able to speak with Ming?"

"He knows we utilized the prototype implants without authorization. He won't be swayed to our side without considerable effort." She paused, considered whether to share the information, and decided to go ahead. "I don't believe all the scientists died when the Implant lab exploded."

"Highly likely. Ming wouldn't waste so much potential, even to make a point."

"It's possible he may be developing an implant of his own."

"We'll find it before he finishes," Henry said with sublime confidence. "That kind of a secret is near impossible to keep. Even you could not do that."

Henry waited for her to respond. She let him.

Finally, he rose and walked to stand in front of her, a tall man with mahogany skin whom the human media had dubbed "patrician." She cared nothing for that, only for his mental and political strength.

Now, he proved his political acumen by saying, "The Sri Lankans broke naturally—the anchor in that region is fluctuating."

Anchors, as Shoshanna well knew, were integral to the functioning of the PsyNet. Since anchors were born, not created, they were identified young and trained to use their abilities to merge with the Net to ensure it remained stable. But those unique Psy also had a habit of failing spectacularly—a disproportionate number of serial killers had come out of the pool of anchors in recent times.

"Do we need to bring it up at the next Council meeting?" With some things, there was better political mileage in taking the initiative.

"I'll take care of it."

"Henry, we need the anchors." They couldn't simply be rehabilitated like the others who broke. Rehabilitation left very little of a functioning mind, and the anchors needed those minds to do their jobs.

Henry's expression didn't change. "He can be brought under control with a little judicious telepathic reshaping."

"That could break his mind."

"I know what I'm doing—I've had some practice." He stared at her. "If we succeed, we'll have an anchor who's bound to us. That part of the Net would be ours to control."

And if they failed, no one would know. "Do you need my assistance?"

"Keep snowing the media. I'll do the rest."

As Henry left her office, Shoshanna did a reassessment. Their previous relationship had been to her advantage, as Henry had obeyed most if not all of her commands. However—and if Henry continued to remain rational—this new partnership could yield even greater fruit.

Henry might not want to rule, but she did. She also knew how to take care of extraneous matter after it had outlived its use.

CHAPTER 20

Dev could still feel the soft curve of Katya's body tucked against his as he ushered her into an apartment on the twelfth floor of the Shine building. The drive into Manhattan had been largely quiet, but he didn't make the mistake of thinking she'd given up her plans of escape—of going north.

Her eyes went to the door as he put down her bag. "You're going to lock me in, aren't you." Not a question, though it was framed as one.

It hit him hard, a two-fisted punch—because no matter his awareness of the calculated evil that had brought her into his life, Katya continued to cut through his defenses like a scalpel, leaving him exposed. "I can't have you out of Shine control." She could be programmed to seek and destroy files, information, specific individuals.

"Out of your control you mean." Her jawline firmed, her delicate bone structure defined against skin that had begun to gain the golden flush of health.

"Yes." Lying would achieve nothing. "My people come first—it's something you can't ever forget."

She gave him her back as she turned to walk toward the windows. "How long do you plan to keep me here?"

Fighting the instinct to bridge the distance, to capture her between his arms as he had in Vermont, he thrust both hands into the pockets of his suit pants. "For now—at least a week."

"That's not an answer, Dev."

"You know the answer." He stared at the slender line of her back, willing her to face him, make him feel less like a monster. "You've always known the answer."

She pressed her hand flat on the glass. "You'll keep me here as long as it takes. Even if it takes years."

It was a kick to the gut, the utter emptiness of her voice. For the first time, she sounded like one of the Psy. As if he'd destroyed something in her. "It won't," he said. "We'll have answers sooner rather than later." He'd set every single one of his contacts into play.

"Then what?" Finally, she turned to look at him, her eyes as empty as her voice. The woman who'd come to him last night was just... gone. "As long as I'm connected to the Psy-Net, I'm a threat. And there's no way to pull me out of the Net. Stalemate."

Dev pushed through the door to another apartment well over an hour later. He'd meant to head there straight after he'd shown Katya to her room, but he'd been in no mood to talk to a traumatized child. Not when he felt like an abuser himself.

His lips set in a tight line. That wasn't coincidence. Nani had been right—someone had put a lot of thought into creating Katya, giving her vulnerabilities designed to play on his deepest instincts. He could deal with sniveling mercenary traitors without losing sleep, even with those who were driven by other hatreds. But he had a big fucking blind spot when it came to women who'd been battered and abused.

Knowing that should've neutralized his response to the

woman he'd locked into the twelfth-floor suite, but all it did was make him aware of the depth of his weakness.

"Dev."

Jerking up his head at the sound of Glen's voice, he glanced toward the open doorway to the left. "Kid in there?"

Glen gave a small nod. "We moved him up here after he started to regain consciousness. It's more homey than the clinic."

"That's fine—but you've got guards on him?" Dev wasn't worried about the kid's physical strength—it was the psychic plane that concerned him. Some of the New Generation abilities could be lethal.

"Tag's here," Glen said. "I realized we'd need another telepath to control this one."

Dev had already picked up the echo of Tag's distinctive mental energy. One of the very few true telepaths in the Shadow-Net, the other man had had a truly horrific childhood. There were some who said it was a miracle he hadn't gone insane. Dev didn't think it had anything to do with miracles—Tag was just one tough son of a bitch. "The boy tell you anything else?"

Glen rubbed at his face, looking haggard in a way Dev had never seen him look—as if the weight of experience threatened to crush him. "Glen?"

"The boy—Cruz," the doctor began, "is worse than messed up. The drugs they kept him on blocked his psychic pathways, but they also stunted his development."

"Fuck." Like the Psy, and depending on the depth of their genetic inheritance, many of the Forgotten didn't react well to human drugs. "Brain damage?" Doctors today could fix a hell of a lot, but even they couldn't heal brain cells after they'd been fatally compromised.

To his relief, Glen shook his head. "No. His intellect is fine—it's his psychic development that's been seriously impaired."

"He's not as strong as he could've been?"

Again, Glen surprised him by shaking his head. "Kid's off the charts. Tag says he's cardinal level."

Dev sucked in a breath. "That shouldn't be possible." Cardinals were rare, so rare, though the populace could've been forgiven for thinking otherwise with the recent high-profile defections of two cardinals from the Net. But Sascha Duncan and Faith NightStar were part of a very, very exclusive club. Across the world, there were millions upon millions of Psy. If there were even five thousand cardinals among that number, it would be more than Dev expected. "He can't have cardinal eyes." White stars on black, the eyes of the most powerfully gifted Psy were both eerie and startlingly unique.

"No—human," Glen confirmed. "His genetic structure is mixed, like the rest of us. But when Tag drops the shields he's holding on Cruz, the boy's power will hit you like a hurricane."

Dev ignored the obvious statement. "You're telling me this boy has no shields of his own?"

The bags under Glen's eyes seemed to grow ever deeper. "Yes. And while he might be of mixed blood, he's got a phenomenal number of active Psy genes, so many recessive pairs..." Glen shook his head. "His psychic channels are blocked as long as he's on the drugs, but take him off and they blow wide open."

"Damn." Dev thrust his hands through his hair, rapidly considering and discarding options. "He'll go insane if we don't figure out a way to give him permanent protection."

"I considered a milder dosage of the drugs," Glen said, "even though I hate putting our children on anything."

"But?"

"But those drugs basically turn him into a zombie." He glanced toward the doorway, compassion in every tired line of his face.

"Does he understand what's happened?"

"Tag hasn't been able to draw him out—Cruz probably sees him as his jailer, so that's not much of a surprise."

Dev recoiled inwardly, remembering Katya's turned back, her empty voice. "I'll talk to him. Is there anything else I need to know?" Shoving everything but Cruz to the back of his mind, he took off his suit jacket, then undid and removed his tie before undoing the top buttons on his shirt and rolling up his sleeves. No use going into a child's room looking like the school principal.

"He's got no family as far as we can figure out—Aryan's team tracked him on the ShadowNet."

"Why didn't we pick him up if he's linked in?" Not every For-gotten needed the biofeedback provided by the ShadowNet—like so many things, it depended on their complicated genetic structure. "This is why we constantly run those seminars, so adults know to look out for minors who might need help."

"Because no one could 'see' him," Glen replied. "Boy's completely isolated."

That, Dev knew, should've been impossible. Everyone had *someone* to whom they felt connected, even if that connection was an unhealthy one neither party would choose. "Aw, hell." No wonder the kid was scared. Making a decision, he rubbed at his jaw. "Can Tag keep a hold on Cruz from outside the room?"

"Yes. You want to be alone with him?"

At Dev's nod, Glen went to the bedroom doorway and waved Tag out. The big man walked into the living area on silent feet, his eyes blazing with fury. "I could strangle his grandparents."

Dev shook his head. "Not if I got to shoot them first." If Cruz had been brought in as per protocol, he would've been taught to develop and protect his powers from childhood. Now, they might be lucky to salvage his sanity. "I could be a while. You okay to hold the shield?"

"I can do it twenty-four hours a day if necessary," Tag said. "Kid's not fighting me—doesn't know how. But I have to remain within a certain radius."

"Can Tiara spell you?"

Tag turned his head but not before Dev glimpsed the dark red flush along the tops of his cheekbones. "She just got on an airjet from Paris."

Glen's eyes lit up with unholy glee. "You must be looking forward to catching up with her."

"I'll beat you both up if you don't shut it."

Glad for the tiny burst of amusement, even if it came nowhere close to easing the ice around his soul, Dev walked into Cruz's room, shutting the door behind himself. The boy was curled up on his side, his ten-year-old body much smaller than it should've been.

His hair was dark and silky—and cut in a bowl shape that would've sent most kids howling to their moms. But Cruz didn't have a mom to complain to. And, until the past few hours, he probably hadn't even realized what he looked like. Now, the boy's huge, dark eyes followed Dev as he grabbed a chair and pulled it forward so he was sitting at Cruz's bedside. That was when he got the first shock.

Glen had said Cruz's eyes were human. They weren't. This close, Dev saw the odd flicker of dark gold in the depths of the near-black irises. Extraordinary. Why had no one noticed? Thinking back, he found the answer—it was possible the drugs had messed Cruz up so completely his gaze had gone dull, too.

"I'm Dev," he said, and waited. Cruz was a ghost to his psychic senses, so slight as to be nonexistent.

The boy didn't say a word.

Smiling, Dev took a different tack. "You're not going to believe this, but I was once your age. If I'd had that haircut inflicted on me, I'd have done serious damage to the hairdresser."

A blink. Nothing else.

"You want me to organize someone to fix it?"

Another blink, but slower this time.

Dev grinned. "Or you could keep it. Women seemed to find it cute on a kid. You'll probably get spoiled half to death."

Cruz raised a hand to his hair, pulling it forward as if to see the color. "My mom used to cut my hair." His voice was quiet...and full of a vicious psychic power he had no ability to control.

PETROKOV FAMILY ARCHIVES

Letter dated May 25, 1975

Dear Matthew,

Your sister Emily sleeps beside me, but even her sweet smile can't stop the grief that ravages my heart. Your father...I always knew that as a foreseer, he was at a far higher risk of mental illness than the majority of the population. And yet I tried not to know. Because he is my heart—I don't know what I would do without him.

He admitted himself to a psychiatric ward today. I begged him not to go. I'm scared of the currents in the Net, the wave of support for Silence. Ever since the Adelajas provided the "proof" of their sons, more and more people are being swayed to the Council's way of thinking. What proof, I ask you. Where are Tendaji and Naeem? Why do we never see them anymore?

No one will answer my questions, and now I'm afraid for my position in the ministry. I'm speaking too loudly. It's not in my nature to close my mouth, but we need the money. So I'll try to listen instead. And I'll pray that your father comes home soon.

With all my love,
   Mom

CHAPTER 21

Katya had been through every room of the apartment. It was a generous space—bedroom, bathroom, and a kitchenette that flowed off the wide main living area. But there was no getting out of it except through the front door, no avenues of escape whatsoever. Even the knives in the kitchen were small, barely sharp enough to cut fruit.

Devraj Santos was not a stupid man.

At least, she thought, trying to find a silver lining, he respected her skills enough to put her in a place from which only a teleporter might be able to escape. Too bad that wasn't part of her psychic skill set.

Another piece of memory slotted into the jigsaw that was her mind.

Her eyes widened. "Of course." She'd been ignoring the very thing that made her different, that made her unique. Yes, she was a telepath—level 4.5 on the Gradient. That meant she was—just—a midrange Tp-Psy. She was also a Gradient 4.9 M-Psy.

Two midrange abilities.

What she'd just realized was that a person with two mid-range abilities could sometimes create an amplification effect—usually on only one of the abilities. However, that effect was so unpredictable that it could be hidden by the user—and she'd hidden hers; otherwise, she would've been pressed into a very different kind of service.

That's why, she thought, seeing a complete chunk of her past in one clean sweep, she and Ashaya had worked so well together in their rebellious activities—Katya had been able to get messages out to almost everyone in the resistance. Because when she exercised her ability to amplify, her Tp skills went from 4.5 to 9 on the Gradient.

And a level 9 telepath could talk to pretty much anyone she wanted. But—she frowned—she hadn't, not for those last months. Why? Her hands lifted to her head, the heels of palms pressing against her temples.

A dart of pain, but it pulled the memory with it.

"Everything that can be done low-tech"—Ashaya's familiar voice—*"we do that way. He suspects you, Ekaterina. And I need you too much to lose you to him."*

"My telepathy would make things quantifiably easier."

"Not if you're dead. It takes energy for you to merge your abilities—it'll be noticed if you increase your intake of nutrients, if you sleep more."

Katya staggered as her mind ricocheted back to the present. Ashaya had been right—the shadow-man...*Ming*—another flash of memory, her torturer's identity delineated with flawless clarity—*had* suspected her. But now there was no one to watch her, to see if she suddenly changed her eating or sleeping habits. Ming had blocked her access to the Net, but he hadn't done anything to stifle her ability to use her inborn talents. A chill spread over her heart—he might even have programmed her to use those talents exactly as she was thinking of doing.

A moment of paralysis. "No." She tilted her chin, forced herself to breathe.

If she let fear stop her, he would have truly won. She had to go forward believing her actions were her own, trusting that she'd somehow risen from the ashes, begun to reform her personality, become the phoenix that lived in her soul.

Surely, *surely* Ming hadn't considered her firestorm reaction to Dev, or how that reaction would make her want to become stronger—so she could hold her own against the relentless strength of him. "The only way to know is to try."

Taking a deep breath, she relaxed into an armchair and closed her eyes. Usually when she used Tp, she was aiming for a specific destination—a particular mind. But, as a telepath, she could also "hear" others if she opened her senses. However, like most of her designation, she kept that aspect of her mind locked tight the majority of the time—even in the Psy-Net, there were individuals whose shields leaked a constant flow of thought. Multiply that irritation by thousands and you had a recipe for madness.

And here, outside the Net? It was likely to be a million times worse. The majority of humans didn't have anything but the most basic shields. Given their history, the Forgotten were likely to be a fraction more sophisticated, but there would still be any number of leaks, of voices.

Soothing the butterflies in her stomach with the knowledge that she could shut off the open pathways at any instant, she gripped the arms of the armchair and dropped her internal shields.

An instant of pure silence.

WHTIOSKTNIHIGHNSTIONTIJO!!!!!!!!!!!!!!!!!!!!

Her head snapped back against the headrest as her shields slammed shut with brutal force. It took several minutes for her head to stop ringing. Her spine was damp with sweat by the time she reopened her eyes, her hair plastered to her forehead.

"Okay," she said, "okay." Calming her racing heartbeat enough that she could force her mind to cooperate took another five long minutes. Finally able to think again, she gripped the chair arms even harder and dropped her internal shields once more—this time, by the merest fraction.

Dev was talking to Cruz about model cars—a hobby the boy remembered enjoying before he'd been placed into state care—when there was a knock on the door. Dev got up. "I'll have to see what that is. They wouldn't interrupt unless it was important."

Tiny lines appeared on Cruz's forehead. "I can almost hear something." He shook his head. "It's gone now. *He* scared it away." Making a face, Cruz fluffed his pillow and glared at the doorway.

Eyebrows raised, Dev opened the door and walked out—to find himself toe to toe with Tag. The big telepath had a thunderous look on his face.

Since the other man usually made an extreme effort to appear nonthreatening, Dev's instincts went on full alert. "What?"

"Close the door." His voice shook with fury.

"I'll sit with Cruz." Walking in, Glen shut the door behind himself.

Dev met Tag's eyes. "You look like you want to kill someone."

"That would be you," Tag muttered succinctly. "I should fucking pound your stubborn head into the ground."

"You could try."

"Pretty boy, I could crush you with one fist." Releasing a huge breath, Tag pointed up. "You've got a goddamn *powerful* telepath up there and you didn't think to warn me?"

Dev froze. "What're you talking about? She's midrange, weaker than—"

"Bullshit," Tag interrupted. "Your little secret is closer to the very high end of the spectrum." Tag shook his head, rubbing at the sides of his temples. "I just caught her mind as it brushed mine. Don't know what she was looking for, but I hope to hell I gave her enough of a scare that she stopped."

Dev was already moving, anger rising inside him in a scalding wave. A telepath that strong could do a massive amount of damage. Katya could tear apart the shields of the weaker members of Shine, leave his people nothing more than vegetables. And he'd brought her here. He'd kept her *safe*.

Slamming out with his senses, he touched every drop of metal in the building. As a result, his fury had turned into a cold kind of rage by the time he reached Katya's suite. Using his abilities to unlock the door before he got to it, he pushed through with every intention of flaying her with his tongue.

That was before he saw her collapsed in an armchair, blood leaking out of her nose.

What had Tag done?

Putting his fingers on the pulse in her neck, he breathed out a sigh of relief. Why, he didn't know. Her death would've made his life considerably simpler. Pushing aside his violent repudiation of the thought, he pulled out his cell and called Tag. "She's unconscious."

"She should be," Tag said. "I sent through a scream along the telepathic line."

Dev's hand clenched on the phone. Tag had done the right thing, but damn if he didn't want to punch the other man in the face for it. God, he was fucking pathetic. This woman had played him from day one, and still he wanted to protect her. "Is she going to come out of it soon?"

"Won't be long. It'll teach her a lesson." Tag's voice changed. "No telepath should *ever* leave themselves that open, Dev. She should know that. If I'd wanted to, I could've sent in something more than a scream."

Even with rage an icy inferno inside him, Dev knew why

Katya had taken the chance. "I put her in a prison. What would you have done?"

"Probably the same." Tag took a deep breath. "That doesn't mean we can afford to feel sorry for her. Your shields are titanium, but she's strong enough to break the shields of half the people in Shine."

"I'll make sure there isn't a next time." Closing the phone, he slid it into his pocket before walking into the bathroom and returning with a damp towel. There wasn't much blood, but he left the stained towel on the little end table as he waited for her to come out of it, an explicit visual reminder of what she'd just chanced.

As he waited, he slid a critical glance over her face. Impossible as it was, it seemed as if she'd dropped several pounds in the short time since he'd last seen her. But that, he thought, rejecting his natural instincts, wasn't his problem. This time, he wasn't going to let her use his weakness where vulnerable women were concerned against him. If she wanted to starve herself, he'd let her.

Katya's head was a pounding bruise, dark and mottled, when she finally managed to open her eyes. Her stomach revolted at almost the same instant, and she pitched forward, feeling her gorge rise.

"Breathe!"

The snapped command cut through everything, chilling her with its utter control. When a glass was pushed under her nose, she took it and rose slowly back up into a sitting position.

"Drink," Dev ordered, his face ruthless in a way she'd never before seen. "It'll get your system up and running faster."

Since she felt like she'd been hit by a truck, she wasn't going to argue with anything that made her feel better. Bringing the glass to her lips, she drank deep. It tasted slightly sweet, with a strong medicinal aftertaste. Guessing he'd laced the water with vitamins, she finished the entire glass before putting it on the table beside the armchair. "Whose blood is that?" she asked, seeing the damp towel.

"Whose do you think?"

She swallowed and looked at the very dangerous man sitting in the armchair across from her, one foot hooked easily over the opposing knee. It made him no less intimidating. In fact, the sheer calm of him set her pulse to clamoring. He was angry, so angry that her very cells spiked with fear. "Dev," she began.

"When precisely," he interrupted, "were you planning to tell me you were a telepath with enough power to conceivably blow out a mind?" Cool tone, flawless enunciation, eyes that tracked her with unflinching focus.

"I didn't know." She wrapped her arms around her torso, feeling unaccountably exposed. "I swear to you I didn't know until just before I decided to go exploring."

"Exploring?" He raised an eyebrow. "Let's leave that aside for a minute—exactly how stupid do you think I am?"

"I don't—"

"Stop." It was a single terse word that cut off her very breath. "The amnesia thing isn't going to fly anymore."

Emotion rose in a cresting wave. "It's the truth. I'm remembering more, but it's not—"

"I don't give a shit." Said in that same scarily calm voice. "All I'm interested in are your orders."

"*I. Don't. Know.*" The swell of emotion was filling her limbs, turning her voice husky. "And it doesn't matter how many times you ask me—I'm still not going to remember until the memories come back. I might not remember even then, depending on the programming."

"We've been over this—as far as Shine is concerned, you're a fully functional covert operative."

Shine.

Not Dev.

"And you?" she asked. "What do you think?"

A cool glance, with a dark edge she'd never before seen. "I think I've been made a patsy." He stood. "But no one can say I don't learn from my mistakes."

"Dev—"

He bent down to put his hands on the arms of her chair, blocking her in. "Don't *ever* try to scan anyone at Shine again. I've authorized the use of deadly force against you."

All the air left her body. Her heart felt as if it had turned into rock. But she refused to let him see, refused to give him the satisfaction of knowing he'd savaged something barely grown inside of her. "Understood, Mr. Santos."

His face, his expression, none of it changed. "Good. Make sure it stays that way."

CHAPTER 22

Katya found herself staring at the door long after it closed on Dev's back. Not that long ago, she'd asked him to kill her if it became necessary. Now, the thought of living was a rebellious pulse inside her. She'd beat this—if only to show Devraj Santos that she wasn't an inconvenience he could lock away out of his sight. She was Katya Haas, and she was a *person*. She'd bled for her right to be a person. She'd survived!

Picking up the glass on the table with cold-blooded precision, she threw it at the door. It made a very satisfying crashing noise. She hoped Dev wasn't wearing shoes the next time he walked into the apartment. In fact, she thought, picking up a vase from the coffee table, she hoped he shredded his feet. Another crash, the porcelain shards mixing with crystal.

As she searched for another breakable object, a drop of water fell on her hand. She glanced down, confused. Where had it come from? The ceiling was dry, and the water, when she raised it to her mouth, tasted of salt.

Tears.

She was crying. Lifting trembling fingers to her cheeks,

she brushed wonderingly at the dampness. She'd cried before; she knew that. In that dark room where Ming had buried her, she'd cried so many tears. But none had been like these. Clean. Angry. Determined. This time, she didn't feel a victim. She felt very much a woman who'd been wronged and who was going to get her vengeance.

Devraj Santos didn't know who he was messing with.

Dev was still riding the red edge of fury an hour later when he coded in a call to Ashaya.

The M-Psy answered almost at once. "Is Katya alright?" were her first words.

"Did you know how powerful a telepath she is?"

Ashaya's eyes went wide. "Yes, but she'd never use it to do harm."

"The woman you knew might not have," Dev snapped. "You have no fucking idea what she might do now."

Dorian's face replaced Ashaya's. "That's enough." It was a snarl. "You fucked up in not asking the question. Don't put it on my mate."

Dev's anger whiplashed back on him. He knew Dorian was right, had known before he called. Taking a deep breath, he said, "I apologize."

Dorian waved it off. "Did she hurt anyone?"

"Not this time." Pure, blind luck that Tag had been on-site. "I need to talk to Sascha."

"She can't do much about a telepath."

"We've got a kid with shielding problems." And according to the info DarkRiver had allowed Talin to share, Sascha was one of the best shield builders in or out of the Net.

"Call Lucas," Dorian said. "Not worth my life to give you Sascha's cell number."

"Why?"

"Just call Luc. Here's the code." A pause. "And the next

time you yell at my mate, I'll rip your throat out. We clear?"
Leopard eyes looking out of a human face.

Dev stared into those eyes, knowing a show of dominance
when he saw it. "Crystal—but don't consider me easy prey."
When talking with predatory changelings, appearing weak
could be fatal.

Dorian's eyes gleamed. "Long as you don't pull that shit
again, we won't have to find out which one of us is more deadly."

Temper now on a leash, Dev input Lucas's number on the
main comm panel. The DarkRiver alpha's face appeared on
the screen an instant later. "Santos," Lucas said, cat green
eyes curious. "This about Noor and Jon?"

"No." Dev shook his head at the mention of the two Forgotten children Talin had adopted. "I need a favor."

"You do realize we keep track?"

"Yeah." DarkRiver hadn't become one of the strongest
packs in the country by being soft touches. "We'll owe you."

"So?"

"I need Sascha's help."

Lucas's gaze went quiet, intent. But all he said was
"Explain."

Dev gave him a bare-bones outline. "I'm hoping Sascha
can teach him to build some shields of his own. I don't know
if it's possible, but if she's as good as Talin says—"

"She's the best," Lucas interrupted, pride in every word.
"But you're telling me this kid is damaged—if the damage is
in the brain itself, Sascha won't be able to do anything."

"All our scans show that his brain is functioning at a hundred percent. He took the hit on the psychic plane."

"Psychic injuries can be as brutal as physical ones."

"But," Dev said, "there's a slightly better chance of recovery."

Lucas nodded. "I'll ask Sascha."

"Thanks."

"Don't thank me yet." Lucas's eyes stayed human, but Dev
knew it was the panther who was speaking. "Even if she says

yes, and knowing my mate's heart, she will, she's not stepping one foot out of DarkRiver territory."

Dorian's earlier words suddenly made sense. "Sascha's pregnant, isn't she?"

A small nod. "Keep it to yourself. We don't want the Council turning eyes in her direction."

"You're saying I'm going to have to travel to you if I want Sascha's help."

"I feel for the kid," Lucas said, "but Sascha comes first. As it is, I'll probably have to hog-tie her to make sure she doesn't get on an airjet and head to you."

"But you'll tell her?" Dev asked.

"When you get hitched, try lying to your mate and see where it gets you. I'll call back after I talk to Sascha."

Knowing he'd done all he could on that front, Dev stepped out to talk to Maggie. "Tell me which fires I need to put out and which ones can wait."

His secretary, an elegant forty-eight-year-old with naturally silver hair that she'd turned into a fashion statement, raised an eyebrow. "Well, where do I begin? Jack and the others want another meeting."

Dev only just stopped himself from gritting his teeth. "When?" Avoidance would get none of them anywhere—and this way, at least he could keep an eye on the problem.

"They're in the city."

"Slot them in this afternoon." Head aching, he nodded at her to go on. "Next?"

"Glen says he'll ensure Patient X will have high-calorie foods delivered to her." There was no curiosity in her tone. Maggie likely knew every single detail about Patient X—there was a reason he'd hired her over the shiny new graduates who'd applied for the position.

"Next." He was still so angry he could barely bring himself to think of the woman who'd slipped under his defenses… then knifed him in the heart.

CHAPTER 23

Even as Dev hung up on Lucas and turned his mind to other matters, something inexplicable was taking place in the Dark-River alpha's territory.

Judd Lauren, Psy rebel, former assassin, and fucking dangerous son of a bitch according to all who knew him, looked mystified at the little girl who was staring up at him, all huge eyes in a heart-shaped face. "Yes?" Crouching down to the forest floor, he tried to appear nonthreatening. "Did you want something?"

She shook her head, glossy black curls bouncing on her shoulders.

Judd had become better with kids since leaving the Psy-Net, but right that second, he felt utterly clueless. Normally when he came down to train with Dorian, it was only Keenan he encountered. And Dorian's son was more interested in copying their moves than chatting. "Noor," he tried again. "Are you looking for Keenan?" He knew the two were fast friends.

Another shake of her head.

He glanced behind her, hoping Dorian would come out and rescue him. No such luck. "Do you want to play?" It was generally what Ben, one of the SnowDancer pups, wanted when he trailed after Judd.

But Noor shook her head again.

Desperation took hold. "Ah . . ." He had nothing.

Then she smiled, pure trust in the sparkle of her eyes. "I have a present for you." She lifted a little fist.

"Oh?" Startled, he held up his hand, palm up. "Why?"

"Because we're the same."

Judd closed his hand over the river-smoothed stone she put in his hand, knowing he was nothing like this bright innocent. His ability had made him an assassin, then a healer, but it would still be so easy for him to kill—only his love for Brenna, for his family and friends, his *pack*, kept him from crossing that brutal line. "Yeah? How do you figure that?"

A beatific smile. "I just know." Then she leaned forward to wrap her arms around his neck.

Hugging her back with all the gentleness he had in him, he rose to his feet, taking her with him. And as he walked back to Dorian's, he wondered what similarities a little girl whose name meant "Light," saw between them.

Once, he would've brushed it off, distanced himself. Now, he kissed her cheek and accepted the gift of her trust.

CHAPTER 24

Katya ate everything sent to her over the next three days. She didn't try to escape—though she did secrete away the over-the-counter pain and flu medication she found in the bathroom, not that it would do her much good—and she didn't try to use telepathy. Instead, she concentrated on strengthening herself using exercise routines she downloaded off the computer console on the wall. That computer only allowed her to access the most basic of sites, but that was fine. She had what she needed.

Pushing all the furniture in the living room to the walls, she made a space where she could stretch out and begin to put her body back into shape. She even cleared away the glass and porcelain shards, loath to let Dev see how deeply he'd hurt her. Her focus was on getting strong enough that she could take the opportunity to escape when the chance came.

And then... she had a nightmare to face.

On the fourth day after she'd been knocked unconscious, Dev finally returned. She ignored him as she began to go through her stretching routine. He came to a stop at the edge of the cleared space. "Pack your stuff. We're moving."

Excitement uncurled in her gut, but she kept her face expressionless. "Where?"

"You'll be near Ashaya."

She was already shaking her head. "We discussed this. I can't be trusted around her."

"That's why you'll voluntarily take a mild sedative."

Her stomach dropped. "No." It would disorientate her, leave her helpless. And she was through with being helpless.

Dev folded his arms across that chest she'd slept so peacefully on mere days ago. "Fine. Be ready by ten."

She could feel her fingernails biting into her palms. "Who's going to punch me to put me to sleep?" she asked, furious enough to draw blood. "You?"

He walked out without answering, shattering her newfound calm.

Tag was waiting outside Katya's room when Dev walked out. "Didn't go well?"

"She won't take a sedative."

"Did you really think she would?"

"No." He wouldn't have either. "But since both you and Tiara are going, she needs to come with us when we go see Sascha. And no way can I take her in when she might be a threat. Lucas'll slit my throat."

"There is another option," Tag pointed out. "Glen could put her into a medically induced coma while we're gone."

Dev felt his entire body hum with violence. "We do that, it's torture." It'd break her, put her back in that room where she hadn't been able to see, hear, touch.

"Yeah." Tag blew out a breath. "You have a little bit of telepathy—can you tell when she's using her abilities?"

"Now that I know to watch for it—if I'm close, yeah."

Tag straightened his big body away from the wall. "Then stay close. Close enough to physically incapacitate her if necessary."

Dev's stomach roiled.

"I'll do it." It was a quiet offer from a man who knew Dev better than most.

"No." He stared at the door he'd only just stopped himself from slamming minutes ago. "She's mine."

"Your responsibility, you mean." It was a very deliberate reminder.

"Don't worry—I'm not being led around by anything other than the brain in my skull." Not anymore.

"Well, she's a pretty thing now that she's started to fill out." Tag shrugged. "And we all know how you are with the helpless ones."

"But she's not exactly helpless, is she?" He almost felt a sense of *pride* in her. God, how fucked up. Yet... if she had been telling the truth—if she'd survived not only torture, but the destruction of her mind, her personality itself, shouldn't that be a cause for pride?

"No." Tag's agreement poured cold water over his thoughts. "What are you going to tell Lucas?"

"The truth." He forced himself to look away from the door, from the fury of a woman who was no longer the broken creature he'd found, but someone far more dangerous... far more compelling. "If necessary, I'll inject her with sedatives myself."

Again, Tag shrugged. "Dev, don't torture yourself like this. Give over the responsibility to me."

"No." Flat. No room for compromise. "You need to control Cruz—that's much more intensive—Tiara can't do it on her own."

"Yeah. Kid's still wide open if we're not blocking him."

If only, Dev thought, they could neutralize Katya as easily. It would make her far less of a threat, but Katya wasn't simply Psy, she was an adult. Even if Tag or Tiara could block her, she'd fight them, and in doing so, drain energy they needed to ensure Cruz's safety. "If Katya let you into her mind," he said to Tag, "if she was able to drop her telepathic shields, could you block her?"

"I'd have to be monitoring her the entire time," Tag said. "She'd hate it. It's different with Cruz—he puts on that sullen act, but there's acceptance there. He knows he needs the shields we put around him. They make him feel safe."

"But they'd make Katya feel violated."

"That and trapped."

"Then we won't consider it." It was an instant decision, made in the primitive core of his soul. "She's already been cut off from the PsyNet. We do this, we effectively maim her."

"So you believe her story?"

"I don't know what to believe." Looking up, he caught Tag's expression. "Say it."

"You know what I'm going to say." Tag shrugged. "You need to hand her off to someone else—her feelings shouldn't count here. We need to contain her in the most effective way possible."

Dev knew that. He also knew it wasn't happening. She was his—whatever happened, he'd allow no one else to interfere. "Maybe this time, the Council did it right." He began to head away from Katya's suite.

"Maybe." Tag fell in beside him. "And maybe they don't know you as well as they think."

"You mean I'm not a sucker for hurt women?" He'd been rewired that way the day after his ninth birthday. No one would ever be able to pull that wiring out.

"You might have a weakness," Tag replied as they stepped into the elevator, "but it won't stop you from doing your job as director."

"So the fact that I'm a stone-cold bastard is my salvation?"

Tag's smile was thin. "The last board was full of nice men and women. The Council almost ate us alive. I'd rather trust a shark at the helm."

PETROKOV FAMILY ARCHIVES

Letter dated September 1, 1976

Dear Matthew,

You played with your father and Emily today, all three of you laughing so hard you made my soul burn with joy. Your father is managing to remain lucid for hours at a time, though I wonder at what it costs him.

Today he received another blow when your uncle Greg decided for Silence. I don't think your father expected his brother to take that step, but Greg's foreseeing abilities are stronger than David's. The nightmares in his eyes... I wish I could help him. But I'm an M-Psy, a scanner.

Some people say that's why I don't understand the importance of Silence, but dear God, how can they think that? I'm married to an F-Psy, mother to two little telepaths. I know the exact cost—down to the last tear, the last shred of fear, the last little bit of light in your father's eyes.

I even said to him that perhaps Greg was right, that perhaps Silence might help those with his gift. He didn't get angry. He knows too well that I love him to the core of my being—the idea of watching his mind fragment, break under the weight of the darkness of his visions... it shatters me. Do you know what he said, Matthew?

He said he'd rather die a madman than live by wiping out

everything that makes him who he is. He'd rather live one day with his love for me, you, and Emily in his heart than a lifetime without feeling that "wild, endless fury." Your father is a poet at times. I bet you didn't know that. I'm smiling as I write this, knowing we've made up our minds. We'll stand against Silence. But Matty, I fear that we might be in the minority.

With all the love in my heart,
   Mom

CHAPTER 25

Katya was starkly conscious of Dev's barely contained energy as he sat beside her on the airjet. Escorted to the very back of the plane, she'd been warned against trying to see who else was on board—though it was difficult to miss the two people moving about in front. One was a big man Dev had introduced as Tag, the other a Venus of a woman with a sleek waterfall of blue-black hair and a dazzling tawny-eyed smile set against a face that was all supermodel cheekbones.

There was, she knew, someone else on the plane, but he or she had been kept from Katya's sight. She made no effort to do a telepathic sweep, to discover the hidden individual's identity. Dev had shown her the pressure injector in his pocket after they boarded. She'd expected a threat, but he'd cut her legs right out from under her instead.

"You force me to use this," he'd said, something dark and painfully old in his eyes, "and I'll never forgive you."

In that moment, she'd had the startling realization that she was seeing the real Devraj Santos for the very first time. He'd retreated behind his walls an instant later, and now, ten minutes into the journey, he was busy working on his electronic datapad. Not a word had passed between them in the ensuing time.

Up ahead, she saw Tag shift his gaze to follow his gorgeous companion's progress as she walked down the corridor to get some water. He snapped his head back around the instant the woman began to return. Katya's lips twitched.

"Something funny?"

She was so surprised by the question that she turned to stare at Dev. He was still looking at his datapad. "How did you know?"

"I know."

In the apartment, she'd made a vow to be civil to him but nothing more. He wasn't her friend—how could he be when he didn't believe a word she said? But at this moment, sitting next to him, she realized that distance wasn't the way to get to Dev. The man obviously knew too much about it—he could outfreeze her any day of the week. But laughter . . . Dev didn't seem to know much about laughter. And while she might be Psy, she'd found a vein of humor in her new phoenix heart.

"Tag," she said, dropping her voice. "He keeps looking at that woman when he thinks no one is paying attention."

"Her name's Tiara." Dev input something else on his datapad. "There's an open betting book at Shine on those two."

Curious, she waited for him to continue. "What about?" she prodded when he didn't.

"When Tag'll get up the guts to ask her out."

Blinking, she stared at the big, solid man with a face like stone. "Your friend doesn't seem like he's scared of anything. I can see him taking on the Psy Council without blinking."

"That's why it's so funny."

"*Oh.*" Now she understood. For some reason, this Tiara rattled Tag on the deepest levels. "When I was in the Psy-Net," she said, catching another wisp of memory, "I never understood how human and changeling females could trust their males without the ropes of Silence."

Dev finally looked at her, those exotic eyes intent.

"Especially," she continued, "when the males were bigger and stronger. Like when Sascha Duncan defected to mate with the DarkRiver alpha. I simply couldn't understand how she could feel safe around him."

"There's no male-on-female violence in the Net?"

"No, not in the sense that you mean. Domestic violence is unheard of—I suppose there's no chance for it," she said, staring into the face of a man who was the effective alpha of his own people, as lethal, as dangerous. "Men under Silence are cold, controlled. But the men outside? You get so angry—there's nothing to stop you from harming a weaker person."

All at once, the temperature dropped, until she could almost see her breath frost the air. "Your research must've been very thorough."

"What're you talking about?"

Dev stared at her, his face holding no emotion whatsoever. After a long, frozen moment, he returned his attention to his datapad. "There's an entertainment module in the datapad in the seatback in front of you."

She didn't know where she got the courage. Reaching over, she grabbed his own datapad and pushed the Off button. He simply held out a hand. "You're lucky that model has automatic memory."

Instead of giving it to him, she put it down the side of her seat. "I'll drop my shields."

An absolute silence, unbroken even by the murmurs of the others on the plane.

"You can't," he said at last. "Unless the whole being-locked-away-from-the-Net panic was another lie?"

It was a surgical strike, precise and deadly, but she refused to let him rattle her. "I'm blocked from the Net, but he did nothing to stop me from using my abilities—"

"Why?" Dev interrupted.

"Probably because that kind of a blackout requires constant policing." Dust in her throat, gravel in her mouth. "Or maybe it's because he wants me to use my abilities, but whatever his reason, it means I have control over my personal shields. I can drop them."

"Is that an offer or a threat?" Cool words, an expression-less face.

"An offer." She was sick and tired of being mistrusted. "You said you had some telepathy. Is it enough to scan an open mind?"

He didn't answer her.

So she went with instinct, assumed he could do what she was asking. "Come in, see what I know, see what I *am*." *Trust me,* she wanted to say. Because anger would only take her so far. She felt so alone. In the days since he'd locked her in that room, she hadn't slept more than a couple of hours a night, too aware of the endless emptiness of her existence.

The skin tightened over Dev's cheekbones. "You trust me that much?"

"You've been up-front—if I prove a threat, I die. Other-wise, I don't think you'll brutalize me."

He flinched, as if she'd hit him. "That kind of invasion, it's nothing a telepath would choose."

"I am. I need you to stop treating me like a fraud. I'm not."

"No." His jaw set.

"Why?" She twisted to face him. "Because you'd feel guilty about invading my mind? I'm giving you permission, Dev."

"That makes it no less invasive."

"And this?" She waved her hand. "This—where I'm treated like a consummate liar—is better?"

He glanced up. Following, she saw Tiara looking at the two of them with unconcealed interest. Dev's tone was clipped when he turned back to her. "We're not discussing this here."

Heat rolled up her body, threatening to color her face. "Fine. But we *will* be discussing it."

The unloading of the airjet went like clockwork. Cruz and his minders were in a vehicle by the time Dev descended with Katya. DarkRiver had sent a welcoming party of four, with two all-wheel drives.

A tall male with distinctive blond hair tied back in a queue stepped forward. "Vaughn," he said, extending a hand.

"Dev." As they shook, Dev saw Vaughn's eyes flick to Katya, then back. Aware the man was a sentinel, one of the highest-ranking men in Lucas's pack, Dev figured Vaughn knew exactly who she was, but he made the introduction anyway. "This is Katya."

Vaughn didn't offer her his hand—a courtesy, since most Psy in the Net preferred not to be touched. "Ashaya's looking forward to talking with you."

"I'm not sure how safe that'll be," Katya said, face drawn.

Vaughn didn't seem worried. "We've got reinforcements. Come on—you two can ride with me and Cory. You met Mercy?"

Dev shook his head. "I heard you mated with a wolf," he said to the beautiful redhead who lifted her hand in a small wave.

"The trauma's just starting to wear off." A deadpan voice, but her eyes sparkled. "I'll be driving the others. This is Jamie." She jerked her thumb at the male beside her, his hair dyed a bright butterscotch yellow streaked with cobalt. "He's riding shotgun."

Vaughn waited until the first vehicle had pulled out before following. He offered Dev the front passenger seat, but Dev chose to sit in back with Katya. The drive passed in easy silence—for the front-seat passengers in any case. Dev was supremely aware of the rigid line of Katya's spine, the knife-edged question that still hung between them.

He wanted to grab her nape, make her turn to face him instead of staring out the window. Battling the urge gave him one hell of a headache. As a result, he was in a shit of a mood by the time they arrived at the location DarkRiver had chosen for the meeting with Sascha.

"Nice place," Dev said. Set on a large plot of land that gave it privacy from neighbors, the single-level house was big enough for all of them. The others had already settled in according to the text message he'd received from Tiara. "How far are we from the city?"

"Fifteen minutes," Vaughn answered. "We'll leave you one of the vehicles—and we can get you another if you think it's necessary."

Dev took a moment to think about it, very aware of Katya standing silently on the other side of the engine. "One more would be good in case we have to split up for some reason. I want both coded to recognize me, Tag, and Tiara."

Katya's hand curled into a fist on the hood.

"Only take half an hour or so," Vaughn said. "Cory'll code you into this one—then you can do your other people."

As the young male leopard worked with the car's computronic system, Dev saw Katya step around to stand near Vaughn. "Is Ashaya well?"

"Yes." The sentinel raised an eyebrow. "Thought she came to see you."

"I wasn't in the best frame of mind then. We didn't talk much."

"She's happy," Vaughn said simply. "Dorian, her, and the cub, they make a good family."

Cory asked Dev to input his thumbprint then so he missed the next few comments. When he turned back around, Vaughn was showing Katya something on his phone, the two of them so close, they were almost touching. If it had been Tag . . . but it wasn't. Dev didn't know Vaughn, didn't trust him. His entire body went taut, ready to strike.

The front door of the house opened in the middle of his fight with a burst of jealousy unlike anything he'd ever before experienced. Mercy and Jamie walked out onto the porch, catching Vaughn's attention. The sentinel put away his phone. "All set?"

Mercy nodded before turning to Dev. "Sascha'll be by this afternoon."

"Thanks." It came out sounding civilized, though he felt anything but.

"Hope she can help the—" The redhead snapped her mouth shut at the swift shake of Dev's head.

Even as Mercy followed Dev's cue, Katya stiffened. An instant later, that stiffness was gone, leached out of her like so much air, her shoulders slumping. He couldn't bear to see her that way. Leaving Cory to complete the verification process, he walked to stand at her side, then thought to hell with it and put his arm around her waist, tugging her into the heat of his body.

She didn't soften for him . . . but neither did she pull away.

"Cory," Vaughn called out, making no comment on Dev's actions, "you done?"

Mercy, however, gave Dev a hard glance. The truth hit him like a lightning bolt—if Katya refused to return to New York with him, the leopards would find some way for her to stay. After all, not only was Ashaya a phenomenally gifted M-Psy, the leopards also had two cardinals in their pack.

He met Mercy's gaze, held it. After a while, she gave the slightest of smiles. "Guess we'll be heading off. See you later, Dev. Katya, here's my number." She handed over a card. "Call if you need me."

Dev waited until the cats had left to say, "You going to call her?"

"No." Rubbing one edge with her fingertips, she slid the card into a pocket. "Ashaya's a good person, but she doesn't understand how badly he changed me. I see him now, you know—Ming—that birthmark on his face is unmistakable. His expression never changed," she murmured, "no matter what he did or how much I begged."

Rage, sudden and uncontrollable, wrapped around his throat as he shifted their stance so that he could look down into her face. But she didn't give him the chance to speak, putting her hands on his chest and pushing. "Why are you holding me?"

"Because you looked like you needed it."

The blunt answer seemed to set her off balance. But only for an instant. "You can't do this, Dev."

"Do what?" He played with a strand of her hair that was flirting with the breeze.

She reached up to push away his hand. "Tell me you've given orders to allow the use of deadly force against me one minute and stroke me the next!"

"I was supremely pissed when I told you that," he said, breaking every one of his rules about engaging with the enemy.

"Because you thought I'd played you." A furious mix of hurt and anger. "And you still think that."

"What else am I supposed to think?" He lost his own temper. "You're a fucking powerful telepath and yet you *forgot*? It's like not remembering you have a limb!"

"It's not the same!" she yelled back, then clutched her head.

He immediately cupped her cheek. "What is it?"

"Shh." Lines formed between her eyes.

He waited for almost two minutes as she stood there, her head cocked in a way that implied listening, as if she was beginning to divine the secrets of her past. But when she looked up, there was only a haunted kind of pain in her eyes. "I'm starting to see even the parts that were hidden deep."

At that instant, he couldn't not believe her. "Good."

"I'm not sure." Her throat worked as she swallowed. "I did things in those labs, Dev, things I don't want to remember."

The fear in her voice rocked him. He'd become used to seeing her as the survivor who'd woken in that hospital bed, the steel-willed woman who'd asked him for a promise of death. But that woman had once been a Psy scientist, might well have done unforgivable things. "Whoever that woman was," he said, voice harsh, "she died in the months you spent with that monster."

"That's too easy." An implacable decision. "No, I have to see, I have to know."

"Then you will." He closed his hand over her nape, soothing his hunger to touch her, claim her. "If there's one thing I know, it's that your will is unbreakable."

"Then you know I'm not going to back down," she said, looking up at him with those changeable eyes. At this instant, in the sunlight, they were so clear as to be translucent. But that made them no less determined. "I want you to scan my mind."

CHAPTER 26

Having read the report his aide had prepared for him on the situation in Sri Lanka, Kaleb walked outside—to the very edge of the patio that stuck out over a jagged gorge—and opened the psychic pathways of his mind. But instead of entering the Net as Kaleb Krychek, Councilor and cardinal Tk, he wrapped himself in a mobile firewall that shifted endlessly, hiding his identity.

Nikita Duncan would've been very surprised to hear who he'd learned that little trick from. He'd monitored Sascha Duncan for some time before she defected—the NetMind had shown a decided preference for the Councilor's daughter and he'd wanted to know why. But he hadn't been able to get through her shields—Sascha Duncan, he thought impartially, might be the best shield technician he'd ever seen. What he'd learned from the glimpses he'd caught of her before she lost herself in the pathways of the Net had been more useful than all the things he'd learned to that point.

Now, using those shields that made him effectively invisible, he shot out through the midnight skies of the Net and toward the spreading stain he'd shown Nikita. Instead of taking the usual route, he found one of the slipstreams that fed into the pool and let it sweep him to the exact spot, much like riding a river into the sea.

He had no fear of contamination—he recognized the dead area for what it was. It held echoes of the DarkMind—the mute, hidden twin of the NetMind, created from all the rage and pain the Psy refused to feel. Part of that echo existed within Kaleb, too. It wasn't that he was a cardinal Tk, it was that he was a *very special* cardinal Tk, one who'd been molded by time and circumstance into the perfect conduit. So he rode the dark rapids with impunity, even as he "spoke" to the NetMind.

The neosentience could tell him nothing about the uprising in Colombo, but sent him a cascade of images from which Kaleb filtered out a single dark thread that snaked almost directly to the anchor in that region. He hadn't lied to Nikita—he didn't think the recent surge in violence by Psy was responsible for this lifeless patch of the Net, but it *was* a factor...and it was starting to undermine the very foundations of the Net. That disintegration wasn't yet an avalanche, and the increase in voluntary rehabilitations might slow it further, but sooner or later something would have to give.

When it did, this stain would spread. And wherever it went, death would follow.

CHAPTER 27

Katya stayed behind the closed door to her room when she heard the others arrive. Dev hadn't ordered her to do so, hadn't even set a guard on her door, but she wasn't going to put people in danger because she felt hurt at being excluded. Maybe she was right and Ming wasn't monitoring her every thought—all the signs pointed to a lack of mind control—but how could she justify playing with lives on the strength of a belief built on such shaky ground?

But if she *was* right and Ming had effectively created a fence around her mind in the PsyNet, how was that fence staying in place? As far as she could see, she had no psychic link to anyone or anything aside from her life-giving connection to the PsyNet.

No link...

"Oh," she said aloud, realizing the depths of Ming's skill at mental combat. The fence, the shield, the prison—*she* was feeding it. He'd locked her inside herself, and then, as a final insult, programmed her own mind to reinforce the walls he'd put in place.

Her hand clawed into the sheets, into the mattress. She wasn't just *inside* a prison, she was part of the prison itself.

Dev watched Sascha Duncan sit down on the other side of Cruz's bed, her mate's hand on her shoulder. Cruz's eyes went from Dev to Lucas and back again. Sascha sighed. "Would you two stop looking at each other as if you're about to get into a shoot-out?"

"No guns," Dev said without taking his eyes off the Dark-River alpha.

Sascha scowled. *"Lucas."* A command to behave.

The leopard alpha's eyes lit with feline amusement. "I will if he will."

On the bed, Cruz's lips curved slightly as he waited for Dev's answer.

"Since you're a guest," Dev said, leaning back against the wall by the door, "I suppose I'll have to let you win this round."

"Generous of you." Lucas moved to echo Dev's position closer to his mate. "See, Sascha, we're all friends now."

Instead of answering, Sascha focused on Cruz. "How old do you think they are?"

Cruz's cheeks actually dimpled as he smiled. "Ten?"

Sascha's laugh filled the room, and for the first time, Dev truly understood what she was. A number of empaths had dropped out with the Forgotten, but so many had stayed behind, hoping against hope that their mere presence would help their people. His great-grandmother Maya had been a child when her parents chose to defect, her empathic abilities in the moderate range. Because of her, he'd thought he knew empaths... but never had he been in the presence of a cardinal E-Psy.

It was, he realized, quite simply impossible to feel hate or anger toward Sascha if you felt any kind of emotion at all. And that, he suddenly understood, was why E-Psy were systemically suffocated in the Net, their powers bound—they were a real threat to Council power. Should Silence break, it was the empaths who might well take control.

But extraordinary as she was, he felt nothing but admiration toward Sascha. She awakened none of the complex, turbulent feelings brought to life inside him by the woman sitting silently in the room at the back of the house.

It destroyed something in him that he couldn't set her free.

Sascha met his gaze at that moment, her own holding nothing but warmth. "I think you can trust me with Cruz." She glanced over her shoulder at Lucas. "Shoo. No one's going to jump through the window with half the pack on watch outside."

Lucas straightened from the wall as Dev looked over to see if Cruz was okay with being alone with Sascha. The boy already had a hand wrapped around hers. "You want Tag and Tiara to continue to shield?"

"Yes." Sascha smiled as Lucas bent down to kiss the back of her neck. "We're going to start with the basic building blocks today. Though I have a feeling Cruz here will catch on fast."

Walking out with the DarkRiver alpha, Dev pulled the door shut so Sascha and Cruz could have privacy. "Sascha's very slender for being pregnant."

Lucas bristled. "Are you saying I don't take good care of my mate?"

"Stop antagonizing him, Dev," Tiara said from her cross-legged position in front of the entertainment screen in the living area. "You know perfectly well how feral predatory changeling men get with their pregnant mates. Tag, go hit one of them."

Tag sighed and looked up. "Is that really necessary, gentlemen?"

Lucas, his eyes human again, looked from Tag to Tiara

and seemed to see something he shouldn't. But he didn't say a word. "I'd like to meet Katya."

Disliking the familiarity with which the changeling male said her name, Dev began to walk down the corridor. "She's staying with me."

"Well, now..." Lucas shrugged. "Ashaya's attached to her."

"No compromise."

Lucas gave him a shrewd glance. "You talk to her like that, too?"

"None of your damn business."

"That's what I thought." A feline smile. "Here's a tip— don't snarl at women. It makes them mad."

"Go screw yourself," Dev said without heat.

Lucas laughed. "I don't have to. I have a gorgeous mate."

Katya opened the door at that moment. "I thought I heard—" Her eyes locked on Lucas.

The DarkRiver alpha was all green eyes and that warm leopard charm as he smiled. "You must be Katya. I'm Lucas."

"Hello." Katya gave a small smile.

Fire rippled up Dev's spine. "Let's go outside to talk." There was no way in hell he wanted the other man in Katya's room.

"Not so long as Sascha's in the house," Lucas said, taking a position against the wall opposite the doorway. "We can talk here."

"What's there to talk about?" Katya asked, gripping the doorjamb.

Lucas's eyes went to her white-knuckled hold. "Ashaya wants you to know you have a way out."

Dev's jaw tightened. "Don't play the alpha here, Luc. I've got no loyalty to you."

"I have to look after my people, Dev, same as you. And Ashaya considers Katya a true friend."

Dev thought of Katya's determination to go north, waited to see what she'd do.

"Thank you," she said, uncurling her fingers only to wrap her arms around herself. His body bucked at the reins, wanting to go to her, crush her close. Then she spoke, and his pride at her turned into a flame inside of him. "I think of her as a friend, too. And because I am her friend, I won't put her family in jeopardy."

"There's your answer," Dev said, making sure Lucas heard the absolute lack of flexibility in his voice. "Anything else?"

"You change your mind, Katya, all you have to do is say so." Lucas's head angled slightly to the right. "I have to go talk to my mate."

Knowing Tag and Tiara would keep an eye on things, Dev stayed behind as Lucas walked away. "You should've taken the chance he gave you."

Katya's eyes went wide at his tone.

Something primitive in him pushed at him to finish his, make his claim in the most final way. "I won't let you leave."

Katya knew she should've been angry, but it wasn't a threat she saw in Dev's eyes. No, what burned in those gold-flecked depths was a possessive demand that she knew would end her loneliness forever . . . but only if she accepted his rules. "I may have been broken when I came in," she said, a deeply feminine part of her sensing that if she gave in now, it would all be over, "but that's not true any longer. The pieces are starting to come together."

"Good." He took her chin in a hold that was blatantly proprietary.

Her stomach filled with butterflies, the steel and heat scent of him in every breath—but she kept her voice. "Even if that means I won't do what you want?"

He rubbed his thumb over her lower lip, his eyes on her mouth. "I never said I wanted a puppet."

"In that case," she said, her lips brushing his thumb, "consider yourself forewarned. Nothing you can do will stop me from doing what *I* need to do."

Dev's expression changed then, filling not with anger but with challenge. "Bring it on."

The kiss was hard, fast, openly possessive—a warning and a promise in one.

Striding down the corridor to find Sascha leaving Cruz's room—to go directly into her mate's arms—Dev nodded at the couple to follow him outside. "Tag," he said, the taste of Katya a lingering sweetness on his tongue, "one of you two should sit in on this, too." They could easily transmit what they heard to the other.

Tiara rose in a graceful movement. "I'll go. Keep your mind open to me, okay, big guy?"

Tag gave a short nod, but Dev saw the flash of hunger in the man's eyes. It made him wonder what it felt like for the two telepaths to communicate—did Tag feel something different when it was Tiara? Part of him couldn't help but think what it would be like to have Katya's mind open to his.

Then you know I'm not going to back down. I want you to look in my mind.

His every male instinct growled in rejection. Such contact would have nothing to do with intimacy—it would be the worst kind of violation, a mockery of what should be.

"Dev, you okay?" It was Tiara, her voice pitched low.

Realizing he'd let his emotions bleed into his face, he nodded. "Sascha," he said, turning to the empath as she came to stand beside him, Lucas on her other side. "What's your opinion on Cruz?"

"He's damaged, but not irrevocably so." An encouraging smile. "The boy can learn to shield."

Tiara blew out a breath. "Damn, I'm glad to hear that. But why wasn't he picking up the things we were trying to show him?"

"His pathways," Sascha said, "are so compromised I had to devise a completely new form of shielding just for him."

"You can do that?" Tiara asked. "Tag wants the blueprint."

"It's a work in progress at the moment—I'm building it from the inside out. Or rather," she amended, "Cruz is, according to my instructions. I'll be happy to give you what I've got so far."

"Luc," Dev said as the two women stepped away, "I've got something else I need to talk to you about."

"Yeah?"

"You have any contact with that new leopard pack up in the Smokies?"

"That's Remi's pack," Lucas said easily. "RainFire."

"Remi?" Dev shook his head. "Sounds like he should be hunting alligators somewhere."

"Short for Remington. Pisses him off big time when anyone uses that name."

"Thanks for the tip."

Lucas grinned.

"How long's RainFire been around?"

"'Bout a year. Remi rounded up a few loners he knew through his roaming, found territory, and sent out the call that the pack was open. I hear they've got a reasonable group now."

"How's that work, the territory thing?"

"You asking for a reason?"

"I've got nervous people in the area, people who own their land fair and square." A lot of Forgotten had settled in that region, finding comfort in the massive shadow of the mountains.

Lucas shook his head. "Won't be a problem. Remi bought up a huge tract of land for his people, and under the amendments to the Constitution after the Territorial Wars, he's got changeling rights to the areas in public ownership."

Dev had read those laws himself. "As long as he maintains the natural landscape and can hold it against other changelings, it's his? Doesn't that go against the Peace Accord?"

"That area was unclaimed," Lucas said. "If it had been claimed but the pack was weak, he could've gone in then, too. Fact it was empty makes it even easier."

"And my people's access to that public land?"

"Still theirs, but if Remi succeeds in holding it, they'll have to follow his rules."

"Not exactly fair."

Lucas shrugged. "If he does hold it, he also pledges to help the people in his territory, so the humans and nonpredatories get leopard protection. It's not a bad deal."

"Unless Remi is a piece of shit."

A grin spread across the leopard alpha's face. "I'll tell him you said that."

"I'd rather you give me his direct line. I can't pin the bastard down long enough to talk."

"He's busy establishing his territory." But Lucas took out his cell and sent the data wirelessly to Dev's own phone. "Remi's okay. It'll be interesting to see if RainFire sticks together—like I said, the pack's based around a group of leopards who chose to walk alone until Remi sweet-talked them into joining up with him."

"You seem to know a bit about him. I thought the packs were independent."

"Times change," Lucas said, no amusement in his tone now. "Intelligence is a useful tool—even for the most isolated packs."

Dev met the other man's eyes. "There are Forgotten across the country."

"Maybe we should talk."

EARTHTWO COMMAND LOG:
SUNSHINE STATION

10 July 2080: *Official incident report: Four staff members appear to have experienced a hallucinatory episode of significant strength. During the period of irregular brain activity, they caused extensive damage to the main sleeping quarters. Repairs are now in progress.*

All the affected individuals were checked by the medics and pronounced stable after twelve hours of observation. The medical team currently has no conclusive data, but is theorizing that the four may have been poisoned by a contaminant in the food chain. Our supplies are in the process of being scanned for toxins.

CHAPTER 28

Katya spent most of the rest of the afternoon watching archived news footage on the small comm unit in her room. More and more of her memory was coming back, and several times she found herself prompting the anchor. When that happened one time too many, she turned off the panel and decided to stretch her legs.

No one bothered her when she went into the kitchen. After grabbing an apple from the bowl on the counter, she opened the back door and stepped out.

"Going to be a nice night," Tiara said from where she was going through a graceful exercise routine on the back lawn, her hair swept up in a sleek ponytail, her body covered by a flowing white top and black leggings.

Taking a bite of the apple, Katya looked up at the early evening sky. "How can you tell?"

"I've got weather-sense, as my *oma* would say."

"*Oma*?"

"My grandmother." Tiara stretched out her long limbs in an almost feline way. "She was born in Indonesia, but her ancestors were all sea-folk over from the Netherlands. No one can read weather like a sailor."

The apple left a sweet, slightly tart taste on Katya's tongue. Relishing it, she took another bite. "Did your family inter-marry with the Indonesian population?"

"Can't you tell? I'm a mutt." A wink from an eye that was uptilted just enough to whisper of ancestors far from Europe.

Katya couldn't help but smile. "You're doing some kind of yoga."

"It's one of the more athletic versions." Spinning in a slow curve, her leg held out like a dancer's, she smiled. "Want to join me?"

Being stronger, Katya thought, would only help in her escape. "Can I do it in these clothes?"

Tiara ran a critical eye over her jeans and sweatshirt. "No, you need lighter gear. You can borrow something of mine."

"You're about a foot taller than I am," Katya pointed out.

"And more than a few pounds heavier." Tiara grinned, one hand on a curvy hip.

She was, Katya thought, the embodiment of the female ideal so many of the human artists liked to draw. All ripe curves and height and an almost electric kind of beauty.

"Right," Tiara said with a nod. "I know what we'll do. Strip off the sweatshirt, and get rid of the jeans. Sun's still out, so the T-shirt will do with some leggings I bought last week."

Katya walked back inside to do as ordered. Tiara threw in a pair of leggings a minute later. Though they were loose enough on her thin frame that she had to use a pin to hold them up, they were otherwise fine, reaching to midcalf—which meant they were likely knee-high on Tiara. Sweeping her own hair into a ponytail, she walked back out to the lawn in her bare feet.

As Tiara began to show her the basic stretches, Katya felt her body flow into the rhythm almost without thought. A few minutes later, the other woman gave her a considering look and said, "Let's try something else."

Katya watched as Tiara demonstrated, then copied the deceptively slow move.

Tiara nodded. "You've done this before."

"Yes." Katya flowed into another move. "My body remembers, even if my mind doesn't." Her brain supplied the information that yoga was considered a valuable form of exercise in the Net, as it meant training the mind as well as the body.

"Awesome. That means we can skip the baby stuff."

"I don't think so." Rubbing at her quivering calf muscles, Katya shook her head. "My body might be willing, but it's not as able as it should be."

Tiara smiled that megawatt grin. "If you're tough enough to mouth off to Dev, you're tough enough for Tiara's Yoga Class."

"How do you know I mouth off to Dev?" Getting into position, she ran her body through a slow, basic routine.

Beside her, Tiara did a much more complex set of moves. "Call it feminine intuition."

"You know," Katya said, feeling sweat roll down her back, "there's a theory that the first Psy were simply humans with a highly developed sense of intuition."

"Well, they do say we originated from the same primordial ooze."

Katya searched the foggy banks of her memory, came up with more data. "If the Council succeeds in maintaining Silence," she said, aligning her body until every muscle was in perfect tune, "and the majority of Psy mate only with other Psy, there's a possibility they'll evolve in a completely different direction."

"That kind of evolution would take a helluva long time. Personally, I don't think it'll happen." An easy shrug as she watched Katya complete her set. "I think the humanity in Psy will rise to the surface."

As Katya's feet came down on the grass, rooting her to the earth, she shook her head. "That assumes there's some humanity still present in them." And after her endless hours with Ming, she knew there wasn't.

Dev was on his way to talk to Katya later that evening when he got a call from Maggie. As a result, he ended up spending over two hours on a conference call with a number of people high up in Shine—all of whom were starting to panic about the rising rate of incidents.

For once, however, the meeting didn't degenerate into an argument—despite the fact that Dev's cousin Jack was pushing for a solution Dev refused to accept. When he finally hung up, it was with a feeling of exhaustion weighing down his shoulders. He wanted to go to Katya, to be with her, even if he couldn't share the fears that threatened to splinter the Forgotten, but the hour was well past eleven, and according to Tiara, both Tag and Katya had gone to bed around ten, after the two women chatted over a late dinner. Dev wasn't sure quite what to make of that. Tiara got along with almost everyone, but she was also fiercely loyal to Shine.

Reaching back to pull off his T-shirt in preparation for catching a few hours' sleep, he froze at the sound of a short, sharp scream, cut off almost before it began.

By the time he slammed into Katya's room, she was sitting up in bed, staring at the sheets.

"What happened?" he asked, sensing Tiara return to her watch in the front.

"The boy," she whispered, "he was such a beautiful boy." Her hand shook as she raised it to her face. She dropped it midway, as if she'd forgotten what she meant to do. "I couldn't help him."

He didn't interrupt, realizing he was hearing an inner nightmare.

"I tried to protect him, but then Larsen asked for him and I couldn't say anything, couldn't stop him." Her throat worked as she swallowed. "I wanted to stab Larsen through the heart with his own scalpel, but if I had, then Ming LeBon would've known we were traitors and *all* the children would've died."

"The boy survived," he reminded her. "I told you that. I don't know why Ashaya nev—"

She shook her head. "It was to protect me. To protect the children. The less I knew, the less they could take from me if I was ever broken."

"You don't have to worry about that anymore—you won't be retaken." Dev did not let go of what was his. "And Jon—that's his name—is safe. The Council knows if they touch the boy, it's a declaration of war."

"Jon...Jonquil Duchslaya," she murmured slowly. "I'm glad he's protected...God, he screamed so much." She dropped her head in her hands, her entire body shaking. "And I had to pretend that it didn't matter, that I didn't care."

His own body strained toward her, but how could he go to her when he'd put her in a cage himself? "You shouldn't have. You were Silent—without emotion."

She lifted her head, eyes shining in the light coming in from the corridor. "There's being cold, and then there's such a thing as being without conscience. I've always had a conscience, and it keeps me awake every single night."

"Katya," he began, not knowing what he was going to say.

"Do you think he'd see me? Jon?" She folded her arms around herself. "I need to say sorry. I need to do that much at least."

Dev knew about demons, saw too many in her eyes. Losing the war to keep his distance, he closed the door and crossed the carpet. "I'll ask."

"Thank you." She scooted back as he sat down on the bed. "You should go now."

"I'm not leaving you like this." Her eyes were stark in a face gone white, her body shivering in spite of the blankets.

"I want to be alone."

"The hell you do." Swearing under his breath, he got into the bed and, ignoring Katya's protests, maneuvered her into his lap. "Quiet," he snapped when she pushed at him.

She went still. "Even I know that's not the appropriate thing to say in this situation."

The overly prim response should've made him laugh. But he continued to feel the remembered terror in her body, her heart racing so fast he thought it might bruise itself against her ribs. Keeping one arm around her body, the other in her hair, he crushed her to him, knowing she needed the sensation, but also knowing she'd never ask for it. Not now.

Slowly, the stiffness drained out of her, one of her hands creeping under his T-shirt to spread out over his pulse. Her hand was cool, or maybe it was that his body was too hot. As always, he couldn't control his reactions around her. It didn't matter. Instead of shoring up his shields, all he wanted to do was offer comfort, give her a way out of that dark room where she'd been trapped without sight, without sound, without touch.

"Tiara told me she was in Paris not long ago."

Startled at her choice of subject, he slid his hand down to her nape, squeezing gently. "Hmm."

"She said she went to visit her parents." Her fingers stroked over his skin in a touch that reached far deeper than anyone else ever had. "She said her mother made her cake and coffee every afternoon, and brushed her hair for her every night, while her dad splurged on a day spa for both her and her mother, took them shopping, and bought chocolate for her to snack on on the airjet ride home."

Dev looked down, but Katya had tucked her head against him, her lashes delicate fans against her cheeks. "Sounds like she was spoiled."

"That's what she said, too." Those fingers stroked lower, curving over his ribs. He knew he should stop her before she inadvertently went too far, but he didn't. Because even now, her skin was a little clammy, her heart jittery.

"What else did Ti share?" Shifting his hold, he closed his hand over her thigh.

She stayed put—though he felt the tremors beneath her skin. "That she expects any man who wants her to spoil her just as badly."

"Was Tag in the room when she said that?"

"Of course."

He glimpsed the faintest shadow of a smile. "You think she was teasing him."

"I *know* she was teasing him. It's amazing how much the eyes can say."

"You must've learned to read expressions very early in the Net," he said, trying to ignore the fact that her fingers were tracing the top edge of his jeans in a maddening caress. "No one can control every minute movement."

"It's much more difficult with the Silent," she murmured, tucking her fingers at his hip, a single aching centimeter under his waistband. "Everything's in very small increments."

"Yeah?" Reaching down, he tugged at her hand—no man was that good.

She resisted. "You feel interesting here." The brush of her thumb over his hip bone.

Dear God in heaven. "Katya," he all but groaned, "unless you want to be stripped naked in about two seconds flat, you can't keep your hand there." He was already hard beneath her. One more touch and he'd snap.

He saw her swallow, but she didn't remove her hand. "The sensations would be incredible," she murmured. "If we were naked."

"Jesus." Pulling off her hand before he gave in to temptation, he closed his own around it. "You're mad at me, remember?"

"Yes. But according to Tiara, sexual contact doesn't necessarily have to involve an emotional tie."

Dev wondered exactly how much time Ti and Katya had been spending together. "She was probably trying to jerk Tag's chain."

A frown. "Even so, it's true, isn't it? People can have sex without liking each other."

"Yes." It was an answer gritted out through clenched teeth.

Her eyes focused on him. "Have you ever had it with someone you disliked?"

"No." He didn't have to think about it. "I tend to take sex seriously."

A pause. "Yet you're aroused by me." Those eyes locked with his again, and his gut clenched against a bruiser of a sucker punch. Because Katya wasn't scared anymore. She was pissed.

"And I," she continued, "am very much someone you dislike."

Leaning forward, he tugged back her head. "I didn't realize you were so good at seduction."

A little flush across her cheekbones. "There's a lot you don't know about me."

"So it wasn't planned," he murmured, feeling his body all but purr. "That means you can't resist the enemy either."

"I'll get over it." A snapped statement. "Now go."

He let her scramble off his lap...only because he knew that one second longer and he'd have followed through on his threat of ripping off her clothes, feasting on the exquisite nakedness of her skin. But he couldn't resist taking her lips. It was a short, wild contact filled with anger on both sides. But there was something beneath the anger, a savage kind of need that shocked the hell out of him and left her staring in confusion.

PETROKOV FAMILY ARCHIVES

Letter dated October 1, 1977

Dearest Matthew,

Emily was sick today. She's got an ear infection, the little darling. It breaks my heart to see tears in her eyes—though of course those didn't last long, not once I got her to an M-Psy, but it was far too long for a mother to bear. You didn't like it either. You were trying to give her your toys so she'd feel better. And you know what? For you, she hiccupped and played for a little while.

As I watched the two of you sitting there, you looking after her, I realized something. I've been so focused on how Silence would affect us that I haven't given a thought to the future, to the unborn. If Silence succeeds, then there will come a time when children are born who'll never be kissed by their mothers, mothers who'll never hold their precious babes and breathe in that sweet, sweet scent as a tiny hand lies over their heart.

It seems such a simple choice, but...

Greg called tonight. He rarely does anymore, so your father tried to keep the conversation away from politics. They always fight when it strays in that direction. But while your father was out getting something for Greg, I made that point to your uncle—about the lack of love between mother and child.

Do you know what he said?

That so many women are falling prey to violence, we've already got a generation that doesn't know what it is to sleep in a mother's arms.

The worst of it is, he's right.

Mom

CHAPTER 29

To Katya's surprise, DarkRiver agreed to allow her to see Jon. A dark-skinned man with intense green eyes drove the boy over. As Katya spoke to him by a tree in the yard, the tawny-haired woman who'd accompanied Jon reached into the back-seat and came out with an armful of giggling little girl.

Noor Hassan.

Her heart clenched to see such open joy on the child's face. Wanting to touch the girl, make sure she really was alright, Katya nonetheless made herself fight her cowardice and look at Jon.

"You've grown taller," she said, wondering why she was surprised. Teenage boys rarely stayed the same from month to month. "Your hair, you cut it."

He shrugged, sending the short strands of brilliant white-gold shifting in the sunlight.

"Thank you for seeing me."

"Tally asked." There was something in his tone that told Katya he'd do anything for the woman who'd asked. "Plus, you never hurt me."

"Didn't I?" She sat down beside him when he took a seat

on the ground, long legs stretched out in front of him. "I didn't stop it either, though, did I?"

He gave her a narrow-eyed glance out of those brilliant blue eyes that had made him so easy to identify. Not many people looked like Jonquil Alexi Duchslaya. "What're you talking about?" he now asked.

"I want to apologize." It was time to face her crimes. "When Larsen hurt you, I didn't stop him." She made no excuses, because there were none.

"I heard your memory was messed up. Is it all back now?"

"Most of it." There were still pieces missing, things, if she was being honest, her mind probably didn't want to remember. She was at peace with that. Because Ekaterina, the woman who'd been a Psy scientist and later a victim, was gone. Katya had risen from the ashes, and she would make her own memories, her own future.

Jon gave her a funny look. "And you don't remember that? He backhanded you fucking hard." He winced. "Don't tell Tally I swore, okay?"

Her entire body went taut. "Who backhanded me?"

"Lizard Man, Larsen, whatever." Despite the careless words, he drew up his legs, putting his arms around his knees. But his eyes held concern, not fear. "He was doing stuff to me, and you said he'd gone far enough, that he was breaking the agreed-upon protocols."

Her mind remained a blank on the incident. "Are you certain? He had drugs in your system."

"Yeah, I'm certain. Not something I'll ever forget, drugs or not." He shook his head. "You tried to move his hand off my forehead and wham, that was when he backhanded you so hard, you ended up unconscious on the floor."

Still no memory, but a bubble of hope. "How did he justify the hit?" Violence was supposed to have been wiped out by Silence, and Larsen had been pretending to be the perfect Psy.

"Dunno. You were out, so it wasn't like you could call him

on it." He stared critically at her face. "I'm pretty sure I heard something crack. I thought he'd broken your nose or your jaw."

A pulse of pain in her nose, a phantom memory. Hazy. Indistinct. But coming into focus. "Yes," she whispered, raising her fingers to the bridge of her nose. "He said he'd had to do it to keep me from compromising the experiment... he did the medical work on it himself."

"So don't beat yourself up about it," Jon said. "You were stuck, same as me. You did what you could."

"That's very wise for someone your age."

He smiled and it was devastating, all charm and youth and a slight cockiness. "Shh. Everyone else thinks I'm hell on wheels."

At that instant, Noor got away from the woman who'd been playing with her and ran pell-mell toward them. "Jonny!"

Rising in a fluid movement, Jon grabbed her up and swung her around to the accompaniment of her delighted laughter. Katya looked at the child in wonder. Larsen, she remembered as she got to her feet, had never touched Noor, Jon having taken her place, but the little girl had known terror. Today, she wrapped her arms around Jon's neck and stared at Katya.

Lines formed on her brow. "Who're you?"

"Noor," Jon said, "that's not nice."

Noor wrinkled up her nose. "Is she your girlfriend?"

"Why do you care?" Jon teased. "You're going to marry Keenan."

Noor leaned close, her next words a loud whisper. "But you like Rina."

Jon went bright red under his golden skin. "This is Katya. She's our friend." His eyes met Katya's as he said that last word, and there was only acceptance in them. "She helped us once."

After another moment, Noor gave a small nod and stuck out a hand. "Nice to meet you."

Katya took it with gentle care, very aware of the delicacy

of the little girl's skin, her bones. "Nice to meet you, too. So, tell me about Rina."

Noor's smile was as bright as her name.

Five hours later, as the house quieted down after dinner, Katya crushed the part of her that remembered only Dev's tenderness as he took her into his arms, and instead picked up the gauntlet he'd thrown down that first night. She should have done it yesterday, but Dev had been so busy, the lines of strain around his mouth so deep, she'd hesitated to interrupt him. It would be so easy to keep doing that—find excuses to put it off—but she would never be allowed any freedom until Dev saw the truth of who she was. And she needed that freedom to escape.

The drive to go north was a clawing need in her throat by now, a hunger she had to physically fight to keep herself from taking irrational risks.

Narrowing her telepathic senses to a fine, fine point, she sent a thought to Dev. He couldn't hear the words, but he'd feel the attempt.

We need to talk.

She snapped back into her mind before Tag could pick up on it.

A curt knock sounded on her door an instant later. "Come in."

"What was that?" Walking in, Dev closed the door behind himself and leaned back on it, arms folded. Instead of the suit she'd become used to seeing in New York, he was dressed once more in those jeans that made him even more dangerously attractive and a plain white T-shirt.

Itching to touch him, she nonetheless remained on the other side of the room. "A way to get your attention."

"You got it."

"It's time." She walked to stand at the foot of the bed. "You need to go into my mind."

A single brutal word. "I told you, that's not happening."

"Why?" She stepped closer. "Because it'll make you feel like a monster?"

He jerked as if he'd been shot. "Yes."

"Tough," she said, refusing to buckle under the urge to just give in, to let him have his way. If she did, they'd never move beyond this point. And every time she looked into his eyes, no matter how much he wanted her, she would see distrust. It *hurt*. So much more than she could have ever imagined. "If I can bear it, you can do it."

He closed the space between them to glare down at her. "But here's the thing, Katya. You can't force me to invade your mind."

She fisted her hands, squeezing so tight her bones ground together in pain. "If I drop my shields and you don't come in, allowing me to close them around your entry point, my mind will be wide open to anyone with psychic ability."

"You think that matters to me?" So hard, so angry.

"Yes, it matters," she forced out through a throat raw with emotion. "Because you've taken responsibility for me. You might have to kill me, but until then, you'll protect me."

"Nice and manipulative of you."

It took everything she had to keep her tone level. "A woman's got to do what a woman's got to do."

"Even if it destroys the other party?" A soft question that cut through her defenses with razor sharpness.

Bleeding, she looked up. "Will it truly be that bad for you?"

A harsh bark of laughter. "Haven't you been able to access the files you have on me?"

"I don't have those memories." She held his gaze, suddenly dead certain that if she forced him to do this, it would kill the last fragments of that indefinable "something" between them. There would be no coming back from it. It wouldn't have mattered to a true Psy, to a person who saw everything as part of a cost-benefit ratio.

But it mattered to her, mattered beyond bearing.

"Okay," she said, dropping her head even as the pragmatic side of her screamed in rebellion. "Okay."

Dev felt Katya's acquiescence like a blow. "Why?"

"Because sometimes the price is too high."

He caught her hand when she would have turned away, tugging her to his chest and taking her mouth in a furious kind of possession before she could do more than gasp. She'd backed away because it would hurt *him*.

It shattered him—he had always been the protector, the one who looked after others. Never had he expected that the enemy would try to protect his heart.

Echoes of sensation, too-soft whispers in his head.

He bit at her lower lip. "Shh. Tag will hear."

Her lips curved into a startled "Oh."

Taking advantage, he swept into her mouth, stroking his tongue against hers, drawing the intoxicating taste of her into his lungs. The whispers ceased, and he was unaccountably annoyed. "I'll have to learn," he said, kissing his way across her jaw, "how to shield your projecting from other telepaths." Because that was an intimacy he'd allow no one to invade.

Katya's hand clenched in his hair as he nipped at the slender line of her throat, only just restraining the savage need to bite hard enough to mark. "That assumes," she said, her voice breathy, "you'll have a lot of chances to practice."

"And your point is?"

Her gaze was dark with arousal when she blinked them open. "Dev."

He waited for her to tell him they shouldn't keep doing this, damn sure he wasn't capable of letting her go. Instead, she stood on tiptoe, put her hands on his shoulders, and stole a kiss that was as delicate as it was passionate, as feminine as it was powerful. It just about broke him, driving him to the edge of surrender. All he wanted to do was tumble her into bed and strip her inch by slow inch.

But she had the reins...and she took her own sweet time. When she finally stepped back, his entire body was vibrating with pure, undiluted hunger.

"I don't understand," she murmured, lifting her fingertips to touch kiss-swollen lips, "how my race could've ever given up such exquisite sensation."

His cock pushed against the zipper of his pants, the metal threatening to turn him into a eunuch. *"Katya."*

As a warning, it had no effect. Dropping her hand from her lips, she clenched it over her navel, as if soothing some inward ache. "I feel so...hungry, so hot, as if my skin is about to burst."

He shuddered, voice lost.

"Is it always like this?" she asked, stroking her hand over her abdomen and back down. Over and over. Until he strode across and replaced her hand with his. She sucked in a breath. "Dev—you're making it worse." But she pressed closer to him, sliding her own hand into the collar of his shirt, seeking skin.

"The things I want to do to you," he said, barely resisting the urge to pull up her top and slip his hand underneath...dip below. He already knew she'd be soft and wet for him, a silken fist he could almost feel.

Her lips trailed up his neck. "You didn't answer my question."

It took him several seconds to remember what she was talking about. "No, it's not always like this."

"So if I kiss another man—"

"I'll kill him." It came out with ice-cold precision, though his body was burning from the inside out. Tangling his hand in her hair once more, he pulled back her head. "We clear on that?"

A slow blink. "If my anthropological knowledge is correct, it's only changelings who're meant to be so possessive." Scientific words, husky voice, a sweet feminine body cradling the painful jut of his arousal.

"Come on then," he said, shifting his hand to cup her bottom. "Push me and see what happens." Changing position slightly, he tilted her up...and settled the heat between her thighs right where he wanted it. She gasped and gripped his shoulders. He smiled.

"D-Dev."

Her stutter was adorable, he decided. Sexy as hell, too. That mouth, those lips, he could look at them for hours, imagine exactly what he wanted to do. "Give me a second," he said, and broke the delicious contact long enough to walk her backward—distracting her with nibbling little kisses that had her nails digging into his shoulders.

She made a startled sound when her back met the wall.

Stroking his hands down to her hips, he ran his fingers to the button at the top of her jeans. Her eyes went huge, but she didn't stop him. Thanking the gods, he undid the closure and tugged down her zipper.

Katya knew she should pull away but she had no willpower where Devraj Santos and his wicked hands were concerned. When he tugged at the sides of her jeans, she shifted back, let him push the garment down. He made her lift her legs one at a time as he pulled it completely off her body.

Then, still crouching in front of her, he ran his hands up the backs of her legs.

The sensation sent waves of blackness rolling through her mind, but this black fire was as hot, as wild, and as masculine as the man who looked up at her with such sensual possession in his eyes. "Give in," he whispered. "Let me make you feel good."

It was an incredible leap for her to make, for a woman who'd never known intimacy, but she had to do this...because there would be no second chance.

CHAPTER 30

Quickly stifling that thought lest it escape, she watched as he rose to his feet and pulled off his T-shirt. Her throat dried up. "I guess all that kickboxing has its benefits." She didn't know where the words came from when her brain was stunned by the raw male beauty of him.

He chuckled. "I'm glad you approve." There was an almost arrogant confidence in him, but she liked it. Better that in Dev's eyes than the terrible pain she'd glimpsed for an instant when she'd spoken of forcing him to invade her mind.

Hands on her hips. Warm. A little rough. *Perfect.* She sucked in a breath, and when he lifted her, it was instinct to wrap her legs around his waist. He moved her until she— "Dev!" she screamed into his mouth as his still-covered cock pushed into her softness, parting her with possessive heat, the thin cotton of her panties no barrier.

His thumb smoothed over the crease of her thigh, inciting her to move impatiently ... but that only rubbed her clitoris against him, further tightening the fist that was her body. Breaking the kiss, she pushed at his shoulders. "It's too much."

"You can take it," he cajoled, kissing her neck, sucking on the beat of her pulse. At the same time, his fingers slid smoothly inside her panties, parting her with even more intimacy. Gasping in a breath, she buried her face in his neck. He smelled of heat and desire and a scent that was pure, aroused male. No, not just any male. *Dev.* She'd asked him if it would be like this with any other man, but she'd already known the answer—no. It would never be like this again. From the start, he was the only man she'd truly seen.

His fingers pinched her clitoris, that tiny nub of flesh she'd always known about scientifically but never really understood until this moment. Pleasure arced through her in an almost violent wave, and she could feel that fist within her tightening, tightening.

"Do you like that?" he whispered against her ear, releasing the pressure to circle the flesh he'd tortured so sensually the instant before.

"Yes." She pushed into him, wanting to rub, but held in place by the delicious heat of his body. The weight, the pressure, it ratcheted up her hunger until she could hardly breathe. "Touch me."

His lips curved. "Demanding, aren't you?"

That smile made her breasts ache, it was so full of promise, of desire. "You're teasing me."

"It's part of the fun." One finger flicked over the bundle of nerve endings she so desperately wanted him to touch much more firmly.

"This," she said, stroking her hand down to graze one flat male nipple, "is not fun."

"On that we'll have to agree to disagree." His voice was husky, his skin hot under her touch.

He was reacting to her, she realized in wonder. Continuing to pet him, she found herself listening to every hitch of his breath, wanting to do what pleased him most. When his ridged abdomen went rock hard as her nails scraped over his nipples, she repeated the caress.

A single word that turned the air blue. Pulling out the hand he had between her legs, he grabbed both her wrists and pinned them above her head. "Now," he murmured, eyes locked with her own, "where were we?" His free hand slid back down, over the twisting ache in her navel, under the edge of her panties, and—

"That's not fair," she somehow managed to gasp.

A kiss that stole her breath. "Who said anything about playing fair?" He rubbed lightly at her cleft, making her entire body clench. "Will you let me in, Katya?"

She shook her head. "No, you should be punished for teasing me." But her body was already silken with welcome for him, her flesh lusciously damp.

"Please?" Another kiss, another intimate touch. And she found herself arching into the finger he stroked gently inside her. The sensation was the most exquisite pleasure-pain, as if her nerve endings were on overload. But instead of wanting less, she wanted more. More and more. Here, in his arms, the torturer's dark room seemed light-years away. How could nightmares invade when there was so much heat, so much feeling?

"That's it," he murmured against her throat as he kissed his way back up to her mouth. "Move on me."

She couldn't stop the strangely fluid movements of her body—part of her knew what to do, how to do it. "More," she ordered, nipping at his ear.

"You're too tight."

"More."

Groaning, he slid a second finger inside her and pumped once. Twice. Pleasure and pain, a stretching ecstasy. Her arousal peaked, hovered there, waiting, waiting...His thumb brushed her clitoris.

Everything exploded.

She felt the back of her head connect with wall as she threw it back, heard Dev's bitten-off curse, sensed her muscles clenching convulsively around him as the orgasm tore her apart. None of it mattered. For the first time in her life, there was so much pleasure coursing through her body that she was delirious with it.

Dev watched Katya's face fill with pleasure and wanted only to undo the zipper on his jeans and take her. But no way in hell was he doing that with Tag and Tiara down the hall, not to mention Cruz. It had been hard enough to keep things quiet this long. A little more and his control would be shot to smithereens.

But no matter that they hadn't consummated their attraction, they'd crossed a line tonight and there'd be no going back from it. His jaw set. He would fight for her, for the woman who'd woken from that hospital bed and started to battle for her right to live. No one would take that right from her.

Soothing her down from the sexual high, he carried her to the bed. Heavy-lidded eyes opened to give him an inherently sensual look as he laid her down. "What about you?" Fingers trailing over his chest.

He caught her hand. "Later." Pressing a kiss to her lips, he thought he glimpsed a fleeting shadow, but when he looked up, her eyes were closed as she gave in to the kiss. "I have to go." He'd have given anything to spend the night by her side, but he needed to sit down and go over the implications of the previous day's conference call. The agitators were becoming more and more vociferous. Something had to be done—but how could he embrace a "solution" that would rip his people apart from within?

Katya's fingers on his cheek. "You have so much weight in your eyes, on your shoulders. I wish I could share it with you."

The honest offer made something clench in his chest. Bracing himself on one elbow so he could look down into her face, he echoed her hold. "That you made the offer is enough."

He wondered what it would be like to have someone of his own, someone he could trust absolutely. The irony was, the only woman he could see in that role was the one woman he couldn't ever trust. "Get some rest," he said, brushing her hair off her forehead. "We'll talk tomorrow."

She opened her mouth, then closed it. "Tomorrow. Good night, Dev."

He wondered if she'd been about to ask him to stay before thinking the better of it. The sense of loss lay heavy on his shoulders as he got off the bed and picked up his T-shirt. Then, unable to simply leave, he moved back to the bed to press a kiss on the exposed curve of her neck. "Have good dreams."

Half an hour later, as Katya finished dressing, she held Dev's final comment close to her heart. There'd been such care in those words, such tenderness. It had made her hesitate, but this was her only option now that she'd given up on getting him to enter her mind. He would be furious, but he'd also be safe—she couldn't hurt him from so far away.

Doubt hit again.

What if her actions weren't her own? What if she was meant to run, to go wherever it was her heart and soul insisted she go? What if the compulsion was only another clever trap?

"No." She knew these thoughts were her own. She *knew.* But how? Frowning in concentration as she laced up her sneakers, she felt a headache coming on. But this time she didn't retreat . . . and the answer appeared from the mists.

"You're a blunt instrument, nothing more." A single finger-tip touching her forehead. "There's no room for subtlety."

"Why?" she asked, too numb to be afraid anymore.

She didn't expect an answer, was surprised when he spoke again. "Subtlety requires mind control. You're not worth that much of my time."

"What am I supposed to do until the triggers activate?"

"You'll exist. Though, of course, not much of you is left anymore." A spreading blackness in her mind, tentacles digging deep, clawing and vicious.

Swallowing a cry of agony, Katya bent over, fist pressed to her stomach. Oh, God, it had hurt when he'd done that. It had hurt so very badly. She'd been little more than the most primitive of creatures by then, but she remembered the final torture, the final obliteration of her psyche.

"But I didn't die, you bastard," she whispered, rising to a standing position though nausea continued to churn in her stomach, a trickle of blood snaking out of her nose. Wiping it with a tissue, she stared at the door. "And when you locked me in this prison, you also freed me." Because no one could strike at her through the PsyNet. No one could spy on her. No one could stop her.

All she had to do was get out of this house.

Which might've proved very difficult had there only been the three other adults in the house. All three were dangerous. And Dev . . . well, she wasn't even going to think about taking him on in a physical fight.

But there was a fifth person here. A telepath.

He'd contacted her yesterday, while Sascha was visiting— Katya didn't know how he'd circumvented Tag. When that curious mind had brushed hers, she'd been so startled, she hadn't pulled back. And he'd talked to her.

I'm sorry they scared you away last time.

Surprised at the clarity of that voice, she'd answered without projecting, hoping he'd pick it up. *They were trying to protect someone.* This telepath, she'd realized at once, knowing that there was no way to wipe the information now that she had it. So she'd have to make sure no one would ever again rip open her mind. *You shouldn't be talking to me. Go back before you get in trouble.*

A quiet pause. *You're like me. You're scared, too.*

I'm trying not to be, she'd answered honestly. *How about you?*

I like Dev—he makes me feel safe.

Me, too.

Another pause. *How come you want to leave?*

She'd sucked in a breath at the ease with which he'd picked out that thought, even if it had been at the forefront of her mind. *That's not good manners, to read someone's thoughts.*

He'd been silent so long, she had thought he'd gone. *Sorry.* Quiet. So quiet. *I don't know all the rules.*

It's okay. We all had to start somewhere. Wanting to help, she'd taken a chance and carried on the conversation. *Just remember—if it's not something you'd want someone else doing to you, you shouldn't do it to them.*

I understand. I won't take your thoughts again.

Thank you.

But since I already did—how come you want to leave?

I have something I need to do. Something that pulled at her until it felt as if her tendons would tear from her bones, a pounding, secretive need. But how could she have any secrets? Ming had taken everything.

A tendril of mischief had brushed her mind and it had had a sense of newness to it, as if the boy had never played. *I can help you.*

No. I don't want you in trouble.

My mom used to say that boys are meant for trouble.

The utter sadness in that sentence had broken her heart. She'd heard wonderful things about Sascha Duncan—she hoped all those rumors were true. Perhaps the cardinal Psy could mend this boy telepath's own shattered heart. *That sounds about right.*

I have a plan. A hesitant whisper.

Charmed despite herself, she'd asked, *Okay, I give. What is it?*

And when he'd told her, she'd realized the stupid simplicity of it might just work better than every other thing she'd come up with. However, it all depended on whether the child could keep himself awake till the right moment.

So she waited, ready.

But when the scream came, she jumped sky-high. Moving to the door as she heard footsteps running toward the front of the house, she twisted the knob and stepped out into the corridor, heading toward that very area. Her breath stuck in her throat as she passed the open doorway of a room from where she could hear a number of voices. The front door was locked and alarmed in spite of the unexpected interruption.

She moved to the windows. Alarmed and locked, all of them.

Aware her time was about to run out, she told herself to *think*. She could break a window, but knew she wouldn't get five feet before Dev, Tag, or Tiara ran her down.

You're a scientist.

Heart thudding, she crept back down the hallway, made a quick stop in her bedroom, then headed to the kitchen, hoping against hope that her young co-conspirator would be able to keep them occupied for a few more minutes.

As she'd expected, a fresh pot of coffee sat on the counter. One of the three would likely not drink it, being off shift, but it would dramatically change the odds. Sliding out the medications she'd lifted from the apartment in New York, she dissolved a highly specific combination into the liquid.

A quick stir and she was done.

The drugs wouldn't hurt the others, just make them lethargic, and if she was lucky, sleepy. She could've used more but she hesitated—the Forgotten did have Psy genes...Unwilling to do serious harm, she retreated, the rest of the drugs still in her possession.

She was back in her room pretending to read when her door opened a fraction. "What was that noise?" she asked Tiara.

"A nightmare." The other woman didn't explain whose. "Wanted to tell you not to worry."

"Thanks."

And then Katya waited.

There was some movement for the next hour, people murmuring, steps to the kitchen, back to the living room. Sometime after nine thirty, a door closed with a quiet snick—one of the three going to bed. Waiting another twenty minutes to give that person time to slip into sleep, she pushed off the blankets and got up.

CHAPTER 31

Heart in her throat, she cracked open the door, knowing her coat and boots would give away her intent if she was caught. And she had no intention of being imprisoned again. Creeping down the hallway, she glanced into the open doorway of a bedroom.

Dev.

He lay with his head on a small writing table, his hair mussed. Knowing she should just walk on, she nonetheless went to him. His pulse beat strong under her fingers. Relief was a cool rain against her cheeks.

Pressing a kiss to his jaw, the roughness of stubble enticing her to linger, she went to leave the room. That was when she saw the stunner tucked in the small of his back. She hesitated. She had no desire to hurt anyone, but if either Tag or Tiara woke, she'd need something with which to warn them off. "Don't hate me," she whispered, and took the weapon before making her way to the entrance of the house.

Tag sat in front of the entertainment screen, a science fiction show playing in the background. His eyes were closed, his head tipped back against the sofa.

A near-empty mug of coffee sat in front of him.

Scared at his stillness, she went to put her fingers on his throat.

He groaned, shifted.

Freezing, she waited for him to wake and raise the alarm. But after a fraught few moments he slipped back into sleep. Relieved, she spread out her senses, searching to make sure the child was okay. Tag's shields were holding—the man was a very strong telepath. Unsure if they'd continue to hold as he dropped further into unconsciousness, she wrapped her own shields over his. Then, with a thousand silent apologies, she ransacked Tag's wallet, taking all the cash he had on him.

The alarm was the next hurdle.

"Help me," she whispered, not knowing who she was pleading with.

A door opened down the hall.

"Tag?" Tiara's voice came closer, husky with sleep. "I thought I felt—" The other woman froze when she saw the stunner pointed at her. Beautiful brown eyes streaked with a hundred shades of gold and amber flicked to the big man on the couch, worry crawling their depths.

"He's fine," Katya said. "I don't want to hurt anyone—I just want out."

"I can't let you do that," Tiara murmured, her hands loose at her sides.

Katya didn't relax her guard. The woman had a weapon on her somewhere. And she was a telepath. Katya held back the powerful psychic assault with her own abilities, creating an effective deadlock. "Do you know something, Tiara?"

"What?"

"I know that if I change the direction of this stunner,"

Katya whispered, "that if I press it to Tag's head, you'll do anything and everything I want."

Tiara sucked in a breath.

"But I don't want to do that." It was a plea. "I don't want to become a monster."

"You won't get away, you know." Tiara's tone shifted. "Dev will hunt you down."

Katya gave the other woman a shaky smile. "So it shouldn't matter if you let me go now."

"Katya, I know you're not going to shoot me," Tiara said point-blank. "So this standoff is pointless."

"The weapon's set for mild stun," Katya said. "You really want to leave the child vulnerable by making me take you out?"

Tiara swore under her breath. "You're not as helpless as you look."

"Thanks. Now walk over to the alarm panel." She shifted to keep Tiara a good distance from her as the woman moved. "Input the code."

Tiara complied without further questions.

Katya felt her lips quirk. "Did you send out a silent distress signal? It doesn't matter—just as long as the alarms don't shriek when you open the door."

"Why do you care?" Tiara arched one perfect eyebrow. "I'm already awake."

"I don't want to scare the boy."

A huge sigh. "I was on the way to liking you, Katya. Now you go and point a stunner at me."

"Open the door," Katya said, knowing the other woman was stalling.

Tiara did so without argument. No alarms sounded. As the Forgotten female strode out onto the porch and took the steps down to the lawn, Katya followed. Knowing Tiara would go for her weapon now that Tag was no longer under threat, she said, "Sorry," and fired the stunner.

"Fuck!" Tiara collapsed onto her knees, her movements jerky and uncoordinated. "Not sporting." It came out slow, uneven.

Tucking the stunner into her pocket, Katya put an arm under Tiara's shoulders. "I know. You can curse me later." Right now, she had to get the telepath to one of the vehicles.

The other woman resisted, but the stunner had short-circuited her nervous system. However, nothing could be done about the fact that the gorgeous woman was taller and heavier than Katya. As a result, Katya was sweating with a mixture of panic and stress by the time she dragged Tiara to the closest four-wheel drive. Taking the woman's hand, she pressed her thumb to the lock.

The door slid open and back.

Pulling Tiara's upper body into the driver's seat, Katya managed to get the woman's thumb on the ignition switch. The car started with a quiet purr.

"Won't restart," Tiara murmured, eyes starting to sharpen.

"I'll just have to keep it running." Lowering the Shine operative to the ground, she took Tiara's cell phone from her pocket. "I used the lowest possible setting—you'll be up and moving in less than five minutes. I'll make sure the boy's shields are solid until then."

Tiara smiled. "Dev is so going to kick your ass."

Taken aback by that smile, Katya hesitated. "The stunners don't have any strange effects on Forgotten physiology, do they?"

"Hell, no." Tiara's speech was beginning to clear. "I've just decided to find this amusing."

Shaking her head at the telepath's strange sense of humor, Katya got in the vehicle and backed it carefully out and onto the drive. She went a hundred meters down, then pulled over into the night-shadow of a large tree. No one would be able to see her if they came down the road. And if she was right about the silent alarm, they were already on the way.

She continued to hold the shield on the boy until she felt Tiara's energy replace hers, snapping back into her mind before the other woman could attack her on that level. In the nick of time. Two vehicles raced down the private road, heading for the house. Katya waited until they turned the corner, then she threw the cell phone—and its GPS chip—out the window and drove like a bat out of hell.

The car's navigation system got her out of the isolated area and onto a major road still heavy with traffic. She drove for twenty minutes before pulling over into the parking lot of a diner packed with monster rigs. The hover-trucks had their own special automatic navigation lanes on the highways, often traveling at speeds three to four times that of cars.

Parking beside one of the rigs, she took a deep breath and turned off the engine. She was now effectively stranded. But if she knew Dev, this car had some kind of a tracking device embedded in it. She left the stunner under the seat, having no desire to cause any more harm.

Conversation stopped the instant she walked into the diner, but she didn't—couldn't—back out. Tiara was probably already putting the trace in motion. Girding herself, she looked around. Most of the people at the counter were men.

Sweat broke out along her spine. Getting into a vehicle with a stranger was hardly the smartest of moves, but it was the only choice she had. And she was a telepath. No one was ever again going to make her a victim. Giving a small smile, she moved to the counter.

"Buy you a coffee?" The offer came from a twenty-something man to her right.

"I'd prefer an orange juice," she said, judging him "safe." If all she had left were her instincts, then she had to trust them.

He smiled, his eyes wrinkling at the corners. "Juice it is. Hope you don't mind me saying, but you could do with some meat on your bones."

Her mind cascaded with images of Dev making her smoothies, sliding granola bars into her pockets. "I'm working on that. Thanks." She took the orange juice and began to sip. "I don't suppose you're going north?"

The trucker gave her a disappointed look. "Aw, damn. South. Jessie!"

A woman with a long blonde ponytail looked up from the shadowy end of the counter. Her face was all freckles and glowing skin. "What?"

"You going north?"

"Maybe." The woman looked at Katya. "You need a ride?"

"If you wouldn't mind."

Jessie shrugged and got up. "I'm heading out now. You can keep me company."

Thanking the man for the juice, Katya followed Jessie out of the bar. The female trucker didn't say anything until they were in the cab of a sleek silver truck with a dash that looked more like something you might find in the cockpit of a small jet.

"Not smart what you're doing," Jessie said as they hit the highway. "Most of the boys, they're okay. But there's a few that think giving a ride means getting something in return."

"I know," Katya said, deciding for honesty. Something about Jessie said that for all her fresh-faced looks, she'd spot a lie a mile off. "But I didn't want to be caught on surveillance at the travel depots."

Jessie switched to automatic navigation after smoothing the truck into its specified lane. The steering wheel slid away as the truck's computronic software took over, accelerating the rig to a speed no human would ever be able to control. "You running from someone?" A concerned glance. "Someone been mistreating you, honey?"

Arms holding her close. A kiss to wish her sweet dreams. "No. But I have something I need to do." A demon she needed to face.

"Fair enough." Jessie kicked back, putting her feet on the dash. "So, you like jazz?"

"I'm going to—" Dev bit off the words, staring at a grinning Tiara. "You just let her walk out?"

"Hey, she stunned me," the woman said, affronted. "And wasn't I the one who tracked the car down to that diner even though she had the devil's luck and took the one with the malfunctioning tracker?"

Knives lanced Dev's stomach at the thought of who Katya might have ridden with, what they might have done to her. "Did Lucas call back?" The leopard alpha had gone to talk to the folks who owned the diner after Dev's attempts had met with stony silence.

His cell phone rang at that moment. Snapping it open, he looked at the caller ID. "Lucas, you got it?"

"She's on a rig heading north," the DarkRiver alpha told him. "With a driver named Jessie Amsel."

"A woman?"

"Yes."

But that, Dev thought, didn't mean she wasn't dangerous. "I've got a contact in the truckers' union," Dev said. "I'll get her route."

"They left about four hours ago."

"Then I better start moving." Hanging up, he called his contact and five minutes later had a printout of Jessie Amsel's route. Eyes narrowing, he made another call. "Michel? I need a favor."

"You going to owe me, cousin." A smile he could almost hear. "What's up?"

Dev outlined what he needed. "Is it doable?"

"Against the rules, but I figure you'll pull my butt out of jail if I land in it."

"Thanks."

"Don't thank me yet. Even if she doesn't switch rides beforehand, Traffic Comp tells me the roads are clear all the way to the border. If she hits Canada before I get to her, nothing I can do about it."

EARTHTWO COMMAND LOG:
SUNSHINE STATION

18 August 2080: Official incident report: Ten members of the scientific team are currently recovering from exposure in the medical bay. It appears they lost their sense of direction in the dark on their way back from a survey mission.

None of the ten contacted base camp for help, and they do not appear to remember the hours they spent without shelter. All ten have been confined to the med bay until they can be fully evaluated.

CHAPTER 32

"**You got the** papers to get over?" Jessie asked as she brought the truck to a stop three hours south of the Canadian border, the world still night-dark around them though it was early morning.

Katya shook her head. "No. I'll have to find a way to sneak through."

"That's not exactly easy. They've got Psy guards now, too—apparently there was a problem with people using telepathy to cloud human guards' minds."

That eliminated the very plan Katya had been counting on. "I don't suppose you know anyone who makes fake IDs."

"Do I look like the criminal type?"

"No, you look resourceful."

Jessie grinned. "What the hell. Come on."

Twenty minutes later, Katya had an identification card that was "good for one use only," according to the wizened little man who made it for her. "They'll get a bounce on it mebbe ten minutes after you scan it through, so make sure you hightail it out of there fast."

Katya nodded and handed over most of the cash she'd taken from Tag. "Thanks."

"And if you get caught, you never saw me." Beady black eyes pinned her in place. "Understood?"

"Got it."

"Are you going over the border?" she asked Jessie once they were on their way again.

The other woman shook her head. "My delivery's to a facility about forty minutes shy of it. You can hitch a ride with another trucker from there—I'll make sure it's one of the good ones."

"Why are you helping me so much, Jessie?" Katya asked, running her fingers over and around the hard edges of the ID card. "I'm obviously someone in trouble, someone who could get you in trouble."

"You heard that thing about paying it forward?"

"No."

"Where you been living, in a cave?" Without waiting for an answer, Jessie quickly explained. "It's like this—if someone does something nice for you, you got to do something nice for another person down the road. It's meant to put good back into the world."

"I see," Katya said slowly. "The world would indeed be a better place if everyone did that. Can I ask—whose niceness are you paying forward?"

"When I was a scrawny little sixteen-year-old, a scary fucker of a trucker picked me up on a dark and deserted street." Jessie's smile turned her striking. "After he finished chewing me out about the dangers of hitchhiking, he fed me, let me shower in his truck, and asked me where I was going. When I said I didn't know, he gave this big sigh."

"And?" Katya prompted when Jessie fell silent.

"And I ended up riding with him for the next five years. Isaac's the one who taught me how to drive the big rigs, who got me my first gig."

"He must be so proud of you. Is he retired now?"

"Hah! He's only six years older than me!"

"Oh." Katya bit her lip, but couldn't contain her curiosity. "You don't see him as a brother, do you?"

"God, I'm pathetic. And obvious." The other woman rolled her eyes. "He still sees me as that scrawny kid he picked up. It hasn't sunk into his tiny male mind that I not only have boobs, I'd like to use them, thank you very much!"

Katya burst out laughing just as dawn began to whisper on the horizon. "You're waiting for him?"

"I'm giving him one more month. I swear, after that, I'm taking the first offer that comes along."

"It's wonderful, you know," Katya said, mind filling with memories of pure molten heat. "Being with someone who touches your heart."

"You don't sound very happy."

"I think he's going to hate me now."

A siren pierced the air, cutting off her breath.

"Damn." A scowling Jessie pulled over to the side of the long, otherwise empty road. "I swear," the blonde muttered, "the hick cops have nothing better to do than hassle law-abiding citizens."

"Jessie, we're actually—"

"Shh. Think law-abiding thoughts." Sliding back her door, Jessie grabbed her coat and jumped down. Katya couldn't see her as she moved toward the officer, but she heard her words. "Michel Benoit, don't you have to go eat a doughnut or something?"

"That's Officer Benoit to you" came the drawling response. "I got a report you're carrying contraband, sweetheart."

"Hell you did!" Now Jessie sounded pissed. "I'm clean and you know it."

"Contraband's about yay-high, dark blonde hair, on the thin side. Ring a bell?"

"I'm sure I don't know what you mean."

Katya had every faith in Jessie's skills, but she had no desire to get the woman who'd helped her so much into real trouble with the law—it wasn't as if the cop wouldn't check the vehicle. Sliding back her own door, she stepped out into the frigid winter air and walked around the front of the truck to stand beside Jessie, the dawn soft and muted around them. Even the snow lining the roadside looked warm in the red and gold light.

"What exactly," Katya said, meeting the cop's ice blue eyes, "am I supposed to have done?"

He smiled, his dark brown hair waving in the gentle breeze. "Might have something to do with firing a stunner."

"They filed a report?" There was something disturbingly familiar about this Michel Benoit.

He raised an eyebrow. "You *want* a record?"

"That means there's no report," Jessie told her, hands on her hips. "He's got no right to pull you in."

Michel's eyes flashed. "This ain't none of your business, Jessie."

"Take your 'aint's' and shove them," Jessie muttered. "Everyone knows you've got a flippin' law degree."

The man didn't seem to take offense, his smile reaching to warm those eyes. "Here's the deal," he said to Katya. "You can come with me nice and easy, or I find something to charge you both with."

"Both? Jessie hasn't done anything."

"Jessie," Michel murmured, "has probably done quite a lot of things."

Katya put a hand on Jessie's arm when the other woman shifted forward, as if tempted to deck the cop. "It's the eyes," she muttered. "The color threw me off but you have the same eyes."

Michel's smile widened. "I have no idea who you're talking about."

"Name Devraj ring a bell?"

"I might have a cousin called Dev, but you know, it's not that unusual a name."

Certain now that there was no way Michel would let her leave, Katya turned to Jessie. "Thank you."

Jessie was still scowling, but she hugged Katya tight. "You ever need help again, you call me. You got my number, right?"

Katya nodded, having memorized the cell code. "So," she said to Michel, "where to from here?"

PETROKOV FAMILY ARCHIVES

Letter dated December 24, 1978

Dearest Matthew,

It's Christmas Eve, but the world is strangely hushed. Normally, the changelings would be playing their yearly tricks—I always half expect to find a tiger sitting on my porch come midnight, as I did once when I was a child. He'd brought me a fresh bough of holly, can you imagine?

But this year, even the human carolers have stayed home. All of us are waiting for the ax to fall—the Council is nearing a decision. If it goes the way I predict, anyone not in the Net will become forever cut off from those we love.

The Council has acknowledged that adults can't be fully conditioned, but those who stay in the Net will have to follow strict guidelines. If they don't, their children will be taken from them—so that they can be conditioned the proper way. My hand is shaking as I write that. No one will ever take you or Emily from me.

Mom

CHAPTER 33

Dev made his way from the airjet to his cousin's home—just south of the border with British Columbia—using the snow-capable rental Maggie had organized. Given the airjet's speed, he wasn't that far behind Michel taking Katya into "custody."

Arriving at his cousin's place, he got out and strode straight to the front door. Michel opened it as he was raising a fist to knock. "She's all yours, Santos." Thrusting his hat back on, Michel said, "If I were you, I'd don body armor."

"Thanks for the warning."

His cousin tipped his head and walked off to his own vehicle. Trying to get a handle on a temper that flat-out refused to respond to the cool brush of metal, Dev walked through the door and followed the echo of Katya's presence to the kitchen—where he found her calmly eating a huge blueberry muffin, a cup of what looked like hot chocolate at her elbow. Jesus—there were even marshmallows in the damn chocolate. "Looks like Michel took good care of you."

A glance that told him nothing. "He knows how to treat a woman."

Okay, that bit. "As opposed to?"

A shrug.

He watched as she picked out a blueberry and popped it into her mouth. "Did you really think you were going to get away?"

"Giving in is not what I do."

It was a slap. And it poured the most frigid water over the temper he'd irrationally feared would turn him into his father. What the hell had he expected Katya to do? Sit meekly while he held her captive?

The woman who'd survived Ming LeBon's brand of torture wasn't the sitting-around kind.

Blowing out a breath, he folded his arms across his jacket. "How close are you to wherever you're going?"

She froze, then seemed to shake herself out of it. "I'm getting closer."

"Still no certain location?"

"It's northwest . . . I think possibly Alaska, though it could as easily be in Yukon."

Dev stepped close enough to play with a strand of her hair. She didn't pull away, but neither did she deviate from the concentrated destruction of her muffin. He was being ignored again. He realized that should've irritated him, but it made his lips curve. Releasing her hair, he moved around to stand at her back, placing his hands palms down on the counter on either side of her.

She took another bite of the muffin.

Grinning, he brushed aside the fall of her hair and pressed a kiss to the delicate skin of her nape.

A shiver. "Devraj Santos," she said with quiet forcefulness, "you are not going to charm me into going back."

He kissed her again, along the slender curve of her neck.

"Who said anything about charm?" he murmured, nibbling at her earlobe. "I'm planning to seduce you."

She put down that damn muffin. "Dev, why aren't you yelling at me?"

Another kiss as he rose to his full height and wrapped his arms around her, dropping his chin on top of her head. "You're too stubborn to respond to yelling." She'd survived something he wasn't sure even he could survive—a man would be stupid not to respect that kind of will in his woman.

"But you're still going to drag me back." Her hand closed into a fist on the counter. "Why? I'm no threat this far from you."

"I have to consider what you might've learned in the time you've been with us, whether you'll circle back and strike."

That hand flexed, then closed again. "Nothing I say will change your mind, will it?"

He knew what he should do. Until he'd walked into this kitchen, there hadn't even been a question in his mind. But— "I can give you three days."

She sucked in a breath. "Dev?"

"We'll take the airjet as far north as you're comfortable, then hire a car."

"I'm glad you'll be with me," she said to his surprise, leaning into his embrace. "Part of me is so afraid of what I'll find—what if there's nothing there?"

"Katya?"

"It would mean my brain really is damaged," she whispered. "If I have this compulsion and there's nothing to back it up."

He suddenly understood her hunger to follow the compulsion far better than he had before. "You aren't brain damaged," he told her, squeezing her tighter. "If you were, you sure as hell wouldn't have managed to sneak out from under my bloody nose."

Katya heard the disgusted edge in that comment and it

made her heart lighten. "I did good, didn't I?" Her smile faltered. "How's Tiara?"

"She opened book on how far you'd get before I caught up to you."

"Oh?"

"Yeah, and she placed the bet for the longest distance."

"And Tag?"

"Let's just say he's not your new best friend."

She winced and went to ask about the boy before realizing that might get him into trouble.

Dev chuckled. "The kid is fine—and we've learned to be extra careful with his shields."

"He's strong," she said, apprehensive about what that might mean. "If the Council finds out the Forgotten have that level of psychic ability..."

"Let me worry about that." He pressed a kiss to her temple, allowing her to turn so they faced each other. "Tell me everything you can about this pull you feel to go north. Do you have any other information?"

"No. But I know I heard something. There...in the black room."

Rage reignited, dark with the need to draw blood. He had to consciously focus to form speech past the vicious power of it. "Why would they have spoken of anything sensitive in your hearing?"

"They made a mistake," she said, her voice halting as if she was reconstructing fragments of memory. "Ming broke me, but even broken, I had ears, I had eyes. He treated me like I was an insect he'd crushed under his boot, not worth bothering about."

The rage in him was a wild thing, animalistic in its anger... its anguish. "What," he forced himself to ask, "did you hear?"

Katya looked up at the sound of Dev's voice, that raw blade. His anger was a lash in the air, a whip of fire. But somehow instead of inciting fear, it made her feel stronger. "Lots of things."

Dev watched her with those amazing eyes, and she knew, she *knew* he would kill for her. It shook her, the knowledge of how deeply they'd bonded with each other. What if—

"No," Dev said. "Don't think about anything but this task. We'll figure out the rest later."

She nodded, her movements jerky.

"I don't have all the pieces yet, but I know I have to go. I have to *see*."

His hand against her cheek. Warm. Protective. "You have no idea what you're searching for?"

"Something bad." She turned into his touch. "When I think of it, I get this oily sickness in my gut." *Evil,* she thought. It was something evil waiting for her, a thing her mind refused to show her, but whose malevolent shadow overlay every other thought.

EARTHTWO COMMAND LOG:
SUNSHINE STATION

17 September 2080: *Productivity has dropped fifty-seven percent in the past three days as staff members complain of increasingly severe headaches.*

It may be advisable to consider a recall of all personnel until the area has been thoroughly tested for biological and/or chemical contaminants. Please advise.

CHAPTER 34

Dev pressed a kiss to her forehead, the unexpectedly affectionate gesture making her eyes burn. "We'd better start as soon as possible."

She knew the three days he'd given her would cost him, but he was going to take the hit—for her. "Dev...I could be leading you into a trap." In spite of how far she'd come, her mind remained a savage maze, full of holes and deception.

Dev rubbed a thumb over her cheek. "Still don't get it, do you, Katya? I take care of what's mine."

"I don't want you to get hurt," she began, but the set of his jaw told her she was wasting her breath. "Were you born stubborn?"

"My mother used to say I was half mule."

It made her smile. "That would make one of your parents a mule. Your mother?"

"She never admitted it." His eyes filmed over with a sadness so deep, she felt her throat lock. "Never had the chance."

She hesitated, unsure of her instincts, of her mind, her soul...but not of her heart. "What happened to her?"

"My father killed her." A stark response that stole her breath.

She was still trying to find the words with which to respond when he continued. "That was when I first understood why some of our ancestors chose Silence. My father—he was never abusive. It was his gift that turned him into a killer."

Reaching out a hand, she closed it over his.

"The ShadowNet," Dev said, looking down at their linked hands, "is a completely different animal from the PsyNet, but we have some similarities."

"Dev," she said, cutting him off though it was the last thing she wanted to do. "You mustn't tell me any more." If she betrayed him, even if it wasn't by choice, it would shatter her—and she knew she wouldn't rise again. Not from that.

His face was suddenly that of the conqueror she'd once seen in him. "We'll break you free, Katya. Even if I have to kill Ming LeBon himself."

"No." She grabbed both his hands. "He's my monster to slay. I don't want you anywhere near him."

"Don't you think I can take him?"

She stared at him, at his cool eyes, his muscular body, his soldier's patience, and said, "I know you could. And that's what terrifies me."

A waiting silence.

"I don't want you to become what he is," she whispered, knowing that Dev had a ruthlessness in him that could turn him cruel, an assassin with a single, brutal objective. She had no doubt that he'd achieve that objective—but he might lose himself in the process. "I'm afraid that if you hunt him, it'll change you, make you a reflection of Ming."

He didn't reply, and she knew that if push came to shove, Dev *would* go after Ming. And if that happened, there'd be only one choice. One she'd make without flinching. She was becoming Dev's weakness. Excise her from existence, and that weakness would no longer exist.

*   *   *

Dev got the phone call from Aubry ten minutes after they took off, the airjet set on a steady course north. Katya wasn't officially on the passenger manifest, which meant they'd technically be smuggling her over the border if they needed to land in Canada, but Dev had ways around the problem if it came to that.

"What is it?" he asked, conscious of Katya putting on her headphones and turning up the music.

"Jack thinks you're dicking him around—he's pissed."

Dev squeezed the bridge of his nose with his fingers. "Can you keep him calm for three days?"

"He's going to last maybe one more day—two at the most." Aubry's tone changed. "Dev, what he's saying, it's not out of his ass. He's making sense."

"I know Jack's making sense." Dev had seen Jack's son William after the first episode, had held Jack as the other man broke down. He had a bone-deep understanding of the anguish that drove his cousin's every action. "That's the hell of it. Look, I'll call him."

"And you'll be back in New York in three days?"

Knowing Tag and Tiara would be able to handle Cruz now that Sascha had become involved, he said, "Yeah. Set up a meeting with Jack."

"I guess you can't escape some things," Aubry said as he hung up, and Dev knew he wasn't talking about the meeting.

Coding in the number for Jack's cell, he waited. The other man answered after a couple of seconds. "About time, Director."

"Cut me some slack," Dev muttered. "You'd think we weren't related, the way you're out to string me up."

"Don't pull the cousin card on me." But his tone became less harsh. "You been avoiding me, Dev?"

"No. We've had some other shit hit the fan." Thrusting a hand through his hair, he leaned back in the seat. "What you're saying—I'm listening."

"Good." A pause. "Fuck, Dev, I didn't set out to be a pain in your ass, and I sure as hell don't want to rake up old memories, but we've got to deal with this."

"There's no way I can support what you want—you know that. Our ancestors gave up everything for our freedom. How the hell can you turn your back on that?"

"Because my *son* is so terrified of his own abilities that he's too scared to make friends." Jack's torment filled the line. "He's a baby, but he's so afraid he'll hurt someone that he stays in his room all day. You deal with that every day and then you tell me the choice isn't mine to make."

Catching the break in Jack's voice, Dev straightened. "What aren't you telling me? I thought Will was stable for now." He'd believed they had time to find another answer—one that wouldn't destroy the very heart of Forgotten identity.

"Something happened. I don't—" A jagged breath. "I need to confirm it. But I know that Will's getting worse."

Dev thought of the seven-year-old boy who called him Uncle Dev, thought, too, of the others on the edge. "It's circled back." The strange new abilities arising in the Forgotten were bringing with them the same madnesses that had driven the Psy to Silence. "But you've seen how Silence isn't the answer to everything—they're not the example we want to follow."

"You go cold, Dev," Jack said. "I've seen you do it. You mainline the machines and you go cold. What if you couldn't?"

Dev knew all too well what it felt like to skyrocket out of control. Especially now, with a woman who slipped beneath the metallic layer as if it didn't exist. "I might go cold, but I stay human, Jack. I *feel*." Too much. Too strong.

"It's a bad choice, I know," Jack admitted. "But if there are only bad choices..."

"We'll find another way." Dev wouldn't lose his family, his people. "I've got Glen and his team on it night and day. And I'm working every contact I have—just...don't make any hasty decisions. Can you give me a few more days? Can Will?" Because if the boy had gone critical, then Dev would turn the plane around. He had every faith that the woman by his side would understand.

"What's so important that you can't talk to me today?"

Dev glanced at Katya's head, turned toward the window of the plane. "I'm fighting to save another life, another mind."

Jack sucked in a breath. "Damn, you know how to sock it to a man. I'll give you a few more days."

"Call me the instant anything changes." Because—and though Dev's protective instincts screamed in violent repudiation at the thought—small, big-eyed William was their barometer, the closest to snapping the threads of his sanity. Swallowing the knot in his throat, he didn't even make an effort to hide his own worry for Will. "You call me and I'll come. You got that?"

A pause filled with things unsaid, and Dev knew Jack understood the brutal truth, a truth no father should have to face. "Yeah," his cousin finally answered. "I gotta go— Melissa's home. This is fucking messed up." The last sentence was tired.

As Dev hung up, he felt the same. Turning, he found Katya looking at him. She took off the wireless headphones only when he slid the phone into a pocket. "I want so much to ask what's put that look on your face," she said, reaching out to place one hand over his.

"Katya, there's a chance we might have to turn back." He tightened his fingers on hers. "But if we do, I'll bring you back. I promise you that."

And though he knew how badly she wanted to reach her destination, she gave an immediate nod. "Your promise is more than enough for me."

His heart expanded, until he couldn't even remember what the metal felt like. "How secure is your mind?"

"It's a vault. Nothing can come in or get out into the Net. But like you said, Ming must have the psychic key to open that vault—he could use it at any time."

He understood what she was telling him, but the possible benefits outweighed the risks in this case. About to ask her what he needed to know, he frowned. "You have a nosebleed."

Making a small sound, she lifted a hand to her nose, taking the tissue he ripped from the pack provided in the seat pockets. "It's the altitude," she said.

He wasn't so sure. "How's your head?"

"Fine." Slipping the tissue into the disposal bag, she made a face at him. "I've never been a good flier. What was your question?"

Still not convinced, he made a mental note to have Glen check her out on their return. "What do you know about the genesis of Silence?"

"Aside from what's in the public domain, I know that it's not as effective as the Council likes to make out—the anchors, the strong Psy the Net needs to maintain itself—they're extremely vulnerable to sociopathy."

Dev had guessed as much. "But it is effective at a certain level?"

"Yes." She nodded. "You know there are abilities that predispose the individual to mental illness—or ones that drive them toward such illnesses because of what they demand."

"Go on."

"For example, some high-Gradient telepaths have trouble building shields—it's as if their abilities are too strong to contain and the power leaks out. With Silence, at least they have an effective barrier of emotionlessness—even if things creep in, those things don't affect them as deeply."

Dev considered that. "Justice Psy—they have a rep."

"Yes. Because the J-Psy work so closely with humans, they're more prone to breaks from Silence."

And when Justice Psy broke, some very nasty people had a way of ending up dead. Dev didn't necessarily think that was a bad thing, but if the highly trained J-Psy weren't able to control their abilities, how could he expect it of a scared seven-year-old? "Is that why the Js always take breaks between cases?"

Katya nodded. "From what I know, they generally work about a month, then go back in for intensive reconditioning before being given their next case." Her eyes lingered on his. "We all came from the same stock," she murmured. "It's inevitable that even in a mixed-race population, mutations and recombination in the gene pool would produce an individual closer to Psy than to human."

He'd known she would understand—she was too smart not to. "Pretty sure the Council's figured that out, too."

"It's a possibility. But there is a certain arrogance among the higher levels of the Council superstructure—the Psy have become so used to thinking themselves the most powerful people on the planet that they fail to take something as simple, and as powerful, as nature into account." This time, her eyes were troubled. "Dev, if your people are considering what I believe—don't."

"You just told me that for some gifts, it's the only choice."

Her hand tightened around his. "But it kills something in the individual and in the group. The PsyNet...it's beautiful, but it's dying, bit by slow bit. How could it not? We give it nothing but emptiness."

Dev understood her speaking of the Net as a living presence. The ShadowNet, too, had an entity of sorts that was its soul, its living imprint, though it was far, far younger than its counterpart in the PsyNet. "I've heard whispers of the NetMind."

"There's a DarkMind, too." Her voice was hollow. "Ming

told me—I guess he thought I wouldn't remember, or he didn't care. The NetMind has split in two."

She didn't have to say any more—if the fabric of the Net itself was being torn asunder, then how could Silence possibly be the answer? And yet… "There are still killers in the Net, but there are fewer."

"Yes." She swallowed. "I think, for a while, it did make things truly better. We were able to breathe without fear of what we might do, what might be done to us. But that soon became replaced with another kind of fear."

"The Council." Dev thought over the implications. "That kind of a power structure is unavoidable once you embrace Silence—it rewards the naturally emotionless, people who have little to no empathy." The sociopaths.

"It's a flaw in the system that we've become blind to." Katya leaned her head against his shoulder. "What will you do?"

"Fight for my people."

PETROKOV FAMILY ARCHIVES

Letter dated January 1, 1979

Dear Matthew,

The decision has been made. Silence is to be implemented. Your father and I knew this was coming. We've been making plans.

I love you so much, my babies. This plan, there's a chance we'll all die. I won't lie to you, won't try to hide the truth. At times, I think I'm being a hypocrite, condemning the others for letting the Council condition emotion out of their children when I'm putting you and Emily in mortal danger, but I know you with my mother's heart.

I know that my Matty is an artist, that you're only ever fully who you are when your face is smudged with paint and your fingers splattered a thousand different colors.

I know that my sweet Emily loves to sing, that she follows you around the house because she adores you so much.

I know that your father would rather go mad a thousand times over than snuff out your bright lights.

So we'll do this. And we'll hope there is a God.

With all the love in my heart,

Mom

CHAPTER 35

"**The situation in** Sri Lanka has been contained." Henry's resonant mental voice filled the psychic vault of the Council chambers. "The anchor in question is now under constant supervision."

"He already was," Tatiana pointed out.

"Yes," Shoshanna said, "but previously, he had a degree of autonomy—as we all know, the anchors are so often cardinals that it's near impossible to monitor them without a huge waste of manpower."

"But in this case," Henry continued, "that manpower is warranted. I've got my personal guard on him, but if the Council is in agreement, I'd like a member of the Arrow Squad to join the team."

Kaleb felt a telepathic knock on his mind. Opening the channel, he found Nikita's voice entering his head. *They're working together again.*

He'd noticed the same thing. *Henry, however, is no longer the beta member of the pair.*

If they've found a way to balance their egos, Nikita

commented, *they stand to become the most powerful force on the Council.*

The fact that Nikita's thoughts had followed his wasn't unexpected—there was a reason he'd allied himself to the San Francisco–based Councilor. Her mind was her most powerful tool, and, unlike the others, she had no thoughts of taking over the Net. Nikita was only interested in her own business interests. It made her an excellent partner for a man who *was* interested in gaining control over the PsyNet itself.

"Agreed," Kaleb said as the Arrow question was put to a quick vote.

Anthony Kyriakus was the single member who didn't immediately agree. "Ming, my question is for you. I've heard a rumor that your Arrows are no longer under your complete control."

Kaleb had also heard that particular rumor, had in fact intended to explore the topic further. Now, he waited to see what Ming would say.

"The rumors are incorrect," Ming said. "The only issue of control relates to the reaction several long-serving Arrows are having to the Jax regimen."

"You're still using Jax?" Tatiana asked.

"Nothing else has proven as effective when it comes to maintaining absolute Silence."

It was more than that, Kaleb knew. Jax—recognized by most only as the scourge of the Psy—had been created for a very specific purpose. When given in the proper dosage, accurately calibrated to the individual, Jax had a way of erasing the personality without erasing the mind. A very precarious balance. "The ones who had the reaction," he asked, "have they been taken care of?"

"I've put them in a facility specifically designed to hold Arrows who've begun to degenerate."

Shoshanna spoke on the heels of Ming's statment. "Why aren't they dead? Surely they're no longer useful."

"Arrows," Ming said, the subtle emphasis reminding them he'd once been one himself, "have only one unbreakable rule—never leave another Arrow behind. It's part of the psychological structure that allows them to function. If I eliminate the defective individuals, it will eventually lead to the disintegration of the near-blind loyalty that binds the Arrows to each other and to me."

"That," Tatiana said, "sounds almost like an emotional attachment."

"It is no more emotional than a chick imprinting on its mother," Ming said. "I'm their leader and they've agreed to follow me—as long as I don't break that one underlying rule, they'll do exactly that."

"How did such a rule ever come into play?" Shoshanna asked, exposing her ignorance of that aspect of human nature.

Kaleb had done his research. He knew about Zaid Adelaja, the first Arrow. Knew, too, that the man had been a soldier turned assassin. And soldiers, no matter their race, lived and died for the team. Ignoring Ming's answer to Shoshanna's question, he rifled through his files, searching for the location of the place Ming sent his Arrows to die.

He didn't have it.

But he would have by the time this day ended. "We also have another matter to discuss." He began to tell them about the dark spots in the Net, doing his ostensible job as the Councilor most attuned to the NetMind. But in truth, he was watching and listening. Each Councilor would have a different response to this knowledge, and, when the time came, each Councilor would either live or die on that response.

CHAPTER 36

It was dark when the airjet landed, having flown at low speed to give Katya's internal compass a chance to focus. She finally stopped them somewhere in the south of Alaska, the air frigid. Thanks to Michel, Dev was kitted out in heavy cold-weather gear, while Katya wore a thick scarf and a jacket much too large for her small frame. It would keep her warm for the time being, Dev thought critically, but no way was he taking her any farther into Alaska that way.

"We'll sort out some clothing for you tomorrow morning," he said, picking up the keys to the all-terrain vehicle that Maggie had organized after his call from the airjet. "The cabin Maggie booked for us is attached to a tourist lodge. They should have a shop of some kind."

Katya's expression was rueful. "I didn't consider the cold up here when I decided to run."

His most possessive instincts spiking at the reminder of just how much danger she'd put herself in, he took her hand. "You'll be fine in the car for the drive."

That drive took less than twenty minutes.

"Your secretary is very efficient," Katya said as Dev opened the door to their unit to reveal a brand new duffel on the dresser to the left. It proved to have everything—clothing included—that she might need over the next few days.

"Why do you think I pay her so well?" Putting down his own duffel, he gave her a flashing smile that had been absent all day. She hadn't realized how much she'd missed it until then.

"This place is lovely," she said, her eye drifting to the huge fluffy bed in the bedroom to the left. "But I still feel like we should keep going."

"You're about to drop from exhaustion, and I'm not in the best shape either—in spite of the nap you gave me last night."

She squared her shoulders. "I refuse to feel guilty."

"It was my own bloody fault for not making sure I checked you for contraband." A scowl. "We'll catch a few hours' sleep, then hit the road with clear heads. Probably get a lot farther."

In spite of the urgency that rippled through her veins, she couldn't argue with his logic. "Okay." Her eyes went right, to the second bedroom. She bit her lip. "Dev?"

"Hmm?" He shrugged off his jacket and dropped it on the sofa before bending to pull off his boots.

She'd already taken off her outerwear, leaving her wearing jeans and a sweater. "Which bedroom do you want?" It wasn't the question she wanted to ask, but her courage deserted her at the last minute.

"Left or right, it doesn't matter to me." He shrugged, finished with his boots, and rose to his feet, a big man with a shadowed jaw ... and eyes full of molten heat. "As long as you understand we'll be sharing the same bed."

The world threatened to crumble from under her feet. "I don't know," she whispered. "Are you planning to tease me some more?"

"Maybe." A playful word, but his face was all hard angles. "And this time, you can broadcast as loud as you like—the other guests are all out on some overnight trip, and the lady who checked us in was human."

He was speaking with utter calm...but making no effort whatsoever to hide the jut of his arousal. "I need to shower." It was true, but came out in a blurted rush.

"Don't take too long." Lifting his fingers to his shirt, he began to undo the buttons. "You do need to get some sleep tonight."

Overwhelmed, she grabbed her things and ducked into the bathroom. The shower cleaned off the grit, but did nothing to cool down her body. After she got out, she quickly dried her hair and was about to dress in loose fleece pants and a sweatshirt when she hesitated, her mind filling with memories of the way Dev had pinned her up against the wall, all heat and barely leashed male power.

Her entire body turned into one big pulse.

Swallowing, she pulled on a long-sleeved woolen shirt over nothing but bare skin. If Dev wanted her, she wasn't going to put any roadblocks in his path. She craved his touch. At first, after she'd woken, she'd thought any human touch would do. But she'd realized different in the days since—it hurt when she wasn't touched, but the idea of being touched by just anyone made her skin crawl.

Her body wanted Dev and only Dev.

Taking a deep breath, she left the duffel in the bathroom and opened the door...to find herself facing a naked sweep of muscled flesh, his chest right there for her to stroke, touch, kiss, his hands gripping the doorjamb above her head. Having decided after last night that she'd take him any way and any time she could get him, she pressed her lips to the rough heat of him, the smoothness of his skin contrasting deliciously with the curling hairs sprinkled over it.

One hand thrust into her hair, holding her to him. Against her bare thighs, the denim of his jeans was a sweet abrasion as he pushed into her space, his erection nudging at the softness of her abdomen. Soft and hard. Male and female. Her skin tightened with pure need.

"Do you know something, Katya?" A husky male voice, his hand keeping her in place. Taking the hint, she began to kiss her way across his chest. It was the most luscious of tasks—he was just so bluntly male that it was impossible to feel anything but deliciously, sensually female.

"Are you listening to me?" A whisper against her ear, a little bite that made her suck in a breath, rise up on tiptoe.

He hesitated. "You liked that?"

Unable to answer with words, she simply angled her head to give him easier access. Taking it, he nibbled his way down her throat before untangling his hand from her hair and closing it about that throat with gentle possessiveness. The touch made her shudder, grip his waist harder. And when he lifted his head to press his lips demandingly against hers, she opened for him at once.

The bite on her lower lip, the sharp dart of pain, sent a rush of liquid to the juncture of her thighs. Dev's eyes were glittering when he raised his head. "Is it the pain or the control?"

Her fingers curled against his skin as shame flooded her cheeks. "I'm aberrant."

He nipped at her lip again, sharper this time. It was all she could do to keep her feet. "No," he said, stroking his thumb over the thudding pulse in her neck, "what you are is sexy as hell." Another kiss, one that threatened to tumble her straight to the floor, it was so full of hunger and demand.

"Bed," she whispered against his mouth. "Please."

Letting go of the doorjamb, he swept her into his arms in a single smooth move. Neither of them said a word until he'd laid her down on the fluffy white comforter, his body blocking out the light as he came over her. "Now," he said, putting one hand on her thigh, below the wool of her shirt, "answer the question."

"I don't know," she said honestly, unable to stop from smoothing her hands over his shoulders, his arms. "But I like it when you crowd me."

Dev's hand stroked up. A harsh exhalation. "You're not wearing any panties." Rubbing his thumb along the sensitive crease of her thigh, he lowered his body until all she could see was Dev, his skin, his eyes, *him*. "Is this what you like? Being covered by me?"

"Yes." She arched into him, wanting to feel his weight, feel crushed by the sheer life of him. "Closer."

"It's the sensation," he murmured, cupping her for a single electric second before returning to his previous maddening caress. "After the dark."

That he understood, it broke her. "There was nothing there," she whispered, nuzzling into his throat, drawing him into her lungs. "When they cut off my senses, when they put me into that chamber where I couldn't even feel my skin… it was like I was floating in nothingness. I went a little more mad with every hour that passed."

Dev brought his body down another fraction, allowing her to feel some of his weight. When she shuddered and grazed her teeth down his throat, he hissed out a breath. "The more contact, the better you feel."

"Yes." She rubbed her body against him—or tried to. He was too heavy, holding her down. Her skin shimmered with waves of pleasure. "But this…only with you, Dev. I trust you."

He pushed a thigh between her own, opening her up, claiming her. "That's a dangerous confession to make to a man like me." Shifting slightly, he braced himself on his elbows above her, a solid wall of muscle and strength. "I'll take everything you offer."

"Will you give anything back?" she somehow found the strength to ask.

A gleam of sensual amusement. "Wait and see."

And she knew that tonight would be a night she'd remember for the rest of her life. Somehow, in this place, everything else had faded away. Here, there was only Dev, only Katya, and a sexual heat that threatened to consume them both.

When Dev pushed to his knees, she couldn't help her sharp cry of disappointment. He pressed a hand to her chest. "Wait." And then he was getting off the bed and heading to the living area.

Tempting as it was to go after him, she obeyed the order. It was another fence, another line of control. The psychologists would have a field day with her, she thought, but if this helped her cope with normality, then who were they to judge? None of them had spent endless mindless hours floating in the dark, unable even to sense their own skin, their own fingers, their own face. It had been like she was dead—alone in a cold, indifferent universe.

"So many thoughts," Dev murmured, walking back into the room with her scarf taut in his hands, the ends wrapped around his fists. "I can hear you thinking. It's like a little knocking at the back of my head."

Her eyes tracked him as he moved across the room with lazy confidence, her toes curling into the comforter. "Do you mind?"

"No." The bed dipped as he got on the bed, prowling up over her body. "What were you thinking?"

"That this need I have, this need for boundaries," she whispered, "it doesn't cripple me. I escaped you, after all."

A little smile that suggested all sorts of wickedness. "Did I punish you for that yet?"

"*Dev.*" He was teasing her again, and this man...God, he was pure addiction.

Taking her wrists in his hands, he raised them above her

head. "No, you aren't crippled. You've just found a way to deal."

She met his eyes. "Does it bother you?"

He wrapped the scarf around her wrists, pulling it tight enough that she could feel the delicious pressure against her skin, then tied the ends around the bars in the headboard. "In case you haven't noticed," he murmured, even as his fingers undid the buttons on her shirt one by one, "I like being in control." One big hand closed possessively over the bare roundness of her breast.

"Dev!"

He stroked and squeezed her with leisurely focus, kissing her each time she tried to hurry him. Sweat began to sheen her body and he hadn't even gone past her breasts. "You'll drive me to insanity," she accused.

"I promise to make it good." A slow smile as he began to kiss his way down the centerline of her chest, pausing to torment her breasts with little bites that had her arching her body upward in silent entreaty.

When he refused to comply, she bombarded him with telepathic requests laced with the fever of her hunger. His eyes glittered. "Playing dirty, baby?"

It was, she realized, the first time he'd ever used an endearment. Something shifted inside her, but she didn't know what it was, didn't understand why her heart beat with a sudden painful ache. "I say anything's fair in bed."

"Remember, you said it." He continued his downward journey, pressing kisses over the dip of her stomach, the curve of her navel.

Her eyes widened as she realized what he planned to do. "Why?" she asked, her voice coming out throaty.

"Why what?" A flick of his tongue along the sensitive skin just below her navel.

She had to take several deep breaths before she could answer. "Why would you do such a thing? What pleasure does it give you?"

Dark eyes meeting her own. "Don't you want to lick me, Katya?"

The image made her nerve endings explode. All at once, it was the only thing she could think about. "Let me try and see."

He chuckled. "Nice try, but I get to go first." Strong hands on the tops of her thighs, pushing her legs apart.

The unadulterated intimacy of it rocked her.

She was so primed that she could feel every square inch of her skin, every brush of his breath against her. Never had she felt more *real*, more alive. "Dev." It was a whisper, a plea, a demand.

The stroke of his thumb against the ultrasensitive skin of her inner thigh. She was still trying to soak it all in when he dipped his head and gave her the most intimate caress of all. The scream tore out of her on a ragged note, and she found herself gripping the scarf to keep herself from jerking out of bed.

Not that he would have let her go.

Strong hands kept her in place as her body tried to escape the overload of sensation—and get closer at the same time. Lights flickered behind her eyes, and she thought surely, surely, something of this would leak into the Net. But she couldn't think about that, could only drown under the waves of pleasure.

The graze of teeth.

Her entire body froze in an almost painful arch. And then she fractured...into a million brilliant sparks. The tremors spread outward from within her center, rippling through her like living fire. She was sobbing with the exquisite ache of it by the time she came down.

"Shh." Dev made his way back up her body, gentling her with a kiss that was as possessive as the hand on her breast. "You're so damn beautiful, Katya."

Somehow, she found a speck of sense. "Not too bony?"

He squeezed her breast. "Not where it counts. And we can work on the rest."

"I'm going to hit you for that," she threatened. "As soon as I get my breath back."

His smile was male and satisfied and unbelievably gorgeous. "Then I should make sure you never do." This time, his kiss was leisurely, but so hungry she gasped into his mouth, wanting only to give him everything and anything he wanted.

His hand slipped down, over her ribs, to the curve of her waist. "How are your shields?"

"Impenetrable." She laughed and it came from the soul. "The bastard locked me in, but I bet he never realized he was giving me carte blanche to do whatever I wanted."

Devraj heard the laugh, but he also sensed the pain behind the laughter. It tore at the masculine heart of him to know that he'd never be able to wipe the memories of devastation from her mind. But there was also a fierce sense of pride. "You beat him once. You'll do it again."

Those huge hazel eyes widened. "That sounds like an order."

"Don't forget it." He stroked up to graze his thumb over her nipple. When she took a whispery breath, the angry protectiveness in him calmed. He hadn't been able to help her then, but he damn well would protect her now. No matter what. "So, where were we?"

"My hands," she said, lifting her mouth to his. "I want to touch you."

He nibbled on her lips. "Hmm."

"Dev."

Smiling at that tart feminine demand, he reached up and undid the soft bonds. Her hands immediately went to his shoulders, stroking and shaping. It was obvious she liked his body, and he was male enough to preen under the attention.

Dipping his head, he kissed her with playful little nips and bites as she took her time learning him.

Of course, his cock had other ideas. He was so fucking aroused it was a wonder he could form a sentence. When Katya's wandering hands moved over his chest, threatening to skim downward, he stopped her. "Not this time." Pressing into her, he reached between their bodies to part her curls.

She made an intrinsically feminine sound of delight, and that, coupled with the damp heat of her, was his undoing. He knew he must have risen to get rid of his pants and underwear, but he had no memory of it. She was wet and slick and wild under his fingers when he next blinked, and his control was beyond ragged.

Sliding a hand under one of her thighs, he urged her to lock her legs behind his body. She followed his lead with an enthusiasm that made sweat bead along his spine, his cock pounding in time with every thudding beat of his heart. Bracing himself on one elbow, he guided himself inside her... and had to grit his teeth from swearing a blue streak as she clenched around the blunt tip of his erection, a hot, wet glove that was such an absolute fit he thought he might pass out from the pleasure of it.

"Dev!" Fingernails dug into his back as he pushed in, trying for slow but knowing he wasn't going to last. "Oh, God, more, please."

It was all the invitation his body needed. Control shattering, he thrust into her deep, so deep, catching her cry with his mouth. For an instant, he thought he might have gone too far, remembering too late that she'd never done this before, but then she tightened her grip on him and rolled her hips in sweet feminine welcome.

"Katya," he said against her ear, trying to draw breath, to not lose himself completely.

Her fingers thrust into his hair. "You feel so good."

The simple statement, made in that erotically husky voice,

stole what small fragments of control he'd had left. Putting one hand on her hip, he pinned her in place as he began to stroke in and out in a hard, steady rhythm that had her clawing at him.

He didn't last long. But it was alright, his hazed brain told him. Because she shattered under him even as pleasure swept over his skin in a scorching wave. For an instant, he felt a strange pull, as if something was stretched taut inside him, but then the sensation just ended, as if it had been summarily cut off. He didn't have time to consider the odd feeling, because his entire body exploded at that very instant, every nerve and tendon taut with ecstasy.

EARTHTWO COMMAND LOG:
COMMUNIQUÉ TO SUNSHINE STATION

18 September 2080: Your status has been noted. A supervisory team will be flying out on the 28th to make the decision as to any possible evacuation. Continue operations as per original instructions until then.

CHAPTER 37

"Dev?" Katya bit lightly at the ear of the man who was crushing her to the bed, his solid male body a perfect, wonderful blanket. Who needed to breathe? "Dev?"

This time, she got a grunt.

Smiling, she pressed her lips to his jaw, loving the roughness under her lips. "I like sex."

She saw the edge of a smile, and it made her own lips curve. "I really like it." Rubbing her heel over the back of his leg, she ran her hand down his muscled arm, wanting only to touch him. "When can we do it again?"

He sounded like he was choking as he said, "You're not acting like a Psy."

"Maybe if they tried sex with you, the others would change their minds, too." She scowled. "Dev?"

"I know, you like sex. Gimme a couple of minutes." It was a laughing complaint.

"No." She drew the sweat and man scent of him into her lungs, luxuriating in the sensations. "Are you planning on having sex with someone else?"

He pinched her nipple hard enough to make her jump. "That's what you get for asking silly questions."

A slow smile spread across her face. "That hurt."

"You're just asking for trouble."

"Am I going to get it?" She bit his ear again.

His hand curved around her breast. "Keep that up and you're not going to get any sleep tonight."

"Sounds good to me."

Groaning, he rose up on his forearms. "No more sex for you. We shower off the sweat, and then we catch some sleep. We need to be ready to head out at dawn."

She reached up to press kisses along his chest, cradling his growing arousal against her lower abdomen. Swearing, he let her play, but only for a minute. "Shower." And this time, he wasn't budging. She found herself being thrust into a fast, hot shower, and then tumbled into bed.

"Sleep." It was an order in her ear as his body closed around hers, protective, and yes, very definitely possessive— the thigh he pushed between her own ensured she wouldn't be going anywhere without him.

For the first time, her compulsion to go north wasn't the overwhelming thought in her mind. And though the heat between them burned white-hot, that wasn't at the forefront either. No, it was the tenderness of the kiss Dev pressed to the curve of her neck, the intensity of his hold. He was, she realized, looking after her.

It was an odd feeling, one that swept warmth through her limbs, turning them heavy. But she found the will to untangle their legs and turn so she could tuck her head under his chin and place her hand over his heart. He thrust his thigh back between hers the next instant. Smiling, she snuggled close. Her sleep was soft, dreamless, peaceful.

*   *   *

Six hours later, the precious interlude was a thing of distant memory. The car was warm, but Katya huddled into her jacket as Dev drove them out of the lodge with grim determination. The dread he'd silenced with the protective warmth of his embrace had a clawhold on her heart once again. She didn't know if it was because of what she'd sensed, what she was leading them toward...or because of her terror that the compulsion was born of nothing, her mind a place of nightmares and lies.

"Don't think about it." A cool order from the director of Shine.

His strength fed her own. "It's hard not to," she said. "I can feel something calling to me, but I know I've never been in this area before."

"Is it possible you were held around here?"

"I suppose. But...I feel no sense of familiarity with anything." The snowy fields passing by on either side as they drove ever deeper into largely uninhabited territory sent a chill down her spine, but not because of any memory of torture.

The world on the other side of the window was actually rather beautiful, the snow glittering with diamond shards under the morning sun, the sky a placid blue that should've made evil impossible. But— "In my mind," she whispered, "everything's swathed in shadows."

The cold, clear-eyed soldier in Dev told him to turn back, that Katya was most likely leading him into a trap, but he kept driving. Today, he was going to follow the gut instinct that had saved his life more times than he could count. This woman—*his* woman—needed this, and he would give it to her.

"Tell me something," he said when she fell silent, her eyes locked on the outer vista.

She started, as if he'd broken into a trance. "What?"

"You mentioned your parents—any memories you want to

share?" He just wanted to get her thinking about something other than the darkness coming inexorably closer. It wouldn't take long, he thought. They'd reach their goal either tonight or early the next morning.

"Well," she said after a long pause, "since my parents had a full coparenting agreement, we all lived together in a family unit. They always consulted each other before making any decision about my welfare."

"Doesn't sound too bad." It was, in fact, far better than he'd expected.

"No. It was a good existence." Folding her arms, she tilted her head to face him. "But it was simply an existence. When I turned eighteen and moved out, there was no difference in my life other than the fact that I could make decisions on my own from then on."

"I thought Psy were pretty strong on family loyalty."

"Yes, but it's a cold kind of loyalty. A month after I reached my majority, my parents—who'd ceased living together the day I turned eighteen—dissolved their coparenting agreement, and my memories tell me that I never knew them to speak to each other again." She shrugged. "They'd achieved their aims, fulfilled their contracts. I have connections to both families, of course, but when I turned twenty-one, I had to choose."

"Why?"

"Because Psy only trust loyalty that is absolute," she said. "I had to formally identify with either the maternal or the paternal side of my family."

"Which did you choose?" Dev asked, fascinated by this glimpse into the forces that had shaped the woman by his side.

"The paternal," she answered. "My father's family is involved in scientific endeavors, while my mother's is more focused on economics. It made sense for me to align myself with the group that would allow me to best utilize my skills."

"And your mother didn't feel like she'd gotten the worst of the bargain?"

"Of course not—genetically, I'm still half hers. But since she did co-raise me, my father had to buy out part of the contract since his family would get the benefit of my training, skills, and connections."

Dev blinked, trying to understand. "He *bought* you?"

"It's a perfectly normal transaction in the Net." She blew out a breath. "Everything's calm and practical and business-like. No fights, no disagreements. All the contingencies are covered in the parenting and fertilization agreements."

Dev couldn't imagine such a cold life, such a cold relationship. "So since you're considered part of your father's family, did you have to contribute financially?"

"Yes. Our family had a central investment fund. I did quite well out of it—we had a good investment strategy." Stretching out her legs, she tapped her fingers on her knees. "I wonder how my death affected things. Likely very little—my work for the Council raised my family's ranking in terms of their influence in the Net, but it was a small contribution. Losing me wouldn't have caused that big a ripple."

To hear her talk of herself in such a clinical way infuriated him. "But your life will cause one hell of a big ripple."

She gave him a startled look. "I suppose that's one way of looking at it. Can I ask you . . . ?" A hesitant question.

"What?"

"About your childhood?"

His hands clenched on the steering wheel. "What do you want to know?" It came out sounding like gravel.

She was quiet for almost a minute. "You don't want to talk about it."

"Not today." Not ever, if he was being honest.

"Is there someone else you—no." She shook her head. "I'm asking for your weaknesses."

"Was the question yours?"

Her eyes were hollow when she glanced at him. "That's just it. I don't know."

Even as Dev and Katya drove ever deeper into the barren wilderness of Alaska, Sascha sat beside Lucas as he drove them to Cruz.

"I do know how to drive," she pointed out, simply to see his reaction.

He shot her a narrow-eyed glance. "Why are you purposefully jerking my chain?"

"Because I can." She smiled. "Seriously, Mr. Alpha Cat, pregnancy doesn't make me an invalid."

"Am I treating you like an invalid?"

She had to concede the point. "No." In fact, with Lucas busy overseeing a major construction deal, she'd actually been handling *more* Pack business. "But you're running yourself ragged—I could've driven myself to Cruz, taken a sentinel as escort. Then you'd have had the morning free to read the revised contracts."

"I can read the contracts while you're working with the boy." Reaching across, he closed his hand over hers. "You know you're not going to change my mind."

She brought his hand to hers, kissed the knuckles. "I know. But I have to try."

"Why? Because it makes me crazy?"

"Because I know I have to train you before our baby arrives." He'd always been overprotective of those under his care. "A baby leopard won't take well to constant supervision."

He blew out a breath. "I'm alpha. Do you think I don't know that?"

She wrapped him in her love on the psychic plane, an invisible kiss.

His cheek creased with a smile she wouldn't tire of if she lived to be a thousand. "I know I'm being a pain in the ass,

Sascha darling, but humor me. I'm working on letting go—I promise our kid will be a wild savage exactly like Roman and Julian."

Laughing at the thought of some of the stunts the two cubs pulled, she blew him a kiss this time. "They wouldn't talk to me when I went to visit yesterday."

"Rome and Jules?" Pure surprise. "I don't believe it—if they were bigger, they'd fight me to claim you."

"Tammy"—the twins' mom—"said they were sulking because they'd figured out I was going to have a baby."

"Ah. Brats are jealous."

Lips curving at the thought of the two little boys who'd brought joy into her life from the instant she'd met them, she nodded. "I cuddled them and told them I'd still be their Aunt Sascha. But I don't think they were convinced until I told them they'd be bigger than the baby—so they could look after it."

"Sneaky." A sharp grin. "Jules, I think, is going to grow up a dominant. Looking after people is an irresistible lure."

"What about Roman? He was just as, or even more, excited by the idea."

"It's hard to say for sure, but I think Rome is going to follow in Tammy's footsteps. And healers *love* taking care of people."

Sascha's eyes widened at the realization that Lucas was right. Roman had the same calm energy as his mother, though his was overlayered with a vibrant childish joy. "Does that happen often? Healers coming from the same family?"

Lucas gave a small nod. "Tammy's family tree has supplied a healer at least every second generation. My mom's side of the family is more sporadic, but we do have a relatively high rate. There are still a few that turn up out of the blue."

"You know," Sascha said slowly, "it could be that healers come from the same genetic tree as M-Psy. I don't know about Tammy's, but your family definitely had Psy members."

"Could be." Sliding into the exit lane, he glanced over at her. "What about this kid, Cruz? He doing okay?"

"Better than okay." Sascha couldn't hide her pride. "He's so smart, Lucas. I teach him something once, and it's like this." She snapped her fingers. "He's a natural."

"Good, the faster he learns to protect himself, the better."

"You're worried about the Council?"

Lucas gave a small nod. "Dev thinks Shine's managed to keep the true strength of some of their people under the radar, but he wants us to be extra careful."

"I don't blame him," Sascha said, a wave of anger building beneath the surface of her skin. "After what they did to Jon and Noor."

"We're almost there, kitten." A brush of his knuckles over her cheek. "You said Cruz needs absolute stability."

Nodding, she took a deep breath and began to settle her emotions step by slow step. But one thing continued to worry her. "I felt Katya that first time we went to see Cruz." She tried not to intrude, but her ability was so much a part of her, she invariably picked up emotional resonances—especially when those emotions were so viciously strong. "She's keeping so much inside—it must physically hurt."

Lucas took almost a minute to reply. "She's strong," he finally answered. "There's a granite will in there."

"Dev is strong, too."

A swift glance from panther green eyes. "You picked that up, too?"

"Hard to miss the intensity between them. But..."

"But?"

She dropped her head back against the seat. "I'm so scared for them, Lucas. Because no matter how hard I try, I just can't see how they could ever find a happy ending."

CHAPTER 38

Ming continued to work as something pinged against his mental shields. It was nothing, simply a reminder that Ekaterina Haas was still alive. He hadn't expected her to last this long—but then again, humans were weak, easily manipulated. And the Forgotten had become more and more human with the passage of time.

Perhaps the little sleeper would complete her task after all.

Putting the unimportant project out of his mind, he concentrated on the problem at hand. *Aden,* he said, telepathing directly to the medic in charge of monitoring the Arrow Squad's response to Jax, *How many Arrows have reacted negatively to the Jax regimen in the past six months?*

The response came almost at once, Aden's primary talent being telepathy. *Seven. We can't afford to lose that many.*

Ming agreed. Arrows were highly trained, many from childhood. There were never more than two hundred overall, and currently, the number of active Arrows had dropped to a hundred and sixty. *Are you close to resolving the issue?*

Something like this happened with Judd Lauren.

Ming recognized the name at once as that of the lone Tk-Cell who'd survived to adulthood in the past generation. Judd Lauren's ability to literally stop the cells of the body had made him an invaluable assassin. *Wasn't he taken off Jax?*

Yes. Along with most of the other Tks. They all functioned as well without it—telekinetics seem to only need a very short stay on the regimen. Aden didn't elaborate but Ming didn't need him to—he knew that after a certain period, the pathways of the brain set permanently, making the use of the drug redundant.

Will that solution work in this case? he asked.

According to available data, yes. It appears some Arrows are in fact being overdosed on Jax since they no longer need it.

Ming took a few minutes to consider the decision. If he lost control of the Arrows, they could conceivably take over the Net. One Arrow was worth thousands of normal soldiers. *Try it on the ones who're already breaking down. See if it has any effect.*

I'd suggest a small number of others who may be close to that point, Aden said. *I can send you a list.*

Do it. Vasic? Is he on Jax? The teleporter was not only an invaluable part of the Squad, Ming utilized him on an almost weekly basis.

No. He hasn't been for years. His brain has reset.

Acknowledging the receipt of the additional names Aden had sent through, Ming ended the telepathic conversation. As long as Vasic was on a leash, there was no problem.

CHAPTER 39

Dev brought the car to a halt in front of the restaurant/bar/hotel/post office in a blink-and-you'll-miss-it town in the middle of nowhere. He'd charged up the engine with enough juice to go for days, and they had supplies, but they needed to stretch their legs at least. "We should stay the night," he said, knowing what Katya's reply was going to be before she opened her mouth.

"I can feel it ripping at me." She stared out at the blackness on the other side of the windshield—it was only six, but night had fallen with the swiftness of a raven's wings. "We're so close."

He'd been more than ready to drive on, but now, looking out at the pitch dark, the flurries of snow, he shook his head. "We have to wait for light. Or we might miss what we're searching for."

"We won't." She fisted her hand, swallowed. "But you're right—we might not see all of it. I can't sleep, but maybe we can wait until the snow passes at least."

And that's what they did. Dev checked them into one of the hotel's two rooms and grabbed a few movies from the elderly owner's vast selection. The movies were on small five-centimeter discs rather than the much more expensive crystals, but they looked in reasonably good condition. Sliding one into the player after Katya told him to choose, he stretched out on the bed, his back against the headboard, his legs straight out.

Katya stood at the window, her body outlined in a lonely silhouette. But she wasn't alone, would never again be that isolated.

"Come here," he said, raising an arm.

Turning from her vigil at the window, Katya crossed the room on silent feet and tucked herself against him. "What are we watching?" she asked, but her eyes kept sliding to the clear square looking out into the night darkness.

Whether it was because of her or because of his own abilities, he didn't know, but he, too, could feel the pull of the evil that awaited. He hugged her closer. "The sacrifices I make for you—just watch."

She was intrigued enough to pay attention to the screen. "*Pride and Prejudice*," she read out. "It's a book written by a human. Nineteenth century?"

"Uh-huh."

"The hero is ... Mr. Darcy?"

"Yes. According to Ti, he's the embodiment of male perfection." Dev ripped open a bag of chips he'd grabbed and put it in Katya's hands. "I don't know—the guy wears tights."

"Shh." She ate a chip. "I have to pay attention. The language is different."

His restlessness calmed as she settled down. He was aware of her attention going to the window, the dark, every so often, but she smiled, too, and once, she even laughed. Sometime around three a.m., she said, "Mr. Darcy is almost Psy in his characterization, don't you think?"

"I try not to think too much about Mr. Darcy."

Laughing, she put her hand on his chest. "No, really. I would've thought the writer based him on a Psy template, but we weren't Silent in her time. Psy were just like humans and changelings then."

He considered that. "I have trouble picturing it."

"Then you haven't been watching—several of the characters in this story are Psy," she pointed out. "Oh, look, it's the villain."

He was amused by the way she deconstructed the whole story scene by scene precisely like the scientist she was. But she had heart, too. He caught her sighing at the end.

He had to kiss her then, had to taste her happiness. Because it wouldn't last. The inevitable was fast approaching, he could feel it in his bones. Thirty minutes later, they were back in the car, traveling toward something neither of them truly wanted to see . . . and yet couldn't *not* see.

"I think we need to turn right at the crossroads."

Not questioning her, he took the direction. The sky finally started to lighten almost three hours into the journey, streaks of pink and orange emerging in the east. But despite the burst of color the world remained desolate. The outpost they'd stayed in had been the last trace of civilization. "Have you ever seen the northern lights?" he asked, watching the car's own lights dim automatically as the sensors picked up the sun's stealthy creep across the sky.

"No." She released a breath. "I'd like to, though."

"You might get lucky—the timing's right and we're far enough north."

"Have you seen them?"

"Yeah. I used to come up here to visit Michel when we were kids. When my mom was alive." The memory ached, but it was one of the good ones. "His mom, Cindee, and my dad are brother and sister." Cindee had wanted to raise him after his father's incarceration, but he hadn't been able to bear the guilt in her beautiful eyes.

Even as a nine-year-old he'd known that if he walked into that house, she'd spend the rest of her life trying to make up for a crime that had never been her fault. It hadn't even been his father's, though that was a forgiveness Dev simply couldn't find in himself. Instead, he'd gone into his *nani*'s spice-and-glass-scented embrace, letting her warmth melt the ice that had grown around his heart.

"But Michel doesn't live in Alaska now?"

"No, he does. He's just on a transfer to Washington State for the year. Some kind of training course."

"He remains a good friend," Katya said, obviously trying to keep her tone light though her eyes were locked on the road in front of them. "He must be—to pull Jessie's truck over because you were looking for me."

Dev scowled. "I still can't believe you managed to get out of the house with *three* of us trained in combat there."

"People tend to underestimate me." It was the first time he'd heard a hint of arrogance in her.

He decided he liked it. "I won't be making that mistake again. And yeah, me and Mischa, we're close as brothers." Cindee had made sure the cousins met, coming down to West Virginia, where Nani had her home and studio, when Dev had refused to go up to Alaska. He hadn't been able to bear the journey without his mom.

"Mischa?"

"That's what his mom's always called him." Dev grinned. "He's given up trying to get anyone in the family to use his actual name most of the time."

"Does anyone call you Devraj?"

"My *nani*—my maternal grandmother." Without asking, he turned left.

Katya leaned forward, her motion almost absent. "Yes." Putting her hands on the dash, she scanned the road in front of them, but there was nothing to see—it twisted this way and that, leaving limited visibility. "What are they like, the lights?"

"Like seeing a piece of heaven." He grimaced at the poetic

words, but they were the only ones he had. "Makes you humble, they're so beautiful. If you don't get to see them this time around, we'll come up here again."

"I'd like that." She gave him a strained smile. "Do you visit Michel much?"

"Now and then." Dev had finally returned to Alaska when Cindee was admitted to the hospital after a bad accident on the ice. His aunt's guilt still lingered, but it had been mellowed by time, by seeing him grow up into a stable youth. These days, they could have a conversation almost untainted by the past. "He comes down sometimes, too."

Katya gave Dev a penetrating look, her attention momentarily caught by the amusement in his voice. "What do the two of you get up to?"

"We used to raise hell when we were younger." A wicked grin. "We're more civilized these days."

"Somehow, I don't quite believe you." She thought of Dev and Michel together, darkly sexy and wickedly charming. Hmm... "I think I need to hear more about these civilized times."

"Male code of honor. No telling."

A shiver crept up her spine even as she went to tease him back. Whipping her head around, she spied the narrow one-lane road to the right. "There."

Dev was already turning, all humor gone from his face. Now he reminded her of nothing so much as a hunter, lean, hungry, and determined. She was suddenly very glad he was by her side—she didn't know if she'd have made it this far alone. The dread in her stomach was a heavy weight, inciting nausea and a panic that told her to run, dear God, *run!*

"No," she whispered. "No more running."

Dev shot her a quick look before returning his attention to the road. "We'll finish this." It was a vow.

Two minutes later, they came over a final, snow-covered rise and into a ghost town.

The sun's rays cut over the houses half buried in snow,

glanced off the broken windows, the ripped and hanging signs. "How many?" she whispered almost to herself.

"Five hundred." Dev pointed to the severely weather-beaten—but still standing—sign to their right. "Sunshine, Alaska, population five hundred."

Sunshine. Every tiny hair on her body stood up. "This place is too small for five hundred."

"Yeah—sign's pretty old." Unclipping his safety belt, he looked to her. "Ready?"

"No." But she undid her own belt, feeling as if she was letting go of her last hope of escape. Shuddering, she shook off the chill, and when Dev came around the car, she was waiting to link hands with him and walk into Sunshine, Alaska. The sense of dread that had been chasing her for days settled into a kind of viscous miasma, at once frightening...and sad. That, she hadn't expected—the sense of sorrow, so heavy it weighed down her very bones. "Where are they all?"

Dev didn't answer, frowning as he looked around. "We're in the town center, but I don't see a bar."

"Why's that important?"

"Human nature," he muttered. "Bars are some of the first places to go up and the last to close in any small town. This far out, it'd probably be the only place people could socialize. Unless there's a church? Could be a religious settlement."

She shook her head. "The buildings are all very uniform. Even the Second Reformation churches have a symbolic shape that makes them stand out."

They kept walking, the snow thick but manageable around their boots. She was glad she'd stuffed a woolen cap over her head before she exited the car, but Dev's hair shone dark under the cool winter sun. "Aren't you cold?" Reaching into his coat before he could reply, she took out his own knit cap and tugged it over his head.

"Thanks." It was a distracted comment as he took her hand again.

"The buildings aren't completely submerged," she said, glancing around. "This place wasn't abandoned that long ago."

"No," Dev murmured. "Look at the way it's packed on the left—there's been a strong wind at some stage. It pushed everything that way."

She turned, nodded. "We can't explore that side, not easily." There was no question they had to get inside. "It's so quiet here." The absence of sound hurt her.

"Listen to my voice, listen to our feet crushing the snow and ice. There is sound." A reassuring squeeze of her hand.

Nodding, she did as directed. They reached the first accessible building seconds later.

"Let's hope this opens inward," Dev said, walking up to the door. "Or we'll have to find something to dig—bingo."

The creak of the door he opened was loud, the thud of their boots on the plain plascrete floor dull and echoey. Snow tunneled inside as she stood looking around. "Appears to be a supply depot." Computronic items lay iced over in the case to the left, while tools and machinery lay in neat rows to the right. In front of her stood a stack of plas boxes stamped with a name that was vaguely familiar. "EarthTwo," she muttered under her breath, moving with Dev as he went to look at the equipment.

"It's mining gear," he told her, picking up a powerful-looking length of rope with one hand.

"That's it." She pointed at the boxes. "EarthTwo is a small mining company that specializes in rare minerals. They sent things to the labs I worked in." Excited now, she found the courage to let go of Dev's hand and open one of the boxes. "Empty." Even that disappointment didn't deflate her excitement. "I didn't imagine this—there *is* something here."

Walking over, Dev pressed a hotly real kiss to her lips. "I told you your mind was fine. You should learn to listen to me."

Her heart raced at the electric burst of contact. "So you can order me around?"

"Would I do that?" He took her hand again, his grip firm. "Let's see what else we can find. This place looks like it hasn't been disturbed since the town was abandoned."

"Or before either." She pointed to the windows, all unbroken.

The next place they stepped into couldn't have been more different. "It's like a hurricane came through here," she whispered, staring at the papers that littered the carpet, the shattered glass from the windows, and even worse, the jagged wires that sprung up from a sofa on one side of the room. Tufts of stuffing—white, disconcertingly pristine—lay scattered on the papers around it . . . almost as if someone had tried to rip the sofa apart in an insane fury.

A touch on her lower back. "Stay here," Dev said as he made his way to the desk.

Listening with a corner of her mind as he went through the drawers, she bent down to pick up a few of the myriad pieces of paper floating in the room. The top one was an accounts list. "Payroll," she said out loud. "I think this must've been EarthTwo's administration office."

"The entire town was a mining op," Dev said, holding up a thin paper file. "Some kind of a prospectus. Sunshine is wholly owned by EarthTwo."

"Strange name for a Psy town."

"Hmm." Dev flicked through the file. "Here's why— the town was founded a hundred and fifty years ago. Before Silence."

"There must be something very valuable in the soil around here, then," she said. "Either something that regenerates or that people only need a little bit of. I didn't see any evidence of heavy drilling."

"Could be anything under all that snow—remember the equipment." Putting the prospectus into a pocket, he crossed back to her. "It's going to get dark fast. We might have to spend the night."

She swallowed. "Why don't we figure out what happened here first." Her eyes lit on something she'd seen but hadn't *seen* until then. "Dev, the specks of brown on these papers... it's not dirt or age spots, is it?"

He looked at the sheets in her hand. "No." His jaw turned to rock. "That's blood."

CHAPTER 40

The papers floated to the ground in serene silence as she unclenched her fingers. "I can see it now." There was a fine spray on the back wall, almost hidden by the way dents had been pounded into the plasboard. And the sofa...some of those wicked-looking metal springs were rusted. Except that wasn't rust.

Dev took her hand. "We need to see the rest."

"Wait." Bending, she picked up one of the sheets she'd dropped. "It's part of the command log. They must've printed out a hard-copy backup because of the risk of power failure."

"Why not keep it on the PsyNet?"

"It takes a lot of psychic power to maintain a PsyNet vault. Some companies prefer—" Chills snaked up her spine as she realized what she held. "Dev..."

Dev took the paper. "'Major incident,'" he read out. "'Request emergency assistance immediately. Repeat, request emergency assistance as soon as—' It just ends."

"A vocal-to-print transcript," she said, tapping a line of code at the top of the page. "Probably set to print out automatically." The thought of the printers working with quiet efficiency while blood erupted around them created the most macabre of images. "It's dated September twenty-fifth." While she'd been with Ming, a creature he thought he'd broken. "The speaker died midtransmission."

"He died trying to save lives—that deserves to be remembered." Folding the piece of paper, Dev put it in his pocket alongside the prospectus. "Let's go."

She'd never wanted to do anything less. But these people, she thought, needed her to keep going. Because they'd been locked in the dark, too, the final moments of their lives erased from existence. "Yes."

The next building housed what appeared to be a mess hall. It was fairly neat, with only a little evidence of trouble—in the food preparation area. "Whatever happened," Dev said, "it happened either very early in the morning or late at night."

"When there would've been only kitchen workers in here."

"Why a kitchen at all? I thought Psy lived on nutrition bars."

"That's the norm, but our psychologists sometimes recommend a more varied diet within an otherwise isolated population—they did for the lab." The scientists working on the Implant Protocol, a protocol designed to turn the Net into a true hive mind, had been buried under hundreds of tons of earth, in a construction Ming had rigged to blow. "Every brain needs a certain amount of stimulation." Her eyes went to a solid steel door at the back of the room. "The cooler." Cold silvered into her very bones.

"I'll do this."

"No." Ripping off a glove, she tangled her fingers with his. "Together."

A pause where she could literally see him fighting his instincts, his face all brutal angles. "These are my nightmares," she said. "I need to see if they're real."

Finally, he nodded and they walked to the cooler, the door growing monstrously larger with each step. "There's nothing on the surface," she said in relief. No blood, no scratches, no dents.

Reaching forward with his free hand, Dev twisted and pulled.

Icy mist whispered out, making Katya take a startled step back. Telling herself to stop being a coward, she returned to Dev's side. "Shouldn't the light come on automatically?"

Even as she spoke, something flickered and sparked and an instant later, a cool blue glow filled the space, illuminating the horror within. "Oh, God." She couldn't get her eyes off the bloody palm print in the very back, a palm print that streaked down over the wall and across the floor until it ended in a pile of blood. "She was trying to get away"—because the print was too small to be that of a man, and her mind simply couldn't accept a child in this madness—"and he dragged her back, killed her."

"More than one." Dev's tone was a blade. "Someone threw bodies in here." He pointed to the other concentrations of frozen blood. "No one else struggled. They had to have been dead by then."

"The entire kitchen staff." She turned, able to see it now. "Whoever it was came in and managed to kill them off one by one. The woman alone figured it out, tried to escape."

"Yeah." Stepping back, he closed the door.

"Where are the bodies?" Her mind jerked from one wall to the next, trying to make sense of an evil that defied understanding. "You don't think they're outside, beneath the snow?"

Dev shook his head. "I'm guessing EarthTwo sent in a cleanup crew."

Neither of them said anything more until they'd walked through the remaining buildings they could access. One was a gym, and it was pristine. The next five buildings had clearly been dormitory facilities. Shattered objects, broken windows, blood and chaos reigned here, most of it concentrated around the beds.

"Night," she whispered. "They were asleep. That's the only way anyone could've gotten so many of them—there had to be telepaths in the group. They'd have warned the others if they'd been awake."

"Unless…"

She looked up from her contemplation of a bunk bed that seemed to have been snapped in half. "Unless?"

"Unless we're talking about more than one killer."

A wave of darkness, a crackle of memory, and the flood-gates opened.

"There's been a major incident, sir."

"Details?" That voice, Ming's voice.

A pause. "The female?"

"She hasn't got enough mind left to understand. Tell me the details."

"EarthTwo received a telepathic and electronic Mayday from its operation in Sunshine, Alaska, approximately two hours ago. The management asked for Council help, as such assistance is a negotiated part of their contract with us. We were able to mobilize a small Tk unit and teleport to the location."

"How many dead?"

"One hundred and twenty." The speaker could've been talking about stocks and bonds, so calm was his tone of voice. "The population numbered one hundred and fifty. Three were seriously injured, while six managed to find hiding places."

"That leaves twenty-one."

"Yes, sir. It appears various members of the team broke Silence at approximately the same time, though not in a central location. They attacked each other and the nonfrag-mented members of the expedition. Of the twenty-one who survived the initial incident, ten died attempting to attack the

Tk team, while eleven were neutralized and put into involuntary comas."

"Sunshine?"

"An isolated outpost. We can send in a team to clean up the immediate mess, but we'd have to take a significant number of Tks off higher-priority tasks in order to fully erase the settlement."

"Viability of the work without telekinetics?"

"There's always a risk of detection with flying in—the op may attract unwanted attention."

A long silence. "Were all the staff members at Sunshine Psy?"

"Yes."

"Have EarthTwo log that the encampment was abandoned after the outbreak of a lethal airborne virus. That should keep anyone else from wanting to go in for the time being."

"Katya!" Dev shook the woman in his arms, having carried her outside to the cold when she refused to respond to him in the dormitory.

Her eyes fluttered. "Dev?"

"It's me, baby. Come on, come back."

"I remembered," she whispered, her voice husky.

"Tell me in the car." Only when he'd settled her in the backseat and crawled in to take her into his arms did he breathe again. "Your eyes . . ." It was like she'd ceased to exist, or gone so deep that he couldn't see her anymore. He'd thought no terror could come close to what he'd experienced as a child. He'd been wrong.

She hugged him, pressing kisses to his jaw. "I'm sorry—I think I must've slipped into some type of a trance state."

He let her soothe him, needing the caresses, needing to know that she was alright. "Tell me." Stroking his hand up her spine, he closed his hand over her nape.

Horror spread its fingers through his chest as she began to speak, the invasion hard and pitiless. "Over twenty people went insane at once?"

"More than that—some would've been killed when they first turned on each other."

"How is that even possible?" He pulled her into his lap, needing to feel the living warmth of her weight. "I've heard that Psy are breaking in higher numbers, but we're talking about a case of mass insanity."

"I didn't believe the rumors," she said. "Not until I heard that."

He waited.

"A number of our—mine and Ashaya's—contacts reported that there were stories of certain parts of the Net going 'dark,' like something was collecting there, something that ate up or buried the fabric of the Net."

"The influence of the DarkMind?"

"Yes, that's a possibility. I just don't know." She shook her head. "No one could ever actually point to an example, so we didn't pay it that much attention. We couldn't—we had to focus on what we could actually see and change."

"Go on."

"You know what it means to be in a neural network—it's like swimming in the sea. There's no way to avoid coming into contact with any pollutants."

Dev pulled off his knit cap with an impatient hand. "You think this 'rot,'" he said, for want of a better word, "seeped into all those minds?"

"The Net isn't locked to any one location," she said, "but your location in the Net is determined partly by where you are in the world. This group would've been in Sunshine, and that means they would've occupied an isolated section of the Net. If they all arrived together, the rot would've started to work on them at the same time."

"Some of the ones who were killed," Dev said, barely able

to wrap his mind around the sheer magnitude of the slaughter, "chances are they would've broken, too—if they'd lived a little longer."

"Yes." Katya wrapped her arms around his neck. "If this has happened once, Dev..."

"We need to record this. We need proof."

"The Council will deny it. No one is ready to believe." A tight kind of anger filled every syllable. "I know—we tried so hard to tell people the truth, but it's like they can only take so much at a time. They'll say you're simply trying to create political—"

"I know." He broke off the flow of frustrated words with a kiss. "I need the records for my people."

Understanding lit those pretty eyes from within. "Oh. I see. Did you bring a recording device?"

"My cell phone has a high-enough resolution and plenty of memory."

Neither of them said anything for several minutes—though they both knew they had to get out of the car to document what they'd found. Katya listened to the steady beat of Dev's heart and in that, somehow found courage. "We can do this."

He dropped a kiss to the top of her head. "Do you know what I see when I look at the blood?"

"Tell me."

"The possible future of the Forgotten." He thrust a hand through his hair. "Why couldn't we have left the madness behind when we left the Net? Why do our abilities always have to come bundled with darkness?"

Katya had spent many hours considering the same. "If they didn't, the Psy truly would rule the world—that flaw, that built-in Achilles' heel, is the only thing that makes us breakable, the only thing that stems our arrogance."

His fingers threaded through her hair, pushing off her cap. "With power comes temptation."

"Yes." She thought of the people who'd worked in the labs

with her, so many of them gifted, so many of them unable to see that what they were doing was monstrous. "That much power, without any controls, changes a person from the inside out." And what emerged wasn't always anything human in the wider sense.

"Emotion is a control." Dropping his hand from her hair, he picked up her cap. "But it's not the complete answer."

"If it was," she murmured, letting him put the cap back on her head, drawing his tenderness around her like a shield, "Silence would have never come into force."

"Circles." He reached out to open the door. "Ready?"

"Yes." But it was a lie. She'd never be ready to face the death that stained Sunshine a dark, nearly black red. It didn't matter. This had to be done. Somebody had to bear witness to the loss of so many minds, so many dreams and hopes. "Yes. Let's go."

PETROKOV FAMILY ARCHIVES

Letter dated January 5, 1979

Dear Matthew,

I almost can't believe that we made it. The ShadowNet, as everyone's calling this new network, is a vibrant, chaotic place. Given our numbers, it's not as dense as the PsyNet, but it's alive. And that's all that matters.

The ostrasizing has already begun. We called your uncle Greg to tell him we were safe. I could see the relief in his eyes, but all he said out loud was not to call him again. He's afraid that if he shows any feelings toward us, the Council will take your cousins away.

I cried afterward. You saw me, wiped my tears. And I knew with every beat of my heart that I'd made the right choice.

I love you so.

Mom

CHAPTER 41

Night fell with predictable swiftness but they were done by then. Neither of them brought up the idea of staying on. Dev simply took the wheel and they headed out. They'd been driving an hour when Katya broke the silence. "I'm starting to remember things I wasn't ready to before."

"Anything like this?"

"No." A long pause. "My memories of Noor's and especially Jon's time in the labs are almost complete."

He didn't try to talk her out of her guilt—that, he'd realized, would take time. The woman Katya had become would never be able to walk away from those darkest of memories. So he kept his tone matter-of-fact, his words the same. "She seems unaffected, and he's a strong kid."

"A gifted one." Katya's voice was quiet. "His ability—it's one so open to misuse."

"Not if he's shown the right path."

"When I was a child," she said, "I used to try to use my telepathy to make others in my crèche group do what I wanted."

"That's a fairly normal developmental stage for telepathic children." Dev, too, had done things as a kid that weren't strictly right—he'd been learning his strengths, stretching his limbs. He wanted to tell Katya that, share the truth of his gift with metal, with machines. "It pisses me off that I can't talk to you like I want." His palms protested the strength with which he was gripping the steering wheel. Relaxing with effort, he blew out a breath between clenched teeth.

"I keep telling myself that things will change, that I'll find an escape hatch."

He remembered what she'd once said about the tentacles of Ming's control. "You haven't been able to work out a way to disengage the programming?"

"No" she said, wrapping her arms around herself in a hold so tight, he heard something tear in her jacket. "Not without damaging my brain. The talons of this *thing* he put in my head are sunk too deep."

"Maybe the programming is too strong to break," he said, pain shooting down his jaw, he'd clenched it so hard, "but it shouldn't have a permanent physical effect. It's a psychic construct."

"Dev...it's not the programming. The prison is anchored in my mind."

His gut turned to ice. "How sure are you?" A long pause. "Tell me."

"I've looked at it from every possible angle. I was hoping I'd made a mistake." The tone of her voice told him she'd discovered different.

Dev was only just a telepath, but he knew everything there was to know about the abilities—both old and new—that might manifest among the Forgotten. So he understood damn well that something that was anchored in an individual's mind, as opposed to the fabric of a neural net, would tear that mind to pieces if it was removed without the proper procedure. And right now, the only person who had a key to Katya's prison was Councilor Ming LeBon.

The decision was simple. "We need to find Ming."

Katya's head snapped toward him. "No, Dev. *No.*"

Having spent the entire day with Cruz, Sascha expected to fall into an easy sleep that night, tired by the psychic energy she'd expended. But she found herself lying awake long after the forest had gone quiet around her. Cuddling into Lucas's changeling heat, she spread her fingers over his heart and tried to match the rhythm of her breathing to his.

Her body began to relax, but her mind continued to spin. Giving up, she decided to read for a while...but Lucas's arm tightened the instant she tried to pull away. She should have let him sleep—instead she stroked a hand down his neck. "Wake up."

His eyes blinked open with feline laziness. "Hmm?" Nuzzling at her in sleepy interest, he squeezed his hand over her hip.

"I can't sleep."

He spread his hand over her abdomen. "Feeling okay?" A tender question, a protective touch.

"Yes." She moved her hand over his biceps. "Just wide-awake."

"Want me to make you tired?" A rumble against her ear, fingers playing over the dip of her navel.

The butterflies in her stomach were intimately, exquisitely familiar. "That's a very tempting offer."

"But you want to talk."

Heart stretching with the force of what she felt for this man who knew her so completely, she kissed the side of his jaw, tangling her hand in the heavy silk of his hair. "Working with Cruz...he's so vulnerable, Lucas, so open to any direction."

"Then it's a good thing you'd never hurt him."

That was what worried her. "That book my mother sent me—it said E-Psy can turn bad."

"No," Lucas said, rising to look down at her. "It said E-Psy often care so much they start to think they know what's best for everyone."

"And then they do bad things," she insisted. "What about that empath the writer profiled—the one who tried to emotionally manipulate everyone to be 'good.' He drove people insane by forcing them to go against their own will."

"He was a loner—without family, without Pack. Do you really think I'd let you turn into a megalomaniac?" An amused gleam in those leopard eyes.

She made a face at him. "This is serious." But he'd succeeded in loosening the knot of fear in her chest. "I never even knew I could feed emotion into someone, literally force them to feel what I wanted."

Lucas played with strands of her hair as she lapsed into thought.

"I wonder why my mother sent the book," she murmured. "Was it to destabilize me, or did she want to warn me of the danger?" With most mothers, it wouldn't have been a question, but most mothers weren't Councilor Nikita Duncan.

"Or maybe she's finally realized what a powerful ally you'd make."

She lifted her face in a wordless question.

"You know what the alpha in me found most interesting in that book?" he asked, bracing his elbows on either side of her head. "The fact that a cardinal empath who has total control of her gift can effectively stop a riot of thousands in its tracks. Imagine how useful that gift would be to a Councilor facing rebellion from within the ranks."

Sascha wrapped her arms around Lucas's neck. "According to Eldridge's book, that empathic skill has saved countless lives over the generations."

"Yes."

"But you don't think that's why Nikita wants it?"

Lucas kissed her with utmost tenderness. "I'm not going to guess at your mother's motives, Sascha. But I can't bear to see you being hurt—be careful, kitten."

His love swept around her, tight and protective and wonderful. "Don't worry," she said, nuzzling into him. "I'm not that vulnerable to her anymore. I just wish I understood why she did this now of all times."

"Ask her," Lucas said, to her surprise. "She might not tell you the truth—probably won't—but you're good at reading between the lines, at reading body language."

"Yes, I think I will." Pressing a kiss to his shoulder, she let her mind meander back to a subject she'd been mulling over earlier that day. "I think something is happening among the Forgotten."

"I get that feeling, too." He shifted so that more of his body tangled with hers. "Those guards on Cruz—I'm not sure Dev is only worried about the Psy. Word is, some of his own people are moving against him."

"Do you think the Forgotten are starting to have the same problems that drove the Psy to Silence?"

"If they are . . . Dev has a hell of a problem on his hands."

Katya felt as if she'd been arguing until she was blue in the face. Dev didn't argue back—he simply refused to change his mind. "Are you insane?" she was finally driven to yell, as they prepared to catch a few hours' sleep at the same little bed-and-breakfast they'd stopped at before. They'd driven half the night, compelled to get away from the malignant violence that marked Sunshine. But from the instant Dev had mentioned going after Ming, she'd had only one thought in mind—stopping him. "That's what he wants! It'll make it so much easier for him to kill you."

Dev pulled down the blankets, having stripped off to his jeans while she changed into sweats. "Get in before you freeze your pretty ass off."

"Dev, you can't just ignore me."

"I said, *get in*. Or I'm dumping you in there."

Anger rose in a wild flood. "Don't treat me like a child!" Picking up the thing closest to her—a shoe—she threw it at him.

He moved out of the way with fluid grace. "That wasn't a smart move, baby." Calm words, but the heat in his eyes was a slow-burning fuse.

Too furious to be able to read whether that heat denoted anger or desire, she said, "Oh, yeah? How about this one?" She threw the other shoe.

He shifted his head aside without really seeming to move. Then he reached for her. She went to spin away . . . only to realize he'd backed her into a corner. "I swear to God, Dev, I'm so mad at you—"

A finger against her lips.

Startled, she stopped talking.

"You're mine," he said in a quiet, implacable voice. "Now and forever."

Her entire body trembled with the force of that vow.

"I will let nothing, and no one, take you from me." Gold-flecked eyes that pierced her very heart. "Do you understand?"

"I'm not going to let you kill yourself," she whispered against his finger. Pushing it away, she put her hand over his heart. "If you walk into a trap because of me, if you die . . ."

"I won't. I'm not stupid and I don't intend to go into this blind. We gather intel and we move when he's vulnerable." He reached out to brush her hair off her face. "He's powerful, but he can't defend against every eventuality."

"He's evil," Katya whispered, her eyes black with memory. "I've never felt anyone so devoid of humanity."

"If good runs when evil rises," he said, his palms braced on the walls on either side of her head, "then the world has no chance at all."

"He won't give you the key."

"Then he'll die."

"Killing Ming"—her lips moving against his—"won't save me. Even if we somehow find a way to undo or block the programming, the mental prison is autonomous, linked to and fed by my own mind."

"But it'll give you freedom. Only Ming knows you're alive—you could live out your whole life with no one knowing about you on the Net."

"Yes," she said, but he saw a flicker of unease in her eyes.

About to ask her what she was thinking, he found his lips taken in a very feminine way—soft, lush, and absolute.

Katya drew the taste of Dev—heat and demand, passion with an edge of steel—deep within, shoving aside a truth that had been bleeding into her mind day by slow day. Today, here, with the thick blanket of snow insulating them against the outside world, she wanted simply to be a woman who'd found herself lucky enough to be in the arms of this incredible, complex man.

When he crushed her into the corner, taking over her world, she shuddered and thrust her hands into his hair. The dark fire of him seeped into her bones, warming her from the inside out. Sliding her fingers through the rough silk, she stroked down over his shoulders and to the temptation of his chest. "I love touching you," she said into his mouth, shaping the muscled planes of him with palms that couldn't get enough. The sprinkling of dark hair was deliciously abrasive—she ached to be naked, feel the sensation on her breasts. "I want to take off my clothes."

He closed his teeth over her lower lip. "That's what I like to hear." Light words, but his face was stark intensity. She knew he could be tender, had felt his care, but beneath the surface, Devraj Santos was a warrior—with a will that was unbreakable.

Shaking with the power of her own emotions, she pressed a line of kisses down his jaw, along his neck. "I'd like to please you this time."

His hand fisted in her hair. "You please me by simply being."

She licked the taste of him into her mouth, felt her body clench. Though his muscles tensed, he stood in place and let her explore the hard male beauty of him. "I don't understand," she whispered, "how my race could've ever given this up." When Silence first began, there would have been lovers, couples who burned for each other.

"Some didn't." Hot breath against her ear as he leaned in to let her better reach his neck. "For some, the price was too high."

His pulse fascinated her, so strong, so vivid, and now, jagged with desire. For her. A little curl of feminine power snaked up her body, heady and hungry. He was such a strong man that knowing she had the ability to affect him like this was a drug of its own. Grazing her teeth along the column of his neck, she ran the nails of one hand gently down his chest, making sure to scrape past one flat male nipple.

He hissed out a breath. "Do that again."

CHAPTER 42

"Like this?" A light caress.

"Tease."

Smiling, she gave him what he wanted—to his husky groan—before pushing at him to shift back. He resisted. She insisted.

A single inch.

Just enough for her to move her head down so she could close her teeth delicately around the nipple she'd tormented. He swore as her teeth slipped, grazing his chest. When she shifted her attention to the side she'd neglected, he accommodated her by giving her another inch.

Warm, golden brown skin under her hands, her lips, the wild, edgy scent of him in her head, a little bit of heaven. Having him all to herself, to enjoy without guilt or worry, if only for this broken instant in time, it was nothing she'd ever regret. No matter what. Shoving the latter thought to the darkest recesses of her brain, she tried to kiss her way down his chest. "Give me room."

"No." He tugged up her head with the hand fisted in her hair.

She licked at his skin, blew out a breath to cool the wet. He shuddered. Nuzzling at him, she pushed. "It's my turn."

"I'm going to embarrass myself if you put that pretty mouth of yours anywhere near my cock." Blunt words, as blunt as the erection pushing against her lower abdomen.

Skin tight with the impact of that erotic image, she pushed again. "I want to taste you. You had your turn already."

The air turned not only blue, but went well over into indigo. "Are you trying to torture me?" A biting, nibbling kiss that sizzled straight down to the dampness between her legs. "What if I don't want to play fair?" he murmured, shimmying one hand inside her sweatpants to cup her bottom with bold familiarity. "What if I want another turn?"

Having his hands on her was scrambling her brain cells, but she wasn't about to give in. Not when this particular fantasy had been driving her insane since the instant she'd first considered it. "Then you better let me do what I want," she ordered, nipping at his jaw. "Or you're not getting it."

"I'm bigger than you are."

She slid her hand underneath the waistband of his jeans to close firmly around him. His body bucked. "You were saying?"

"Witch." He moved back just barely enough, widening his stance to give her room.

It was all she wanted. Being hemmed in by Dev added an exquisite layer of sensation to her sensual exploration. Not only did she love being surrounded by the burning sexual heat of him, she felt protected—more than safe enough to give in to her wildest fantasies. Removing her hand, she dropped a kiss to the center of his chest and ran her fingers down his sides, stroking over his skin with a playfulness she'd never thought to find in herself.

"I'm keeping score," he warned. "Payback's going to involve screaming on your part."

She'd come to associate screaming with pain...but, well,

with Dev, she had a feeling it'd take on a whole new meaning. "I can't wait." Kiss by kiss, she progressed down his body, until she was kneeling, her fingers on the top button of his jeans.

Looking up through her lashes, she met his gaze as he looked down, his hands braced on the wall above her. The gold in his eyes seemed to have spread, creating something akin to a glow. "Am I imagining it?" she whispered, flicking open the button.

"No."

Fascinated by that electric gaze, she wanted to ask more questions, but then he shuddered, shattering her thoughts. She'd been playing her fingers over his erection—now she realized she'd driven him to the edge. Wetting her lips, she took hold of the zipper tab.

"Fuck," he muttered through gritted teeth as she tugged it over the push of his erection and down. The next few instants passed in a kind of sexual haze. All she knew was that she'd somehow managed to release him from his clothing, and now the aroused length of him lay in her palm. It was a compulsion to lean forward, to flick her tongue across the head.

He jerked, but didn't pull away. "So?" It was a hoarse question.

She looked up, closing her fingers around the silken heat with a possessiveness that surprised even her. "So?"

"You"—he cleared his throat, took a couple of deep breaths—"you asked what the pleasure was in doing this."

Dipping her head back down, she leaned forward and took him into her mouth. This time, his shout wasn't contained. One hand tangled in her hair, his thighs iron hard, erotic tension in every single muscle.

Drawing the taste of him deeper, she moved her hands to his thighs, giving herself more room to play. She heard him swear and felt him tug gently at her hair, but no way was she ending this when she'd barely begun. Instead of withdrawing, she dug her fingers into those rock-hard muscles in silent reproach.

When he jerked and released her hair, she knew she'd won. At least for the next little while. So she took full advantage, sucking and licking and learning. There *was* pleasure in this, such extreme pleasure that it felt as if her bones were melting from the inside out. The taste of him intoxicated her, but more, feeling his response, knowing it was because of her... it pushed her arousal to a fever pitch.

"Enough." He stepped back before she could hold him to her.

Frustrated, she glared. "I wasn't finished."

"I'm about to," he muttered, and pulled her to her feet, shoving at her sweatpants.

She stepped out of them and her panties at the same time, exhilarated at the raw edge of him, the glittering gold in his eyes. "Dev, wha—"

He lifted her with a display of strength that stole her breath. "Legs around my waist." It was a clipped order.

She obeyed immediately. He rewarded her by sliding into her in a single hard thrust. Her scream echoed off the walls as pleasure short-circuited her body. His hands gripped her bottom, holding her tightly in place as he moved in and out. She clawed at his shoulders, feeling herself hanging on the precipice.

"God damn it!" Dev's body went taut against her and she knew he'd lost every bit of his steely control.

That was all it took.

Electricity rocked through her, as wild and as hot as the man who held her pinned to the wall in helpless surrender.

Katya lay boneless as Dev dropped her on the bed. "I still have my top on," she muttered, not the least bit interested in moving. Her bones were jelly, her inner muscles continuing to spasm in little bursts of pleasure.

Dev, having finally gotten rid of his jeans, sprawled down over her, burying his face in her neck. She managed to find enough energy to thread her fingers through his hair and hold him to her as his chest rose up and down in long, deep breaths. "You've killed me," he muttered.

"I plan to do it again as soon as I recover." Which would be in about a week.

"Insatiable."

"Only for you."

A silence unbroken but for their jagged breaths. "So honest." He pressed a kiss to her damp skin. "Don't ever change that about yourself."

Her free hand curled into the sheet. Was a lie of omission still a lie? *Yes*, she thought, honest with herself, even if she couldn't be with him. "I'm hungry."

"Give me a minute to find the strength to hunt and gather."

Her lips quirked. "Devraj Santos, brought down by a woman half his size."

"With a mouth like heaven." Another kiss. "You can do that again anytime you want. I insist."

A laugh burst out of her. "Ouch, my stomach muscles hurt." But she'd take this kind of pain any day. "Tell me about the eyes." Surely that knowledge was nothing that would hurt the Forgotten even if Ming found her before she could end this?

"Hmm." His lashes moved against her in an incongruously delicate caress. "We had cardinals drop out with us. The eyes disappeared within a generation."

"Because of the dilution in your abilities," she murmured. "No cardinals, no night-sky eyes." Cardinal eyes were eerily beautiful. Even Psy in the Net rarely met those at the extreme end of Psy power—white stars on black, their eyes seemed to reflect the Net itself.

"But some of us are starting to be born with these eyes."

"Brown and gold?"

"The color doesn't matter." He rose up on his elbow, damp strands of hair on his forehead. She liked him this way—sexy and disheveled. "I don't think you're listening to me." He mock-scowled when she reached up to lave kisses over the muscled curve of one shoulder.

She smiled. "Sorry."

"As I was saying before I was so rudely interrupted"— she laughed at his severe tone—"there's some kind of psychic feedback in times of either great emotional stress or arousal." A gleam in those beautiful eyes. "I think you gave me both today."

"That's what I like to hear," she said, in deliberate echo. "Jonquil," she whispered. "I thought his eyes were simply an extraordinary blue, but I think he exhibits the phenomenon."

Dev cupped her face in his hands. "It's not connected to the level of power," he told her. "It seems to be a random mutation that's occurred in a certain percentage of the population."

"Maybe you're in the process of developing your own version of cardinal eyes," she murmured. "Even if it's not connected to power now, it might one day end up being so."

"I hope to hell not," Dev said, jaw firming. "It'd make the strong ones easier to identify and target."

"I thought this was a safe question." Chest tight, she closed her hand over his shoulder. "Don't worry, Dev. I won't let anyone take the knowledge from my mind." Not this time. Not ever again.

"Why do you think I told you?" A tone that left no room for doubt. And then he said the words she'd waited what felt like a lifetime to hear. "You won't betray us, Katya, no matter what the cost."

"*Dev.*"

"You beat him. You survived," he said quietly. "Ming has no claim on you anymore."

PETROKOV FAMILY ARCHIVES

Letter dated July 17, 1982

Dearest Matthew,

You're growing so big and strong, my boy. Your talent shines ever brighter. I wish we didn't have to uproot you at such a critical time, but I'd rather be safe than sorry. Several of the defectors have recently disappeared without a trace. They were all at the powerful end of the spectrum. There's specula-tion the Council is eradicating us.

Your father...he had a vision yesterday. He's so rarely truly with us these days that I wanted only to talk to him, but he used the minutes that he was awake and lucid to warn me. They're going to come after you, Matthew. You're too power-ful a telepath. So we have to run. And we have to keep running until they can no longer find even a trace of the Petrokovs.

Your father won't come with us. He calls himself a liabil-ity. And he won't listen to me when I say different. Before Silence, I used to tease him by quoting the Manual of Psy Designations. It says that F-Psy are considered some of the strongest individuals among our race because of what their ability demands. But today, he proved the definition true to the last word, my strong, courageous David.

He made me promise to go tomorrow. I don't know if I can. I don't know if I can leave the only man I've ever loved.

Mom

CHAPTER 43

You won't betray us, Katya, no matter what the cost.

He was more right than he knew, Katya thought two hours later, pain beating at her temples. Reaching out, she whispered her fingers over Dev's cheekbones, conscious he'd wake to anything but the most butterfly of touches. Even then, he shifted.

"It's just me," she whispered, as the exquisite ache in her heart threatened to tear her wide open. This, she thought, was love. She'd never felt it before but she *knew*. This feeling, it went soul deep, and it ravaged even as it healed. Devraj Santos had become an integral part of her. She couldn't let him go after Ming—she had every faith in his abilities, but she refused to lose him to a fool's errand.

There was no way to save her.

She'd realized that the instant after Dev had said she could live out her whole life without anyone being the wiser. True. Except that her whole life might only equal another month...if she was lucky. The thing with being in a prison was that after a while, your skin got pasty, your body got weak, and your mind began to beat itself against the walls in a vain effort to escape.

She was Psy.

She couldn't survive being permanently cut off from the Net.

The biofeedback alone wasn't enough. She had to be *some* part of the fabric of a neural network. Psychic isolation... It would drive her mad, increment by slow increment.

Her fingers lifted to her nose. Dev hadn't seen it. She'd hidden it. But there, in Sunshine, her nose had bled again. Just a little. But more than on the plane. It had been easy to shrug off the incident as being a consequence of the bitter cold—yet even then, part of her had begun to wonder. And now, tonight, as her skull threatened to implode from the agony of a sudden spiking headache, she accepted the truth—her brain was already starting to lose the battle. Her mind had begun its slow, steady beat against the walls of its prison.

Even if she somehow managed to hang on to her sanity, Ming had assured her end. She'd told Dev she was remembering more and more. She hadn't told him she'd remembered the final session.

Talons sinking into her mind, deep, so deep she knew she'd never get them out. "It hurts," she said tonelessly. It wasn't a complaint. He'd ordered her to tell him her reactions. She didn't understand why, when he could simply read her mind, but she wasn't going to rebel without reason. That brought pain so excruciating, one more episode might snap the final, fragile threads of her very self.

"Good." A "snick" that she heard with her psychic ear. "It's done."

She waited.

"Open your psychic eye."

It took her almost a minute, she'd been forced to keep herself contained for so long. All she saw was blackness. Then, as her eye adjusted, she began to make out the spiderweb linked to every part of her mind. Those thin threads fed back to thicker, darker, obscenely jagged roots.

Chilled, she moved around those talons . . . and slammed into an impenetrable black wall. Panic gripped her throat but she didn't make a sound. Instead, she padded around the walls until she was back at her starting point. "I'm locked inside my mind." It was the worst kind of nightmare. Even the rehabilitated, those Psy who'd had their minds destroyed by a psychic brainwipe, had access to the Net. Ming might as well have buried her alive.

"We wouldn't want your aberrant mental state affecting the Net." A small pause as he took a seat. "Your personal shields are under your control—you'd be useless otherwise. Telepathy appears to be your only offensive capability."

So, she thought, ignoring his deliberately belittling words, she could still do that much at least. But it wasn't the same— she'd never been so alone, her mind surgically excised from the herd.

"Why does it hurt?"

"An incentive to complete your mission within a particular time frame. The longer it takes, the less chance you have of actually obtaining any useful information before the Forgotten realize what you are."

"Incentive?"

"If you complete your primary task and return to me by the date imprinted in your mind, I'll consider removing the controls that are effectively starving parts of your brain into cell death."

"Those parts won't regenerate, no matter what. That's no incentive."

"On the contrary—all the parts that'll fail before the deadline are nonessential. After that point, your motor skills and ability to reason will go, followed quickly by the involuntary controls."

"Like breathing?"

"What else?"

She sucked in air, savoring something that was going to be lost to her soon enough. "If I come back, if I complete the primary task, you'll allow me to access the Net again?"

"I might even decide to retain you as one of my operatives." Coal black eyes with the rarest specks of white stared into hers. "You'd be a most effective assassin—after all, you don't exist."

Katya spread her fingers over the steady pulse of Dev's heartbeat as the pain of the headache dissipated, leaving only a dull bruise. More pain would come soon, but it didn't matter. She'd never complete the primary task. Not consciously. But she knew damn well that Ming wouldn't have left that to chance. How could she guard against a threat she couldn't see, couldn't even guess at?

If she were truly selfless, she'd slit her own throat.

Dev's eyes snapped open, startling her into a little gasp. "Dev?"

"What were you thinking?" Gold glittered in the depths of the rich brown that had come to mean everything to her.

"A nightmare," she said, and it wasn't a lie. "That's all."

He tugged her until she was almost under him. "I've got you. Sleep."

Heart thudding in reaction, she put her hand on his shoulder, let him tuck her close, and tried to find sleep. The thoughts that had somehow awakened him, she shoved to the back of her mind. Suicide, she realized belatedly, would destroy Dev. He'd blame himself. That was simply the man he was—protective to the core. She'd have to find some other way to save him from the loaded gun that was her mind.

Because killing Devraj Santos was simply not on the agenda.

CHAPTER 44

Judd Lauren walked into the church that Father Xavier Perez called home and took a seat in the last pew, beside the guerrilla fighter turned man of God. After a moment of silence, the other man sent him a slow glance. "No questions today, my friend?"

"I thought I might give you a break."

"And yet I see a question in your eyes."

"The Psy won," Judd said quietly. "In your corner of the world, the Psy won."

They'd first met in a bar in a no-name town in Paraguay. Judd had been there to liaise with a contact who never showed. Xavier had been sitting on the bar stool next to his and, tongue loosened by tequila, had begun to talk. Back before he became a no-good drunk, the priest had said, he'd been a man with simple needs— but one who believed in fairness. And there had been nothing fair in the way the Psy had effectively shut out the humans in his region from any kind of trade with the neighboring sectors.

First, it had been a political protest. But things had quickly escalated . . . until the Psy had crushed the human rebellion so thoroughly that not even an echo remained.

Xavier gave a slow nod, his skin gleaming ebony beneath the soft church lights. "Yes."

"And yet you believe in God."

Xavier took several minutes to answer. "There was a girl in my village," he said, his tone a caress. "Her name was Nina. She was...a bright light."

Before, Judd wouldn't have understood. Now he'd held Brenna, now he knew what it would do to him to lose her. "Did she die in the fight against the Psy?" The assassins had whispered into the village in the depths of the night, death their only agenda.

"We thought they might come," Xavier told him. "We never imagined they'd be as brutal as they were, but we got our vulnerable out."

Judd waited, knowing the story wasn't over.

"Nina wouldn't go. She was a nurse—she knew she'd be needed. She, like all of us, thought they'd rough us up some, leave us to lick our wounds."

"That must've put you in one hell of a mood."

Xavier's lips curved. "I threatened to tie her up and throw her on the back of a donkey if that was what it took."

"She stayed."

"Of course. Nina was pure steel beneath that sweet surface—I figured that out when we were six." The smile faded. "Then the Psy came, and I saw man after man fall, blood pouring out of their ears, their noses, their eyes."

A huge burst of psychic power, Judd knew, could do that. "If they'd had a full Squad, they could've done the whole village at once."

"Yes. But I suppose our little rebellion only merited two or three men. The ones who did come were powerful— ten men died in the first three minutes." Soft words, Xavier's hands remaining flat on his knees. "I managed to run Nina out through the jungle...and then I told her to jump in the river."

Judd had seen that river, seen the crumbling remains of what had once been a thriving village. "It was the only way out."

"It was a four-story fall—and Nina was never the strongest of swimmers." Xavier's hands curled, crushing the fabric of his white pants, part of the simple clothing of a Second Reformation priest. "But I promised her God would look after her, and then I kissed her good-bye. As she jumped, I prayed to God to keep her safe, to watch over her."

Judd knew without asking that Nina had never been found. "Why didn't you jump with her?"

"You're a soldier—you wouldn't have left either." Xavier took a deep breath. "Turns out my head is harder than anyone knew. The Psy blast knocked me out, but I regained consciousness hours later."

"A natural shield," Judd said. "Pure chance that you had it, that it was tough enough to deflect the hit." It was likely, he thought, that the Psy team had been using as little power as possible, because not even a natural shield could protect against a full telepathic blow. "You should be dead."

"The assassins obviously didn't bother to check to make sure I was—though I guess I *was* dead for the six months I spent drunk." He spread his hands again. "You're quiet, my friend."

From behind them, the Ghost finally spoke. "I'm waiting to hear the answer to Judd's question."

Judd had heard the other man come in, heard him lock the door, but hadn't turned. It was part of their unspoken code, one that kept faith with the Psy rebel who was both ruthless and—in his own way—utterly loyal.

"The answer," Judd said, "is that so long as Xavier believes in God, he can believe that Nina lives, that she somehow survived."

"That logic is inherently flawed," the Ghost pointed out, but there was something in his voice that Judd couldn't quite catch.

Xavier shook his head. "There *is* no logic to it, my friend.

It has everything to do with the heart and nothing to do with the head."

The Ghost said nothing. Judd hadn't expected him to. A man didn't survive the high-stakes game the other rebel was playing by being anything less than pure ice.

"So," Judd said, "why did you want to meet?"

The Ghost passed a data crystal over Judd's shoulder. "There have been some changes in the Arrow Squad."

Catching the crystal, Judd slid it into a pocket. "Deaths?"

"Seven men are currently being held in a facility deep in the Dinarides, a remote mountain range along the Adriatic. There's a possibility they've all been taken off Jax."

Judd took several minutes to think of the implications of such a radical shift. "Either it's as a result of a medical reaction—"

"—or the Arrows have decided Ming is no longer the leader they want to follow," the Ghost completed.

"Would it be that easy?" Xavier asked. "Won't the M-Psy be monitoring their reactions?"

"The medic in charge of monitoring Jax reactions is always another Arrow," Judd said quietly. "If that Arrow is no longer loyal to Ming..."

"What will they do if it's the latter?" the Ghost asked. "If they intend to take the leadership from Ming?"

"I won't betray my fellow Arrows." Each and every Arrow had been shaped by his or her ability, all of them lethal, all of them destroying their chances of a normal life. The fact that Judd was now on the other side of the war did nothing to sever that bond.

"The PsyNet can't handle rogue Arrows," the Ghost argued. "They could destabilize the entire system."

"No," Judd said. "An Arrow's first task is to maintain Silence. They'll do nothing to undermine the stability of the Net."

The Ghost didn't say anything further. Theirs was an alliance of equals, and the rebel knew Judd would not bend on this, as the Ghost wouldn't when it came to protecting the Net. It was Xavier who next spoke. "And you, my friend, what is your first loyalty?"

That was a question the Ghost had never answered. But it wasn't, Judd thought, the simple need to put the Net into better hands. Something far more personal drove the rebel.

Now, the Ghost rose. "I'll answer that question when I've completed the task demanded by that loyalty."

Until then, Judd thought, they'd continue to fight this war, not knowing if, when push came to shove, it would be the Ghost's logic or his ruthlessness that would prevail.

CHAPTER 45

Dev had the jet fly them to a private landing strip near his home in Vermont. Having had to make the long drive from the isolated bed-and-breakfast to the airstrip where the jet was waiting, they arrived in the late afternoon. Jack had called earlier to delay their meeting till the following day, so Dev had a few hours' grace, and he needed that time to think, to plan. Not only about what he'd say to his cousin, but also about how to end Ming's terrorization of Katya.

His hand fisted so tight, his bones ground together.

"Stop it." Katya put her hand over his. "Don't let him destroy you." Her voice was husky, she'd been trying to talk him out of his decision since before dawn.

"Should I let him destroy you instead?" He curled his fingers around hers.

"Dev."

He didn't say anything, and she finally went quiet. The rest of the trip passed in an edgy silence, but he didn't make the mistake of thinking she'd given up.

"I thought you needed to return to New York," she said as

they walked into his home. She frowned. "Dev, was the door unlocked?"

"No."

Her concern evaporated as she realized he'd probably had some kind of a remote in the car. "New York?"

Striding upstairs to throw their duffels into his bedroom, he called back over his shoulder, "I need some quiet time."

As she watched him come back down the stairs, she found a thread of laughter inside her. "So we'll be sleeping in separate bedrooms tonight?"

Leaning against the wall, he crooked a finger. "Come here and I'll tell you."

"Do you think I was born yesterday?" Folding her arms, she shook her head. "I'm staying right here, Mr. Santos."

He straightened, the barest hint of a smile curving his lips. "Then I guess I'll have to come to you."

An almost desperate need took hold of her as he walked over. Her time was running out. She hadn't had a nosebleed today, but a headache pounded at the back of her skull with relentless force. Bang. Bang. Bang. Bang. It made her want to curl up in a little ball and whimper.

But she wasn't going to waste time doing that, not when she had so little left.

Dev's smile turned grim as he came to stand in front of her. "How bad is it?" His fingers settled gently on her temples.

She melted into the touch. "I thought you weren't that strong a telepath."

"I was waiting for you to tell me," he said. "Or were you going to pretend you were fine?"

She recognized that she was being reprimanded, even though it was being done in that quiet, reasonable voice. "There's not much we can do. I have to deal with it using the usual mental exercises."

"They haven't worked for the past ten minutes, have they?"

Realizing his mind was far too acute to miss anything, she gave in. "Do you have an alternative?"

"Possibly," he said, to her surprise. "My ancestors were a rebellious lot, in case you hadn't guessed."

"Really?"

That got her a small smile. "Cheek suits you." A kiss so tender, tears burned at the backs of her eyes. "Sometime after they dropped out of the Net, one of the M-Psy started questioning the accepted knowledge that Psy react badly to all narcotics and painkillers." His fingers drifted down to the back of her head, pressing lightly.

It felt so good, she couldn't stop her little murmur of relief. "Did the M-Psy find a solution?" she said after almost a minute.

"Not a drug one." He shook his head. "You full-bloods are appallingly weak."

"And you half-bloods can't even telepath a foot."

A nip at her lower lip. "But, he did figure out a way to alleviate pain through the use of pressure points during massage."

"Did your ancestors pass the knowledge on to those in the PsyNet?"

"What do you think?"

Sighing, she placed her forehead against his chest, realizing the pain was already starting to fade. "The Council wouldn't have wanted any such close-contact healing when Silence was so young, so easily broken."

His fingers went down her neck, to her shoulders, then back up. "Yes. And then later, the touching would've gone against the conditioning."

"Sounds about right." Her arms were around his waist, the heat of him a familiar stroke. *I'll miss you so.* Dev trusted her enough to let her roam the house and grounds alone now. He'd never expect her to run. But she had to. Because if she didn't, she was terrified she'd lose herself to Ming's control, try to spill Dev's blood.

And once she was gone, Dev would have to drop his idea of going after Ming—no plan would work without her active participation. He'd be safe.

"Come to bed," he murmured against her ear. "I'm in a good mood—I'll give you a full-body massage."

"How generous," she teased, headache less than a dull throb now. "This has nothing to do with getting your hands on my naked body?"

Kisses brushed along the shell of her ear. "Of course it does—I don't massage for free."

She let him tug her into the bedroom, let him shut the door, strip off their jackets. *Just once more,* she told herself. Afterward…after he was asleep, she'd sneak out. He hadn't reset the house alarm, and that would have been the biggest hurdle. It would take an hour to reach the main road on foot, perhaps longer, but she had time. All the time in the world. Because she had no destination…aside from getting away from Dev.

But right this moment, she wanted simply to breathe in the scent of him, until it was imprinted into her very cells. When he pressed her back against the door, his hands on either side of her, she wrapped her arms around his neck and smiled in welcome. "Do I get a kiss before my massage?"

"Since you asked so nice." His lips were smiling when they touched hers, and she'd never guessed until this moment what it was to kiss a man you could laugh with. They smiled through the entire kiss, as he sipped at her, before slicking his tongue over her lips.

She danced her own tongue playfully over his, flirting but never delivering. He nipped at her in sensual punishment before taking her mouth with a dominance that was as natural to him as breathing. And through it all, he kept her pinned to the door, his heavier body a delicious source of pressure.

Smoothing her hands over his shoulders, she slipped her fingers under the sleeves of his T-shirt, glorying in the quint-essentially male strength of him. "Take off your T-shirt."

"I'm starting to think the headache was a ploy so you could have your wicked way with me."

A teasing Dev, Katya found, was a devastatingly sexy Dev. "You look hot—I thought it would cool you down."

That got her another laughter-filled kiss. He backed off only for the moments it took to strip off his T-shirt and throw it to the floor. She couldn't help but spread her fingers over the silky-rough surface of his chest as he returned to claim her mouth, his own hand closing possessively over her hip.

A single squeeze and she trembled. Feeling him smile at her response, she scratched her nails lightly down his back. "Again," he ordered, his voice husky.

When she did, she had the pleasure of feeling his big body shudder before he raised one hand to the back of her neck, kneading the tense muscles in a firm yet gentle sequence that made her moan as the last vestige of pain was replaced by pleasure, her body softening even further for him.

"Good?" An intimate murmur as she nuzzled against him.

"Mmm."

He continued to use those strong fingers on her, his head dipping to kiss the sensitive skin of her neck. Stroking her hands down his sides, she undid the top button of his jeans. He stilled but didn't stop her. And when she lowered the zipper, he sucked in a breath. Feeling bold and free and unashamedly female, she slid her hand beneath the waistband of his underwear.

"Katya."

Biting down gently along the tendon stretched taut on his neck, she caressed him, slow and easy, knowing it would drive him crazy in the best way. "How did I get to be the one giving the massage?"

A strained chuckle against her ear, a bitten-off curse. "Harder."

She did the opposite.

"You're going to get in trouble if you keep doing that."

Pressing an openmouthed kiss to his neck, she resumed her lazy stroking. "I'm not scared of a little trouble."

He pulled off her hand with such speed—pinning her wrists on either side of her head—that she barely had time to gasp in a breath before he kissed her...before he *took* her. She let him. Because, quite simply, there was something to be said for a man who knew what he wanted and made no bones about demanding it.

The feel of his strong hands on her wrists simply enhanced her pleasure. She tried to pull away, but only because it amplified the sensations. Dev knew. He used his body to hold her in place, even as his lips insisted she return every kiss, every little bite, every breath.

She gave him all she had.

And still he asked for more.

Melting, she ran the back of one foot over his calf, urging him closer. Her reward was the release of her hands, as his own slid down her back, pulling her up. Instinct had her putting her legs around him in a shockingly intimate embrace, the hottest part of her pressed to the hardest part of him.

But even then he wasn't satisfied. He shifted her until she was *exactly* where he wanted her. The pressure on her clitoris made her suck in a gasp, grip at his shoulders. "I can't—"

"Yes, you can." Another thorough kiss, their tongues dancing, tangling, loving. "Just a little more." He moved his body against hers, not gently, not hesitantly—no, this time, Dev was determined to push her over. And push her over he did. Into an erotic whirlpool from which there was no escape.

When her lashes finally lifted, she found herself being dropped lightly on the bed. Looking up, she watched as Dev pulled off her shoes, kicking off his own as he prowled up onto the bed from the other end. "You," he said, his eyes taking a slow journey down her body, "are seriously overdressed for the occasion."

"I'm too sated to move."

"I'm too happy to assist."

Feeling another smile bloom on her face, she let him unbutton her shirt. His fingers danced over her breasts as he pushed the fabric to either side of her body, half baring her... but making her feel far more naked than if she'd been stripped. The paradox intrigued her, but nowhere near as much as the golden heat in Dev's eyes.

Her body beginning to coil again, she bit her lower lip as he shifted to undo her jeans. Pulling both the denim and the soft cotton of her panties down in two quick tugs, he threw the clothing to the side and returned to her—taking a seat between her thighs.

Cheeks flushing as he ran his hands down the upper slope of each thigh, his eyes locked with hers, she swallowed. "I'm not completely naked, and yet, I feel so exposed."

"You look beautiful," he murmured, his gaze on the unsteady rise and fall of her breasts. Reaching up, he tugged at the cup of her bra until it slid aside to reveal a nipple, taut and begging for his touch. "Beautiful," he said again, dipping his head to take the hard nub into his mouth.

She cried out, the suction reaching straight through to the liquid heat between her thighs. Dev's knuckles brushed over her damp curls at that very moment. "Oh."

"So soft." Grazing her nipple with his teeth, Dev rose to look down at her.

She felt an absolute creature of the senses at that moment, flushed and without inhibitions. Reaching up, she went to caress him, but he stopped her hands. "It's my turn, remember?" And the wicked glint in his eye was the only warning she had before he began to kiss his way downward. She tried to grab at his shoulders, but he simply chuckled and kept going.

His kiss was hot, dark, wicked.

It was all she could do not to sob from the pleasure of it. Clutching at the sheets with desperate hands, she made no protest when he spread her thighs even farther and settled in to taste her as if she were some exotic banquet, and he a connoisseur.

"Shh." Strong hands stroked her down as he laved kisses on the delicate skin of her inner thighs.

But just as she'd almost gotten her breath back, he kissed her with that same devastating intimacy a second time, the tenderness of his touch doing nothing to hide the possessiveness. Part of her was convinced he knew she'd decided to leave him, but that thought was less than a flicker in the back of her mind. Right now, the endorphins flooding her body left no room for anything but pleasure.

Slow, seductive, sizzling.

A single lick and it was too much. She twisted away, desperate to escape . . . yet wanting more at the same time. *"Dev."*

Holding her hips in place, he pressed his lips to her navel. "Trust me."

She trusted him more than she'd ever trusted any other being. "I need you." It was a dangerous confession, but she had no barriers left.

His hands tightened on her, and then he was moving over her body in a molten wave of kisses, touch and pure heat. She found her lips taken again, even as he reached between them to free himself, shoving his clothing down just enough. It was still too slow—she was rubbing herself against him by then, hungry, so desperately hungry.

"Katya, baby, stop." It was a groan. "I can't hold on if you do that."

She raised her lips to his again, infusing her kiss with every ounce of passion in her. Shuddering, Dev gripped her hard on one hip. "I sure hope you're ready, sweetheart."

"Yes, yes!" Crying out as her body stretched around the hard thrust of his entry, she wrapped both legs around his waist. And then she let him lead.

He took her on a ride that eclipsed anything they'd ever before done. Wild, untamed, and vividly physical, they danced. The last thing Katya remembered was seeing Dev's eyes shimmer gold.

CHAPTER 46

"**Shower**," Dev said, all but carrying her to the bathroom.

"Later."

He pressed a kiss to her shoulder. "We're both sweaty—and I need to get some work done."

Holding on to him, she let him turn on the shower. The warm spray washed off the sweat of their lovemaking, and that was all they were capable of then. Dragging her out of the bathroom, Dev rubbed her down before doing the same to himself, while she tried to keep herself upright.

Just when her legs threatened to go out from under her, he dropped the towel and grabbed her. "We do that again," Dev muttered, "and I might not live to tell the tale."

Nuzzling her smiling face into the damp heat of his neck, she let him carry her to bed, lay her down on the tumbled sheets. "I'm so sleepy."

"Yeah, might be a good idea to catch an hour's shut-eye," he said with a yawn. "We didn't get much more than three hours last night."

As he pulled the blanket over them, her lashes fluttered

down. Body sated and wrung out, she tried to remember what she had to do. Leave. Yes, she had to do that.

But then Dev put an arm around her waist and pulled her close, and she surrendered to the selfishness in her that wanted another moment, another minute, another hour with him. *I'll go once he falls asleep,* she promised herself, never realizing that she was sliding into the same dreamless void herself.

Dev felt Katya leave the bed, his senses coming half-awake as he waited for her to return from the bathroom. It took him too long to realize he couldn't hear the tap running, any sounds at all. "Katya?"

He opened his eyes just in time to see her run into the room, the light from the setting sun dancing off the deadly blade in her hand. Snapping to full alertness as she lifted the murderous blade high above her head, he went to roll away, but something stopped him. The angle of the knife, it was wrong—"Katya!"

Blood spurted as she thrust the knife into her own thigh, crashing to the floor with a shattered cry of pain.

He was kneeling beside her almost before he remembered moving, his heart a hammer against his ribs, his entire body taut with adrenaline that had nowhere to go. "God damn it, baby." His words came out harsh, angry, even as he flicked on the light and focused on the wound, trying not to let the sound of her pained breathing distract him from doing what he had to do to help her.

But he couldn't stop the stream of angry words. "What the hell did you think you were doing? You could've hit your femoral artery." He was fucking glad to see that she hadn't. The knife, however, had gone in deep. "If you wanted to die, you should've told me. I'd have done it for you."

He gripped her leg hard, holding her in place as he reached for a nearby bureau, yanking out an old but clean shirt. "Leave it," he snapped when she went to pull out the blade. Her silent tears grated on his every protective instinct. But he was tearing the shirt and using the material to put pressure on the wound—working around the knife embedded in her—even as she sobbed. "It'll heal fast with the proper care, though I've a mind to sew you up myself. The stupidity—"

"Dev." Fingers on his stubbled jaw. Tear-stained eyes met his. "I was trying to kill you."

"So why did the knife end up in your thigh?" Under his touch, her skin was delicate, so easily bruised. "Talk."

A slow blink. "I *couldn't* drop the knife." She lifted her hand to her mouth as if ashamed.

He gripped her chin. "You call me next time. You fucking scream. You don't stab yourself."

"I couldn—"

"You could," he said, his tone hard. "If you can fight the compulsion enough to stab yourself, then you can fight it enough to let me know something's wrong." Continuing to keep pressure on her thigh with one hand, he used the other to rip away the hand she'd been using to cover up a nosebleed. "How bad?"

"Not so bad." She went to turn her head away but he forced her to face him as he used a strip of fabric to wipe away the blood.

Her cheeks pinkened. "I can do that."

It was the sheer normality of the reaction that convinced him she wasn't lying about the consequences of fighting what had clearly been an implanted suggestion. "It's fine." His voice was still sandpaper raw, and when she flinched, he knew it wasn't from the pain. Putting down the strip of cloth when it became obvious her nose had stopped bleeding, he dropped his head to press a kiss to the top of her knee.

An indrawn breath...then gentle feminine fingers in his hair, stroking, calming. He shuddered, felt his hands clench on her thigh, forced himself to loosen his grip. "We need to get you to a medic."

"You can do it." Another stroke through his hair.

He lifted his head. "No. The wound's too deep. I want someone qualified to look at it."

"I can't be DNA scanned." Fear glittered in her eyes.

Leaning forward, he gripped her nape and held her in place for a kiss that had no tenderness in it, he was so fucking scared for her. "I'll take care of it." But first he wanted her dressed, warm. "Keep the pressure on." Slapping her hand onto her thigh, he found his T-shirt, pulled it over her head, then wrapped her in a blanket.

She took a gasping breath and watched as he grabbed his cell phone from the bedside table without getting up. Flipping it open, he coded in a familiar number. "Connor," he said when the phone was answered on the other end. "Can you make a run to my place?"

"You hurt?" Instant alertness.

He could hear movement, as if Connor was already grabbing his gear. "No. But bring your full kit. Knife wound, deep."

"Bleeding?"

He glanced down, parting the blanket. The cotton of the shirt wasn't soaked through. "Contained, but there was some loss of blood before I got it stopped." Holding the phone between ear and shoulder, he used a couple of strips of fabric to wrap the makeshift pads into place.

"Patient conscious?"

He looked into hazel eyes gone a muddy green with pain. "Yes."

"Keep him that way. I'll be at your place in ten."

Hanging up without correcting Connor's assumption on the gender of his patient, Dev put the cell phone back on the table and got up. "Connor lives close. He'll be here soon." As he bent to pick her up, she protested. He ignored her. "Katya, I'm going to do exactly what I want, and you're going to let me."

She held on to his shoulders as he carried her to the bed and sat down with her in his lap. "I am?"

"Yes." His lips were on hers before he even knew he was going to kiss her, his hand once more at her nape, his knuckles brushed by the soft fall of her hair. He licked his tongue across the seam of her lips, gained entrance, and then he turned the raging animal in him loose. Because, how *dare* she hurt herself?

Katya just held on as Dev took total possession. Not long before, she'd thought she'd scaled the greatest heights of emotion with this man. She'd been wrong. Never before had she felt so utterly overwhelmed. Dev was no longer holding back even an iota of what made him the powerful man he was.

Trembling from the wild fury of the kiss, she gripped the solid muscles of his shoulders and did precisely what he'd told her she would—she let him do exactly what he wanted. Because this man was as wild as any changeling, as dangerous, and right now, so on edge, she had a feeling any resistance would be read as the wrong kind of challenge.

Not that she wanted to resist. His kiss, it was melting her from the inside out, the ice of the compulsion no kind of a barrier. She shifted even closer, wanting to strip off the T-shirt and press her body to his, to soak in the essence of him. Nothing and no one would stop Dev from taking what he wanted.

And right now, he wanted her.

But he broke the kiss far too soon. "How bad does it hurt?"

It took her a few seconds to realize what he was asking her. "Hardly."

"Shock." Lips compressing, he raised one hand to push her hair off her face. "Are you cold?"

"Not when you kiss me."

His eyes flared with a deeply sexual fire. "Oh, I plan to kiss you. After Connor's gone."

Dev watched as Connor cleaned out Katya's wound. When the man's long-fingered hands touched her skin, Dev had to grit his teeth to keep himself from ripping Connor's damn arm out of its socket. The reaction made no rational sense—not only was the quiet male a friend, he was also a highly qualified doctor. Though he chose to live in Vermont, he was a critical part of Shine's diagnostic team. It was Connor who'd worked out a way to pinpoint those at risk of the Talin Process Degeneration. Taking its name from the first identified case, TPD came about because of a lack of biofeedback—biofeedback the victims weren't aware they needed, because their need was so very small.

Dev knew all that. He also knew he wasn't rational. "How bad is it?" he snapped when Connor finished and turned to get something from his kit.

The other man arched an eyebrow at Dev's tone, but his own response was civil. "Not serious. The sealant will repair most of the damage, but I'm going to have to put in stitches first." He took out the stitch stapler.

"Those things hurt like a son of a bitch," Dev said, walking over to place his hand on Katya's hair. "Put yourself under," he told her, having already explained her genetic makeup to Connor.

She shook her head, and that stubborn angle to her jaw made it clear she wouldn't be changing her mind. Instead of forcing the issue, he nodded at Connor. "You got anything that'll numb the area?"

"Sure," the other man said, "but full-bloods react badly to anesthetics. Even that much might mess her up."

"Just do the stitches," Katya said. "It'll be a quick, fast pain, and then it'll be over."

Connor gave her a long look. "The wound will ache overnight, while the sealant works. After that, it shouldn't be worse than a deep bruise."

Katya gave a small nod and reached up. Instead of letting her take his hand, Dev sat down on the bed so he could look into her eyes, and tugged her face to the curve of his shoulder. "Do it," he ordered Connor.

As the other man went to work, Katya flinched and wrapped her arms around Dev in an iron-tight embrace. But she didn't make a sound, and a few seconds later, Connor was finished. Dev felt her body go limp as the doctor put a thin-skin bandage around her thigh.

"The staples will dissolve as the skin knits," Connor told him. "The bandage is waterproof so she can shower with it. No need to change it for three days unless she complains of heat or severe pain in that area—call me if that happens."

"I've got some of those bandages," Dev said when Connor held up a pack.

Nodding, the other man put them back in his kit. "Good night's sleep and she'll be fine." He got up.

Stroking a hand down the back of Katya's head, Dev settled her on the pillow and stood. "I'll be back in a minute."

She didn't say anything, but her eyes followed him as he exited the room. It took everything he had to leave her there, but Connor obviously needed to talk to him. The other man didn't say anything until they reached his car. "You going to tell me what you're doing with a full-blood?"

"No." The fewer people who knew the truth, the better. "You didn't see her."

"See who?" Throwing his medical kit into the passenger seat, Connor slid his lean form into the vehicle. "Let her rest."

Dev stopped in the process of turning around. "That's none of your business."

Connor met his eyes, the lines of his face even more austere in the early evening light. "Never thought I'd have to tell you how to take care of your woman."

Dev felt his fingers curl into a tight fist. "Lot of assumptions in that statement, Connor."

"Just telling it like I see it." He pulled the door shut.

Dev was inside the house before the other man finished reversing down the drive. Closing and locking the door, he strode down to the bedroom. Katya wasn't on the bed.

CHAPTER 47

Dev's eyes zeroed in on the bar of light showing under the bathroom door. He pushed through without knocking.

"Dev!" She pulled a towel in front of her body.

Lust kicked him hard—as if he hadn't all but killed himself with her mere hours ago. Every bit of the anger, the rage he'd felt at seeing her hurt seemed to have transmuted into pure need. Ignoring the savage hunger to teach her exactly how badly he took her hurting herself, he walked over and wrapped the towel more firmly around her damp body. "What the hell do you think you're doing?"

"I wanted to wash off the blood that dripped down my leg," she said. "It only took a minute."

"Then why are you trembling?" He swung her up in his arms without waiting for an answer. "If you've pulled out the stitches, I'm going to redo them, and I'm not as gentle as Connor."

Instead of snapping back at him, Katya nuzzled her face into his neck and said, "I'm sorry."

He knew she wasn't talking about the shower. "It wasn't

your fault." Placing her on the bed with all the tenderness he had in him, he lay down beside her. "They messed with your head."

Shimmering green-gold eyes met his as she shook her head. "I'm a walking weapon. I *knew* this was coming and I stayed. I should've left yesterday!"

He knew she was right. But he also knew it was far too late. "I told you—you're mine. I don't let go of what's mine." Pressing a kiss to her temple, he raised himself up on his arms.

She gripped his biceps. "Don't leave."

"I need to clean up the floor. I'll be back in a few minutes."

But the cleanup took a little longer than he'd expected, and she was asleep by the time he returned to the bed, curled up on her uninjured side. Sliding in beside her, he tugged away the towel with careful hands—he needed to wrap his body around her instead, feel her safe and warm, protected in his arms.

Only then did he allow himself to accept the fear that had gripped him when he'd seen her bleeding on the floor. Trembling, he pressed a kiss to her shoulder, drawing the clean, warm scent of her into his lungs. For the second time in his life, he was watching a woman who was everything to him slip from his fingers, and he could do nothing to stop it.

The agony of it ripped through him, until he half expected to see his own blood stain the sheets.

"No," he said, and it was a vow. He'd find a way to get Ming to undo or permanently block the compulsions, because no way was he ever again watching Katya cry because her mind had been violated, her limbs turned into a marionette's. And if Ming refused to cooperate—"I'll kill the bastard." He had to believe that once the Councilor was dead, Katya would be able to live a life free of fear.

She shifted in his arms, and he realized she'd woken. "It won't help, Dev—the shield will hold. And being trapped inside it...it's killing me cell by cell."

He refused to accept that, to give in. "Can he stop it, release the pressure?" He felt her body tense. "Don't you dare lie to me."

Another pause and he knew she wasn't going to give him the truth. "Don't do this to me, baby." He hugged her tight. "Don't make me helpless." Never again, he thought, never again would he be helpless while a woman he loved died in front of him.

Her body shuddered. "How can you ask me to lead you into death?"

"For me, Katya. Please." He wasn't a man used to begging, but he'd do anything it took to protect her.

"He *may* be able to," she said at last "He said I'd make the perfect sleeper assassin. I'd have to be alive for that, but I don't know what kind of a life it'd be."

Dev's anguish shifted to grim determination. "It'll be life. We can work out the rest later."

"He's a cardinal, Dev. His power...I can't describe it—it's endless, vast. He could turn your mind to putty with a single thought."

Dev had some abilities of his own, not all of them psychic. The director of Shine didn't need to be a powerful psychic— he needed to be ruthless enough to slit enemy throats if necessary. "You let me worry about that." Stroking his hand over her hair, he promised himself that Ming would pay for every second of pain, every injury, every drop of blood.

Even as Dev made his silent vow, the man in question was walking through the doors of the Dinarides facility. "All of the Arrows confined here," he said, "they're being monitored, restricted from using their abilities?"

The M-Psy beside him nodded. "Yes. All seven are cooperating at present."

At present. Ming knew he'd have to implement a much more final strategy if and when that cooperation stopped.

Arrows—even damaged Arrows—couldn't be contained indefinitely. "Where's Aden?"

"With one of the men—monitoring the effects of Jax withdrawal. It can sometimes cause sudden cardiac failure."

Ming looked at the M-Psy. Unlike Aden, and like most of the medical team, Keisha Bale was not an Arrow. "Aden," he said now, "is he showing any signs of unusual behavior?"

"As you know," Keisha began, "he was never put on Jax—it would've made him incapable of the value judgments required to monitor the effects of the drug on others." The M-Psy paused as they walked through a security checkpoint. "However," she said after the computer cleared them, "that shouldn't be a cause for concern. Aden's psychological profile makes him highly unlikely to deviate from the rule book."

That was what Ming was counting on. As a boy, Aden had been trained not only by other Arrows, but also by his parents—both members of the Squad at the time. He was the solitary living Arrow who'd been taught to become so from the cradle. Those were not easy bonds to break. Even had he wanted to, Aden lacked the medical knowledge to truly interfere—he'd had specialized training when it came to the effects and side effects of Jax, but aside from that, he was only a field medic.

Opening his telepathic channels, Ming contacted another one of the Squad. *Vasic, is the situation in Argentina under control?*

The answer came fast, though it wasn't as clear as Ming's voice, Vasic's Tp skills hitting just below 6 on the Gradient. *It's going to take a little longer than predicted.*

How much longer?

At least four more days. We can do it faster, but you specified no deaths.

Stick to the plan. Ming didn't want to kill the humans, not because humans weren't expendable, but because too many things had already been played out on the public stage. Even he had made that mistake with the destruction of the Implant lab—but he'd learned since then. It was time the Council returned to the old way of doing things—behind the scenes, where no one could stop them.

Dev's heart was still filled with a potent mix of anger, worry, and a furious kind of possession when he walked into the meeting with Jack, Connor, Aubry, Tiara, and Eva—the manager in charge of educational development—the next morning.

Jack and Tiara sat side by side, while Aubry and Eva sat opposite them. Connor, as the representative of the medical team, had positioned himself alone at the other end. Taking in everything with a single glance, Dev looked at Tiara. "Switched camps?" He knew she'd flown back from California specifically for this meeting, leaving Tag to watch over Cruz.

"Always been in this one," she said with a languid wave. "I'm sane, but there for the grace of God…"

"So you think we should encase our emotions in ice?" Aubry asked, obviously bewildered. "Damn, Ti, you really want to stop driving Tag crazy?"

Tiara shot him a cool smile. "What's between me and Tag is between me and Tag."

"Aubry is right," Eva interrupted, her accent lending an exotic music to her words. Born in Puerto Rico, she'd only been in New York for two years, since Dev relocated her from a field office on the island. "There'll be nothing between the two of you if we do what Jack wants and implement Silence."

"Hold on." Jack leaned forward, arms crossed on the table, face lined with grim determination. "You think I want to lose the light in my son's eyes? You think I *want* to teach him that love isn't something precious? You think I want to break his mother's heart?" He shook his head in a violent negative. "But my boy is already losing that light. He killed Spot."

A shocked silence.

Dev was the first one to speak. "That raggedy old dog of

his?" He couldn't believe it. William doted on the mutt his father had rescued from the pound.

"Yeah." Jack dropped his head into his hands. "Will cried so hard as we buried the dog. I knew we'd need the body, but I couldn't do it, couldn't put Spot in a chiller in front of him."

"Of course not," Dev said, and it was a gut reaction. "But you went back, didn't you?" He knew his cousin. Jack hadn't graduated at the top of his class in medical school without having a spine filled with pure grit.

"I did an autopsy the night of the day I talked to you, after Will was in bed." A glance at Dev. "I figured I could be of some use to my son—give him proof that he didn't kill his pet. I thought I'd find the old guy had had a heart attack or something."

Eva moved her hand across the table, as if to reach Jack. "He didn't?"

Jack shook his head again. "His heart was just...pulverized. Like a little bomb had exploded inside. The crazy thing is, there wasn't a mark on him on the outside."

"Hell." Connor spoke for the first time. "William's adamant it was him?"

Jack nodded. "His eyes that day—I've never seen such terror. Before...before we thought he might be a telekinetic. He's so accident-prone and the notes the rebels left behind say that young telekinetics are notoriously clumsy because they move things without realizing it."

Telekinetics, Dev thought, were also obsolete from the Forgotten population. The ability to move things with the mind had been one of the first gifts to go, which wasn't surprising as telekinetics had formed the smallest group among the rebel contingent. Dev's great-great-grandmother on his father's side, Zarina, had left a journal that Dev had read as a child. He'd never forgotten her words about the Tks.

I'm an M-Psy. My chances of insanity are low, but if I do go mad, I might possibly kill someone. However, if a strong

*Tk goes mad, he will almost certainly kill. And because Tks
are disproportionately male, as E-Psy are disproportionately female, he will kill his sister, his wife, his daughter.*

*That's a burden that crushes the Tks, makes them
turn inward. I don't blame all the telekinetics who chose
Silence. How can I? When I prayed every night that my
child would not be born a Tk. Only the X designation is
more cursed, and thankfully, that gene is so recessive it
rarely makes an appearance.*

"Did you have a genetic chart done on William?" Dev
asked his cousin. Things were in flux—there *was* a chance
the Tk gene had risen to the fore once again.

"We were about to when that happened, with Spot. I didn't
want to scare him by asking him to come in for tests."

"Do you have a genetic sample? Glen can run the DNA tests
with that," Dev said, looking to Connor for confirmation. He continued at the doctor's nod. "We'll have a starting point at least."

"Here." Jack put a sealed plastic bag on the table. "I
planned to ask for a DNA chart anyway. Got some of his hair
in there, his toothbrush, even a swab of blood from when he
cut himself running into a wall." His body jerked, those solid
shoulders of his shaking. "It's killing Melissa to watch him
literally will himself to death. Yesterday, I had to threaten her
with a sedative so she'd get some sleep—we're so afraid to
leave him alone for even a second."

Dev walked to stand beside his cousin, putting a hand on
his shoulder. "Don't give up, Jack. I promise you, we'll find
an answer."

"Silence is an answer," his cousin whispered, but there was
a weariness to him. "I wish it wasn't, but it is."

Meeting that familiar gaze, Dev knew what he had to say,
what he had to decide. "And if it is the only answer, then we'll
find a way to teach William to be Silent."

No one disagreed with him.

CHAPTER 48

Dev considered everything Jack had told him—both during and after the meeting—as he headed down to Katya. She'd volunteered to be confined to an isolation ward in the clinic while he wasn't able to be with her. It tore at his every protective instinct that she'd effectively imprisoned herself, but there was no knowing what grenades Ming had put in her head.

Soon, he promised himself. Soon, she'd be free. Today, however, he needed her help. But first—"How's your leg?" he asked, after kissing her gently on the forehead.

"Healing normally according to Dr. Herriford." A soft smile. "You want to ask me something."

It didn't surprise him that she knew. He knew her unspoken secrets, too. "What are the abilities that can cause death?"

"Pretty much all the strong offensive gifts," she told him, eyes troubled. "Telepaths and telekinetics are near definites. M-Psy, less so—it depends on whether we have an offensive gift we can couple with our M potential. Ps-Psy occasionally—"

"How?" As far as he knew, psychometrics used touch to

divine an object's past. Many worked for museums or private collectors, appraising which items were genuine, which fake.

"If an object has a violent past," Katya explained, "it occasionally 'short-circuits' one of the Ps-Psy, causing some kind of a temporary psychic injury. But I've heard rumors that some Ps-Psy can also absorb that violent power purposefully." She turned up her palms. "I never really had much reason to research them so my knowledge isn't that good. I'm sorry."

"You're doing fine. Any other designations?"

"Some of the old texts mention an ability more destructive than telekinesis, but to be honest, I can't think what that would be. Tks can collapse buildings on top of people—the truly powerful might even be able to cause small quakes."

None of which explained William's killing of his dog. There was, Dev knew, a very good chance the boy had been born with a violent New Generation ability. And if so, Silence might not be the cure Jack was hoping for.

"The person you really need to talk to," Katya murmured, "is an Arrow."

"The Council's bogeymen?"

"You know about them?"

"They're mentioned in our records." Dev's own ancestors had been hunted by the Arrows, families torn apart, loved ones forever lost.

"Well, they deal in death. They'd know all about the destructive abilities." She put her hand on his arm. "Unfortunately, I don't know any in the resistance. Ask Ashaya—she has more contacts."

Loath to leave Katya in a sterile environment that had to awaken terror-filled memories, he pressed a kiss to her lips. "One day, you'll be free of him. Then you can walk through any room you want, any place you want."

"One day."

But as he headed back upstairs, he knew their time was running out at an inexorable pace. According to the text Glen had sent to his phone half an hour ago, Katya had suffered a severe nosebleed that morning. And as he'd looked into her eyes before he'd left, he'd glimpsed a pinprick hemorrhage.

Rage tore through him, leaving devastation in its wake. Forcing himself to the comm panel in his office, he put through a call to Ashaya. Her eyes widened at his request. But all she said was "I need more information."

Dev sent through Jack's notes on his son—and on what William had done. "Ashaya, whoever you share this with, make sure you trust him absolutely."

"Understood. I'll get back to you as soon as I can."

Switching off the screen, he walked to the window. It was a cloudy winter's day, with snow an ominous threat in the sky, but New York moved with clockwork precision below him— there were so many Psy in the financial center of the country that efficiency was less striven for than expected. But even from this far up, he could spot the humans, the Forgotten, the changelings. They wore color. Splashes of bright red, azure blue, even shimmering gold.

The Psy shunned color, and if there was no other hope for William, the boy Dev had held as a newborn would learn to shun it, too. Why color? Perhaps, Dev thought, it was because the vibrancy of it spoke to something within the Psy soul, the same as music. No Psy ever sang, ever attended a symphony. He'd heard it said that their voices were uniformly flat, but he didn't believe it. No, what was more likely was that their voices had been flattened by Silence, by the cold control it took to maintain a stranglehold on emotions so powerful, they should never be contained.

The door opened behind him. "What is it, Maggie?"

"Is that any kind of greeting for your *nani*, Devraj?"

Spinning on his heel, he crossed the office with long strides to pull his grandmother's rangy form into his arms. "What are you doing here?" The scents of spice and paint filled the air, overlaid with an edge he'd always thought of as glass. As if Kiran Santos's love for her work had infiltrated her very being. "Where's Nana?"

"I left him at home." His grandmother winked as he drew back from the embrace. "I wanted to spend time with my other favorite man." Strong hands, scarred by a thousand nicks and cuts, closed on his upper arms. "You look tired, *beta*."

"You shouldn't be here," he said. "You know that."

"Don't you think the Psy spies know about me?" A squeeze of his arms. "Of course they do. They see me as a weakness, but I'm a strength."

He'd never yet won an argument with his grandmother. Giving in, he took the hand she held out to him. "Why are you here?" She'd always left him to run Shine as he saw fit, no matter that she hadn't agreed with all his decisions—such as the one that had precipitated a heart attack in a member of the old board earlier in the year. Dev hadn't apologized for that. He couldn't. Because the old board had been hiding from the truth, burying their heads in the sand.

Meanwhile their children had been dying, systematically culled by the Council.

"You needed me," his grandmother said, switching from English to Hindi without pause. "Why didn't you call or come to me on the ShadowNet?"

"Because there are no answers here."

"The woman," she said. "You care for her a great deal."

"Yes." A stark answer. "Yes."

"Tell me."

And he did. Because she was one of the very few people he trusted implicitly.

"I want to kill Ming—tear him apart with my bare hands— but what I really need from him is the key that'll release Katya from her psychic prison, wipe out the compulsions. For that, I need him to talk."

"Devraj, you must realize...holding a gun to Ming's head

will achieve nothing. Not unless you can somehow cut off all his avenues of escape."

That's why he liked his grandmother. She was practical. "It has to be a short, hard hit." A brutal hit. "Even if he gets out a telepathic cry for help, I have to convince him he'll die before that help reaches him."

"That assumes he has no teleporters at his command, and I wouldn't assume that."

"There's only been *one* report of a true teleporter, and our intel says he's currently somewhere in South America—not attached to Ming," Dev argued. "The others are Tks. Able to teleport, yes, but not as fast."

"Fast enough." His grandmother leaned forward, frown lines marking her forehead. "We need to discuss this with the woman. With your Katya."

"No. I can't risk—"

"Hush, Devraj." A fond smile. "Do you really think you're going to win this argument?"

He tried to scowl at her, but there was simply too much love in his heart for this woman. "I'm not putting you in danger. Katya tried to kill me," he said bluntly. "It may be that she's programmed to strike out at others close to me if she gets the chance."

"That's why I have a big, strong grandson to protect me."

And that was how Dev found himself in the subbasement level, standing at one end of the table while the two women who meant most to him in the world looked across at each other. Physically, they couldn't have been more different.

His *nani* was a tall woman with nut-brown skin and sparkling dark eyes. Katya was just barely of medium height, her skin almost translucent, though it had gained a little more color recently, her eyes a soft, wary hazel. His grandmother was tough, looked tough, her arms ropy with muscle. Katya in contrast, appeared soft...delicate.

An illusion.

The woman who'd walked through Sunshine, Alaska, without screaming was no weakling.

"So," his grandmother said, "you're the one who has my Devraj staying up nights."

Katya didn't turn to him, holding his grandmother's gaze. "Actually," she said, "I blame him for the sleepless nights."

Nani laughed. "I like her, *beta*." Reaching forward, she closed her hand around Katya's. "You should meet Dev's paternal great-grandfather, Matthew; he's the one Dev gets the stubborn from. Old goat's well over a hundred, but I haven't yet seen him back down from a fight."

Katya's eyes widened. "Was he—"

A nod. "Yes, he was alive when Silence first came into effect. His parents, Zarina and David, were part of the original rebellion."

Katya didn't speak for almost a minute. "He would've been a contemporary of the very first children who were Silenced in the Net."

"He remembers a cousin, said he saw him on the street years later, and it was as if the man's soul had been wiped away." The older woman shook her head. "Two different paths...though perhaps the paths are merging once again." There was a troubled note in her voice. "But that's not why we're here—we've been discussing how to disable Ming long enough that you can get him to set you free."

To her credit, Katya only blinked once. "We could render him unconscious, but that would defeat the purpose. If there is a key to unlock the shield, it has to be a telepathic one."

"There's also a high chance he could use the opportunity to kill you." Nani's tone was pragmatic.

Dev had already considered that. "Not if he knows that if she dies, he dies."

"Which brings us back to the point of how to disable Ming." Katya frowned.

And in that instant, Dev realized exactly what they had to do. Pacing from one end of the room to the other, he swept out a hand. "Leave that for now." His every instinct rebelled against the plan his brain told him was the only possible answer. "We'll need an exit strategy, too."

"Make him meet you on your ground," his grandmother suggested. "Turn him into the intruder—it'll make it much easier for you to get away."

"Getting him to come to us will be close to impossible," Katya said. "He's extremely security conscious." When Dev didn't reply, Katya looked up. And said, "Oh. You've already thought of the answer, haven't you?"

He didn't bother to lie. "Yes."

"When were you going to tell me?"

"Never—I planned to come up with another way." Thrusting his hand through his hair, he walked over to pull her up from her chair. "I don't like the idea of using you as bait."

"It's the best shot we've got." Cupping Dev's cheek, she made him meet her gaze. "We're doing this."

"Then you're damn well obeying every order I give you. Understood?" His voice was pure frost, protective rage barely contained.

"Yes."

Dev's grandmother sighed. "That's not the way, beti. With men like my grandson, you have to be disagreeable on principle."

Laughing at the amused advice, Katya reached out to take the other woman's hand, feeling so at ease it was as if she'd known Kiran forever. She never got that far. Her spine twisted into an unnatural shape as agony spiked down her body. The last thing she heard was her own high-pitched scream.

"What happened?" she asked Dev hours later from the hospital bed.

His cheekbones were razors against his skin as he gripped her hand. "Glen thinks your motor controls somehow shorted out at the same time that you had a problem with your nervous system." His voice was ragged, raw with anger.

"The countdown's speeded up." Even if Ming gave them the key, even if that key unlocked the shield, even if it miraculously released the talons sunk into her brain, whatever was already damaged could never be fixed. "There's more, isn't there?"

He swore. But he didn't let go of her hand, and she held on tight. Or tried to. "Please, I need to know."

His eyes were tormented when he looked at her. "We took a scan of your brain. Parts have been permanently compromised. You'll always have problems with your fine motor controls, your memories."

That explained why her fingers didn't quite grip right, didn't quite feel right. Rage boiled within her, but she didn't let it rise, afraid that if she did, it would be all she was, all she'd become. She loved this man too much to waste time on useless anger. "You won't reconsider trying to take Ming?" If Dev died . . . no, she'd make sure he didn't.

"No."

"Then let's put the game into play."

CHAPTER 49

Judd slipped into the child's room without anyone being the wiser. The boy stared at him wide-eyed as he shifted out of the shadows twenty minutes after the boy's parents had finally gone to bed. If Judd's intel was correct, however, both of them would be back to check on their son within the hour.

"Have you come to take me?" The child sounded both terrified and strangely glad.

Judd understood—in a way William's loving parents never would. "No. I've come to see if I can help you."

"You can't. I'm a monster." A tear leaked out of his eye, a tear he brushed off with an angry fist. "I hurt Spot."

Crossing the room to sit on the boy's bed, Judd raised a hand. "I need to touch you." This would have to be a very delicate telepathic investigation. If he activated the wrong trigger, the boy would try to strike out, and while Judd was well shielded, there was no need to make the kid feel worse about himself than he already did. "Will you lower your shields?"

"Okay." Dull compliance. As if he hurt so much, he'd given up.

Judd touched his fingers to William's temple, his psychic senses arrowed to a fine point. Then he went looking. According to the notes Ashaya had shared, the doctors at Shine had found an unusual version of the Tk gene, but what Judd saw was blindingly familiar. It seemed the Tk-Cell mutation didn't discriminate against the half-blooded.

This boy, this bright, beautiful young boy, was a murderer waiting to happen.

Judd's jaw set. No way in hell was that future ever going to be. "I want to tell you something and I want you to listen."

William nodded, but his eyes were dull.

Judd took the boy's chin in his hands, made him focus. "I can do what you can do."

"No one—"

Taking a pocket knife from his jacket, Judd flicked it open and ran the blade across his palm, releasing a thick line of blood. "Watch." Piece by piece, cell by cell, he closed the wound, until nothing remained but the blood. Using a tissue from the bedside table to wipe it off—and ensuring the tissue ended up in his pocket so he'd leave behind no trace of himself—he showed the boy his palm. "I can do what you can do."

This time, William's eyes were anything but dull. "Can you fix me?" he whispered.

Once, Judd would've answered with a yes or a no. That was before he fell in love with a woman who saw no evil in him. "There's nothing to fix. What I can do is teach you to control it. So you can use it for good things."

"Like what?"

"Like putting broken bodies back together."

He saw the boy consider that, his teddy bear clutched tight to his heart. "That wouldn't be so bad."

"Actually," Judd said. "It's better than that—it's pretty damn good."

A shaky smile. "Yeah?"

"Yeah. So, you ready for your first lesson?"

CHAPTER 50

Dev woke to the insistent beeping of his phone at two a.m. on the day they planned to corner Ming, very aware of Katya cuddled against him. Only when he felt her breathe did his heart settle into a steady rhythm.

Turning to the screen of the small comm unit on his bedside table, he flicked it on to find Jack's shaken face looking at him. "Dev, William's sitting here eating chocolate crunch cereal."

Dev shifted his brain into gear. "Weird time for it, but that's still good news, so why do you look like you saw a ghost?"

Shoving a trembling hand through his hair, Jack said, "Because my son tells me an Arrow came to see him tonight and started teaching him how to be good."

"Damn"—Dev whistled softly through his teeth—"she came through."

Jack wasn't listening, his attention fixed on something to his right. "I'll be there in a second, sweetheart." Returning his attention to Dev, Jack shook his head. "Melissa's just sitting there, petting his hair like she's afraid he's going to disappear. But he keeps on smiling."

"The Arrow isn't a threat to William," Dev said, knowing Ashaya Aleine would never harm another mother's son. "I have a feeling he has to worry about his own name getting out—that's probably why the night visit."

"I don't care if he wants to visit at three in the fucking morning if he can do this for my son." A shaky laugh. "I'll do whatever the man wants. All you have to do is tell me."

Three hours later, Dev called Jack back. "He wants you to move to San Francisco." The information had been relayed through Dorian.

"Man's got family to protect," Dorian had said. "Less people who know what he can do the better. I didn't even know before he decided to tell me today."

Dev raised an eyebrow. "This guy sounds secretive."

"I'd have him at my back anytime." A steady gaze. "He's determined to help that kid—determined enough to share a secret he's kept for a hell of a long time, so if I was you, I'd do exactly as he says."

Now Jack didn't hesitate for even a second. "I'll start packing."

Hanging up, Dev met the eyes of the woman who'd just exited the bathroom. "Come to bed."

She didn't argue, but as she walked across the room, he saw something that made his spine knot. "Your balance is off."

"Yes." Sliding into the bed, she ran her fingers down the roughness of his jaw. "But I don't want to talk about that right now. Love me, Dev."

And because he could deny her nothing, he did as she asked.

If Dev had allowed himself to acknowledge the enraged helplessness that twisted around his mind in a thousand coils, he might've done something stupid. As it was, he compartmentalized. It was a skill he'd gotten very good at as a child.

The machines, the metal, usually helped, but never when it came to Katya. She reached too deep, made him feel too much.

"I didn't think the non-Silent could do that," Katya said to him that evening as they discussed the final preparations. A bare two hours remained. Dev would've preferred a longer lead-up, but not only would Ming be in the city today, but the longer they waited, the more Katya would lose of herself.

"Do what?" he asked, looking up from his sketch of the location where they planned to lure the bastard.

"Shut away emotional responses." Rising from her seat on the sofa in front of him, she walked over to sit on the arm of his chair. "You've gone cold."

His slid his own arm around her waist in an instinctively protective gesture. "It's necessary." Tugging gently, he brought her into his embrace. "A soldier can't operate unless he's completely focused on the target."

"How long were you a soldier?"

"Few years after high school." He frowned and annotated a gap in the net of snipers he planned to have cover the meeting spot. "I decided it'd be the easiest way to get the kind of training I needed."

"Needed for what?" A warm hand along his nape, a kiss pressed to his cheekbone.

"Katya." It was meant to be an admonishment, but he was lost the instant he met those hazel eyes. Groaning, he pulled her down with a hand on the back of her head and bit at her lower lip in sensual punishment. "I know what you're trying to do."

Her gaze darkened to jade shot with tiger's-eye. "Let me."

"I can't."

It took her long minutes to release a sigh. "I don't want to lose you."

He looked at her, waiting for her to understand.

"No," she said after almost thirty seconds of silence. "I wouldn't choose safety either if it was you."

He kissed her for that, for accepting his need to protect her, keep her safe.

Afterward, she nuzzled into his throat. "Just a few minutes."

"Just a few." He needed to have every piece in its absolute accurate place or it would all turn to shit. If they worked it exactly right, the Councilor would find a physical meeting more expedient than a psychic one. Because a meeting on the psychic plane would leave Katya ultimately vulnerable—Dev was sure Ming had a hidden back door into her mind, one that would allow him to easily skirt the shields he'd put in place and take anything he wanted.

"Is it all from being a soldier? Your ability to compartmentalize?"

Shadows whispered at the back of his mind, voracious and grasping. He fought their attempts to drag him back into the grief-shrouded past. "Why?"

"There's a sense about you . . . as if the need for control is ingrained into your soul."

"One way to put it." Releasing a slow breath, he ran his hand over her hair. "I told you my father killed my mother. What I didn't tell you is that I witnessed the murder." He kept his voice even, his words clear. That emotional stranglehold was the only weapon he had to fight the shadows' insidious taunts.

"Oh, Dev." A soft whisper, his pain echoed in her voice. "How old were you?"

"Old enough to understand that my father shouldn't have his hands around my mother's neck like that but not old enough to pull him off." The memory haunted him every day of his life. If only he'd been stronger. But he'd been a slight boy of barely nine, his father a big man who outweighed him four times over. "He probably would've killed me, too, except that my mother managed to broadcast a telepathic scream for help."

He could still hear the jagged shock of the door being

broken open, the stamp of booted feet, shouting, then people thumping fists onto his mother's chest and breathing into her mouth. Her chest had begun to rise and fall, feeding his hope...until he'd realized that she wasn't doing it on her own, that she wasn't really breathing.

"It took the rescuers ten minutes to realize I was in the room." He'd been thrown into a corner by his father's back-hand, had lain there dazed and bleeding as his world shattered in front of him. "I saw them drag my screaming, crying father from the room. Then I saw them pronounce my mother dead."

Katya's kiss was a benediction against his forehead. "Honed in fire," she murmured. "Did your father suffer a psychotic episode?"

"Yes. And he never really came back. He spends almost all of his time in a room in a facility in Pennsylvania. It's a nice place, lots of gardens, trees, real peaceful, but he only ever leaves his room when he's forced to, or if I visit."

"Do you visit him often?"

"No." He closed his hand around her hip, his grip tight. "The adult in me, the reasoned being, understands that he didn't do what he did out of choice. So I go. But then I see him, and I'm that child again, watching him snuff out my mother's life. And I can't go that last step—I can't forgive him."

"At leas—" Katya began, just as Dev's watch beeped.

"This can wait," he said, shamefully relieved. "It's time."

Forty-five minutes later found them sitting in a car outside a row of storage lockers located on the eastern edge of Queens, Katya at the wheel. Dev had chosen the location for two very important reasons—one, it was out of the way, lessening the chances of interruption, and two, it gave the snipers an excellent line of sight.

"Okay," he said, checking his phone. "The business association dinner's about to wind up. He'll be on the road within the next ten minutes. Surveillance confirms the teleporter isn't with him—this is our best shot."

Rubbing her hands on her thighs, Katya looked at him. "I don't know if I can do this."

"You have to, baby. If he decides to utilize a back door into your mind, he needs to see what he expects." Reaching over, he pulled her out of her seat and into his lap. "Hopefully, his arrogance will have him accepting everything at face value."

"I don't want to share this with him." She put her hands on his face. "I don't want him to know how much you matter."

"He won't," Dev whispered, the gold in his eyes electric in the hushed dark inside the car. "He has no comprehension of what it is to feel this much for someone." He brushed her hair off her face.

She had no defenses against him. So she leaned forward and took his mouth in a soft, sweet kiss. Tenderness and pain ravaged her in equal measures as he put his arms around her. Taking the taste of him inside her mouth, she allowed him to seize the lead, to kiss her as if he'd never get enough.

Fire licked up her spine, passion rising even in the midst of chaos. When his hands slipped under her sweatshirt to move up her back, she shivered. Focusing only on the sensations, on the heat he could stoke so easily, she moaned in the back of her throat and moved her hand to his neck, playing her fingers over his pulse.

He nipped at her mouth, his own hands sweeping around to cup her breasts. Hunger rocked through her, but it was then, while he was distracted, that she dropped the pressure injector hidden in the sleeve of her sweatshirt into her palm. "I'm sorry, Dev." Pressing the injector to the pulse in his neck, she pushed the trigger.

His body jerked. Breaking the kiss, he stared at her. "Katya?" Betrayal snuffed out the gold and an instant later, his head slumped back on the seat.

CHAPTER 51

Swallowing tears, Katya picked up his cell phone and input a number she'd found embedded in her memory.

Ming's voice was an ice-cold blade at the other end. "Councilor LeBon."

"I have him," she whispered, letting her desperation, her fear, her anguish flood her mind.

A pause. "This is unexpected." The crawling brush of fingers slithering over her mind. "A double cross, Ekaterina? I wouldn't have thought it of you."

Nausea roiled as those fingers probed and violated. "I want to live." She kept her thoughts mired in the torment she'd felt the instant Dev understood what she'd done. "You promised you'd release me if I delivered Devraj Santos."

"I ordered you to kill him."

"I thought you'd prefer him alive if you could get him that way." The fingers retreated from her mind, but she didn't breathe a sigh of relief.

"True." Another pause. "Where are you?"

She gave him the coordinates. "There are sharpshooters waiting for you."

"I see that. Since I'm without a teleporter at the moment, I'll drive to you. Wait for further instructions."

Hanging up, Katya dropped her forehead to Dev's, wanting to sob but knowing she couldn't indulge the need. Instead, she shifted back into the driver's seat and took a deep breath, feeling her chest muscles strain against the pressure. Her fingers trembled on the steering wheel, but it wasn't from fear. She was losing more and more pieces of her body, her self.

The cell phone rang seven minutes later.

"Drive out of your current location," Ming told her. "There's an empty lot ten blocks to the left."

"I'm on my way." Closing the phone, she started up the engine and headed out into the late evening darkness. Dev's phone rang almost immediately. She knew it was his team, trying to figure out what the hell was going on.

She snapped the phone open. "Change of plans," she said to Aubry. "We've been directed to another meeting point."

"Where? I need to get my men to—"

She gave him the coordinates to a location ten minutes from the correct one. "Hurry."

"Give the phone to Dev."

Knowing the other man would never believe anything else she said, Katya hung up. And drove like a bat out of hell, certain Aubry and his people wouldn't be able to get to their vehicles fast enough to follow her.

She screeched into the empty lot behind a huge warehouse less than five minutes later. Ming's dark sedan was waiting for her, the windows opaque. Bringing her car to a stop beside it, she got out, her left leg shaky but still capable of keeping her upright. And her fingers…they were strong enough to complete this.

The back window lowered to reveal Ming's face. "I have to admit," the Councilor said, "given what I glimpsed in your memories, I would have expected you to have turned traitor."

"I want to live." Repeating her earlier words, she folded her arms as Ming's driver/bodyguard got out—pinning her with a cool stare from the other side of the car.

"Your memories didn't come back early enough," Ming mused, looking at her as if she were an experiment. "Unfortunate that you were handicapped for such an extended period. The amnesia was only meant to give you a cover long enough for them to trust you."

She ignored his words. "You said you'd be able to fix me."

Ming leaned back in his seat. "You've left it too late. There's no way to repair the damage."

"Stop it advancing then."

Ming spoke to the driver. "Get the Shine director."

As the Arrow—and the driver was unquestionably part of the Council's most lethal private army—came around the front of Ming's sedan, Katya said, "Stop."

Of course he didn't. She turned to Ming, feeling the hairs on the back of her neck rise as the Arrow reached Dev's side of the vehicle. "You lied, didn't you?" she asked, letting him hear her anger. "You were never going to be able to undo what you did to me. The shield is unbreakable."

"Yes, and as the lines of programming are linked directly to it—ah, you didn't know that."

"I was dead the moment you took me."

"You did well, Ekaterina." Pincers closing around her brain. "If I'd known you'd prove this useful, I wouldn't have anchored the shield in your brain, but what's done is done."

And now, she thought, hearing the Arrow push back Dev's door, it was time for her to die. "You know, Ming," she said, as a line of wet trickled out of her ear, as her left leg began to spasm, "I'm really not as stupid as you think." Bringing out the sleek little gun hidden in her lower back, she shot him in the head.

A solid thump sounded from behind her...the impact of a body hitting the ground.

Blood covered her, having spurted through Ming's open window, but her attention was elsewhere. "Dev?"

"He's down. Stunned." Getting out of the passenger seat, Dev ran to her. "Damn it to hell, Katya, he could've—"

She shook her head, dropping her gun hand to her side. "No. Part of me always knew it had to be a lie. You can't undo a trap that severe."

Something flickered on the other side of Ming's vehicle.

"Get in the car!" Shoving her inside, Dev crashed in behind her. As he spun them out of the lot and away, the car reacting unbelievably fast, she turned to look.

Ming's car had somehow collapsed inward, as if someone had crumpled the frame like so much paper. "Dev?" she whispered.

"Turns out that frame had some metal in it" was his cryptic answer. "How many men teleported in?"

"Four." She could see them silhouetted against the New York skyline. All were wearing the unrelieved black of the Arrow Squad. The fact that they were still at Ming's vehicle as Dev's car disappeared around the corner made her jaw tighten. "Ming's not dead."

Dev hung up the phone, meeting Katya's eyes as she sat on their bed, her arms locked around raised knees. "You're right, the bastard survived." DarkRiver's Psy contact had come through again. It made Dev wonder how high up in the superstructure that contact was, but he wasn't idiotic enough to jeopardize the man's cover by asking too many questions.

"I shot him in the head."

"He has the devil's luck." Climbing onto the bed, he sat with his legs bracketing her, his hands cupping her face. "The bullet blasted through and straight out the other side, along the very top of his skull. He's unconscious but predictions are he'll make a full recovery."

"Will it all come back on you? On Shine?"

"No, baby." He moved his body closer around hers, hating to see her like this, so quiet, so shattered. "This is simply another chapter in a war we've been fighting since my ancestors dropped from the Net. It's just out in the open now."

"Are you mad at me?"

"Yes." He could still remember the sheer panic he'd felt at being trapped in the car while she stood so close to Ming. "You weren't supposed to actually knock me out." The dose had been small—he'd started to come out of it even as they peeled out of the first meeting spot, but the injector had been meant to be empty.

"Because I know how thorough Ming is," she said, her fingers curling into his T-shirt right over his heart. "He'd never have missed that. I had to make him think I'd pulled off the ultimate double cross, made you believe I cared for you... then delivered you up to save my own life."

"And he's so sure of his power, he didn't bother to look beyond the surface."

"No." A tight smile. "I'm nothing to him—he can't comprehend that I might have a mind of my own."

He locked his arms behind her, his fingers clenched. "Where did you get the gun?"

She'd wondered when he'd ask her that question. "Guess."

"My grandmother."

"Yes." Katya had expected an immediate "no" to her request. Instead Kiran Santos had looked into her eyes for a long moment before reaching into her purse and retrieving the weapon. "At first, I couldn't believe she trusted me, then I realized it's you she trusts." She spread her fingers over his heartbeat. "Will you tell me about why locks open for you?"

"Figured that out, did you?" A lighthearted comment, and yet his soul went cold. Because if she was asking him for secrets... *"No."*

"Please—I'm so curious."

And because he could deny her nothing, he told her about his affinity to metal. "At first, it was just metal. I could sense it, feel it, taste it. The chill of it keeps me calm when everyone else is exploding." Except with her. Never had it worked with her. "As I grew older, I found I could manipulate objects with metallic components, like deadbolts."

"Did it develop further?"

"This year," he said, "I've begun to 'connect' with machines that have very few metallic components—I'm talking a single circuit. I can now command computers on a basic level, such as those in cars. In time, I might literally be able to 'talk' to much more sophisticated systems—Glen and Connor think it's possible I could grow beyond the need for metal altogether."

"Extraordinary," she whispered. "You're developing the ability to interface with machines on the mental level." For an instant, the pain receded from her voice as the scientist took over. "It's a skill specific to the technological age."

"That's what the docs say." Releasing the death grip he had on his own hands, he cupped the back of her head, stroked her nape. "Want to see a cool trick?"

A little nod, weak, too weak. Pain shot along his jaw, down his spine, but he didn't let the emotions out, didn't break when she needed him to stay strong. "Watch." Focusing, he drew metal to him.

"Oh!" Katya ducked as a small metal sculpture attached itself to his arm. "You're magnetic?"

"No." He pulled the sculpture off, placing it on a nearby table. "Though the effect is the same. You should see me with spoons."

A smile that tried so hard to hold on. But he *knew*. "Katya?"

"I'm so sorry, Dev." She blinked in a rapid burst. "I can't feel my lower legs anymore."

His entire body jerked. "*No*. Not yet."

"Not yet," she agreed. She couldn't let him go. "We don't

have to worry about any other embedded compulsions—I'm not strong enough to be dangerous."

"Ming?" A single harsh word.

"As long as Ming's unconscious, his Arrows won't be able to find me. He did too good a job of hiding me." She'd been his pet project, his little perversion. "But when he wakes—"

Dev kissed her, halting her words. She surrendered, more than willing to delay the inevitable. Just a few more days, she thought, a few more hours with this man she adored to the deepest core of her soul.

Dev wanted only to hold Katya every second of every minute, but the director of the Shine Foundation didn't have that luxury. "I'll be back as soon as I can," he told her the next morning as she lay curled up on the sofa in the sunroom of his Vermont home.

"Don't worry. I'll be fine." She glanced toward the hallway. "Your friend Connor will be here."

"I can't leave you alone when you're so getting so weak," he said. "Don't ask me to."

"According to your grandmother, I should disagree with you on principle, but you already have bags under your eyes." Lifting a hand, she placed her fingers on his pulse in that way she had. "I'll be waiting for you."

He kept that promise close to his heart as he walked out the door. Cutting the travel time short by using a jet-chopper instead of driving, he arrived in New York twenty minutes later. His first task was to check in with Cruz. He'd talked to the boy on his cell phone a couple of days back, but it was good to see that dimpled smile on-screen.

"He's even starting to like me," Tag said when Dev transferred over to Cruz's current guardian.

"You okay on your own?"

"Cruz is behaving. And Ti'll be back after the meeting today." A pause. "Good luck, man."

Dev knew he'd need that luck as he walked into the meeting. With Jack having withdrawn his appeal for Silence, the fractious situation within the Forgotten had calmed, but it was by no means over.

"I can't stop any of you who want to practice some kind of conditioning," he now said to the men and women around the meeting table. "But here's what I think—we found a way to help William, could be, we find a way to help the others, too."

"Lot of coulds and maybes, Dev."

He met Tiara's distinctive eyes. "Case-by-case situation." He'd thought this over, would go to the floor to save his people. "And Aubry had a point—can you honestly tell me you'd be happy living a life where you didn't spend half of it teasing Tag? Jesus Christ, his balls must be fucking purple by now."

"Way past," Aubry muttered. "I'm pretty sure the pitiful things are about to fall off."

Tiara's cheeks went red as several people around the table snickered. But she wasn't one to back down. "Since when are you interested in other men's balls, Aubry? Something we should know, hmm?"

Another round of snickers as heads turned toward Aubry.

"Look at us," Dev said, rescuing his second-in-command, "we're on opposite sides and still able to laugh about it. That doesn't happen with the Psy."

A few nods, troubled glances. "But Dev," another woman, a solid member of the board, said, "this is the tip of the iceberg. What if we can't find a way forward?"

"The Forgotten have always been known for their courage under fire. We *will* find a way." He had to believe that—not only for his people, but for his Katya. "I'd like to read you all something," he said. "This is a letter that my great-great-grandmother wrote to her son. She was an M-Psy, her husband a foreseer. It's dated November eighth, 1984."

He waited to ensure everyone was listening. "'Dearest Matthew,'" he read, "'We buried your father today. Do you know what his last words were to me? "Damn stubborn woman."'"

A ripple of restrained laughter.

He continued reading. "'You better believe it. I wasn't going to leave my husband behind when the Council's murderers came after us, no way, no bloody how. We only had two more years together, but those two will last me a lifetime.

"'So now you know—you come from the stubbornest stock this side of the equator. No one is going to stop your star from shining.'" Putting the page on the table, he met each gaze in turn. "Zarina buried her husband, and still she fought for her children's right to be free. How can we do any less?"

The meeting disbanded an hour later, with the unanimous agreement that they'd make no move toward any kind of a Silence program. The Forgotten had fought too long, and too hard, to give in this easily.

Dev called Katya on the comm panel as soon as he was able. "How are you?"

"Fine." Her lips curved. "Connor brought me a smoothie—he said you threatened to cut his legs off at the knees if he forgot."

"Damn straight." Heart a forever ache in his chest, he simply looked at her for a long moment. "I should be home around eight tonight."

"How did the meeting go?"

He'd stopped hiding things from her the instant he'd understood the truth, understood how little time he had to share his world with this extraordinary, beautiful woman. "There are going to be no easy answers for the Forgotten. We'll have to ride the tides and see where they take us."

"That's freedom, Dev," Katya whispered. "Don't ever give it up."

CHAPTER 52

Katya had thought hard all night about what she was about to do, knowing that at this moment, she could ask anything of Dev and he'd give it to her. She didn't want to take advantage of that, and yet, at the same time, she knew she'd never again have the chance to do this.

Crossing over to him, her lower legs encased in computronic black carapaces that gave her the strength to move, she put her hand on his shoulder.

He looked up from his contemplation of the snow-draped woods. "Sit on the steps with me."

"I want to ask you something."

"Anything."

"I'd like to meet your father."

His shoulder turned to rock under her hand. "Why?"

"There are so many things I want to do with you," she whispered, "things I know I'm never going to get the chance to do, but maybe, there is one thing I can do."

"I'm not going to forgive him now if I haven't all these years." He stared straight ahead.

"I know." She slid down to sit beside him. "But maybe you can see him through new eyes."

"It'll be a waste of time."

"Please, Dev, do it for me."

"Below the belt, baby," he whispered, wrapping one strong arm around her shoulders. "Damn unfair."

Her eyes burned at the pain she could feel in the big body beside hers. "A woman's got to use what she has with you."

The faintest hint of a smile. But it was layered in a heavy wave of darkness, of loss. "Alright. I'll take you to him."

Four hours from the time she'd asked him, they walked into the large, sunny visiting room of the place Dev's father called home. It was, as Dev had said, a lovely place. Cane chairs with soft white cushions lay in easy conversational groupings, while indoor plants soaked up the sunshine coming in through windows that looked out over the sprawling gardens. The plants outside lay in winter sleep, but even so it was a peaceful vista.

But the gardens apparently held no appeal for the lone man who sat by the windows. His attention was locked on the doorway.

Katya's heart stopped as she met those eyes. "Dev, you look so much alike." Except for the color of his skin, Massey Petrokov was the mold from which Dev had been cast.

"Yeah." Dev's hand clenched around her waist.

She waited for something more, but he went silent. Massey watched them approach with the same silence. But when she reached him, what she saw in his eyes made her own burn—the abject apology as he looked at his son, the complete lack of hope…it broke her heart. "Hello, Mr. Petrokov," she said, taking a seat opposite him.

The older man—his face aged far beyond his years—finally looked away from Dev. "You belong to my son."

"Yes."

"He'll take care of you," Massey said, his gaze following Dev as his son walked to stand facing the windows on Katya's left. "He won't hurt you."

"I know." She waited until the man turned back to her. "Will you tell me about her?"

"Her?"

"Dev's mother."

Dev's entire body froze, but he didn't say a word.

Massey swallowed. "I don't have the right to say her name."

"Please."

After a long, long moment, Massey began speaking, his eyes locked on his son's back. "We were teenagers when we met. She was the bright, funny girl. I was the jock. But we always found something to say to each other. She made me feel smart." A smile as he fell into memory. "She used to say I made her feel strong."

At that moment, there was nothing insane or broken about Massey Petrokov. He was a young man, his whole life ahead of him.

"I asked her to marry me after I finished college—on a football scholarship. I knew even then that she was going places, but that was okay with me." A small laugh. "I used to say I'd be the househusband while she took over the world."

"Were you?"

"Yes." Another smile. "I played for four years, then got injured. But I made good money those few years, and my Sarita was already on the fast track at her investment firm, so we were okay financially. We decided to try for a child. She got pregnant almost immediately."

Katya didn't dare glance at Dev, but she could almost feel his concentration. "Did she like being pregnant?"

Massey blinked at the words, as if he'd forgotten her presence. "It surprised her how much she liked it. She'd thought she'd have trouble bonding with her baby—she never really saw herself as maternal. But right from the word go, she adored everything about the child in her womb." Massey turned to his son again, speaking to the rigid line of his back. "Grape juice and bananas, that's all she wanted to eat half the time."

A quiet pause, filled only with the soft shush of a nurse's footsteps in the corridor on the other side.

"She was meant to go back to work twelve months after Dev was born, but she took another year off. We managed." His eyes glazed over again. "But after that, it was mostly me and Dev. We were thick as thieves—I used to make him his lunch, take him to kindergarten, then school, help him with his homework. Sarita used to call us her Two Musketeers."

The depth of Dev's sense of betrayal made so much more sense now. He'd adored both parents, but he had to have been closer to his father simply because of the amount of time they spent together. "It sounds like a good life."

"It was." His shoulders began to shake. "But then..." A jagged sob. "I never meant to hurt her. She was the only woman I ever loved."

Unable to stand his pain, Katya reached forward to take his hands. "It wasn't a conscious choice," she whispered. "Your mind wasn't your own." She knew all about that, about being made a puppet.

Massey just shook his head as he cried. "But I killed her. And I'll carry that guilt for the rest of my life." Shifts in his eyes, as if something was trying to get out. "I'm not lucid much these days," he said clearly, even as tears rolled down his cheeks. "I wish I was never lucid." Another pulse of darkness, fragments of a broken mind trying to retake control.

Katya felt movement, then saw Dev's hand close over his father's shoulder. "You weren't you," he said, his voice raw with emotion. "Not that day." He didn't seem to be able to get out any more words, but they weren't needed. Massey's face filled with such joy that it hurt Katya to look at it.

"My boy," he said. "My Sarita's precious Devraj." One of his hands left hers to close over Dev's.

They sat that way for a while...until Massey Petrokov could no longer hold on to his sanity.

"How did you know to ask about my mother?" Dev asked as they walked back into his home. It was the first time he'd spoken since they left his father.

She dared go to him, slide her arms around his waist. "I thought it was something you'd likely never asked him."

"I used to copy everything he did." Arms clenching around her body. "I used to want to be exactly like him when I grew up."

"He was your hero."

"Yeah." A pause. "Afterward, I couldn't even bear to keep his name. I chose my mother's instead."

"Maybe one day, you'll be ready to reclaim it."

"Maybe."

Neither of them said anything else, but Katya knew Dev would return to visit his father again. It didn't make her want to stop railing at fate, but it did give her a little peace. "Promise me something, Dev."

"No." It was implacable.

She smiled. "Stubborn man."

"It's in the blood."

"I'm selfish," she admitted. "I want you to promise to love again, but at the same time, I want to scratch out the eyes of any woman who even looks at you."

His chest rumbled, and then, for the first time in what seemed like forever, he laughed. Delighted, she grinned. And when her spine twisted under a fresh wave of pain, she tried not to let him know. But he did. Of course he did.

"Hold on, baby," he whispered against her temple. "Hold on."

She tried...but Ming had stolen that from her, too. Her

arm muscles spasmed and fell silent. Inside her chest, she could feel her heart laboring to beat another beat. The bastard had won. She was dying. But she'd do it on her own terms.

Reaching up with an effort that had Dev bracing her neck, she brushed her lips against his jaw. "Let me go, Dev."

"No."

They both knew he couldn't stop her. The link to the Net—her lifeline—was inside her mind, a deeply personal thing. And yet they both also knew she wouldn't take that step until he gave her permission. Because she understood him. If she did this, if she left him without a final good-bye, Dev's rage would destroy him from within. "I need to know you've made your peace with this."

He squeezed her nape in gentle reproof. "I'll never make peace with this."

"Dev."

"Forget it, Katya." A stubborn line to his jaw that she knew too well. "It's never going to happen."

Dropping her head to his chest, she swallowed the tears in her throat. He was strong. And his heart, it was breaking. She could hear it. "I can't live this way," she whispered, knowing she was asking the impossible, knowing, too, that he was strong enough to bear the pain. If he had asked it of her... "Ming's out right now, but when he wakes, he'll find me."

"We'll get you out."

"There is no way out." Wrapping her arms around him as well as she could, she soaked in his warmth, his strength... his devotion. It was the last that stunned her. This man, this beautiful, strong, powerful man, adored her beyond reason, beyond sanity, beyond anything she'd ever expected. And she had to leave him. "No matter if I survive the physical disintegration, this prison I live in, this darkness that locks me away from the PsyNet, it'll eventually steal my personality, steal everything I am." She'd already felt the hovering edge of a rapacious madness.

"I talked to Ashaya," he said, still fighting for her, her lover with the heart of a warrior prince. "Her sister, Amara, isn't a full part of the neural net that keeps Ashaya alive. If—"

"They're twins, Dev." She'd seen the two interact in the labs, understood something about them she'd never been able to put into words. "And Amara's...unique. She probably doesn't care as long as she's connected to Ashaya. My mind is different." And it was starting to crumple under the pressure.

"How close?" he asked, his voice sandpaper rough.

"Too close."

"Link with me when you drop," he ordered. "It's possible we can find a way to give you the biofeedback you need through the ShadowNet."

"No. It won't work."

"We can do it," he said, misunderstanding. "You're a strong telepath and I've got enough telepathy—"

"No," she interrupted, reminding him of the unalterable facts. "The claws he's got in my mind, the spiderweb—there's no way I can pull out safely."

"What if you're wrong, what if you can? Promise me you'll link then."

She shook her head. "There's a chance the spiderweb is designed to spread. What if that's what I am? A true Trojan horse." Meant to infect the ShadowNet with a plague that would stifle all life, snuff out every bright light.

His arms tightened to bruising strength around her. "Viruses can't travel through the fabric of any net. That's been confirmed over and over."

"He did something," she replied, even as she fought the desperate urge to grab the chance at life and hold on with all her might, "and there's no way to know where his evil stopped. We can't play with the lives of your people—what if I come in and we discover that Ming *did* find a way to engineer a virus that'll survive in the ShadowNet? What then?"

"Ming isn't known to be a viral transmitter."

"No," she acknowledged. "Everyone says only Nikita Duncan can do that. But Councilors keep secrets."

"The risk is low," he argued. "We can quarantine you with shields if necessary."

Her vision blurred in one corner. She kept her face buried against him, somehow knowing it was blood spreading across her eye. "Please, Dev. Let me go."

Dev could have withstood anything except that soft, sweet plea. She was hurting. His Katya was hurting, and though she tried to hide it from him, he knew damn well she was starting to lose more and more control over her body. This, now, was her chance to go out on her own terms, with the dignity and grace Ming had tried to steal from her. Cupping the back of her head, he buried his face in her neck and felt his body shatter from the inside out.

She held him as he broke, her arms so very gentle. A kiss pressed to his cheek. "I love you, Dev."

"I'll never forgive you." It was torn out of his soul.

"I know."

He went to raise his head but she held him to her. "No. I don't want you to see me like this."

"You'd be beautiful to me no matter what."

"That's what they all say. But leave me a little vanity."

How could she make him smile even now? Stroking his hand over her hair, he pressed his lips to her temple. "Go then, *mere jaan*." My life. Because that was what she was. The best part of him. "Just remember—the next ten or so lifetimes, you're spending with me."

"Yes, sir." A final, sweet touch of her lips.

Taking the taste of Dev into her lungs, into her heart, Katya retreated to the psychic plane and began to make her way through the jagged minefield of her mind—skirting the numb, dead spots, the distorted pathways, the epicenters of pain—to the very core, to the place where she was connected to the PsyNet itself. The last time she'd seen it, it had been a strong, vibrant column laced with a bright blue energy that seemed to surge with the bold purity of life itself.

Today, that column was pitted and dull, the energy a sluggish mud. If she didn't do this now, death would only be delayed, not halted. And when she died, she'd do so paralyzed and broken, locked within the hell of her own mind. At least today, she could still feel Dev's body around hers, still hear his murmurs of love and devotion, still understand that she'd touched something extraordinary when she'd fallen in love with this man.

Standing before the dying column, she took a deep breath. "Oh, how I love you, Dev." It was incredibly easy to cut through the weakened link. One psychic slice and it was gone, her bond to the Net, her final anchor.

She waited for the agony and it wasn't long in coming. Iron pokers tore through her insides, ripped open her flesh, splintered her bones. But she hardly noticed. Because Dev had been right. No kind of virus or created matter could travel outside the Net. As she fell, Ming's cage didn't fall with her.

Instead, the prison, the spiderweb, the talons, they all wrenched out of her mind with brutalizing force, ripping through her brain itself. The pain was so acute that she couldn't even hear her own screams. And then one too many of those sadistic spikes tore free, and her mind just stopped.

CHAPTER 53

Dev had never before heard a sound of such sheer agony. Holding Katya as she convulsed, as her screams turned into ragged, gasping breaths, he prayed for the first time since the day he'd watched his mother's eyes go forever dull. "Please," he whispered. "Please." Asking for mercy, for deliverance.

Liquid spread over the front of his shirt, where she'd pressed her face, and he knew it was blood. But still her heart beat, still her fingers clawed. How much more would she suffer?

"Let me take it," he pleaded to the heavens.

Agony speared through him on the heels of that wish. He held on to Katya even as his knees hit the floor hard enough to send pain rocketing up his body. Gritting his teeth, he swallowed the pain, opened himself up for more. Against him, Katya had gone quiet, and for that mercy, he'd pay any price.

It felt as if his skin was being sliced from the inside out, a thousand knives cutting him open.

Then, as abruptly as it had begun, it ended. He found

himself kneeling on the floor, Katya's unmoving body held to his own, his breath coming in jagged pants. There was blood everywhere. Some of it was his, he thought, realizing that whatever had happened had literally forced blood through his very pores, but that wasn't important.

Because Katya was breathing.

"Katya." He cupped her cheek. It was warm. But her eyes were closed. And when he reached for her with his mind, he found...almost nothing. Less than the barest echo of the vibrant woman she'd been.

Not brain-dead, but close to it.

Shoulders shaking with grief, he brought her limp body to his chest and collapsed against the wall.

Dev ignored the insistent beeping of his phone.

When it wouldn't stop, he threw it at the wall in front of him, the throw angry enough to snap the casing in half.

Two seconds later, someone began knocking at his mind, the knocks so hard they stole his concentration, his time with Katya. Baring his teeth, he opened his psychic eye and "punched" Tag.

It should have made him retreat. Instead, the telepath shook off the hit and began to speak using their ShadowNet link. "There's a new thread, Dev." The mix of frustration and wonder in the other man's tone finally got through Dev's grief. "Are you listening? There's a new—"

But Dev was already staring in anguish at the twisting silver thread that linked his mind to a fading star. It was so small, that star, the light within it the barest flicker. And the silver thread, it was so fragile, a single careless push might jar it loose. When his *nani*'s love surrounded him, he didn't protest, didn't do anything, too broken inside his soul.

But part of him, the Shine director part, was able to

think, to process. "I thought the ShadowNet couldn't take full-blooded Psy."

"We can't do it by choice—not like the PsyNet," Nani said. "We tried that with a would-be defector back in my day."

"But she's here."

"We made a critical mistake—we forgot to factor in the thing that sets this net apart from the PsyNet. Emotion, Devraj." Her voice held wonder interwoven with sorrow. "The Forgotten's bonds to the ShadowNet itself are of need, but the bonds *between* those inside our net are bonds of emotion."

Dev heard, but that dull silver thread, that barely-there connection, couldn't be his love for Katya. "I love her more than that." She'd become his reason for being.

"She's dying, *beta*, that's why the thread is so faded. You know that."

He knew, but he didn't want to. "She wanted to die on her terms, but I can't let her go. Not now." Not when she'd fallen into his arms.

"I don't think your Katya would begrudge you the time to say good-bye."

Rising from his collapsed position on the physical plane, Dev carried Katya to the bathroom and drew her a bath. He took the utmost care with her, washing her hair until it shone, drying her body with the softest of towels. Then, dressing her in her favorite T-shirt and the boxers she'd stolen from him two days before, he laid her down in their bed. She looked so peaceful, as if she was sleeping.

Connor flew in from Manhattan later that day and hooked up a feeding tube. "Take this out when you're ready," the doctor said before he left. "She'll slip away without pain."

Leaving Connor to make his own way out, Dev crawled into bed beside her. She was so warm, her heartbeat so strong, it seemed possible she'd wake at any moment. But he knew that was a cruel lie. Still he couldn't help hoping.

And though he wanted to keep her only to himself, when Ashaya rang two hours later, having heard what had happened through Tag, he knew he couldn't. "Okay," he said to her request for permission to come say good-bye.

He spent the night holding Katya, trying to find the courage to let her go.

His grandparents drove in before dawn. "My Devraj." Walking to Katya's side of the bed, his *nani* took off the ring she'd worn on her wedding finger since the day his grandfather proposed. Her withheld tears glittered diamond bright as she handed it to him. "Here."

Accepting the gift, he slid it gently onto Katya's ring finger. "She told me she wanted to be you when she grew up," he found the voice to say, forcing himself to rise from the bed. "Are there messages for me?" It was a hollow question.

"Aubry and Maggie have everything in hand. Your *nana* and Marty will take care of what they can't." A tender hand passing over his hair. "This time is yours."

Ashaya and Dorian arrived not long afterward, bringing both Keenan and his "girlfriend" Noor. "They're inseparable," Ashaya said to him, as if afraid he'd mind.

"It's good to have them here," he said, glad for the sound of laughter, of life around Katya.

Sascha Duncan had flown in, too, Lucas by her side. Dev knew the empath had come for him, to help him, but he didn't want any help, didn't want to hurt any less. "Cruz?" he asked Sascha.

"He's starting to hold his shields," the empath told him. "I think he'll be fine."

"Good." Leaving Sascha, he returned to Katya, wanting to tell her about the boy who'd helped her escape.

Ashaya found him there forty minutes later. "There's only one choice." The M-Psy's eyes were shimmering wet as she placed a tentative hand on his shoulder.

"I know." And his heart broke impossibly more with

every hour that passed. "I just need a little more time to say good-bye."

Keenan and Noor ran into the room at that moment, skidding to a stop at the end of the bed. "She's sick?" Keenan asked, his face solemn.

Ashaya put her hand on her son's head. "Yes, sweetheart. She's very sick."

Little Noor went around Ashaya to pat Katya's hair, smoothing it out on the pillow. "She's Jon's friend."

"Yeah." Dev tried to smile for the girl, but couldn't quite make his lips move.

Ashaya picked Noor up and settled her in the curve of one arm, taking Keenan's hand with her free one. "Come on, babies. Let's leave Katya and Dev alone for a while."

Barely aware of the door closing, Dev lay down on the bed alongside the woman who held his soul, his heart, his everything. Her heart still beat, her breath still came, but her mind, that beautiful, sharp, courageous mind, was damaged beyond repair. She'd never wake now, but he could keep her alive for years on machines.

A sob shook his body.

How could he do that to her? To his laughing, spirited Katya? The truth was, he couldn't. He'd have to let her go, press a final kiss to her lips, and hope that heaven was real, that one day, he might look up, and there she'd be.

CHAPTER 54

Ming LeBon lay severely injured in a sealed chamber accessible only to telekinetics with the ability to teleport—and the M-Psy they brought with them. It was meant to be the safest possible of all locations, since the Tks on the Arrow Squad would quickly take care of any intrusions.

"We could kill him now," Vasic said without inflection.

Aden nodded. "It wouldn't even take much effort."

Yet neither of them made the move.

"He dies," Vasic finally said, watching two M-Psy move carefully around the fallen Councilor, "it creates a vacuum."

"It'll destabilize the Net. No knowing who or what would fill that vacuum."

"You could." Aden was far more stable than Vasic, than any of the other Arrows. "We'd stand behind you." And no one—*no one*—had ever been able to withstand the combined might of the Arrow Squad.

"It's not time." Aden's almond-shaped eyes swept over Ming's body, and Vasic knew his fellow Arrow was noting every minor injury, every weakness. "We can't show our hand.

We've lost enough men that there are a couple of Councilors who might be able to gather the resources to get in our way."

"Kaleb Krychek," Vasic said, "would've made an excellent Arrow."

"I checked his files." Aden was nothing if not thorough. "The public ones and the private ones I was able to hack into. He was considered for Arrow training—until Santano Enrique decided to make him his protégé."

Santano Enrique, as Vasic knew, had turned out to be a sociopathic killer. It was meant to be a well-kept secret, but Arrows were shadows, impossible to trace or see. It was their job to know the Net's darkest truths. "Is he showing any signs of sociopathy?"

"None that I've been able to see—but he's on the far end of the Silence continuum."

"So are we." He stared at Ming. "We might be able to work with Kaleb."

"What makes him any different from Ming?" Aden asked. "He was an Arrow, and still he betrayed us."

"Kaleb has blood on his hands," Vasic replied, knowing too much about death himself, "but I haven't been able to find one instance of him eliminating an individual who'd remained loyal to him."

Aden was quiet for a long time. "How many Arrows do you think Ming had killed?"

"Too many." In doing what he'd done, Ming had broken the cardinal rule of Arrows—it was the integrity of the Net, of Silence, that was of prime importance. Everything else, every other concern, was secondary. If getting rid of other Arrows had furthered that aim, the Arrows would've followed Ming to their graves. But Ming had done it for power. And lost his hold on the entire Squad.

CHAPTER 55

Lucas knew Dev had made his decision when the other man came out of Katya's room that night. The Shine director's face was haggard, his eyes blank with loss. "One more night," he said, almost to himself. "Tomorrow morning..."

Knowing no words would ever be enough, Lucas watched silently as Sascha walked across the room to touch her hand to Dev's heart.

The man stood there like stone, and eventually, Sascha turned away, tears streaking down her face. "He won't let me help him," she said, tumbling into Lucas's arms.

"Some pain a man needs to feel." He dropped a kiss on top of her hair, understanding Dev in a way not many men could. He'd almost lost Sascha once, would carry the terror of those moments in his heart forever.

Dev was still standing in place when Keenan and Noor ran past, laughing. Lucas saw them go into Katya's room and was about to call them back when Dev shook his head. "Let them be. Katya would've loved seeing Noor this way." Seeming to shake himself out of his shocked state, the other man looked around the room. "Is Connor here?"

"Outside with Dorian. Ashaya and your grandmother are making sandwiches in the kitchen. Your grandfather's in the office."

Nodding, Dev turned left, undoubtedly heading to talk to the doctor who would tomorrow note Katya's official time of death. "Is this better, kitten?" he asked the woman in his arms. "That Dev has the chance to say good-bye?"

Sascha shook her head. "His heart is shattered, Lucas—I have a feeling Dev will never truly recover." Her voice broke.

"Shh." But Lucas, too, had to swallow a knot in his throat.

Dev came in from talking to Connor, wanting only to crawl into bed beside Katya and feel her heart beat for one last night. But when he entered the bedroom, what he saw made him come to a standstill in the doorway.

Noor lay curled up beside Katya, one tiny hand on Katya's chest. Keenan lay on the other side, his hand over Noor's.

"Dev, have you seen—" Ashaya came to a stop beside him. "Oh, I'm so sorry. I'll get Dorian to help carry them out."

"No," Dev found himself saying. "They're just doing what the cats do—trying to heal her with touch because she's hurting."

Ashaya put her fingers on his arm. "They're too little to understand that she can't be fixed."

"I think," he said, "she'd have liked to know she spent her last night surrounded by hope."

"I know you want to lie with her," Ashaya began.

"I won't sleep." He needed to watch her as long as possible.

And he did. Taking a seat on the bottom of the bed, one foot on the sheets, the other flat on the floor, he watched her as twilight turned to midnight, then slowly to the darkest hour of night, when everything seemed to go silent. Sometime after three a.m., he was distracted by a kind of ache in his head... no, that wasn't right, it didn't hurt—it was more like a shift inside his skull, not uncomfortable, just different. Frowning, he checked his psychic shields. Holding.

Keeping his eye on Katya on the physical plane, he stepped out into the ShadowNet to check for outside interference— he'd allow nothing and no one to cause her any more pain. He didn't see it at first. But the longer he stared at the flicker of Katya's mind, the more he became convinced that he wasn't imagining it. Her flame was getting stronger.

Heart in his throat, he dropped back down to the physical plane and tried to find any indication that he wasn't simply creating phantom images, wasn't simply going mad with grief. But she still slept as peaceful and motionless as always, two little hands on her body. On her *skin*. Why hadn't he noticed that before? Both Keenan and Noor had moved their hands... to either side of Katya's head.

Half certain he *was* losing his sanity, Dev forced himself to remain on the physical plane for an entire two hours. Only then did he allow himself to open his psychic eye. "Dear God." It was a whisper full of wonder.

Terrified any disturbance would destroy the miracle, he stayed in place for the next four hours, making sure no one came into the bedroom. When Noor and Keenan finally woke, within seconds of each other, he looked into their groggy little faces and barely kept himself from crushing them close. "Good morning."

"Morning," Noor mumbled, rubbing at her eyes. "Want Tally."

Keenan reached over to pat her arm, moving as if his limbs were too heavy to lift. "Tally's at home, but I'm here."

A little smile. Yawning, Noor got up and crawled around the bed to Dev's side, exhaustion in every line of her body. "Pancakes?" she said hopefully as he cuddled her as hard as he dared.

"Pancakes," he whispered in a voice that threatened to shake, raising his hand to muss Keenan's hair when the boy came over to lean against his knee.

While his grandparents and Sascha distracted the kids with pancakes, Connor and Ashaya began to check Katya over using the equipment Connor had in his mobile kit. Dev could tell both doctor and M-Psy were leery of his hope, that they were doing it only to humor him, but he didn't give a damn. And when Ashaya's mouth dropped open and Connor began to swear under his breath, he didn't allow himself to collapse in relief.

That would have to wait until she woke.

"Her brain," Connor finally said, "is healed, according to this scanner." He stared at the equipment, thumping it with his palm as if to recalibrate it. "I need better gear."

"Get it," Ashaya muttered, staring at Katya. "I don't have the ability to see the damage, but all her responses are within the normal range."

Connor got out a cell phone. "Glen," he said a moment later, "I need you to fly out with one of the..."

Dev tuned out the rest of the conversation, knowing what he knew. "I can see her on the ShadowNet," he told Ashaya. "Her flame is bright enough to burn." Her mind, it was different; her psychic self cut with crystal clarity. She was already drawing curious looks from the Forgotten in the ShadowNet, none of whom had ever glimpsed the razor-sharp psychic presence of a Psy born in silence.

"You don't need the scans," Ashaya said with a nod. "But the rest of us do. Because if she's healed..."

He spread out his senses, found two innocent and deeply vulnerable minds in the kitchen. "Yes."

* * *

Three hours later, there was no question about it—not only was Katya healed, but she was likely to wake from her unconscious state at any time. Forcing himself to go out onto the porch with the others so they could discuss what had happened, he found himself watching protectively as Noor and Keenan—bundled up like little penguins in jackets, boots, mittens, scarves, and hats—tried to climb a tree at least ten times their combined size. Both had just woken from a two-hour nap and weren't moving with anywhere near their usual level of energy.

"Which one of them did it?" Dev asked, still shell-shocked.

Every single person on the porch shook his or her head. Ashaya was the first to speak. "When I asked Keenan if he had helped Katya, he told me 'they' fixed her."

"They?" Sascha leaned forward, watching the kids as they chased each other in circles.

"Yes."

Noor ran to the porch at that moment, scrambling into Dorian's arms. "Ha-ha!" She teased from her high perch. "You can't get me."

Keenan grinned and jumped up to grab her booted foot. "Can too."

"Uncle Dorian!" It was a laughing scream.

Lucas grabbed Keenan and turned him upside down, to the boy's delight. "So," the alpha said easily, "you two helped Katya."

"Yeah," Keenan said, walking on his mittened hands across the porch as Lucas held him up. "Noor can't go in by herself."

Dev held his breath, waiting to see if the children would add anything else.

"Yeah, I had to do a lot of weaving," Noor said. "Kee is my truck."

Both of them found that hilarious. Keenan was still

giggling when Lucas turned him right side up again. "Does it make you tired?" Lucas asked.

"Yeah." Noor nodded. "My head is full now."

"Keenan, how about you?"

But it was Noor who answered. "Kee's head is quiet."

Seeing something dart across the snow, Keenan jumped across the porch in excitement. "Come on, Noor!"

"Okay, okay." Kissing Dorian on the cheek, the little girl asked to be put down and then she was off after Keenan as he ran back toward their climbing tree.

"There were rumors," Nani murmured, "that in the past some Psy were born with gifts that only worked in tandem with another."

"Noor didn't show any active abilities when we tested her at Shine," Dev said, knowing he owed a debt to those two babes that could never, ever be repaid. "But she *does* carry a high percentage of Psy genes."

"My son," Ashaya murmured, "is a telepath. He's midrange, but in that range, he's crystal clear. A truck . . . a conduit."

Sascha nodded. "For whatever it is that Noor does, her 'weaving.' "

Dorian blinked. "Huh. She told the Arrow who helped William that they were the same. But I'm pretty sure even he can't do this. She's—they're both—unique."

"Yes," Ashaya agreed. "I've never heard of an M-Psy—of *anyone*—who can heal that kind of an injury."

"It doesn't matter whether or not we can define her gift— we have to protect her, protect them both," Dev said, meeting Lucas's eyes. "Tell Talin and Clay that they have every Shine resource at their disposal. If others find out what she and Keenan can do . . ."

"We'll all protect them," Lucas said, and it was a vow. "No one will take advantage of those two."

"Yes." Sascha's voice held awe. "Keenan's clearly exhausted, and what Noor said—about her head being full—I think she's flamed out, her gift has gone numb from overuse. Ashaya, can you tell about Keenan?"

Ashaya nodded after a moment's pause. "He's flamed out, too." Worry laced her tone. "It might take days for them to recover."

"But they will recover," Sascha reassured her. "They've just overstretched their psychic muscles."

"We'll have to be careful who and what we expose them to," Lucas said. "Keenan adores her so much, he'll follow her lead, and she won't be able to help trying to heal the injured even if it means hurting herself." A glance at his mate.

As Sascha made a face at the DarkRiver alpha, Ashaya whispered, "A tandem gift…It's extraordinary."

"Not really," Dorian murmured, surprising them all. "Keenan has a twin for a mother, after all."

A frozen silence.

"Oh." Ashaya blinked. "Yes, of course. Amara and I have always been able to merge."

"So maybe," Sascha theorized, "Keenan was born with an innate ability to merge with another mind. Perhaps it was only that he needed the right mind." A pause. "And the right environment—tandem abilities are unlikely to flourish in a network that punishes any kind of an emotional connection."

"Yes." Ashaya nodded. "It's a very intimate link."

Sascha turned to her packmate. "And it's probably not one you could forge with simple practice. That's why they ceased to exist. But the potential was always there."

"We have to monitor them," Ashaya said, eyes worried. "I don't want either of them unduly influencing the other. Keenan's my baby, but young telepaths don't always understand right from wrong when it comes to their psychic abilities."

Dev shook his head, watching Keenan help Noor onto the

first branch. "That, I don't think we have to worry about. They enjoy each other too much to try to change the other person."

"It would be considered bad form to mind-control your future mate," Dorian said dryly.

Ashaya laughed at Dev's surprised look. "Those two are quite determined that they belong to each other. I have a feeling we'll have a hard time keeping them from jumping the gun when teenage hormones hit."

The thought made everyone grin. The kids played on, unaware of just how extraordinary they'd proven themselves to be.

CHAPTER 56

Dev wanted so badly to talk to Katya, but she remained unconscious. He kept going into the ShadowNet, checking to see that the fine silver thread that connected them was still there. He got a surprise the fifth time he checked.

Silver had turned to gold.

The next day, gold had become platinum, a solid, unbreakable rope.

His *nani* found him in the ShadowNet. "Look at that, *beta*. Beautiful."

"It's stronger than any other thread." He kept running his psychic fingers along the length of it, amazed and delighted in equal measures.

Nani laughed. "Of course it is." A wave of affection surrounded him. "It's love."

"Yes." He felt his heart expand. "It's also because she can't access the biofeedback by herself. She has access to the ShadowNet because her mind is close enough to ours to allow it, but she's linked to me, not jacked into the network itself. I have to draw in the biofeedback for both of us."

"Does that bother you?"

"No—there's more than enough to go around." His heart swelled. "I wish I'd known it would work like this before."

"Love is unpredictable, Devraj. Those bonds, we can't control."

"Never liked surprises," Dev said. "But I think I've changed my mind."

As his *nani* laughed, he felt Katya awaken, their link to each other so deep and true, the knowledge was instinct. Dropping from the net, he strode into the bedroom just as her eyes lifted. "Hey, sleepy." It took incredible control to keep his tone light, his face calm.

Dev? A confused look. *But—*

"Shh." Kissing her gently on the temple, he helped her sit up, his heart thudding double time. She'd spoken telepathically and he'd *heard*. It was another piece sliding into place, another joy. "I'll explain everything."

And he did. No one interrupted them—knowing his grandmother, she'd played sentinel and barred the doorway.

"Those two are miracles," Katya whispered. "Dear God, Dev, if the Council ever—"

"They'll never find out," he promised her. "All of us, Shine, the cats, we'll all protect them."

Her face twisted. "And to think," she said, "that Larsen would've destroyed Noor had he had the chance. He'd never have understood the gift of what she is."

"You did." He ran his hand over her hair. "Lucas plans to apologize to you for chasing you in panther form."

That made her smile. "I thought I was done for that night."

"No," he said, closing his arms around her. "You had to live to meet me."

Her hand spread over his chest. "How am I hooked into your ShadowNet?"

"Through me," he said. "My grandmother agrees—your

connection is only through me. It's our 'mating bond,' as the changelings put it, that's keeping you in the ShadowNet."

"A mating bond." She smiled. "I like that."

"Katya—that means if I die," he told her, "so will you."

A shining look up at him. "That's what happens to change-lings, you know. One dies, the other doesn't last long."

"How do you know?"

"I did some research once. I was curious." Fingertips strok-ing over his cheek.

Dev understood. "It's not only changelings. Humans pine away, too."

"But," she said with a smile, "I'd like to have a long life-time with you, so stay safe."

"You, too." He reached up to cover her hand with his own, holding it against his cheek. "Because if you die, so will I."

A smile that held a spark of mischief, a bright new thing. "Will you pine away?"

"It's no laughing matter." But he was smiling, too.

"Dev, my Dev." She rose to straddle him, her face glowing with happiness.

Placing one hand on her hip, the other on her lower back, he bent his head and let her press kisses all over his face, fleet-ing touches of love, of affection, of promise. "You saved me, you know," he said between kisses.

A curious look.

"Everyone's been worrying the metal would take me over." He drew in the scent at the curve of her neck. "But how can it when you have a line straight into my heart?"

"*Dev.*" More kisses, gentle touches. Then a whisper against his ear. "I'm afraid to look at your ShadowNet."

He found himself whispering back, playing with her. "You? Afraid?" He slid his hand under the sheets to close over her thigh. "Not my Katya."

"Will you hold my hand?"

"Always."

Dev was waiting for Katya on the psychic plane when she opened the mental doorway of her mind and took the first step out into the shimmering chaos of a network of thousands of minds, millions of emotional connections. He felt her shock, but she held on to their bond and stayed in place, looking, learning.

"It's..." He felt her wonder, her terror.

"You get used to it."

"You do?" A laughing question. "Dear God, Dev. How do you navigate this?"

"Follow the threads."

"But I only have one to you."

"You can bounce off the threads of others," he explained. "As long as you don't actually try to hook into an emotional line without permission, no one minds if you use the threads as navigation points."

"And this," she said with a deep breath, "is definitely a place that requires navigation."

"You're wrong, you know," Dev said, nudging her attention sideways. "You have got other threads."

"But I don't know anyone else in here." She touched the thread. "It's your grandmother!"

He felt her follow the thread, knew when she'd reached the end. "I see her, but I also see... your grandfather?"

"Yes, you have a link to him through her. As you have a link to thousands through me."

He could see her thinking that over. "When I form more connections, you'll be able to access them, too?"

"On a certain level," he said. "It depends on my own emotional bond with the individual. Look."

She followed his finger to a sparkling silver-blue thread that glittered diamond bright. "Who is that and why am I linked to her?" Curious as a child, she touched her psychic hand to the silver-blue thread. "Tiara." He saw her smile on the physical plane. "She likes me enough that this link's formed."

"She's always been a lunatic."

"I think she has excellent taste." She played her fingers over the thread. "It's very fine."

"You've just begun a friendship. If you grow apart instead of together, the thread will fade, too."

"I guess," she murmured, "lovers in the ShadowNet always know where they stand."

"If both are psychic," he pointed out. "If a Forgotten forms an intimate bond with a human, that human is pulled nominally into the net. We can see the mind, but it's automatically shielded—we think the ShadowNet does that because otherwise humans would be too vulnerable. But it has the side effect of blocking their access to the network." A sound of frustration. "We never even considered that it would be otherwise with Psy, that the ShadowNet would recognize you as different."

"You had no reason to think that," she said, calming him. "The ShadowNet's acceptance of me is a gift—but it's only an answer to those who love."

"Those who dare to love."

"Yes." Another pause as she scanned the multitude of intertwined and entangled threads around them. "This network is very, very complex."

He smiled. "That's my Psy."

A playful mental slap came down the line as she began to figure out how things functioned. "It's open, that's what the difference is. Your ShadowNet is open to outside connections and influences—even shielded, those human minds bring something to the network."

He took time to consider it. "Yes, I think you're right."

"But that also means," she pointed out, "this network can't retain information with the same efficiency as the PsyNet. Or can you still find data in this chaos?"

"Not without searching a whole heck of a lot. Easier to use computers." He laughed at her expression on the physical plane. "It can be useful in that way sometimes, but mostly, the

ShadowNet is about feeding our psychic need for connection, for family."

"What about the biofeedback?" she asked, worry a jagged thread in her emotional signature. "I'm taking so much. If your network leaks energy—"

"It doesn't matter. Look around. We're overloading with it."

"You are, aren't you?" she murmured. "It's because you feed things back to each other, somehow increasing the output. Love goes out, love comes back, and the energy grows with each exchange..." Another pause. "Dev, the psychic pathways are different. It's as if my mind is slightly out of sync."

He knew that, had hoped she'd be able to navigate them. "Can you move along them?"

"Not easily or instinctively, but yes." Almost a minute of silence. "Actually, I think I'll enjoy the intellectual challenge. There's so much to explore."

In spite of her intrigued comments, he could feel her beginning to overload with the intensity of the emotions in the ShadowNet. Making a command decision, he bullied her back down to the physical plane.

"I wasn't finished," she almost growled at him.

He held her close. "You're exhausted."

"It was just so much input." She snuggled into him, tugging up his shirt to touch skin that tightened at the first brush of her fingertips. "The PsyNet is full of pure data—there are uncountable pieces flowing past every split second."

The Shine director in Dev could see the appeal. "You'd be able to know what was happening every minute of every day." That, he had to admit, would be highly useful.

"Yes. But it's cold. Data is always cold—it just exists. But the ShadowNet—each thread tells a story and each carries a different emotional flavor. I want to touch every one, know every one!"

"That, my beautiful Psy rebel," he said, speaking against the lush fullness of her lips, "will take at least a million years."

Husky feminine laughter, playful fingers dancing along the waistband of his jeans. "I guess I'll have to take it one kiss at a time."

PETROKOV FAMILY ARCHIVES

Letter dated May 5, 1995

Dearest Matthew,

Today, as I watched you promise to honor and cherish the woman you love, I saw the beginning of a dawn so bright, nothing will dare stand in its way. Our hope, our courage, our very heart carries on in your willingness to love, to be vulnerable, to hurt.

Those in the Net call us weak, but they're wrong. It's easy to ignore emotion, to bar the pathways of the soul. If I hadn't loved your father, his death wouldn't have forever broken a part of me. But if I hadn't loved your father, I'd never have known what it is to be human.

As the years pass, I hope you'll remember that, that your children's children will remember that. And when the shadows return, as they eventually will, remember this, too—we survived once. And we'll keep on surviving.

Nothing is stronger than the will of the human heart.

With all my love,

Mom

Turn the page for a sneak peek at the next novel
in the Psy-Changeling series, *Bonds of Justice*

JUSTICE

When the Psy first chose Silence, first chose to bury their emotions and turn into ice-cold individuals who cared nothing for love or hate, they tried to isolate their race from the humans and changelings. Constant contact with the races who continued to embrace emotion made it much harder to hold on to their own conditioning.

It was a logical thought.

However, it proved impossible in practice. Economics alone made isolation an unfeasible goal—Psy might have all been linked into the PsyNet, the sprawling psychic network that anchored their minds, but they were not all equal. Some were rich, some were poor, and some were just getting by.

They needed jobs, needed money, needed food. And the Psy Council, for all its brutal power, could not provide enough internal positions for millions. The Psy had to remain part of the world, a world filled with chaos on every side, bursting at the seams with the extremes of joy and sadness, fear and despair. Those Psy who fractured under the pressure were quietly "rehabilitated," their minds wiped, their personalities erased. But others thrived.

The M-Psy, gifted with the ability to look inside the body and diagnose illnesses, had never really withdrawn from the world. Their skills were prized by all three races, and they brought in a good income.

The less-powerful members of the Psy populace returned to their ordinary, everyday jobs as accountants and engineers, shop owners and businessmen. Except that what they had once enjoyed, despised, or merely tolerated, they now simply *did*.

The most powerful, in contrast, *were* absorbed into the Council superstructure wherever possible. The Council did not want to chance losing its strongest.

Then there were the Js.

Telepaths born with a quirk that allowed them to slip into minds and retrieve memories, then share those memories with others, the Js had been part of the world's justice system since the world first had one. There weren't enough J-Psy to shed light on the guilt or innocence of every accused—they were brought in on only the most heinous cases: the kinds of cases that made veteran detectives throw up and long-jaded reporters take a horrified step backward.

Realizing how advantageous it would be to have an entrée into a system that processed both humans, and at times, the secretive and pack-natured changelings as well, the Council allowed the Js to not just continue, but expand their work. Now, in the dawn of the year 2081, the Js are so much a part of the Justice system that their presence raises no eyebrows, causes no ripples.

And, as for the unexpected mental consequences of long-term work as a J . . . well, the benefits outweigh the occasional murderous problem.

CHAPTER 1

Circumstance doesn't make a man. If it did, I'd have committed my first burglary at twelve, my first robbery at fifteen, and my first murder at seventeen.

—From the private case notes of Detective Max Shannon

It was as she was sitting staring into the face of a sociopath that Sophia Russo realized three irrefutable truths.

One: In all likelihood, she had less than a year left before she was sentenced to comprehensive rehabilitation. Unlike normal rehabilitation, the process wouldn't only wipe out her personality, leave her a drooling vegetable. Comprehensives had ninety-nine percent of their psychic senses fried as well. All for their own good of course.

Two: Not a single individual on this earth would remember her name after she disappeared from active duty.

Three: If she wasn't careful, she would soon end up as empty and as inhuman as the man on the other side of the table . . . because the *otherness* in her wanted to squeeze his mind until he whimpered, until he bled, until he begged for mercy.

Evil is hard to define, but it's sitting in that room.

The echo of Detective Max Shannon's words pulled her back from the whispering temptation of the abyss. For some reason, the idea of being labeled evil by him was . . . not acceptable. He had looked at her in a different way from other human males, his eyes noting her scars, but only as part of the package that was her body. The response had been extraordinary enough to make her pause, meet his gaze, attempt to divine what he was thinking.

That had proved impossible. But she knew what Max Shannon wanted.

Bonner alone knows where he buried the bodies—we need that information.

Shutting the door on the darkness inside of her, she opened her psychic eye and, reaching out with her telepathic senses, began to walk the twisted pathways of Gerard Bonner's mind. She had touched many, many depraved minds over the course of her career, but this one was utterly and absolutely unique. Many who committed crimes of this caliber had a mental illness of some kind. She understood how to work with their sometimes disjointed and fragmented memories.

Bonner's mind, in contrast, was neat, organized, each memory in its proper place. Except those places and the memories they contained made no sense, having been filtered through the cold lens of his sociopathic desires. He saw things as he wished to see them, the reality distorted until it was impossible to pinpoint the truth among the spiderweb of lies.

Ending the telepathic sweep, she took three discreet seconds to center herself before opening her physical eyes to stare into the rich blue irises of the man the media found so compelling. According to them, he was handsome, intelligent, magnetic. What she knew for a fact was that he held an MBA from a highly regarded institution and came from one of the premier human families in Boston—there was a prevailing sense of disbelief that he was also the Butcher of Park Avenue, the moniker coined after the discovery of Carissa White's body along one of the avenue's famous wide "green" medians.

Covered with tulips and daffodils in spring, it had been

a snowy wonderland of trees and fairy lights when Carissa was dumped there, her blood a harsh accent on the snow. She was the only one of Bonner's victims to have ever been found, and the public nature of the dump site had turned her killer into an instant star. It had also almost gotten him caught—only the fact that the witness who'd seen him running from the scene had been too far away to give Enforcement any kind of a useful description had saved the monster.

"I got much more careful after that," Bonner said, wearing the faint smile that made people think they were being invited to share a secret joke. "Everyone's a little clumsy the first time."

Sophia betrayed no reaction to the fact that the human across from her had just "read her mind," having expected the trick. According to his file, Gerard Bonner was a master manipulator, able to read body language cues and minute facial expressions to genius-level accuracy. Even Silence, it seemed, was not protection enough against his abilities—having reviewed the visual transcripts of his trial, she'd seen him do the same thing to other Psy.

"That's why we're here, Mr. Bonner," she said with a calm that was growing ever colder, ever more remote—a survival mechanism that would soon chill the few remaining splinters of her soul. "You agreed to give up the locations of your later victims' bodies in return for more privileges during your incarceration." Bonner's sentence meant he'd be spending the rest of his natural life in D2, a maximum security facility located deep in the mountainous interior of Wyoming. Created under a special mandate, D2 housed the most vicious inmates from around the country, those deemed too high risk to remain in the normal prison system.

"I like your eyes," Bonner said, his smile widening as he traced the network of fine lines on her face with a gaze the media had labeled "murderously sensual." "They remind me of pansies."

Sophia simply waited, letting him speak, knowing his

words would be of interest to the profilers who stood in the room on the other side of the wall at her back—observing her meeting with Bonner on a large comm screen. Unusually for a human criminal, there were Psy observers in that group. Bonner's mental patterns were so aberrant as to incite their interest.

But no matter the credentials of those Psy profilers, Max Shannon's conclusions were the ones that interested Sophia. The Enforcement detective had no Psy abilities, and unlike the butcher sitting across from her, his body was whipcord lean. Sleek, she thought, akin to a lithely muscled puma. Yet, when it came down to it, it was the puma who'd won—both over the bulging strength that strained at Bonner's prison overalls, *and* over the mental abilities of the Psy detectives who'd been enlisted into the task force once Bonner's perversions began to have a serious economic impact.

"They were my pansies, you know." A small sigh. "So pretty, so sweet. So easily bruised. Like you." His eyes lingered on a scar that ran a ragged line over her cheekbone.

Ignoring the blatant attempt at provocation, she said, "What did you do to bruise them?" Bonner had ultimately been convicted on the basis of the evidence he'd left on the battered and broken body of his first victim. He hadn't left a trace at the scenes of the other abductions, had been connected to them only by the most circumstantial of evidence—and Max Shannon's relentless persistence.

"So delicate and so damaged you are, Sophia," he murmured, moving his gaze across her cheek, down to her lips. "I've always been drawn to damaged women."

"A lie, Mr. Bonner." It was extraordinary to her that people found him handsome—when she could all but smell the rot. "Every one of your victims was remarkably beautiful."

"*Alleged* victims," he said, eyes sparkling. "I was only convicted of poor Carissa's murder. Though I'm innocent, of course."

"You agreed to cooperate," she reminded him. And

she needed that cooperation to do her job. Because—"It's obvious you've learned to control your thought patterns to a certain degree." It was something the telepaths in the J-Corps had noted in a number of human sociopaths—they seemed to develop an almost Psy ability to consciously manipulate their own memories. Bonner had learned to do it well enough that she couldn't get what she needed from a surface scan—to go deeper, dig harder might cause permanent damage, erasing the very impressions she needed to access.

But, the otherness in her murmured, he only had to remain alive until they located his victims. After that . . .

"I'm human." Exaggerated surprise. "I'm sure they told you—my memory's not what it used to be. That's why I need a J to go in and dig up my pansies."

It was a game. She was certain he knew the exact position of each discarded body down to the last centimeter of dirt on a shallow grave. But he'd played the game well enough that the authorities had pulled her in, giving Bonner the chance to sate his urges once again. By making her go into his mind, he was attempting to violate her—the sole way he had to hurt a woman now.

"Since it's obvious I'm ineffective," she said, rising to her feet, "I'll get Justice to send in my colleague, Bryan Ames. He's an—"

"No." The first trace of a crack in his polished veneer, covered over almost as soon as it appeared. "I'm sure you'll get what you need."

She tugged at the thin black leather-synth of her left glove, smoothing it over her wrist so it sat neatly below the cuff of her crisp white shirt. "I'm too expensive a resource to waste. My skills will be better utilized in other cases." Then she walked out, ignoring his order—and it *was* an order—that she stay.

Once out in the observation chamber, she turned to Max Shannon. "Make sure any replacements you send him are male."

A professional nod, but his hand clenched on the top

of the chairback beside him, his skin having the warm golden brown tone of someone whose ancestry appeared to be a mix of Asian and Caucasian. While the Asian side of his genetic structure had made itself known in the shape of his eyes, the Caucasian side had won in the height department—he was six foot one according to her visual estimate.

All that was fact.

But the impact was more than the sum of its parts. He had, she realized, that strange something the humans called charisma. Psy professed not to accept that such a thing existed, but they all knew it did. Even among their Silent race, there were those who could walk into a room and hold it with nothing but their presence.

As she watched, Max's tendons turned white against his skin from the force of his grip. "He got his rocks off making you trawl through his memories." He didn't say anything about her scars, but Sophia knew as well as he did that they played a large part in what made her so very attractive to Bonner.

Those scars had long ago become a part of her, a thin tracery of lines that spoke of a history, a past. Without them, she'd have no past at all. Max Shannon, she thought, had a past as well. But he didn't wear it on that beautiful— not handsome, *beautiful*—face. "I have shields." However, those shields were beginning to fail, an inevitable side effect of her occupation. If she'd had the option, she wouldn't have become a J. But at eight years of age, she'd been given a single choice—become a J or die.

"I heard a lot of J-Psy have eidetic memories," Max said, his eyes intent.

"Yes—but only when it comes to the images we take during the course of our work." She'd forgotten parts of her "real life," but she'd never forget even an instant of the things she'd seen over the years she'd spent in the Justice Corps.

Max had opened his mouth to reply when Bartholomew Reuben, the prosecutor who'd worked side by side with him to capture and convict Gerard Bonner, finished his conversation with two of the profilers and walked over. "That's a good idea about male Js. It'll give Bonner time to stew—we can bring you in again when he's in a more cooperative frame of mind."

Max's jaw set at a brutal angle as he responded. "He'll draw this out as long as possible—those girls are nothing but pawns to him."

Reuben was pulled away by another profiler before he could reply, leaving Sophia alone with Max again. She found herself staying in place though she should've joined those of her race, her task complete. But being perfect hadn't kept her safe—she'd be dead within the year, one way or another—so why not indulge her desire for further conversation with this human detective whose mind worked in a fashion that fascinated her? "His ego won't let him hide his secrets forever," she said, having dealt with that kind of a narcissistic personality before. "He wants to share his cleverness."

"And will you continue to listen if the first body he gives up is that of Daria Xiu?" His tone was abrasive, gritty with lack of sleep.

Daria Xiu, Sophia knew, was the reason a J had been pulled into this situation. The daughter of a powerful human businessman, she was theorized to have been Bonner's final victim. "Yes," she said, telling him one truth. "Bonner is deviant enough that our psychologists find him a worthwhile study subject." Perhaps because the kind of deviancy exhibited by the Butcher of Park Avenue had once been exhibited by Psy in statistically high numbers . . . and was no longer being fully contained by Silence.

The Council thought the populace didn't know, and perhaps they didn't. But to Sophia, a J who'd spent her life steeped in the miasma of evil, the new shadows in the Psy-Net had a texture she could almost feel—thick, oily, and beginning to riddle the fabric of the sprawling neural network with insidious efficiency.

"And you?" Max asked, watching her with a piercing

focus that made her feel as if that quicksilver mind might uncover secrets she'd kept concealed for over two decades. "What about you?"

The otherness in her stirred, wanting to give him the unvarnished, deadly truth, but that was something she couldn't ever share with a man who'd made Justice his life. "I'll do my job." Then she said something a perfect Psy never would have said. "We'll bring them home. No one should have to spend eternity in the cold dark."

Max watched Sophia Russo walk away with the civilian observers, unable to take his attention off her. It had been the eyes that had first slammed into him. *River's* eyes, he'd thought as she walked in, she had River's eyes. But he'd been wrong. Sophia's eyes were darker, more dramatically blue-violet, so vivid he'd almost missed the lush softness of her mouth. Except he hadn't.

And that was one hell of a kick to the teeth.

Because for all her curves and the tracery of scars that spoke of a violent past, she was Psy. Ice-cold and tied to a Council that had far more blood on its hands than Gerard Bonner ever would. Except . . . Her final words circled in his mind.

We'll bring them home.

It had held the weight of a vow. Or maybe that's what he'd wanted to hear.

Wrenching back his attention when she disappeared from view, he turned to Bart Reuben, the only other person who remained. "She wear the gloves all the time?" Thin black leather-synth, they'd covered everything below the cuffs of her shirt and suit jacket. It might have been because she had more serious scars on the backs of her hands—but Sophia Russo didn't strike him as the kind of woman who'd hide behind such a shield.

"Yes. Every time I've seen her." Frown lines marred the prosecutor's forehead for a second, before he seemed to shake off whatever was bothering him. "She's got an excellent record—never fumbled a retraction yet."

"We saw at the trial that Bonner's smart enough to fuck with his own memories," Max said, watching as the prisoner was led from the interrogation room. The blue-eyed Butcher, the media's murderous darling, stared out at the cameras until the door closed, his smile a silent taunt. "Even if his mind isn't twisted at the core, he knows his pharmaceuticals—could've got his hands on something, deliberately dosed himself."

"Wouldn't put it past the bastard," Bart said, the grooves around his mouth carved deep. "I'll line up a couple of male Js for Bonner's next little show."

"Xiu have that much clout?" The trial of Gerard Bonner, scion of a blue-blooded Boston family and the most sadistic killer the state had seen in decades, would've qualified for a J at the trial stage but for the fact that his memories were close to impenetrable.

"Sociopaths," one J had said to Max after testifying that he couldn't retrieve anything usable from the accused's mind, "don't see the truth as others see it."

"Give me an example," Max had asked, frustrated that the killer who'd snuffed out so many young lives had managed to slither through another net.

"According to the memories in Bonner's surface mind, Carissa White orgasmed as he stabbed her."

Shaking off that sickening evidence of Bonner's warped reality, he glanced at Bart, who'd paused to check an e-mail on his cell phone. "Xiu?" he prompted.

"Yeah, looks like he has some 'friends' in high-level Psy ranks. His company does a lot of business with them." Putting away the phone, Bart began to gather up his papers. "But in this, he's just a shattered father. Daria was his only child."

"I know." The face of each and every victim was imprinted on Max's mind. Twenty-one-year-old Daria's was a gap-toothed smile, masses of curly black hair, and skin the color of polished mahogany. She didn't look anything like the other victims—unlike most killers of his pathology, Bonner hadn't differentiated between white, black, Hispanic, Asian. It had only been age and a certain kind of beauty that drew him.

Which turned his thoughts back to the woman who'd stared unblinking into the face of a killer while Max forced himself to stand back, to watch. "She fits his victim profile—Ms. Russo." Sophia Russo's eyes, her scars, made her strikingly unique—a critical aspect of Bonner's pathology. He'd targeted women who would never blend into a crowd—the violence spoken of by Sophia's scars would, for him, be the icing on the cake. "Did you arrange that?" His hand tightened on a pen as he helped Bart clear the table.

"Stroke of luck." The prosecutor put the files in his briefcase. "When Bonner said he'd cooperate with a scan, we requested the closest J. Russo had just completed a job here. She's on her way to the airport now—heading to our neck of the woods as a matter of fact."

"Liberty?" Max asked, mentioning the maximum-security penitentiary located on an artificial island off the New York coast.

Bart nodded as they walked out and toward the first security door. "She's scheduled to meet a prisoner who claims another prisoner confessed to the currently unsolved mutilation murder of a high-profile victim."

Max thought of what Bonner had done to the only one of his victims they'd ever found, the bloody ruin that had been the once-gamine beauty of Carissa White. And he wondered what Sophia Russo saw when she closed her eyes at night.